Vann Turner

SOMETIMES LOVIN' IS HURTFUL

feather books

cosby, tennessee

For Robert Simmons, my husband.

~

Here it is, all dusted off.
That's what you asked of me
on *that* bed.

~

Just days after we had met I explained,
Why, that's jasmine, night-blooming jasmine.
Kelsie and Sophie were on leads
—Remember?—
as we walked my neighborhood in St. Pete.
You told me then I needed to publish *this* novel,
spend my years writing.

~

Twenty-five years ago.
Seems like last evening.
But the Muses are again whispering,
sculpting in fog or swirling in breath.
You wanted me to write.
I'm doing it now…
for you.

~

Continue, Packman, to stand beside me,
your hand on my shoulder.

~ Contents ~

SOMETIMES LOVIN' IS HURTFUL

Are you drawn forth in a world of men
To slay the innocent?
— Richard III
— Act I, Scene 4

PROLOGUE

A gray mutt pressed fearfully against the apartment's wall. Although he was unheard in the physical world, the dog was speaking with God in a simple, child-like voice: "People can be awful mean, God. Do you think he wants to hurt me? He didn't bark at me, though. He didn't throw cans at me. I was scared when he tricked me and got me inside that moving thing. But he got inside with me. And my belly's now full and I'm not cold anymore, just wet. I used to have people who fed me, taught me things and played with me. I miss little Johnny and Suzy, God. Could you make things go back to how they were?

"Look! The man is reaching his paw to the floor and he's calling me. Do you think it's okay if I go up to him? He's not trying to trick me again, now is he, God?"

God answered him and the dog said, "All right, then. If you think it's okay, I'll go see."

CHAPTER 1

Billings, Montana. 1980.

Slowly, hunching close to the floor, the three-legged mutt dared to approach. In fits and starts he inched his way toward the man who beckoned in gentle voice. The dog would creep along a couple inches, then pause and in the pauses renew his resolve.

"It's okay. Come on over here," the deep voice said from an armchair.

The clangor of doorbell—like a bolt of thunder—smashed his courage. He hunched close to the floor, then scurried back to the protection of the wall.

Irritated, Bob clenched his jaws. His new dog was again cowering, ears pulled back, eyes wide and outlined in white.

"The bitch!" After that single ring and a brief pause, the doorbell started ringing without let-up, a familiar way of summoning. Bob stood, dashed to the kitchen and tossed his journal into the cabinet with the pots and pans. *You'd froth at the mouth if you ever saw what I've written about you, baby*, he thought. With a kick he slammed the cabinet shut.

The bell demanded him and demanded him. *Hold on, won't you!* In his rush he tugged at the belt of his old blue terrycloth robe that he might flaunt nakedness to her in greeting. That was her stipulation whenever feasible.

He unbolted the door and stepped out onto the landing. "Hi, hon," he said, hugging her. Around them raged November's early blizzard, white and silent. The wind caused his robe to flap against his legs. The wind swirled upward, raw and cold.

"Aren't you affectionate?" Carmen said, hugging him in return. "After standing you up, I was half expecting words."

"Would my saying something change anything?" he said.

"That's a good boy," she said. She slid one hand under the robe to his bare back. Her other hand coursed through the brown hair on his chest, then began its downward trek.

He curled his toes from the coldness of the melting snow, saying, "Come on in. We don't have to put on a show for the neighbors."

"Audiences can be fun." She brushed past him. "We've changed our plans for tomorrow night. Tonia and Bennett somebody will be joining us. Textiles. He's in textiles."

Just inside the door Bob leaned against its jamb to remove his wet socks. He noticed Carmen had tracked snow across the hardwood floors and a clump of it fell from her suede boot onto the Navaho-style rug. Though he now paid the monthly rent, she had made the initial first and last month's payment and had purchased most of the furnishings for him — expensive furnishings, oak and beige leather. He dropped his wet socks next to the door. "Run that by me again," he said.

"We've changed our plans," Carmen said, unbuttoning

her coat. "Tonia and Bennett somebody will be joining us. Your maroon suede jacket and tie, please. I'll be wearing beige and pink."

He was fully aware that his tattered robe still hung open to reveal his nakedness as he approached her. "We sat right there on that sofa and made those plans together. Were we just playing charades or something? It was supposed to be a romantic evening, just the two of us, not your whole entourage again. I had earmarked it so we talk, heart to heart, and work some things out." He cinched the robe around him tightly. "And now you go and change everything without even asking me? Well, the three of you be sure to have a good time, because I may not be going."

"It's all set, Bob," she said, flinging her red scarf on the sofa.

"Haven't you been listening? We made those plans together," he said standing beside her. "We've been through all this but it never sinks in: I'm a man. A full man. Not just something to amuse you, like your Corvette, your stable full of championship Morgans. I'm not on auction for you. You can't just buy me with clothes and furniture and dinner. You can't keep playing games with me because I'm getting damned tired of it."

"I don't know what the big deal is. It's just dinner. You should like being seen with me. Everybody says we make a striking couple," she said.

He looked into her dark eyes. A bit of lipstick had worn off a portion of her bottom lip. With her long dark hair, dark eyes and full breasts, she was attractive, though unusually tall for a woman, only half a head shorter than his six-feet-two.

"There comes a point in a man's life, baby," he said gently, "when he sees the fun and games as froth like bubbles on beer. And he starts to dream real dreams. It may have come to me a little later than to most men, but I've started to dream the wholesome dreams of a real future."

"And just what future do you see in that crystal ball of yours?" she asked with a snicker.

He noted melting snow had left a wet spot on the pastel rug, then looked into her brown eyes and said, "Would you like children, Carmen?"

"Oh," she said, turning from him and nodding toward the sliding glass doors that opened onto the lanai. Against them hung a framed piece of stained glass. Three shades of brown glass formed an Indian's head whose dark brown hair streamed—motionless and for eternity—in gale-force winds against a blue sky. "The piece I bought you looks nice up there. Moss does fine work, doesn't he?"

There you go! I talk about children and you talk about things. He exhaled audibly. "He's got talent. Would you like a drink?"

"I was wondering when you were going to ask," she said.

He headed for the kitchen which was separated from the living room by a breakfast bar.

"The roads are terrible," she said. "Saw two accidents on the way over. You should be out plowing."

"Well, hon," he said from the kitchen, "I've put in fourteen hours of overtime this week already. The State's not going to pay me any more."

"They still need to be plowed," she said. "Run down and bring up my overnight bag, would you? It's not locked."

"You're spending the whole night?" he asked.

"If you're amusing."

"Wouldn't you like that drink first?"

"Sure," she said, "and fix yourself a strong one. It'll get you ready for things."

"I've had three already. I'm well on my way." In silence he tended to ice cube trays, glasses and bottles. *More games! Just pour the booze down the drain! Kick her out, Bobby!* He was unsure if he had thought that or had heard it.

Neither spoke, till he heard a clipped, icy voice. "What's that!"

From behind the breakfast counter he looked at her. Her outstretched arm and pointing finger accused the mutt who was pressed against the wall, ears flattened, eyes fearful. "Beats me, baby," he said. "What does it look like?"

"You asked me if you could get yourself a puppy!"

"I did, doing a hundred miles in this storm—slippery, couldn't see—for one of Redman's shepherds."

"That's not a puppy!" she spewed.

"Well, think about it. Think hard, Carmen. He *was* a puppy once, I guess."

"You don't say?!"

"And he's had enough," Bob went on, "more than enough. People throwing things at him, chasing him off. At the diner—And you did stand me up. I had just gotten a new puppy and didn't want to be there in the first place. I wanted to take him home, not meet you for lunch. But you insisted we meet there and you never showed!"

"Something came up, okay?" she said.

"Yeah, sure," he said, slowly dropping ice cubes one by

one into the glasses. *Maybe I will kick you out.* Each ice cube made a clunking sound. "Anyway I was sitting there, waiting for you, and noticed something outside in the swirling snow. It was just a small, gray something—couldn't see what it was—but it fell, got up, lumbered, and fell again. It was struggling through drifts, plodding toward the light from the diner. I cupped my hands around my eyes to block the glare and just feet from the steps, the gray something became a dog. He nestled to the bottom step, where the wind and overhang left a bare patch of concrete. He was shivering, snow pelting him. It was pathetic. He bent down and chewed and tugged at ice encrusted on his paws, baby. Then he looked up into the light from the line of windows."

Bob had stood up, called for his check, wadded the burger in a napkin, wrestled with his coat and bracing himself with an arm on the table, awaiting his check, had watched out the window.

"Here you go, Bobby," Della said, still tallying on a small pad as she shuffled over. "Let me go get your puppy. He's so tiny, ever so cute, and all curled up in a box right now. But I'll go bother him and wake him up for you."

"Why don't you just go ahead and keep him!" he said. He strode to the register.

Della tagged behind. "But Jesus Crockett, he's yours," she said.

He gave Edna the check and a five, then turned around to crouch at eye-level with the waitress. "Listen, Della. You like him, you'll be good to him, so keep him."

"Oh! Oh!" she said, putting her hands to the sides of her face and shuffling toward the kitchen.

Edna handed him the change and looking over bifocals said, "Now that was an awful nice thing to do, Bob."

"It's nothing, okay?!" All along the counter men paused from their coffees, conversations and newspapers to turn their heads and watch. He stuffed the change into his jeans.

Della was rushing back from the kitchen—snuggling the little shepherd to her face, and saying, "Look, Mrs. Clement, he's all mine! Bobby gave him to me, a present!"

He went out into the cold.

"Who did you give that expensive puppy to again?" Carmen asked.

"The waitress, Della."

"The cabbage-faced one?"

"Yeah, Carmen, the one you call Cabbage Face. Okay?! Outside I had to trick the mutt into the truck with bits of hamburger, but I couldn't leave him out there in the cold. He's not a wild dog. He came to the light from the diner for help. He wouldn't have survived out there."

"So a common waitress has Redman's puppy of championship line?" she said.

"Yeah," he said from behind the breakfast bar. "She'll be good to him."

"You give a simple-minded moron a pedigree, and drag home a mongrel?! Look at that thing! It's deformed! Ab-so-lute-ly dis-gusting!"

"Watch it, baby!" he said, slamming a bottle of vodka onto the counter. He cinched the belt to the robe even more tightly around his waist. Tall, erect, he came toward her from the kitchen.

Just feet from her he stopped and pointed a finger into her face. "People who go around insulting a man's dog don't end up living too long."

"You have no standing to threaten me!" she said, squaring her shoulders, and moving back a step.

Easy, boy! He inclined his head a little to the side and smiled weakly. "I wasn't threatening, hon. I was just explaining how things are in this world. No, the little guy just needs a friend and a little help, too. He's fended on his own long enough. He's had enough of people throwing things at him. How would you like it if you had to paw through people's trash to find just enough to stay alive?"

"It could never happen to me," she said.

"But think about it," he said. "It could."

"Not to me!"

"Well aren't you the fortunate one," he said.

"But what do you want *a thing* like that for?"

"He's not a thing. And he might not seem like much of a dog right now, scared and huddled in fear like that," he said. "But I know about dogs, have known about them from childhood. He'll come around."

"Have you forgotten about my drink, Grunt? Be a good boy and bring me my drink."

Again she had changed the subject and the muscles of his jaw pulsed. "It'll take just a minute." He returned to the kitchen where—in silence—he poured soda water into her vodka and topped his bourbon with a splash of water.

In silence he walked back into the living room and handed her the vodka. She took it without comment. He noted how the snow swirled outside the glass doors.

"Oh, Bobby, Bobby," she said, with gentle smile. "Can't you let it sink into that hard, proud, sexy head of yours that I love you and only want the best for you?"

He sipped his bourbon and watched the snow. "I've tried to call it love, this thing we've got," he said. "It's not a storybook kind of love, Carmen. It'd never be fit for children to witness. But the thing is, Carmen, I can't imagine us growing old together, gray hair, wrinkles and all."

"Well I'm not going to get old!" she exclaimed.

"Yeah," he said, unconvinced.

"There are ways, Bob," she said, gesturing nonchalantly. "Surgeons, and this and that."

"For your sake, hon, I sure hope so."

"I don't want to have words," she said. "I love you. I love you more than I've ever loved anybody. Of all the men I've dated, I love you the most. And I think that says it all."

Half a head taller, he glanced down into her eyes. Then, silent, he watched the swirl of ice in his glass. "I don't doubt that," he said. "That's probably the most truthful thing you've ever said. The most naked thing."

"It's true," she protested.

"But sometimes people in love think about," Bob went on, "and sometimes talk about getting married, raising a family. How many boys and girls they want, what would be good names, what type of schools they should go to, those things. But the funny thing is, I can't imagine us getting married."

"Well good! Don't try! It could never happen. But even when I do get married, you'll be there on the side, Bob. We'll continue to see each other, have our good times and our games."

He lifted his bourbon in toast. "Well thank you for that, baby!" he said. "That's what I'm dreaming about, longing for—being the kept boy on the side!"

"Bob," she said tenderly, lengthening the syllable. She put her arms around him. "I love you, love you for today. Isn't that enough?"

"If you did, if you really did, I could probably get by with that."

"I do, in my own way," she said, pressing up close. While she held her drink in her right hand behind his back, she slid her left under his cinched robe, to rub his chest, entwine the hair around her fingers. "You've got such a beautiful, healthy, strong body. I love it, and all the fun we have with it. If you'd run down and get my overnight bag, we could have a good time. That's why I came over." One of her fingernails caught in a long loose thread of his robe. "But why do you insist on wearing that old rag, instead of the red and black silk one I gave you? With such a sexy body, you should want to present yourself well. I know, you'll say it's comfortable, but *really*!" She found his left tit and started pinching it and twisting.

"Easy!" he said, pushing her hand away. "That one's still sore."

She put her hand back, still pinching but more lightly now. "Poor *ba-by*. Drink up, Bob, and have a couple more," she said, then—pressing her body flush to his and straddling his leg with hers—added in a whisper, "Get yourself ready for me and amusing. Drink up, Grunt. Real drunk. Sloppy drunk, so your head will confuse pleasure and pain, have them blur together like they do. I *will* please you. So run down and bring up my overnight bag. I've got new toys to play with."

He pulled from her. "I don't need to endure more toys."

"We'll start the festivities off tonight with you in fatigues, Grunt…One of the new ones is called the Jaws of Hell. As I recall you've been there."

His brows creased and lips parted in a pained expression. "Lots of guys were there," he said and left her standing mid-room as he crossed to the sliding glass doors.

Silent, he stared into the snow. *It was hell*, he remembered a guy saying at the diner that day. He didn't know the man and only spoke to him for a few minutes, but he remembered his name, Zane Carlson, remembered his dark wavy hair, his eyes the vibrant brown of roasted chestnuts. He remembered his words and the timbre of his voice: *I was there too, Rangers, '67 to '68. Hue, Khe Sanh, Tay Ninh. But I don't like talking about it. We lifted too many men onto the choppers.*

Outside the sliding glass doors the snow swirled and eddied, with nothing visible except the whiteness. "It snows in Nam, too," he confided softly. "You didn't know that, did you, baby?"

There was no answer.

"And most people think Nam's one huge rice paddy. They're wrong. There are mountains there, many of them beautiful mountains. And if a man just started trudging through the snow that way," he said, pointing into the whiteness, "he'd come to mountains."

"Mountains in Montana? Really?!" she interrupted. "You

don't say!"

Bob ignored her and continued on, "Anyway, in the bad years when I was trekking from place to place looking for a job, sleeping in my truck and working day-labor whenever I could, and although I had to sell piecemeal whatever I had in order to buy some cans of beans so that I could keep my pride and stay out of the lines at the soup kitchens, in all that time, Carmen, I never even once thought of selling my backpacking gear." He paused and in the silence heard the clink of fresh ice cubes dropping into her glass. He continued to gaze into the snow. There was the sound of liquid being poured. "Would it be okay with you if I went backpacking next weekend?"

"Maybe," she said, "I'll see. Tonia and I could fly down to Denver, I guess."

"Then I can?" he said, his voice rising. He turned around.

From behind the breakfast counter she said, "I said I'd see."

"Maybe I'll invite the guy I met at Edna's today, and we'll go winter backpacking, snow-shoes, two-man tent and all."

"Who's this you met?" she asked.

"A guy I told who to talk to about a job, an ex-Ranger. He was in country only one tour, though, '67 to '68. I served three."

"No, what does he look like?"

Bob's head lifted upward and he smiled broadly. "I know what you're up to, baby. Good-looking, just let it go at that," he said. "Real good-looking."

"But if he's a friend of yours, I'd like to meet him." She had a fresh drink in hand coming from the kitchen.

"I'm sure you would! See how he fares on that four-poster bed you bought me, huh?"

"It could be interesting. Put the two of you on that bed and watch what happens."

"Nothing would happen!" he said.

"But you're so cocksure eager to dash off into the woods with some good-looking guy you just met. 'Two-man tent and all.'"

She's mocking me!

"Is there something you haven't told me?"

"I know what you're getting at, but you know better."

"It's no big deal," she said. "Tonia and I have been…Shall I say, *friends?*…for years."

"But I'm not. Sure I've been in the Corps so I've seen men doing it firsthand. Even my Pa's a fag. He ran off with a hairy guy and left me. I was twelve…"

"Drink up, Bob, and fix yourself another," she said. "Whatever happened when you were twelve is your business, and I'm waiting to try out the Jaws of Hell on your balls — so get yourself drunk."

He didn't respond to that, but, enmeshed in the memory of his abandonment, continued on. As he spoke his voice got softer and softer. "But at least Pa thought enough of me to leave me forty dollars and my dog. Three times me and Rusty set out to find him…"

"Bob?" she said.

He resumed in a voice a little louder than normal, "…but the farthest we ever got was forty miles. Three times we returned to the oak on Bullrush Creek."

"Bob, I already told you, fix yourself a drink!" she said.

As the recollection of his Pa's abandonment wrenched anew his heart, twisted it, knotted it, he stared at her. He had come face to face with the reality of Carmen.

"Now, boy!" she said.

Obedient, he drained the contents of his glass and headed toward the kitchen. As he passed by she told him, "Stop." He did. She tugged the robe's belt once, and his bare flesh again came into view. "Okay," she said.

He continued toward the kitchen.

"No, all of it off," she said.

He stopped and let the tattered terrycloth robe slip from his shoulders and arms. It lay in a blue heap on the floor. He was now completely naked, Carmen fully clothed.

"Now fix yourself a tall one," she said.

He did, replacing his rocks glass with an iced tea glass from the cabinet. He started to drop ice into it but she interrupted, "No, straight, with just a little water."

He complied.

"Now come over here," she said.

He did. He stood before her naked, head bowed.

"Start drinking," she said.

He drained half the glass. It wasn't cold, wasn't diluted enough. It burned his throat.

"Good boy," she said. "Now there are three things I want you to do for me. First, go down to my car, bring up my overnight bag, set it on the sofa, open it and bring me the Jaws of Hell."

"Okay," he said. He noticed there was a run the length of a finger in her hose. Her black suede boots had shiny splotches on them left by the melting of the snow.

"And you are to do it naked. I don't care if you get cold. It snows in Vietnam, I hear, but you already know that. Don't you, Grunt?!"

"Yes," he said.

"Second, you are to get rid of that disgusting mutt. You can throw him out in the snow, take him to the pound tomorrow, or to a vet and have him put down if you have to. But you are to get rid of him."

"He just needs a bath and a little time to get accustomed to things around here," he protested, looking up.

"You don't seem to understand. I never want to see that disgusting freak again."

"Carmen," he said, looking her square in the eyes, "a vet amputated his hind leg, so somebody cared about him once. Was it a little boy, a widow, an old man? We'll never know. And all this is new to him now, and he's scared, but he'll come around and be a good dog."

"Reagan hasn't taken office yet, and with Carter's recession there aren't many jobs to be had out there."

"And what do you mean by that?" he said, his voice rising.

"Just pointing out how things are *in this world*," she said, mocking his words.

"And what's number three?" he asked with a controlled tightness in his voice.

"We're changing *again* our plans for tomorrow night, that's what. I'll call and make our reservations for five."

He forced a chuckle, then said, "But I already told you I may not be going. It was supposed to be just you and me, a romantic evening, remember?"

"But you will be ready, jacket and tie please, six o'clock.

You will go, Bob, and be your simple, transparent, masculine self. That's the bargain."

"What bargain?" he asked.

"You keep yourself available and amusing and you get to keep on working your job."

"You couldn't do anything there," he said.

"Couldn't I? While your father owns some bar in San Francisco—It has to be a faggot bar, now isn't it, Bob?—my Daddy's on the Executive Board of the Moral Majority. He hates perversion, and wouldn't like it, not one little bit, what you've made me do with you."

"What who makes who do! Who ties who up, huh?"

"I think Daddy would believe his Pumpkin if I told him you would always tie me up and make me choke on you."

"That's not how it is. You put collar and leash on me, drag me around and you tie me up!"

"That's just a detail he'll never hear about. And it was his influence that got you that job, and got it for you in spite of the hiring freeze. It would take only one phone call from him and they would suddenly discover the error in your hiring."

"In my nine months with the State I've had two excellent evaluations!"

"I'm not positive, but I would think clerical errors are above civil service review, but even if not, Daddy will fix it. So you will be ready tomorrow at six, or you can go live out of your old, rusting pickup truck again if you want. It wouldn't be too nice with winter set in, but if you want to, I can arrange it. Your choice."

He stared at her as the memory of his homeless years trekked through him. Living in his truck, sleeping in it, eating in it. He remembered standing in the lines at day-labor hoping to be one of the chosen who are sent out to scrub pots for a day, or scrub cooking grease from floors or a hood. And most days he would sit with dozens of men, and wait and hope from five A.M. on. And at noon, as hunger gnawed at his stomach, they would be sent away without work, without pay, with only an announcement to be early the next morning. He and the other men sitting in folding chairs would disperse, hang-dog in silence.

But I survived! Managed!

He put his drink down on an end table, went over, picked up his robe from the floor and put it on.

Meanwhile Carmen put her drink on the breakfast bar and was clapping her hands together close to her chest, fingers spread like a child's. "So you can forget about number one, we'll use the Jaws on your balls tomorrow night when we get back. And number three, I never did tell you all of number three except being ready. I want you to go find that guy you met—the good-looking guy, the ex-Ranger?—and invite him, and have him here with you when I pick you up. Is he hung?"

"I wouldn't know!" he said, his voice tight and clenched.

"I hope he is," she said. "Big ones are amusing. I'd like to show you how amusing they are and watch you choke on it."

Anger surged, but—yet again—he checked himself. *Easy now, easy!*

"That's what you need," she went on, "a man to get you all worked up, then whip you, beat you, use you like a little fuck-boy. A lot of damn good fuckin' men got killed in Nam," she said. "Their flesh has rotted into the ground by now, but not yours, boy. You weren't good enough to die with men, real men. I ought to cut your fuckin' balls off."

"Did you know," he said in a whisper, "Sir Charlie used to do that to the corpses?"

"With your balls cut off," she went on, "you wouldn't be so damn rambunctious, so head-strong, now would you? It'd keep you in your place. My Grunt, the gelding!"

"Yeah," he said, his knees giving way until he knelt on the Navaho-style rug. His shoulders shrugged and again the robe fell from him. It lay across his lower legs. His head bowed and his arms went to behind his back and stayed there as if they were bound at the wrists.

Again he was kneeling in a bamboo shack, a Prisoner of War. "Robert Newell," he said in a lifeless voice as if abuse and deprivation had sapped it of any spirit. "Corporal, US59884526, United States Marine Corps."

"I ought to tie you up right now, Grunt, whip you, beat you, make you squirm."

"Robert Newell, Corporal," he said, lifelessly. "US59884526, United States Marine Corps."

She didn't respond. The room was silent. *Come on, baby,* he thought. *You know all the right strings. So pull 'em. Pull 'em fuckin' hard. Do it, baby.*

"Well, Grunt, I've got to go," she said.

He opened his eyes and looked up. She already had her coat on. "No!" he exclaimed. "I'll get that thing from the car and I'll amuse you."

"I'm leaving," she said. "We'll have festivities tomorrow night when we get back. And I expect you to be charming at dinner and amusing afterwards. Make sure your Ranger buddy goes with us. But don't worry, Bob, it'll be okay. I'll put the whip into his hands myself."

She went to the door, opened it and held it open. The snow swirled into the room. "Cold out there, nice and warm in here. And with so many good men dead, mangled, how is it you two boys got out alive? You must have a lot in common."

He was still on the floor, his arms behind his back. "Don't go, baby," he pleaded, raising one eyebrow and lowering the other. It was a boyish expression, questioning and pleading at the same time.

She laughed, tossing her head, her hair streaming in a swirl of wind into the room. "You *are* most amusing. Just look at yourself on the floor there—naked, raging hard-on." She laughed. "So simple, so easily toyed with, *so many* hormones. If you keep on being a good boy, maybe I'll let you and your Ranger buddy go off into the mountains next weekend, two-man tent and all. Romantic."

"Carmen?" he said as the door closed behind her.

"Carmen!" he yelled.

Against the wall, the gray mutt's eyes were on him.

CHAPTER 2

Naked on the floor, he dreaded the next night. *It's not just Carmen and her toys,* he thought. *It's the prospect of ushering something new into my life. Another man in my bedroom? In MY bedroom?! The man would have a man's body, a man's strength, passions and will. He might even have a need to prove something— to Carmen? to himself or me? What difference in outcome would that make? Carmen would whisper in his ear and goad him on. She stated she wants to watch it. Drunk, it could happen. It must not. Pa? No, Pa! Never!*

In the dead quiet of the room the only sound was the faintest crinkle of snow hurling itself against the glass doors. He turned his head to stare into the swirling whiteness. It was albino universe out there, a universe without horizon, landmarks or points that define. *Without compass bearings I could wander in that whiteness for a lifetime, lost for a lifetime, struggle all my days, and in the end the white coldness would still win.*

It matters that people should cling one to another, huddle together for warmth. Huddle together for encouragement. That's the one solace in it and that's important, to cling together. In Nam we always helped one another. You had to or you wouldn't survive.

On the day of his arrival in Billings, Montana, he had met her in a barroom. An hour later she was moaning under him in the motel room she had rented. Within days he suddenly had a good job with the Transportation Department, his first decent job since the start of his downward spiral. Within a week, with her financial assistance, he moved into an apartment. He owed her the roof over his head, the food he ate, the job he worked, the booze he drank—the booze she encouraged him to drink. *Gratitude and appreciation are important. I must never let the world strip me of a sense of gratitude. Nobody makes it on their own.*

If I were drunk enough, maybe I could satisfy both of them, please them. 'I was there too—Hue, Kay Sahn,' the ex-Ranger had said as he was standing there by my table, inquiring about work, any type of work. Hair dark and curly, jeans faded. Good sized bulge. "Yes, baby," he said softly into the silence of the room, "I think he is well hung." A shiver went up his spine.

A thumping sound in the room drew his attention. Against the wall the dog was now sitting up, wagging his tail. This wasn't the championship German shepherd puppy he had driven a hundred miles that day to get. This was a pathetic, middle-aged mutt.

From kneeling on the floor, he changed to a sitting position, pulled his tattered robe from under him and draped it on his shoulders. With a weak outstretching of a hand and a patting on a thigh, he beckoned the dog. "Come on, boy.

Come on over here."

The dog stood, looked at him with head tilted to the side and ears perked, then started hobbling toward him on three legs. Just beyond arm's reach he stopped to sniff the tips of his fingers. Then daring to approach closer, he sniffed the palm of his hand. His quick short breaths felt warm, light and fragile. The dog came closer to sniff his side, then, insinuating his muzzle under the robe, sniffed his armpit.

"Sit," he said. "Do you know how to <u>sit</u>?" he said, emphasizing and elongating the syllable.

He did.

"Good boy!" In silence he stroked his flank—still damp with the melting of snow and odorous in the air. He gazed again out into the storm. *One day an eternal whiteness will come to me and take me by the hand. Cold, it will bid me give up the struggles and the dreams. One day I'll have to, and will.*

With the dog beside him, he watched as encroaching night smudged the whiteness with gray. He was chilled, his skin in goose flesh.

With nothing resolved he pushed himself heavily from the floor. He took the robe—only draped on his shoulders—and put it on, then moved to the thermostat to turn it up. In the kitchen the dog had a second serving of Puppy-Chow, which he ate, not greedily this time as he had with that first dish, not with eyes fixed on him, wary, fearful, and outlined in white. This time he ate contentedly, as if enjoying the flavor of the kibble. Yet though Bob watched him, that watching didn't cheer. He watched until the liquor bottles on the counter drew his gaze.

He could see an iced tea glass half-full on the oaken end table in the living room—"No," she had said, "a tall one, straight, with just a little water."—but instead of getting it he took another iced tea glass from the cabinet. Ice cubes went into it, and bourbon to the rim.

"You know what she wants, Grunt, and you don't have that many choices," he said aloud. "And you heard her: Get yourself drunk." He lifted the glass to his lips, inhaled a deep breath, drained it empty, then refilled it. He took his journal, a large spiral notebook, from the pot cabinet where he had stashed it. As his new dog chased the last morsels of kibble around the bowl, he went to his chair of beige leather and sat.

The bourbon he had already consumed was working its alchemy on his senses. His nose and lips were numb. Soon, he thought, it'll start working on my brain. *So drink up, boy, and it'll muddy up your thinking, confuse things, confound pleasure and pain.* With a single lift of the glass he drank three-quarters of it, then poured the one he had been told to fix without ice into it.

He opened his journal. Though he neither read it nor scanned it, poignant words, carefully printed in a draftsman-like precision, burned into his retina: "…hog-tied me with her money…just using me…" The date, 12 Aug 80, astonished him.

Was it really that long ago, last summer, that I figured it all out? But I'm still here, being a good boy, still pandering myself at her command. So she wants to get me drunk, does she? Wants to teach me some new games, does she? Would that please you, Pa? Would you like to watch it too? I want to say fat chance. That's what I _want_ to say.

He watched as the gray dog bathed himself at his feet on the light pastels of the Navaho-style rug. *Carmen doesn't like you.*

Outside, twilight was darkening into night. He stood up and, wobbly, carried his drink to the bedroom, putting it on the dresser and stumbling on into the bathroom where he ran water into the tub and stood there, steadying himself with a hand on the wall as he watched it fill. *Once bathed, he'll stand a better chance at the pound of being adopted. A little better, not much. People don't usually adopt three-legged dogs.*

He carried the mutt from the living room and put him in the tub where he endured the water, shampoo and rinsing without fuss. As the water drained, he dried him with a monogrammed towel, then got into the shower.

Steaming water cascaded over him. Slowly he lathered, running a soapy hand over his body, and remembering the hands of women he had known before Carmen, their softness and tenderness. *The women before had no need for toys, games, costumes and a man who, for whatever reason, would allow it. Those other women didn't see a man as just an amusement, a plaything for their lusts. But I'll be honest, Pa. Carmen's toys rouse my horniness, too.*

He held his head, face up, under the cascade of water. *With her money maybe she has dozens of men down on their luck. Keeps them in a stable, like her Morgans and quarter horses. Rows of bunk beds on both sides, like barracks. The men tethered to their bunks. The Drill Instructor will ask, 'Which one tonight, ma'am?'*

Their relationship didn't need adjustment. It needed

severing. In spite of Carter's recession, he ought to pack up the truck tonight and get the hell out of here while he still could. *If she could get away with it, she would castrate me!*

He turned off the water, stepped out of the tub and started to towel off. The dog was watching from the doorway with head at a quizzical tilt. He wiped the fog from the floor-length mirror and his nakedness, strong, healthy, and six-foot-two, was there before him. *No way in hell am I a fuckboy, Pa! I'm a man!*

With towel limp in one hand, he gazed at his reflection, pleased with his appearance, his body. Yeah, he was every bit as good-looking as his Pa had been. Veins coursed down his arms. Light brown hair flared over his chest then descended as a single line, then flared again below belt line. That hair was a deeper shade.

Leaning closer to the mirror, inches from it, he gazed into the depths of his eyes, eyes a pale and vibrant blue. He gazed into the soul behind.

And eyes like his, pale as faded denim, stared back at him. His Pa stared back at him.

Bob leaned away, gasped—startled at seeing his Pa in his apartment.

His Pa leaned back too.

Slowly, hesitantly, fingers were reaching up until—through glass and years—fingers touched fingers and he was a child again, living with his Pa, doing the best they could, as his Pa restlessly searched for somebody who wanted him, or "If God forbid me love, Bobby, then I'd settle for earning a mite better living."

In that quest they trekked from place to place. From town

to town they sojourned throughout the South. In school after school, in Selma and Ft. Walton, in Shreveport and Savannah, Bobby's schoolmates nicknamed him The New Kid. That nickname the same everywhere. Bobby didn't like that. Those school-year phantoms halted abruptly with his Pa's abandonment in his twelfth year—with the sofa gone, Grandma's clock gone and forty dollars taped to a brown paper bag.

And it was again his own, mature nakedness that the mirror reflected to him now.

A dozen years ago his Pa had rejected him. Four years ago his Pa had again rejected him. *Two rejections and still I'm entwined with you, Pa. Shouldn't be—I'm a grownup now!—but am. And besides I'm as hairy as you! You ain't got nothin' on me!*

With a hand coursing over his chest, he reveled in his hair. His hand followed the line of hair downward, descending, descending till fingers entwined pubic hair, enmeshed them, entangled them in a fist and pulled.

But that doesn't belong there! Who the hell am I trying to fool? No way does it belong, that jungle of dark hair at my crotch. I'm not a man, not a real man. It's bogus, that hair, no more real than a child's costume for a dress-up party. It doesn't belong! To you, Pa, I'm a throw-away boy. To her, Pa, a fuck-boy!

His hand was inching over for the shaving cream.

White foam, from beltline down, clung to him in ribbons until a hand smeared it around, covering the dark hair in whiteness.

In the mirror his Pa smirked, one corner of his lips higher than the other.

And as Bobby stood before the man out of whose sinews he had been fashioned, with definite and repeated strokes, changing the blade twice and washing the hair down the drain, he shaved off the pubes.

Stroke by stroke his Pa watched the disguise being removed, watched the emergence of smooth boyish whiteness.

At last the razor was dropped into the sink, and he returned to the bedroom for his bourbon. His four-poster bed was neatly made. *There it is—the Adult Playpen, Carmen. That's what you called it when you bought it for me. Or maybe I got it all wrong. Maybe you bought me…for it.*

In the gloom—the only light coming from the bathroom—he picked up his glass from the dresser but the reflection in the mirrored wall—a reflection only half-seen—made him pause midway to his lips. The virgin whiteness of freshly shaved skin seemed to glow in supernatural light to contrast with the dark heaviness that hung below. He snickered at the absurdity of his image, half-man, half-boy. *As absurd as the bearded lady in the circus. Without the beard. Carmen will be amused.* Yet at the next moment he realized what he saw was cripplingly honest. The humor vanished and he was ashamed of what he had done.

He put his drink on the dresser untasted, backed up a few steps and flopped across the four-poster bed. Around him the walls were lonely and stark. *If I call her maybe she'll come back over, or maybe I could drive out to her place if she'd have me. Then I can find out what the Jaws of Hell looks like, feels like. I'll probably like it. I'm drunk enough.*

Around him the walls swirled, the ceiling swirled and

distant memories of long ago swirled. They leered at him and smirked.

"Go on, Bobby, give Mommy the flower. It'll be the last thing you ever give her. Go on, boy, drop the flower in the hole."

~

"Pa, can I ride the Thunderbolt again?"
"Can't afford it, boy."

~

"Most folks be saying they'd have given ya to the State and let them raise ya. But I ain't done it, 'cause it's only fit your own folks should tend ya. Ain't been easy doing it all alone, but I ain't done livin' yet, boy—not at thirty-three!—not by a long shot!"

~

"But Pa, you promised! You promised we'd stay here and Ft. Walton and Selma! You promised!"

Two weeks later his Pa and Grandma's clock were gone, only a few stray coat-hangers in Pa's closet. On the kitchen counter lay a brown paper bag with a note written on it:

13 is old enuf and youve got gristle. Youll be okay. I wish I could really explain but your not old enuf to under stand. I do love you, Bobby, and someday youll ken what love demands. So dont think bad of me pls. There is Grady you see. I see his eyes how he looks at you. Cant be. But he says he loves me and I deserve to get something out of life too. So it has to be this way. Sometimes, Bobby—Someday youll ken this for yerself—sometimes lovin is hurtful. Sorry. Sometimes it is.

Pa

He had taped forty dollars to the bag and had left Rusty for him. She was tied to the longleaf pine out back.

Such memories from childhood jeered at him as he lay on the four-poster bed. His hand moved and he felt the bristle of freshly shaved skin. The hand descended lower to pull on his balls, hard, to twist them until they ached. *This is what you wanted when you bought that thing for me, right? Well, your contraption works, Carmen. Hurts like hell! So do it, baby! Do it hard!*

CHAPTER 3

As one hand pulled scrotum and wrenched testicles, the other grasped flaccidness and sought to consummate manly, physical love. Against the effects of bourbon his hand pistoned, struggled and tried. The attempt was in vain, for bourbon and sleep thwarted the attempt.

And with sleep there came a release from his passion, pains and fears. There was a smoothing of brows as sleep bid him lay down his defenses. His chest began to rise in deep, slow heaves as he lay atop the spread. His head was now limp on the pillow, lips gently parted. He appeared to be not Carmen's toy, but a mother's son, fully grown perhaps, but still a mother's son.

Gray mists shimmered before him like a heavy fog. Without thoughts or pain he watched the gray undulations. Gradually there was a lightening in color: The fog became first a lighter gray, then took on a tinge of blue. And through those timeless mists a woman approached, swirling the fog with steps serene and matronly. She was enveloped in light—It was from her that the pale blue light radiated.—and there were swallows encircling her and darting on the wing against the blue sky.

He pretended to be asleep, yet peeked through slitted lids as she stood over him. Her dress was a simple house dress, tiny flowers against an ivory ground. She bent to tuck him under a patchwork quilt and there was a pure, clean scent about her—soap, starch and ironing boards. It was a scent he vaguely recognized from earliest childhood. She kissed his forehead.

"I'm glad you've come," he said, opening his eyes.

"Nothing could have hindered me tonight, Bobby. Do you want to tell me about it?" she asked.

As he pondered how much to tell her, he bit his lower lip and scrunched his face up like a boy's, with one eyebrow raised and the other lowered.

She sat down on the bed, taking his hand in hers and stroking it tenderly. She waited for him to begin. In the darkness of his bedroom the pale blue light surrounded the bed and the two of them now, and swallows, flitting on the wing, encircled the two of them.

"I hurt," he finally said.

"Is there more?"

He averted his gaze from her to the spirited swallows so fleet on wing. "It's my heart that hurts." He couldn't look at her, but looked at the patchwork quilt.

"I know," she said.

"That's all, I guess," he said.

"I too have been in the world, have known its struggles

and its sorrows. There is more you have not spoken."

He gazed into her eyes, into the tenderness there. He again lowered his gaze, avoiding her eyes. "I've let her do things," he said. Then, in a whisper such as a child might use to impart deepest secrets, he added, "I've pandered myself to her money."

"Very good," she said. "Wisdom cannot begin until we learn to call things by their rightful names."

"But after the years of wanderings it is comforting to have things and go places I can't afford myself. It is because of her that I now eat well and drink well."

"Is that enough to fill your soul, Bobby?"

He shook his head no. "I love the outdoors, you know, and woods and backpacking and critters and birds and all. But not even once since I've been here, with the austerity of the Rockies looming in the distance and beckoning me, has she let me spend a weekend in the wilderness."

"Is that what you long for, a weekend in the wilderness?" she asked.

"No, not really."

"Then what?" she asked.

"Love. I long for love. A woman to love me and cling to me, and I to her. A woman to be home when I drive up after work, and to be there regardless whether I drive a clunker held together with rubber bands, spit and a prayer, or a new Trans-Am or Camaro. To wander a park toward sunset, my arm around her."

"Such a love is a beautiful thing," she said. "I know, for your Pa and I had just such a love."

"And with soft breasts and figure," he said. "A woman I

can be proud of saying, 'And this is my wife.' A woman who, years away—when the children are grown and starting families of their own—who, eons hence, when we are beginning to think of having to say goodbye to this world—a woman who, in our grayed years, would still smile at me a funny wrinkled smile. An old woman, but still my princess and my bride."

"You ask well," she said.

"That is what I want. I'll let other men chase after their heart's content, whether it's houses and boats, clout or fame. For me love would be enough."

"I shall pray, beloved, for a love that surrounds you like a quilt, and for a love…"

"But will I get it?" he interrupted.

"…and for a love that overflows your heart and flows out to all the world."

"But will I get it?" he asked again, a desperation in his voice.

"I can but pray, as you could. But I think the Father will smile upon your request for it keeps with what He pleads with us to do." She stood up. "I shall pray He grant it before the appointed time."

"But if you're not sure if I'll get it or when, I'll settle for a friend or a buddy for a while, okay?"

"His wisdom. It will be granted according to His wisdom, my son," she said as she stood up. "But for now there is Quasi, the dog you saved from impending death. The Father loves all his critters equally. And Quasi has much love to give. So let it rest in His wisdom and sleep now," she said, stroking his forehead and running her fingers through his hair. "Sleep now, my beloved. My child."

Though he closed his eyes, he peeked and saw his mother kneel beside his bed. Surrounded in light, with hands clasped and face lifted heavenward, her lips moved in ardent prayer. Gradually the blue light dimmed and grayed into darkness and he slept.

During his hours of sleep the blizzard abated and morning followed the night in its ordained course. With a stretching and a rubbing of the eyes he awoke into that Sunday morning, crystalline and bright, with sunrays streaming into his room. Strange, his first thoughts were of his mother. Strange, for she had died before his earliest memories. His recollections of her were not memories, but vague associations with print dresses and the scent of ironing boards.

Among the crumpled spread and sheets, Quasi was curled on that bed with him. It surprised him that he knew his dog's name, Quasi, but shrugged off the source of that knowledge. In the warmth and brightness of the sunlit room he scooted down in the bed to curl around him and rub his belly. Quasi didn't have to raise his hind leg, for that had been amputated at the hip. "Don't be ashamed, boy," he said. "Lots of guys got maimed in Nam, maimed or worse." Quasi seemed to smile, his pink tongue drooping from the side of his mouth.

"You would have died out there in the storm. But you'll be safe now. You won't have to wander in the cold, not alone anyway. That's what she'd like to see. It won't happen. We might not always have a grand apartment like this, but rather the rusting roof of my truck for shelter, but I promise you'll be safe now and you'll never be alone.

"She doesn't like you, but don't feel bad. She doesn't like

me either. Or maybe it's men she doesn't like and I'm just a specimen. She wants to get me drunk and stand there and watch another man humiliate me.

"It won't happen tonight. Getting out of it tonight is easy—I'll just lie to her about not being able to find him. But the idea is in her head now. She wants to watch another man use me, rut with me. And someday, somehow, she will work it out.

"With that sin upon me, I could not stand in congregation with other men with my head held high.

"She would probably love to cut off my balls for the fun of it, and would, if she could.

"I know, Quasi. I know. In spite of her money, influence and power I have to sever this thing with her. I will. Somehow. Someway. And while I live, I will again live in the dignity of being a man.

"Thanks for the advice, little guy. And maybe, along the way, I might even find love."

CHAPTER 4

Although Carmen was displeased that Bob had been unable to find the ex-Ranger, the flight by private jet to Denver that Sunday evening was amiable enough. A limousine waited on the tarmac to take the four of them—Carmen, Bob, Tonia and Bennett—to the Maison D'Or. As Bob held the door for Carmen to get situated, Bennett commented on what an attractive couple they made.

Once all were ensconced Carmen grasped Bob's knee, kissed him on the cheek and said, "Bennett, I can honestly say I love him more than I've ever loved anybody."

And there's been a stable-full, right, baby? Bob thought.

"He's had a lot of pain in his life," she went on, "but he hasn't let that crush him. Just last week he worked fourteen hours overtime. My only complaint is he's a little provincial in some of his attitudes, but he's learning to loosen up a bit."

"What type of work do you do?" Bennett asked. He had a mane of shoulder length hair and was closely shaven.

Extremely close shave. Has to be Ivy League. That's their hallmark, Bob thought. "For the State," he answered. "Department of Transportation."

"And he's very good at what he does, Bennett," Carmen chimed in. "He plows the roads well and fixes the potholes just like new."

You bitch! He continued to look at Bennett without a glance in her direction. "But it's decent pay and good benefits. What do you do?"

"Not much, really. Home base is Houston, but I travel a lot. We opened a new plant in Thailand a couple of months ago. Bangkok is the wildest city on the face of the earth! Absolutely anything goes, anytime of day or night."

"Now, honey," Tonia said, putting a hand on his sports jacket. A solitaire diamond sparkled on her wedding finger. "You of course do not indulge, do you?"

"Me? Of course not," Bennett replied. "All it takes is money, Bob, and not an awful lot of that, either. But besides traveling, I just sign my name to whatever papers my people put in front of me."

"That doesn't present very well," Tonia said. "You must read them first, and if you agree, you sign them."

"Matter of fact, I don't, Tonia. I trust the people working for me and their judgment. If I didn't, they'd find themselves standing in the lines at the Missions."

"The number of the homeless in the country is a real problem," Bob said.

"No it's not, Bob," Carmen said. "It's not a problem for me. It's not a problem for Tonia or Bennett. It's only a problem for the homeless."

Bob's mouth opened, then closed as he checked himself. He looked out of the limousine's window and recognized the highway they were on. Before his unwitting plunge into the downward spiral, he had lived here in Denver, had worked for the Manville Corporation as a security guard. At day's end he would change clothes in the men's locker-room, then get into his jeep and drive this same highway out to Boulder, to the University and his classes. He had wanted to become a teacher, elementary level.

As the elevator took them up to the Maison D'Or at the top of a skyscraper, Tonia chatted with Carmen about possible locales for the upcoming honeymoon. The two men stood silently side by side.

The *maitre d'hotel* greeted Carmen by name, then held the chair for her as she sat. Bennett held Tonia's chair. As the four of them settled into their chairs and places, Bob looked out the plate glass window. The city lay at their feet. Lights sparkled here and there in the encompassing mountains, while overhead—stretched out against the darkness of interstellar space—lay the Milky Way. He scooted his chair closer to the window, cupped his hands around his face to block the glare and gazed in awe. "That's the galaxy we're a part of, Bennett," Bob said. "Can you see it from there? I forget if it's a hundred million or a hundred billion stars. But if you could travel at the speed of light, it'd take you a hundred thousand years to cross it. Beautiful, huh?"

"Yes, Bob," Carmen dismissed. "But where's the waiter?"

Just then a busboy arrived at the large round table and started to remove the fifth place setting. "Leave it," Carmen said. The busboy, a teenager with red hair and freckles, asked if they were expecting another. "No," she replied, "but leave it in honor of all the men who have died and rotted in jungles. But you are a little too young to remember any of them, aren't you?"

"Yes, ma'am," the busboy said and left.

"But you remember them, don't you, Bob? Pity what happened to those good men."

Bob repositioned himself at the table and looked at the chair being left empty in honor of Lt. Loomis, Lance Corporal Robbins, Stemmle, Blue.

"So," Bennett said, "you were in Nam?"

"Yeah," Bob said absently as he gazed at visages, at the faces of men, the grime of dozens, hundreds.

"What branch were you in?" Bennett asked.

"Corps," he said, then shook off the hauntings of the past. "But I went to the VA for counseling—me and Doc—and it helped. There are just some people, Bennett, who know all the right strings to pull." He scowled at Carmen then said, "Where's the waiter? I need a drink." He scanned across the candlelight of the room, the coiffures.

Carmen reached over and put her hand lovingly on top of his. The pink of her sleeve contrasted nicely against the deep maroon of his suede jacket, a gift from her. A tuxedoed waiter approached, followed close behind by the same busboy. The waiter was maybe a year or two older than Bob, with blond hair and mustache. As the busboy began to fill water glasses, the waiter inquired about cocktails.

"Bourbon and water," Bob said.

The waiter gasped as he looked at Carmen's hand atop

CHAPTER 4

Bob's on the table. In spite of his professional etiquette he appeared distraught, eyes wide and gulping. He cleared his throat and inquired, "Any special brand, sir?"

"No."

Carmen glanced up at him and a grin came over her face. "Well, Jesse!" she said. "Are you in a wedding party or something tonight? Just look at you!"

"Smirnoff and soda, Carmen?" he asked.

"Everybody, please meet Jesse. I trust you didn't starve too long."

"Getting back to the drinks, please."

"Should I remember him?" Tonia asked Carmen.

"Of course, a couple years ago. Jesse Parker. You know, *Smegma*," Carmen said. "Prodigious gobs of the slime. So much he could put K-Y out of business! That Jesse!" The women snickered together. Then Carmen looked up at him. "No offense—that's just girl talk, Jesse." She opened her evening bag—pink with bold purple and crimson swirls to match her gown—and took out a bill. "Here." Bob could see it was a hundred dollar bill she was pressing into his hand.

"Thank you," Jesse said. Without a glance at the bill, he slid it into his trousers. "But getting back to the drinks."

"Oh, skip all that and join us for old-time's sake. I could set you up in the complex where Bob lives. It's nicer than where I had you," she said, squeezing Bob's hand. "Join us. It might be fun."

Bob pulled his hand away from her.

"I have a job to do, Carmen," Jesse said.

Bennett spoke up, "I'll have a J&B and water, Jesse, and please bring Tonia a dry Manhattan on the rocks, Crown

42

Royal."

"Thank you," he said and left.

"Proud and foolhardy," Carmen said. "Look at him, a lowly waiter."

"I'd say he's maintaining," Bob said. "His haircut's fresh. And he may be in school."

"But going around and asking people what they want to drink and what they want to eat. How demeaning!"

"He's the guy you picked up hitchhiking, right?" Tonia asked. "He was thumbing alongside the road. A backpacker who had broken his leg. Yes, I remember now! You took him to the emergency room, visited him, and then rented an apartment for him as he healed. And he's the one you said you got on film."

"That's right!" Carmen said, then bent to whisper in Bob's ear. "Many fine attributes. Huge, uncut, and he can beg just like a dog and eat out of a dish on the floor. So guzzle your drinks tonight, boy."

There was a tinkling overhead. While the others at the table craned their heads upward to the single swaying chandelier, Bob fixed his gaze on the redheaded busboy standing attentively against the wall. His face became a mask, lips contorted, nose scrunched, eyes bulging and brows raised. His expression confounded revulsion, nausea and fear.

Bob had seen that look before and had himself seen the Hag before, in Nam. He did not join all the others in the room in looking up at the one chandelier swaying among the dozens. He would not gaze at her, the Hag with her toothless grin, the matted hair, the flies on her belly, maggots on her toes. He kept his eyes on the horror on the busboy's face. But now he knew the Hag had followed them—or just him?—back to the States.

A fine gentleman stood and made a lighthearted remark. Another sought to top it and the clientele resumed their chatter.

The busboy retreated into the kitchen.

"I can't understand why just one chandelier was swaying," Bennett said. "It couldn't have been a little earthquake—all of them would have moved."

Tonia said, "You men like figuring things like that out. I'll let you worry about it. Doesn't matter to me."

"Men are most curious animals," Carmen said.

Bob recalled Jesse's gasp for breath at seeing Carmen's hand atop his. *Jesse hadn't gasped because Carmen had found another man. He gasped in apprehension as to what it entails for me.* "Did you love him, this Jesse?" Bob asked for all at the table to hear.

"That's hardly fair," Tonia said, coming to her defense, "to ask a woman the tender secrets of her heart."

He laughed an insincere laugh. "It's fair...and significant! Did you?"

"No!" she said.

He looked at her. *You bitch!* were the only words throbbing in his head. Without response he stood up and began to walk. Behind him came Carmen's voice, and Tonia's, calling his name. With carriage proud, erect and military, he went past the *maitre d'*, got onto the elevator.

On the ground floor he crossed the lobby and exited onto the street. The cold wind was bracing. He pulled the collar of his sports jacket around his neck and began to walk toward where the Greyhound station used to be. He hoped it was still there.

It was a sixteen hour bus ride from Denver to Billings. Once there he made a quick stop at Edna's 24-Hour Diner where Della paid for his burger from the money in her apron and where a machine dispensed a pack of Winstons, his first in a couple of years. *It's something Marines do. All of us smoked. All except Doc and he wasn't really a Marine anyway. A Navy Corpsman.*

Outside, he made two phone calls from the booth, the first one to his boss, "I got stranded in Denver and had to take a bus back." The other call was to Foster's taxi.

And finally Quasi! Out to pee. A double serving of kibble. A ride to the vet's. And then his first heeling lesson in the vet's parking lot. Quasi did well on three legs.

Back home he took a chicken from the freezer and put it still frozen into the oven to roast, then found his copy of *The Hunchback of Notre Dame*. During his homeless years, he had had no access to television, so he had read voraciously. At day's end he would sit in his pickup truck, and by moonlight or street lamp would read paperback copies of SciFi, Western, Classics. He purchased them cheaply at church bazaars and yard sales. Six large banana boxes of them were stashed in his closet.

As Quasi munched the first of his rawhide chews and as the chicken slowly roasted, he sat in his chair, struck a match, lit a cigarette—only the second from the pack—and began anew Hugo's timeless tale of mismatched love.

He had not read thirty pages when the doorbell rang. Though it rang only a single short ring with no annoying continuance, he knew who it was. Quasi's dark eyes were questioning him as he stood up and crossed the room.

"What do you want?!" he demanded. His body blocked entrance into the room.

"Can't we just talk?" Carmen asked.

"I think it's all been said. Weren't you listening?"

"Bob, may I please come in and apologize?" Her hand was reaching timidly toward his.

He stepped back from the doorway and she entered to mid-room.

"Is that chicken roasting I smell?"

"Go ahead and apologize," he said, closing the door.

She was unbuttoning black leather driving gloves. "I see you still have *that dog.*"

"Where's your apology?" he said. As erect as a recruiting poster he was standing beside her now.

"I was thinking about that old truck of yours. If you'd like, we could go out this evening and you could test drive something you'd look good in."

"That ain't much of an apology, baby," he said.

She put her arms around him and laid her head on his chest. "I do love you. There's a strength about you...I can even hear your heartbeat. Solid. Firm. It sounds like the heartbeat of ten thousand men. Forgive me. Forgive me, Bob. I never realized you had fears so deep within you. Other people can have sex and just take a shower and wash it off. But not you. I promise I'll never force you into sex with another man. You're too strong for that. Too provincial."

Hesitantly he put a hand on her head and started to stroke her hair. "Well maybe the Pastor had something to do with that outcome."

"Who?" she asked, pulling back a little and looking into his face.

"Reverend Negley. No, I didn't live in the woods with my dog from the time Pa left until I was old enough to enlist." He chuckled. "No. The Pastor found us there, and maybe some of his water and blood seeped in."

"I never realized you were religious," she said, hugging him and putting her head back on his chest.

"I was baptized, but no one who's been through what I've been through and who's seen what I've seen, could possibly keep on believing in God."

"Oh, Bob. I do love you. I'm just beginning to appreciate the depth of you. Let's go to bed and make up properly. And if we hurry, we can go out and get you a new truck, or MG, Trans-Am, whatever you want." She held him tightly.

"If we hurry, huh?" he said.

Clinging to him close—with her gaze averted to the floor—she whispered, "I'll even let you fuck me as long as you use some grease."

"Some grease, huh?!" he said.

"Come on, Bob." She took him by the hand and pulled toward the bedroom.

He didn't move. "One question first, baby…Can I go back to school? I would like to be a teacher."

From arm's distance she looked at him. Her brows knitted briefly, then her free hand went on top of Bob's to surround it. "But if you did, with your job and the classes and the studying, how much time would that leave us to be together?"

With increasing backward pull, he extracted his hand from

her grasp. "That was a test, baby. You failed. So you can get the hell out of here. You talk about love," he said, "but you know nothing about encouraging, nurturing, loving."

"Bob?"

"Go."

"Bob?" she said entreatingly.

"Get the hell out!" he bellowed.

Without further protestation she began to put on her gloves. He watched in silence. At the door she paused and turned. "It's not as cold out there as it has been. But it's only November and winter hasn't really set in yet. I think I'll stop by the Mission and give them a donation. There are so many homeless. Pathetic. Then I'll go visit Daddy. *Ciao!*" The door closed softly behind her.

He got his journal from its stashing place and a pen from a kitchen drawer. He sat in his chair, lit a cigarette. Quasi was against the wall now, again chewing absently on his rawhide stick.

He put the date on the page and under it wrote:

1. Give notice.

2. Close checking.

3. Lights/Phone.

4. Dispose of things.

Scary. Having served on the front lines meant something after previous wars. Now it's a liability. Even my Decorations mean nothing when you're looking for a job. But maybe I'll find something anyway. And even if I don't, I'll manage somehow with my dignity intact.

The first thing next morning, Tuesday, he told his boss he

was quitting and gave four days notice. At noon he went to the bank.

On Wednesday he found several good boxes behind the supermarket and purchased a blue plastic tarp and some rope.

On Thursday the telephone was disconnected.

On Friday evening the Salvation Army arrived. They were pleased to receive such fine furniture and clothes in such beautiful condition.

That last night he and Quasi slept on the floor in the empty apartment.

By first light they were in the truck. He stopped by the diner for breakfast and to say goodbye to Della. Then, with Quasi snuggled so close it made shifting difficult, they set forth, headed south, headed to the land of his childhood.

CHAPTER 5

Atlanta, Georgia.

While Bob and Quasi curled together on the floor in Montana, a couple thousand miles away Blaine Shirer found no parking spot at Graffiti's. He circled around again to the off-duty policeman hired to protect the vehicles. With his red MG still running he got out to speak with the officer.

"Jamie, if I left you my keys, would you move it into a spot when somebody leaves?"

"Of course, Mr. Shirer, not a problem. We got a babysitter for tomorrow night and we'll be front and center for the opening. How's it going? Will it be as good as *Macbeth*? *Is this a dagger I see before me, / The handle toward my hand?...*"

"Five curtain calls. That's the most we've ever gotten and after opening night it was standing room only. That's what you guys did! I can only hope it'll be as good. We've worked hard enough but we're having a little problem with the blocking. We're doing it just as it would have been done at the Globe. The only difference is we're using women—except for

Nursie. We've *got to use* drag for her!—and we're using lighting. The lighting's the problem. In the dimmer scenes the students can't see their blocking marks. And the opening's tomorrow night!"

"Did you know your Juliet—Margaret—is our next door neighbor?"

"Yes, she's mentioned that."

"Well, you'll remember Carl was *our* stage manager. He was always spot-on when any little problem came up. He'd ponder it and find a solution, every time, never failed. Maybe he'll have a workable suggestion for you. He's inside."

"I'll check him out and thanks for tending my car for me."

"Anytime, Mr. Shirer."

Blaine showed his ID, paid the cover charge and merged into the crush of men and the throb of tom-toms. Strobe light cast its fairy dust over sweaty torsos.

In an abandoned textile factory, not six blocks from Graffiti's, dogs barked, then snarled, then whimpered. The loser was dumped into a black trash bag while some men cheered, others cursed and money exchanged hands.

Observing it all from a loft was Bronc and two of his bodyguards. He noted one of his lieutenants enter by a side door and run across the floor to the stairs. Bronc was already standing when he barged into the manager's office.

"O'Neil's storage unit is empty!" he shouted.

"All sixty-four kilos?"

"Empty! *Nada!*"

One of the two bodyguards spoke up. "And that was good shit, boss."

"Best powder money can buy!" Bronc said. "Horse, to Graffiti's! Extract Tony! We've got a fuckin' war to wage!"

CHAPTER 6

Locketville, Missouri.

Slowly, not daring to push the old pickup faster than forty-five miles per hour, yet with the dream of a future drawing them on, Bob and Quasi made their way. Seventy miles west of the Mississippi smoke bellowed from the engine. It bucked and lunged to a grinding noise. It shimmied and stalled.

When the tow truck arrived, the burly mechanic—with baseball cap turned backwards—said the towing alone would cost sixty-five dollars.

"Okay," Bob said, "I don't have much choice."

The mechanic held his hand out. Bob paid him in advance, watched him attach chains and climbed into the passenger seat. While knitted dice swung from the rearview mirror, Quasi snuggled comfortably on his lap.

Once in town the two of them pushed the pickup into a bay. While the mechanic searched for the problems—which he asserted in advance would be many—Bob and Quasi went out to the sidewalk and stood on the curb under oak trees.

They were skeletal with winter and rattling in the wind.

This was a cameo of a town, one from a by-gone era, one time and progress had overlooked. Across the street was a white steepled church with plywood nailed across the door and onto the windows, and even the plywood was gray with age. *If there is a God, He wouldn't let that happen to His churches*, Bob thought. The sign out front mocked the hope that once thrived here: The First Baptist Church of Locketville. *As if there'll ever be a Second!* Besides the church, there was the service station, a tiny post office, a one story brick elementary school, a little grocery store, barbershop, feed store and restaurant. That was Locketville, all of it, Locketville, Missouri.

He pulled his wallet from his jeans and sat down on the curb beside his dog. Without taking the bills out but thumbing through them, he counted three hundred sixty-four dollars. *I started with six hundred ninety. Where'd it go? There was food and tips for the waitresses, gas, three quarts of oil, a motel room one night—but only one night—a new retread on the right front and the tow charge. That's it.* He gulped. He wished he had a cigarette, and considered walking down the block to the little store. *Can't afford it.* He went back to the service station.

The mechanic was under his truck on the hydraulic. "What do you think?" he asked.

"Come over here," the mechanic said, coming up steps to point to a gizmo in the engine. "Here's the first problem, guy. The water pump's shot. And see all the burned wires? But back here's a bigger problem." He moved back, squatted and pointed to something under the bed.

Bob at least knew enough to know that what he was

pointing to was part of the axle. As a teen, living with the Pastor, he never had a car, and then on his eighteenth birthday he had enlisted, so he had never learned about auto-mechanics.

"Look in there," the mechanic said, pointing into a joint. Bob looked. "See how it's all worn? See the metal shavings? Well, that's the universal and yours is dangerous. Let that thing fall off while you're high-tailing it, and wham-bam-thank-you-ma'am, you're a goner."

"That dangerous, huh?" Bob said.

"Yep. If it'd start—and it won't—I wouldn't drive it around the block," the mechanic said, standing up.

"How much is all this going to cost?"

"Mighty old truck there, buddy."

"Ball-park figure?" Bob said, raising his eyebrows.

"I'll have to call around to see if I can find the parts first. If I can find them, I'll have you an estimate in about an hour. But don't get your hopes up, guy. And I guess it'll take four or five days to get the parts here, and then another one or two for the labor."

"Is there a cheap motel anywhere near by?" Bob asked.

The mechanic pointed caddy-corner out the bay door. "Thirteen miles down the road in the next town over."

"Je-sus Christ!" Bob said.

"But then you might check with Mrs. Sloan about taking you in. She used to take guests in, hasn't in years, but used to."

"Where would I find her?" he asked.

He walked Bob out to the sidewalk, and pointing, gave directions.

He found the clapboard house a block and a half down a side street. A gutter, long since pulled free from the eaves, wavered in the strong north wind. The front yard was overgrown with weeds, brown with the solid onset of winter. He went around to the back. Burdock had grown up in the chicken yard where hens hadn't cackled in years. He had Quasi sit beside him as he knocked at the kitchen door. There was a tapping across the floor and the door opened.

"Yes?" a gray-haired woman said. She was plump and of translucent complexion.

He said he was in a jam, his truck had broken down, and his name was Bob. "And I'm told you used to take in boarders."

"Well I don't know. A body hears about strange happenings on the radio these days," she said.

"I'm not strange. Honest," he said with his best Sunday-school smile.

"And who was it told you come here?"

"I don't know his name. At the station, the mechanic. A big guy, black hair, a little older than me."

"You must mean Willie. Growing up he wanted to be a teacher—I might have had something to do with that, or I like to think so anyway....But I really don't know," she said and hesitated.

He explained about the water pump and the universal and about having to order all the parts in, and he was just trying to return to the South, the land of his childhood.

She took from the pocket of her house dress a white handkerchief. It had lace on the edges. She dried the palms of her hands with it, then said hesitantly, "Well, I guess if Willie told you, I imagine it would be all right."

"And my dog, too?"

"You have a dog?" she asked.

"Yeah, right here," he said.

"What type of dog is it?"

She was blind. "He's an awful good dog, never messes or bothers things. I haven't had him too long, short gray hair. The vet said he's forty seven pounds. And he has only three legs."

"How'd he lose his leg?" she asked.

"I don't know. I've only had him a week and a half or so. His name's Quasi."

"From Quasimodo?"

"Yeah," he said.

"Have you read it? *The Hunchback of Notre Dame*?"

"Sure. I've read lots of things."

She made clicking sounds with her tongue against the roof of her mouth as she pondered, then set the price at twenty a week, room and board.

"It probably won't be a week," he said.

"Then we can divide it out."

He agreed to the price and accepted her invitation to come in. Except for the kitchen with its yellow linoleum floor and glass curtain, the house was dark, with dime-store bric-a-brac cluttering the tops of surfaces. There was no television, but books, books in cases from floor to ceiling in the living room, books in smaller cases in the hallway, and even stacked in the corner of what was to be Bob's room.

She fixed two cups of instant coffee from a kettle, and they sat together at the Formica table. The preliminaries about the cold front passed quickly and Mrs. Sloan talked about herself. Her husband had died forty years ago, but she had managed by teaching school. All the knickknacks throughout the house were gifts from her students accumulated over the years. Now and then she used to take in the occasional boarder to supplement what a schoolmarm earned. It was diabetes she had, but got by okay on her Social Security and two visits a month from the county nurse.

He surmised she was a lonely, old woman—she had talked on so long. "This is all very interesting," Bob said. "But I've got to go back and check on the truck now. We can talk some more when I get back."

"I was planning on tuna casserole for dinner," she said. "Would that be okay with you? I make it special—I put green olives in it. It makes it special."

"That sounds great, Mrs. Sloan."

"And would you mind leaving Quasi with me? It'll give us a chance to get acquainted. And would it be okay if I gave him a Saltine?"

"Spoil him all you want, ma'am."

"Thank you," she said.

"Sure," he said and left.

He arrived back at the station almost exactly one hour from the time he had left. Through the plate glass window he could see Willie sitting on a high stool in back of the counter. "So, Willie," he said as he opened the door and entered, "I hear you once wanted to be a teacher. I still do."

"Yeah, a ton of years ago when I was a kid. You're lucky it's a Chevy, guy. I found the parts in St. Louis. The universal is brand new. The water pump's a salvage, but what the hell, it should be okay."

"Great," Bob said, "but uh, how much is all this going to cost?"

Willie picked up the pad on which he had written. Bob noticed his fingers were stained with grease. "Three hundred and twenty, maybe plus a little, maybe minus."

That depletes my funds! He inhaled a deep breath, held it, then exhaled. "Okay," he said. "Go ahead, get the parts in and do what you got to do. But if you can keep the cost as low as possible, I'd appreciate it."

"Sure will."

"Thanks," he said. His head was spinning and he was a little wobbly by the time he reached the sidewalk. He placed a hand on the bole of an oak to steady himself. When the truck broke down, he had foreseen a day or two of rest from the highway, not this.

If I were alone I'd stick my thumb out, hitchhike, and get there with hundreds still in my pocket. But I'm not alone anymore. I've made a commitment. And no way will Quasi be cast out again. The commitment isn't our problem. Money is.

There are jobs in Atlanta but I'll need at least two hundred to rent a room and eat while I look for work and then wait two weeks until I get paid.

Three hundred sixty-four dollars. That's it. Period. If the repairs cost only three hundred, that would leave sixty-four. And then minus twenty to Mrs. Sloan for room and board. No way can I get to Atlanta on forty-four dollars. That's not even enough for the gas.

And no way in hell will I defraud an old blind woman. No way can I, upon leaving, hand her a one dollar bill and tell her it's a twenty. She's putting herself out to help me and I can't do that.

Divine intervention would be helpful, if Divinity existed. That was a beautiful pipe dream while it lasted. But it's just that. It's all up to me, my actions. Mine alone.

He glanced upward through the rattling branches. Against the crystalline sky, high aloft, soared a raptor. The triangular shape of the tail told him it was either an eagle or buteo, but he couldn't see the size of her head so identification couldn't be made. *I wonder if they even have buteos here. If not, then it's an eagle. Can't see what type.*

Across the street doves searched contentedly in the leaves while a swallow darted in the air. He followed the swallow toward the restaurant.

CHAPTER 7

At the counter of the Blue Plate Diner Bob draped his sheepskin coat—an expensive gift from Carmen—on the back of a stool. He scanned the room. Two men were bent over newspapers along the counter. Three tables were taken: two women and a child at one, a young couple at another, and an elderly man and grandson at the third.

He sat, ordered black coffee, got it, and moments later asked the waitress—as she was carrying an order to a table—if he could speak to the owner.

He watched the plastic clock on the wall tick off the seconds as he waited. A middle-aged man came out of the kitchen and approached. He wore a soiled apron, had deep lines drooping from nose to chin around his mouth, and his salt-and-pepper hair was cut into a flat-top. Wiping hands on his apron, he introduced himself as Mr. Atchity, the owner. Bob explained about his truck breaking down and being towed in from the Interstate, and about trying to get to Atlanta, where he'd heard the recession hadn't depleted all the jobs yet. "So what I'm getting at is I need work. Do you have anything that needs doing or do you know of anybody who does?"

Mr. Atchity massaged swollen arthritic fingers. "Things are right tough in these parts too. But in a couple months we'll have a new President and maybe he can do something to change things around."

"But I need a job now," Bob said.

"Are you a veteran?" Mr. Atchity asked.

"What difference does that make?"

"To me a lot," Mr. Atchity said.

"Yes, sir, I served."

"What branch?"

"Marine Corps. Three consecutive tours in Nam, sir. So you don't have a job for me and you won't help me either, right?"

Mr. Atchity took off his glasses and wiped them on a handkerchief from his hip pocket. "I was in the Corps, too. And war, son, is not pretty. The only difference with you guys and us is you had reporters swarming all over the place and cameras."

"Well can you help me find a job then?"

"Would you like a piece of pie?"

"It's a job I need, not pie!"

Mr. Atchity took a slice of apple pie from the glass display case, put it in front of him and filled his coffee cup. "Tell me what you think. I make them myself from my wife's recipe," he said and left.

Maybe! I've got to tell him what I think about the pie, so he's planning on coming back. Please. Through the pass-through window he could see Mr. Atchity in the kitchen. He was talking into the black receiver of a telephone mounted onto the wall. *Please!*

He hadn't eaten half the pie, its crust full flavored and flaky, when Mr. Atchity was again standing in front of him. "This is not for public knowledge," he said, "but the health department is threatening to close me if I don't fix the place up, and that right soon. Now I can't afford to pay that much, no more than minimum wage, but I'll throw in meals for you, as much as you can eat. So it's not much of a job I'm offering—not for a veteran who served honorably—but if you want it, you got it."

"What time do you want me here, sir?" Bob asked.

"You can cut the *Sir,* I was enlisted too. You can call me Mr. Atchity. Now there's not a lot of dishes first thing in the morning, so I'll come in early, get breakfast going and you can come in about seven."

Bob stood up and offered his hand. "Thanks! I'll be here at seven," he said.

Mr. Atchity shook it and nodded.

When he got back at Mrs. Sloan's, she was keeping the casserole warm in the oven. He tried to help her carry things to the table. "No, you go sit, young man," she said. "This is woman's work." Slowly, using the sense of touch rather than sight, she placed things on the table. He noticed her lips moved with each step across the room. She was counting them. The tuna casserole was tasty, enlivened with the green olives.

As they ate, he explained that, from now on, she wouldn't

have to bother to fix him anything. He'd take his meals at work.

"No," she said.

"But Mrs. Sloan, it comes as part of my pay."

"The deal we made was twenty a week for room *and* board," she said.

"But I'm just trying to help. It must be an awful lot of bother, having to do it, you know..."

"Blind?" she asked.

"Yeah."

"A body learns to manage, Bob. And planning the meals and then cooking them will give me something to do with my time."

"Well, then," he said, "I can at least do up the dishes for you every night."

"And just how would I ever find anything if you go and put them away?" she asked. "We have our deal, young man. We'll stick to our deal."

"Okay," he said. "Then I guess I'll take a walk. I need to go to the store anyway."

"What do you need at the store?" she asked.

"I probably shouldn't tell you, but I'd like a cigarette."

"Well, right around the corner there you'll find a pack. I don't know what kind they are, of course, but a church lady left them here last month. She's probably forgotten about them by now, but even if she hasn't, I don't think she'd mind."

He found the cigarettes and lit a Kool as Mrs. Sloan scraped all the dishes into an iron skillet. She put it on the floor for Quasi. It was too much food for him, but Bob checked himself from saying anything. He smoked that cigarette and another as she did the dishes and tidied the kitchen.

Back at the table she said, "See, being blind isn't all that bad. A body can still manage. The one thing I really miss, though, is not being able to read."

Bob asked if he could read aloud to her and they talked about what she would like to hear. She finally decided on *Middlemarch*, which, after much searching, he located on the top shelf of a bookcase in the living room.

In the weeks that followed he would read aloud every evening—at the table, after their chat—a chapter or two. At passages her plump face would light and blind eyes would twinkle like a girl's.

She would wake him every morning by making the sound of a rooster crowing—It was pretty authentic.—and there would be a full breakfast waiting, biscuits, honey and all.

In those weeks he worked for Mr. Atchity with the strength of unfailing gratitude. He scrubbed the kitchen hood inside and out, he painted walls, and tinkered with plumbing. He did pots and dishes, stripped twenty years of grease from the floors, and working through the night, singlehandedly ripped out the carpet from the dining room and replaced it with new.

When his pickup was ready, he paid for the repairs, but left it parked on the street in front of the house and walked the two blocks to and from work. The only time he used it was on Thursday evening when he and Mrs. Sloan would drive thirteen miles to the nearest supermarket. Through the aisles Mrs. Sloan would push the cart, and walking beside her would be Bob, towering above her, handsome with his light brown wavy hair and eyes of palest blue. As they slowly made their way up and down the aisles, he would describe what they were passing and she would ask a hundred questions—Did he like this or that? Or did they have *baby* lima beans? Back home he would hand her item by item, telling her what each one was, as she patiently placed things where she could find them.

After three weeks on the job, he began to leave the restaurant for an hour in the slow part of the afternoon to return home to check on Mrs. Sloan and Quasi. During those hours he tried to teach three-legged Quasi to play Frisbee. As long as he kept the Frisbee low, Quasi did almost okay, but jumping was not his thing. They changed the game to Fetch the Stick. He did great with that.

He was off Sunday afternoons—The restaurant closed at two.—and under brilliant blue skies or gray, he would walk, content and happy, along dirt roads or woodland paths. Quasi went with him, hobbling at his side, or sniffing in the dead leaves, or dashing into this bush or that. Once Quasi discovered why skunks aren't called a dog's best friend. Mrs. Sloan told Bob to bathe him first in tomato juice. And no, he could take it from the pantry—fourth shelf up, far right. When he had accomplished the proper order of bathing as Mrs. Sloan had explained it—and had dried Quasi the best he could—he found a bottle of cheap perfume sitting on the kitchen table.

A few days before Christmas she asked if he would cut a little tree. "Oh, I know what you're thinking," she added, "but it does smell good and brings back memories." The next day he got permission from Mr. Atchity to extend his afternoon break by an hour. With a shovel resting on his shoulder and with three-legged Quasi hobbling beside him, he wandered woodland paths until he at last came upon the perfect tree.

He didn't cut it but dug it, and back home found a large earthenware pot among the brambles of what had once been the chicken yard. He put their tree on the Formica of the kitchen table, washed up and drank a glass of warm milk before returning to the restaurant.

When he got home that evening, a little after seven as always, he found their Christmas tree decorated with a porcelain angel on top and twenty-four fancy red ribbons blind Mrs. Sloan had tied and placed the best she could. He asked how she knew which spool was red, and she explained she had carried all of them to the variety store and there had asked Peggy to pick out the red.

"You mean you walked to town?" he asked.

"Of course. It wouldn't have done at all to have purple ribbons, or green or something, now would it?"

"You're a remarkable woman, Mrs. Sloan," he said.

"A body finds you can do a lot in the dark as long as you go slow," she said.

On Christmas morning there were four packages under that tree: a flannel shirt for him, a small bottle of Chanel Number Five for her, and two boxes of dog biscuits.

One day during his afternoon break Mrs. Sloan broached a subject she had previously avoided. She asked why he wasn't married.

"Well, I guess I just haven't found her."

"But that's where your future lies, Bobby," she said, "in

67

home, and caring and providing."

Don't you think I dream of that, long for that, need that? "Well one of these days, I guess," he said. "But uh, I've gotta get on back. Uh, we've had a real busy day at work, you know? The dishes will be stacked high for me. And, uh, I just wanted to make sure you were okay, but I really need to get back to those dishes now. I'll see you tonight."

The week before Reagan was to take office, they were sitting and chatting over their hot Ovaltine—Coffee kept Mrs. Sloan awake and Bob had enough of that at work. Into their conversation fell one of those peaceable lulls that sometimes befall among those who are comfortable with one another and have no need to impress. Into that silence Bob said, "I've been thinking, Mrs. Sloan. I've been able to save up a little money, and I'm wondering if it would be okay with you if I used some of it to buy some paint. I'll do the inside first, and come spring I'll get the outside done. And maybe I'll fix up the chicken house and we could have some hens."

"No," she said. "It's time you and Quasi left."

"But why?! I think we get along pretty good!"

"That we do, and it's been nice having you here. And Quasi's been company for me during the day. But it's time for both of you to leave."

"But I'm happy here," he said.

"And I've been happy too," she said. "I never knew how lonely I was with just the radio for company. But you've got to find your future, Bobby. That's not here. We can stay in touch."

"You don't even have a telephone."

"You can write," she said.

"But how'd you…"

"Mrs. Hutchinson, the traveling nurse, can read them to me. And you can come back and visit an old woman now and then. And maybe bring the wife and kids? My first name is Ethel in case you have a little girl."

"Yeah!" he said, "come back and visit. Excuse me!" He stood up—the chair scuffing roughly on the floor—went to his room and slammed his door with a thud.

"Bob?" she called after him.

He flopped face down on the bed and hit it with his fist. *Rejection! What the hell's wrong with me?! After that shit with Pa, those years of homelessness, that debauchery with Carmen! Shit! I thought I'd found a home here and maybe a little love. And now she's kicking me out. 'My first name is Ethel in case you have a little girl,' she had said. Is there meaning in that or is it just senile babble?*

He sat on the edge of the bed and into the darkness of the room said those words aloud, slowly, in his deep masculine voice. "My first name is Ethel in case you have a little girl." And then he understood. She wasn't rejecting him. She was demonstrating something about love.

His chin quivered. Now he understood. She probably needed him more than he needed her. Yet she was sending him away, for she knew—as he did if he were honest with himself—that his future and dreams didn't lie here. He stood from his bed, went to her door and knocked.

"Come in, Bobby," she said.

He opened the door. In the meager light he could see she was already in bed, with the blankets up to her neck.

"Come, sit," she said, patting the bed.

He did. "You're one hell of a woman, Mrs. Sloan."

"It's just you're young, and healthy and you've got to set forth, Bobby."

"I know," he said. He found her hand and squeezed it.

"Now what would the church women say if they found us here like this, young man? Or what would my Papa say? He would insist you marry me. Now wouldn't that be a sight!"

"Goodnight, Mrs. Sloan," he said, rising.

"Sweet dreams," she said.

He was going to leave Friday morning after getting his pay Thursday and a final trip to the supermarket.

It snowed heavily late Thursday night.

Morning came and Mrs. Sloan woke him, as usual, by crowing like a rooster. As usual, she had prepared a full breakfast—oatmeal, eggs, sausage, biscuits, honey.

He made three trips carrying armfuls of clothes out to his truck and put them under the tarp with his six cartons of paperbacks. He came back, hugged Mrs. Sloan, and said his thanks and his goodbyes. He called Quasi to come with him this time.

From his truck he gazed for one last time at the house. He saw her at the front window, her hand parting the glass curtains. Above her the gutter still hung free and water from the melting snow dripped from the eaves. The weeds in the yard, draped in that heavy wet snow, assumed the enchanted appearance of snowdrifts.

It wasn't a grand house, but here within those clapboards

he had found, after his years of wanderings, had found, for a little while at least, a home. Here he had paused from his downward spiral. And here he had learned something about love, something that his thousands of hours of sitting in church as a teen, of his thousands of hours of studying the Scriptures, hadn't even hinted at. Stripped of the gilded babble of preachers, love—working itself out in the real world—was, indeed, sometimes hurtful.

He had learned about self-denial from the old blind woman standing in the window there, her hand foolishly parting the curtain as if she could see. He promised that if she couldn't come to Atlanta for the wedding, they would honeymoon here, in Locketville, Missouri, in a clapboard house with gutter hanging loose.

He leaned across the seat and Quasi and rolled down the passenger window. Mouthing widely the words, he said, without sound, "I love you." How he wished blind eyes could see, but maybe they did. While the glass curtains were still parted, he shifted into gear and headed onward toward his future.

FROM THE JOURNAL

When I was crossing the bridge from Indiana into Kentucky the car in front of me skidded on the ice and plunged through the railings. I slid to a stop and jumped feet first into the darkness below.

Somehow I managed to pull a little boy from the car and get him onto a sheet of ice. But I couldn't find the car again—what with the ice floes and it being dark and the current and all. If it hadn't been like that maybe I could have seen bubbles or something. But I couldn't find the car again. Anyway, I'm told a helicopter rescued the little boy three miles or so down the river and Fire Rescue tossed me a line.

The Church of the Black Brethren put me up in a motel room. TV crews came and wanted to interview me, but I wouldn't go out and talk to them. Quasi and I just lay in bed watching a Redford movie.

Angels singing awoke me in the morning. That's what it sounded like. I looked out the window and dozens of black men and women with tons of kids were there. All were dressed in the black of bereavement and their voices, what heavenly voices! I never heard voices that celestial before.

I put on my jeans and opened the door. And here they come, all piling in, the women carrying cakes and two cardboard boxes with gobs of homemade food, some of it still hot. One of them had even baked dog biscuits. They weren't all perfect like in a store-bought box, but Quasi loved them.

The men wanted the keys to my truck to take it to some garage. I told them no, so they hot-wired it and brought it back an hour later with new tires all around. Michelin. They bought me Michelins.

I left that afternoon, foregoing a church service and banquet in my honor. I had to invent a lie, so I told them I was headed to Atlanta for my wedding. A little white lie, but I think they believed it. They were still going to have their banquet, though, to celebrate little Isaac's survival.

A little ways out of town I noticed they had even filled my gas tank up. I wish they hadn't gone to all the bother. I'm not the hero they say I am. I managed something but it wasn't enough. There will still be a double funeral, for mother and son. I wish I were a better man.

At least little Isaac will have the church to raise him and tend him and love him. To be all alone in this world is not how it's supposed to be.

Atlanta lies only eight hours down the road. Perhaps I'll land a decent job.

CHAPTER 8

Atlanta, Georgia.

In all the much ballyhooed city, the only job he could find was that of roofer. Yet it was enough to keep him out of the lines at the soup kitchens where the well-meaning seasoned the chili with despair. For several weeks he had been dating Linda, a graduate of the Culinary Institute and formerly the chef in a now defunct restaurant. "The *Journal* gave us two rave reviews, Bob. And we were on the way to making it a real destination, but with this economy, kaput! you know." She was now working as a cook in a diner located about mid-way along the route he took between King Roofing and his room.

As he walked from work to the diner this Thursday—his denim jacket folded and perched on his shoulder—he was puzzling over Linda's avoidance. On Monday, Tuesday and Wednesday he had seen her busy at work in the diner. Each time she had smiled and waved, but each evening when he had called her from the pay phone, her mother had offered excuses why she couldn't come to speak. He wondered if today she would find time to come from the kitchen for a moment.

There was nothing wrong with last weekend, that's for sure. Saturday had been her daughter's birthday and he had attended the little party, had given her a stuffed Dalmatian and, later, the three of them had gone out to see Disney's *101 Dalmatians*. Sunday he and Linda had taken a long walk through the city, gazing into the window displays of department stores and jewelers. They had stopped at Burger King for dinner, then, for the first time, had made love. Although it had been in his shabby room, it had been wonderful love, first slow, tender, and building to passion and writhing.

He wondered why she was avoiding him. She said she understood how tight jobs were, that the only work he could find in the whole city was that of roofer, and how she understood it was only temporary. She said she understood that his truck wasn't starting dependably since his arrival here and that it would take him another week or so to save enough to have it fixed. She said she understood. That's what she said.

Along cracked sidewalks and new, for twelve blocks, under ancient oaks and past azaleas already budded, he walked. Gray-haired women, wrapped in bright afghans, rocked—in their timeless way—on porches. On the telephone line overhead, a flock of grackles perched—thousands of them, stretched out for three blocks or more, each grackle identical, each with an iridescence on the wing, all but four facing the same direction.

Half a block ahead he saw Linda coming out of the front door of the diner. She was getting off work early and had already changed into slacks and a multicolored sweater. Her blond French-cut hair was freshly done. *Must have had it done yesterday after work.* At the sidewalk she got into a red Camaro, double-parked, the engine running.

He slunk into a doorway to watch her leave in the sporty car, a young man with mustache behind the wheel. He hoped she hadn't seen him pressed in the doorway there.

He watched the traffic go by. *I don't have a Camaro, baby. I don't have a nice apartment. I don't even have a decent job. But damn it, I'm doing the best I can!* He hit the wall with his fist. *It would just make things easier to work toward a future with you by my side. I never should have allowed you to see my dumpy room.*

Still in the doorway he lit a cigarette. *I'll never stop here for dinner again, but I do understand, Linda. You have a daughter to worry about as well. There'll be needs and bills that I myself could not meet. I can barely support me and Quasi, so I can't blame you for looking at my empty wallet, baby. So I'll miss your laugh, your smile, and our future together that I've been imagining. That was foolish of me, wasn't it?*

Maybe I should have told you I've got something up my sleeve, something I'm working on. Some magazines pay ten thousand dollars for a short story. Imagine, Linda! But if I could just get paid a hundred or two at first, that would help, wouldn't it? But with you passing by in a Camaro that's just a would-a, could-a, huh, baby? I promise you'll never see me again, never hear from me. And as somebody used to say, Ciao....But that's kinda harsh, what I really mean is Good luck, Linda. Really.

I wish I hadn't written Mrs. Sloan about you. I'll have to write again and explain, or maybe I'll just stop mentioning you. That's easier. For the time being I'm not going to date. I'll just maintain, keep myself out of the soup kitchens. I've got paper, pencils and maybe I can tell a story. Maybe a magazine will buy one.

The kids in the school yard over there are cute, all bundled up in their jackets and sweaters and playing. I'd love to play with my kids when they got home from school, or maybe walk them to a park and watch them play with their chums. But it all depends on having some bucks. Can't watch too long. Someone will think I have motives, but they are so cute.

Against the chain-link fence around the schoolyard two policemen shoved a black man, his hair braided into dreadlocks. As the children tossed balls and jumped rope, they frisked him. On numerous afternoons that man had beckoned to Bob, hawking euphoria.

The evening chill was starting as he crossed caddy-corner through a little park. He paused to take his denim jacket from his shoulder and put it on. He noticed his jeans and tennis shoes were stained black with tar. Cars streamed by as he walked, and delivery trucks, occasionally a limousine.

He passed the Laundromat where he did his wash on Saturdays, and passed by the adjacent storefront church, The Church of Penitents. The afternoon service was beginning with a piano pounding block chords of a hymn he recognized from childhood.

He entered the next doorway down, Bud's Place Cold Beer, and although the transition from sunlight to gloom blinded him, he knew the layout, went straight in a dozen steps and turned left a couple more to the bar. He sat.

Bud, a bald, bespectacled man, put a draft in front of him.

"Why is it your little lady ain't been in with ya all week?" he asked.

"She's anybody's lady now. Want her phone number?" Bob said, putting two quarters on the bar.

"Sorry, man," Bud said.

"Plenty of fish, ya know?"

"Well, here's something to cheer ya up. We're having a drawing. Chance for a pitcher of beer for a nickel."

"Sure," he said.

Bud scooped Bob's two quarters into his hand. "I'll take it out of this," he said. After ringing up the cash register, he took a clean pitcher, turned it over and dropped Bob's change, a nickel, into it. Bud handed him the stub of a pencil and a bar napkin. "Got to write your name on it now." Bob did and gave it to him. Bud repositioned his bifocals and held the napkin beneath the light under the bar.

Bob scanned the room. The heavy jowled cigar smoker sat on his usual stool to his right. Four young men in white tee-shirts, all familiar, stood around the pool table in the back. At a table behind him two women sat with a pitcher, one rocking a baby carriage, the other with curlers in her hair. To his left, nearer the door, three businessmen sat at the bar.

Bud stood upright, held the napkin before him and proclaimed in loud voice, "Ah yes, Robert Newell!"

Bob started with bafflement at the loudness of his announcement.

"Them dudes down there been asking 'bout cha," Bud informed. He motioned with his head toward the three businessmen.

Bob snapped his head to look. Two of the businessmen,

dressed in matching blue blazers and white turtlenecks, were standing up. The one in the center, in sunglasses and suit, leaned toward the bar and looked Bob's way. "Hey Newell!" he called.

In the back of the barroom the cue ball smacked into the rack. The baby burst into wails.

The businessman put his sunglasses into his breast pocket. "Hey, Newell!" His voice was syrupy. "Hey, buddy." The pallid scar at his temple, like a tree blasted by lightning, seemed to glow.

"Bronc?" Bob said, astonishment in his voice. Grinning, he stood up and went down to him. "Gees, it's good seeing you, Private," he said with a jovial punch on the shoulder.

"Don't muss the clothes," Bronc said, swiveling to him. His companions were standing by their stools, one tall, Bob's height, the other shorter, with dark Italian complexion.

"You really look good," Bob said. "Are you doing okay?"

"A hell of a lot better than just okay," Bronc said. "The limo out front's mine."

"That's great!" Bob said.

"And I've got pads," Bronc went on, "acreage in the country, power. I've got 'most anything a *man* could want."

"That's great," Bob said. "Have you heard anything from Sgt. Hollinger, or Tanner, or Frog? I know Doc Preston's doing okay. He's got a lovely wife, home, and he's working for his uncle. Gees, it's good seeing you." Again he punched his shoulder.

"I done told ya, don't muss the clothes," Bronc said, leaning back on the barstool. The two men in blazers moved half a step closer to Bob, one on each side. "So tell me, what's happening with you?" Bronc asked.

Bob shrugged. "I, uh, just got off work and, uh, broke up with my girl friend, you know?" He gave a little chuckle. "And well, I'm just working as a roofer, but it's a temporary thing."

"We know," Bronc said. "We seen you walking lots of times, seen you come in here, too. Lots of times."

The two men in blazers were nodding. The taller one on Bob's right started working his jaws as if he were chewing on something.

"Well by next Tuesday or Wednesday I'll be able to get my truck fixed, so I won't have to walk everywhere. Since I've been here it's not starting right—sometimes it does, sometimes it doesn't. If you saw me walking, though, you should have stopped and said Hi, maybe given me a lift."

"But you stink of tar, Newell," Bronc said.

Bob glanced at the black stains on his jeans and shoes. "Let's see you do roofing work and not get dirty!" he said, his voice rising in defense.

Bronc looked down at his nails. He held his hand out to the shorter, dark-haired man on Bob's left. A switch-blade was put into it, its blade flashing open with a solid cling. Bronc cleaned his nails. "I will pick you up in the limo one day, give you a ride you'll remember," he said.

"You know," Bob said, "I had nightmares—me and Doc—for a while. But we went to the VA for counseling and it helped. Did you have nightmares?"

Silent, Bronc pretended to pare his nails. In the back of the room pool balls clinked one against another, thudded against felt, and rumbled down pockets. "Was your last time fuckin' your girl friend super?" Bronc asked, looking up. A broad grin came over Bronc's face, his eyebrows raised, the pallid scar at his temple taking on an inhuman orange tinge.

"Bronc, I wasn't responsible..."

"To hell you weren't! You had to run off like that, didn't cha!"

The two men in turtlenecks looked past Bob at each other.

"What do you mean, *run off*?!" Bob said. "I escaped!"

"Did you hear that, boys? He e-scaped."

The men in turtlenecks nodded.

"It's not my fault..."

"Shut up!" Bronc said. "I knew someday. Knew it!" His lower teeth were bared, the scar on his temple pulsing red.

"I don't have to listen to this," Bob said.

The men in turtlenecks moved in so close he could feel their warmth through the blazers. From the church adjacent the piano started pounding chords again.

"But you go and high-tails it, and Charlie fuckin' takes it out on us!"

"But who brought the Regulars?" he protested.

Bronc shook his head. "You had nightmares, but I have a fantasy—Ever have a fantasy, Newell?—and my fantasy is going to fuck the hell out of your nightmares. It's about a little bamboo cage somewhere, Corporal. A *little* bamboo cage, not big enough to sit up in or lie down in, and set up on stilts, just like it was, remember? And maybe I need a pet for my little cage."

"I'd break the fuck out. Charlie couldn't hold me and you fuckin' can't hold me!" The baby in the carriage howled.

"That's what I told you he'd say, right, boys?" The dark-haired one nodded; the taller one continued to chew. "Well Newell, I've got that cage and I need a pet for it."

Bob turned to leave, but the two men grabbed his arms.

"Stuff you in that cage naked. And stuff something else in there with ya. A demon maybe."

"You're crazy," he said.

"But funny thing about demons is you've got to keep feeding them to keep 'em happy because it's not nice when they get hungry. Demons get mean and nasty when they're hungry."

Both men nodded. Bob noticed that in the back of the room one of the pool shooters indicated Bob with an upward nod and all four stood around the pool table looking at them. *Hey guys*, he thought, *I don't know you and you don't know me, but we've seen each other lots of times. How about giving me a hand, huh?*

"You're crazy, Bronc," he said, sweat now trickling down his sides.

"Naw. Not me. Just got fantasies about putting a demon inside ya, in your blood and in your head. He'll keep a real close eye on ya. But my boys here will keep him fat and happy, give him demon food every couple hours. Demon food comes in a needle, Corporal. Have my boys here stick your arms every couple hours. Every couple hours for three or four days, till you're hooked real good and the demon is big and strong, but fat and sleepy. But then the boys stop bringing the juice because I told 'em to, and the demon starts getting hungry and mean, and takes it out on you."

"I'd fight it."

"Yeah, fuckin'-A, Newell! But when you've eaten almost

the whole turkey and your guts stop cramping and you stop belching up blood, my boys here will start feeling sorry for the poor little demon and will bring him more needles and keep feeding him till he's again big and strong, and then—you know how forgetful boys can be—they again forget to feed him and he gets mad at ya. Again. How much cold turkey can you take, Newell? Way out in the country, without food, water? Naked in that bamboo cage, with the sun and the mosquitoes and the cold at night? Remember? Could you take a week, Corporal? Maybe two? Or maybe there might be a little food, some water. Could you take it month after month in that cage? Bronc's pet?"

With sharp snap of his shoulders Bob turned but failed to break free from the men's grasp of his arms. They tightened their hold and moved in, their bodies flush with his.

Slowly Bronc inspected the switchblade, looking at it close to his face, rotating it. In the gloom the bright metal glowed and glinted with a light of its own, a supernatural, unholy light. Bud, the owner, was no longer in back of the bar. The cigar smoker got up from his stool and headed for the rest room. The women scurried out the door. The four pool shooters stood at the table, watching. *Hey, guys?* The shorter dark haired man on Bob's left started grinning and grinding his crotch up and down Bob's leg. The hymn, "O What a Friend," came through the walls. One of the pool shooters dropped coins in the jukebox.

Bronc moved the blade, agleam in the darkness, before Bob's face. It wavered before his eyes, then lowered in graceful, serpentine scrolls. He held it, still twisting it, at Bob's crotch. "But you've got one uncle," he said, his voice now calm, measured, distant. "All you've got to do for your uncle, is do to your balls what you did to mine. I've got to hear ya telling me how sorry you are. And I've got to hear ya weeping and crying with the pain where your balls used to be. And when I'm sure you're really sorry, and not just cutting 'em off for some more juice, but really sorry—when I'm sure, we'll drop you off at some hospital. But if detectives ever ask me one fuckin' question—Just one!—you're dead, boy."

"I'm not responsible…"

"Fuck you ain't!" Bronc flared. "Charlie beat 'em till they were coconuts."

"The doctors…"

"Fuck the doctors!"

"Well, Bronc," Bob said with a snicker, "maybe lots of little boys and girls are sleeping safer because of it."

Bronc jabbed the blade at Bob's crotch. It missed its intended mark, sticking two inches into his thigh instead. With a fierce twist of torso Bob freed himself from the grasp of the taller man on his right and slammed Bronc backwards against the bar.

Both men seized his wrists, twisting them behind his back and pulling them upward toward his neck. The pain that radiated from his shoulder, elbow and wrist forced him to arch his back, forced him to strain his chest unnaturally and uncomfortably high. It was a horrible, intense pain. *Don't dislocate them! I can't work if you do!*

Bronc, standing now, looked at his prey. A crazed smile flickered on his lips. It vanished into a blank gaze, then flickered again.

Suddenly he kneed Bob's crotch, which doubled him over,

the breath knocked from him. A right upward hook to the jaw straightened him, until a knee again crushed the balls, then another hook, another knee. And again, and again.

He was limp in the men's clutch when at last Bronc grew tired. A hand grasped his hair and pulled his face upward. Bob tried to open his eyes. Everything was blurred under a red haze. His hair was released, his head fell and there was a wiping of hands across his back. His arms were released and he collapsed with a hollow thud onto the floor, his hands moving meekly to protect genitals.

"Your little, tiny balls hurt now, boy? Aww. We'll fix it so you don't have to worry about 'em no more. You *do want* to cut 'em off for me, now don't you?" Bronc said, then shouted, "Fuckin' answer me!" He kicked Bob in the abdomen, which caused him to cough and to choke on the very coughs. "Now get that fuckin' asshole out of my sight."

His armpits and legs were grabbed, and his back dragged across the ground. They dropped him on the sidewalk, his head hitting with a clunk. He slowly curled up into a ball. The concrete was cool under him.

Blood flowed from his forehead and mouth to form a puddle. It seeped from the gash on his thigh to darken his jeans. And he lay there, curled up, his hands protecting genitals from the pain which radiated up from them, a pain so intense it usurped all thought, a sick, nauseous, unmanly pain.

Women carrying grocery bags passed by. Groups of high school students parted left and right. Old men walking their dogs tugged on the leash as they commanded No, No. In hushed silence they gawked at him who hovered in and out of consciousness.

CHAPTER 9

Bronc, massaging his knuckles, followed his bodyguards and Bob out. He paused on the sidewalk to take the sunglasses from his breast pocket and put them on. "Oh my!" he said mockingly. "Look what we have here. Must be a drunk." He stepped over Bob and climbed into the open door of the limousine.

The taller man, Spider, got into the rear with him while Tony, the dark Italian-looking man, went around to drive. As they pulled from the curb, Spider in the rear said, "You weren't serious about taking him to a hospital after he's made himself a girl, were you?"

"Shit!" Bronc said, scooping white powder up into a spoon. "Picture it. All naked and bloody, howling with pain, but sticking his arm out through the bars and begging for more poppy juice…"

Tony, driving, interrupted: "Why don't you make him cut off his cock too?"

Bronc ignored him. "But under the cage we'll have a pile of straw. And as his blood flows and he howls and begs, you guys will have marshmallows on sticks and roast them. And I'll roast his balls. And there he is scrambling in the cage, trying to get out and clinging to the top of it. But his scrambling won't do no good as his flesh grows red, then blisters, then blackens."

From the front seat Tony asked, "What the hell we waiting for, boss?"

"Sure ain't no huntin' blood in you," Bronc said.

"Hey, Spider," Tony said, pointing to his left at a slight frizzy haired man loitering in a park. "You can have him tonight."

"Actually I wouldn't mind going out on the town, picking up a whore and fooling around."

Bronc had the powder melted into a clear liquid over a cigarette lighter and with his teeth was uncapping a hypodermic needle. He spit the plastic cap out. In silence he stuck the needle into his forearm.

"What do you say, boss? Can I?" Spider asked.

Still in silence Bronc pressed a button to lower his window and tossed the used hypodermic out. He rolled his sleeve back down. "Tony, drive over to the girlie district and let him out. Spider's got some business to tend to."

"Can I have some bucks?" Spider asked.

"That frizzy haired freak in the park," Tony piped up, "wouldn't cost nothing. I'll turn back if you want me to."

The men in the rear ignored him. Bronc took his wallet from his breast pocket, opened it and handed Spider three one hundred dollar bills. "Pick out a real young one," he said, "just learning the trade, still tight and not all stretched out. And teach her things she never imagined and never even heard of. Use her good."

"Thanks," Spider said.

Bronc scooted way down in the seat to stretch out. "Good stuff...and we might even film it."

"Not me, you're not!" Spider said.

"No," Bronc said. "The cage, the fire under it. Film it for posterity's sake. Then when you're out fucking whores and Tony's out with some guy, I'll watch that bloody, ball-less punk burn. But we can't have too much straw under it, just a little pile, do it slowly and watch him scramble. And the last laugh is mine."

"Can I go out later, too?" Tony asked.

"No. I'm thinking about calling Mrs. O'Keefe, have her send over some entertainment, some young stuff. You picked up the manly juice at Dr. Olstein's like I told you to, right?"

"Yeah, he did," Spider said. "Four vials. Two for here, two for the country place."

As the limousine turned toward the red light district, the frizzy haired man Tony had mocked continued to loiter in the park.

With his short stature, his receding jaw and reddish hair— so frizzy no one could do anything with it—God had not blessed Blaine Shirer with a commanding facade. Instead, he had other gifts. Four years ago the Diocese had voted him Teacher of the Year. In the slanted late afternoon light he was standing under an oak. This park was too small to be a major attraction—only one block—but it occasionally proved profitable and was convenient to home.

Though clouds scuttled against the sky, though children played on teetertotters and pairs of morning doves pecked in the grass, Blaine was not watching them. He was watching a man in white tee-shirt smoke a cigarette. With his back toward Blaine, he was sitting on a bench, his legs well spread, a white hard hat on the bench beside him. Dark curly hair descended to the neck of the shirt, soiled from the day's labor and the underarms still wet. *Hot,* Blaine thought. *I'd love a chance to satisfy you. If you were drunk, it'd be easier.*

With a flick of the cigarette butt onto the ground the man stood up. He turned his head to look at Blaine watching him. A sneer came to his lips, then he picked up his hard hat and continued on his way.

At a discreet distance Blaine followed him, not close enough that it was blatant, but close enough that he could hear each strike of metal cleats against concrete. The strides were measured, arrogant. He remembered the last time he had had a construction worker, months ago now, around Thanksgiving, two of them, brothers, both drunk. They had been abusive and wonderful, until the end, anyway. He followed the man with the hard hat out of the park, up the street.

Ahead, something was on the sidewalk outside a barroom. An old man tugged on a cocker spaniel's leash. School kids, slowing their pace, gawked at the something on the sidewalk. The construction worker he was following did not slacken his stride or even glance down. It looked like a person lying there.

Blaine quickened his steps, then knelt over a man who was curled into the fetal ball, hands on genitals. Blood, thick and sticky, was on his forehead, in his light hair, on the sidewalk. Blaine looked up and around. Standing in the doorway of the barroom were four young men in tee-shirts. "Call an ambulance, will ya?" Blaine said.

The men shot quick glances at one another until the most athletic-looking one said, "Shit! Maybe he deserved a beating. We don't know."

"But he still needs help," Blaine said.

The athletic man shrugged. The others shook their heads. They turned from the doorway into the darkness within. From the storefront church came the strains of "Amazing Grace."

"I'll get you to a hospital," Blaine said.

"No," the man on the sidewalk said, then coughed. He spit bloody sputum onto the ground. "Just help…" Again he coughed. "…home." He was laboring to push himself from the ground, struggling to his feet. His arm went around Blaine's slight shoulders. "All I need is some help…walking," he said and coughed.

For three slow blocks Blaine steadied and supported the weight of the man, Blaine's hand at the man's waist, his arm around Blaine's shoulders. The man's torso was firm and tight, not an inch of flab. Sexy. The scent of him mingled the honest aroma of a day's labor with the acridness of asphalt. In the acridness was also a tinge of brimstone.

Along century old cobblestone streets, under majestic oaks, past pairs of mourning doves on lawns they went at a plodding pace. People paused on the sidewalk to gawk at them. Blaine knew what they were seeing—one tall, athletic and bloodied, the other slight, frizzy-haired and jawless. On Hyacinth Street, the street on which Blaine lived, they turned left.

"There," the man said, "second house down."

Blaine knew the house. Brown weeds rioted in the yard. Years ago the front door had been removed, its entrance now a black yawn. A storm shutter hung askew on the second floor and paint peeled from the clapboards. The house was attracting undesirables into the neighborhood and a year ago he had joined his neighbors in signing a petition that the building be razed.

When they reached the cracked walk leading to it, the man said in feeble, irresolute voice, "I can make it on up," but did not protest as Blaine continued to support him through the doorway, into the dark mustiness within.

Beer cans, McDonald wrappers and newspapers littered the floor and somebody's radio was blaring out rock and roll. The rag rug on the stairs—once charming in an Old World way—was black with grime, though on the portion that ascended each step it still held a tinge of color.

The man grasped the bannister—creaking and wobbling under his weight—as they went up the stairs. He laboriously probed in his jeans for keys at a door on the second floor. Blaine still supported him and steadied him. *Poor guy,* he thought, *wanting to live like this.*

Together they crossed the room eight feet to a narrow bed. It was neatly made with an olive drab US ARMY blanket. With a moan and hand to his head the man lay gingerly back and Blaine lifted his legs onto the mattress. They were heavy and muscular, and through his jeans he could feel the hair on his legs.

He began to unlace the tar-stained tennis shoes until a dog's sudden jump onto the bed startled him. He stepped back as the dog snuggled close to the man and started licking at the blood on his chin.

"Can I get a washcloth and towel and clean you up some? Undress you, see how bad your wounds are?" he asked.

"No," the man said with difficulty, then added, "but take a beer from the fridge." He coughed.

Blaine stood motionless at the foot of the bed and watched the dog tend his master.

He licked the blood from the man's chin and cheek, his long pink tongue making slow strokes. As he licked a soft, high whine started to come from him. He licked more quickly, more urgently. At last he sat, lifted his head and, with his eyes closed, howled a long, piteous, and desolate howl.

The man patted him on the shoulders. "It'll be okay. It's okay," the man said. The sound of master's voice calmed the dog and he stood over the bloodied face and started slowly licking at the blackened blood in his hair. It was a gray three-legged dog, the man's arm around him.

Blaine looked around the room. The single bed jutted out between the windows. An overstuffed easy chair overflowed with tar-stained clothes. Against the wall to his right stood a tiny closet someone had built of plywood and not bothered to paint. Beside it were two stacks of cardboard banana boxes, each stack three boxes high. He read the labels, Sci-Fi, Western, Poetry/Sci/Text, Am/Br Lit. The one on top, Sci-Fi, was open to reveal paperbacks. Next to those boxes were two larger boxes, unlabeled, with tee-shirts visible in the top one.

To Blaine's back was a make-shift wall, not extending to the ceiling. He went around it, and past a table set against the outer wall, into what was supposed to be the kitchen. He opened the refrigerator, half-heartedly going after the offered beer. Icicles hung from the freezer. There was a carton of eggs, half a loaf of bread, a package of bologna, a bottle of catsup and two beers. He closed the refrigerator without taking a beer.

The little table, painted green, had initials, hearts and obscenities from previous occupants carved into it. An ashtray served as paperweight to a stack of white handwritten pages. The page on top bore the words, "Not Rusty Too, by Robert Newell." Under the title the handwriting commingled, curiously, script and printing. At the place the man apparently sat were other pages with a plastic ball-point pen on top. The page was numbered sixteen, apparently a draft, for words were scratched out and arrows directed the text to smaller words in the margins. Blaine leaned forward and twisted his head to decipher a portion of that page. It was either fiction or biography.

He looked again at the man, at Robert Newell, lying on that bed, the dog licking at darkened blood. On the wall at his head, between the windows, hung the only adornment on the walls, a document in a simple black frame. From its general format he knew it was a military discharge. He hoped it was from the Marine Corps—those men were rougher/wilder, because they had something to prove about their manhood both to themselves and to others.

CHAPTER 9

As he approached to find out what branch of service, bared fangs and deep growls warned him off.

He went to the open door and turned to gaze again at the man, his stained tennis shoes still on. *You've got a hot body, and maybe you're handsome too, so I'll be back. We could make a deal. You could use some financial help, and if you're hung, we might even make it a weekly thing.* He threw the lock on the knob and checked to make sure it was securely locked: *The poor guy doesn't need to be robbed tonight. He's had enough trouble for one day.*

Four houses down and on the opposite side of the street was a large brownstone with white swans at the bottom of the landing and leaded glass sidelights flanking the door. He entered the building and in his apartment, the entire second floor, fixed a gin and tonic. He took it and sat in an antique wing-back chair, richly upholstered in a fabric of white magnolias and green leaves on a crimson ground.

He recalled that the only adornment on the walls in that room across the street was a military discharge—no crucifix, no pictures, no calendar of pin-up girls, only a discharge. *The best men are military. We couldn't possibly meet here—couldn't bring him into my home!—but I could go across the street once or twice a week to his room. I could take a bottle of booze and a fifty dollar bill.* He chuckled at a joke Russ had told him last weekend: What's the difference between a straight Marine and a gay Marine? A six-pack.

He conjured an image of that Robert Newell drunk and

bare chested—a drunken Marine on leave. *So, you really want it, huh?* he would say, rubbing the bulge in his jeans. *So, how much is it worth to ya, per inch, huh fag?*

In late-afternoon light his huge oriental carpet—patterned of off-white, pale blues and greens—seemed to glow and colored the air itself with a diffuse pastel light. His eyes fixed on the ornament on the coffee table in front of the sofa. It was a marble replica of Michelangelo's Pieta, a souvenir of his grandmother's last tour of Italy. He crossed himself at her memory. There, on the coffee table, a Man lay limp across a woman's lap, His arms languid at His sides.

As he gazed at it, he saw, superimposed on it, a man languid in a shabby room, a military discharge proudly displayed on the wall. Although he wanted to fantasize about Bob as he wanted Bob to be, he found himself wondering about the real man. He wondered why he had gotten beaten up, what his stories were about, how his dog had lost a leg. He wondered what swirling elements in his past, in his history, in his accumulated days, had brought him to dwell in that derelict room on the fringe of society.

A strange thought came to him: *For Dr. Holzhauer I have explored every insignificant nuance of my own past. Both the traumas and the insignificant thumb pricks. Carl, Russ, Sofonda, they all have pasts. I know about them. They've told me. I've asked questions. But I don't believe I've ever, not even once, thought about the histories of the men I prowl for. Strange. No! Not strange! Pathetic. I suppose even those men have histories, each of them a common tale of hopes and dreams, disappointment, failure, and happenstance. And maybe some achievements along the way. I hope so. But I don't know! I never asked! I never cared!*

Heretofore, he admitted, he had been so preoccupied with his own desires and the exciting adrenalin of the search, he had never thought of the hearts of the men, their sorrows, hopes and aspirations. He had seen them not as full, real people, but only as Manhood, for that was what his own needs, his physical and psychological needs, needed to see.

Not even once had he wanted to talk with them, get to know them on a personal basis, maybe become friends. For they existed in this world to be searched out and used. And over the course of years he had used many hundreds of them while on his knees — construction workers, truckers, soldiers, punks — had used them in parks, restrooms, abandoned factories, locker rooms, alleys, cars, culverts and bushes. Occasionally he would hear a "Thank you," or "That was good," but whether he heard it or not, he would walk away satisfied, and back home, would write a slash mark for each one on his calendar.

It was more than a slash mark, though, because his kneeling before each one of them wrote a sentence or a paragraph not only in his history, but in theirs as well. And his contact with hundreds of men, or thousands, had injected into their lives, into their indelible histories, incidences of indiscretions. Some would see it as more than indiscretions. They'd see it as homosexual sin. He saw it as homosexual sin.

Across the street a man, a veteran, lay bloodied, while on his table lay handwritten stories. On that same table previous occupants had carved their initials and inarticulate messages to posterity. Maybe the man had a story to tell, a story worth hearing. The man was hurt and only his dog was there to minister to him.

Perhaps I should have sat up until morning with him, keeping watch. And if he took a turn for the worse, at least somebody would have been there to call an ambulance. But in the morning there would be no telling how he would have reacted on finding that a stranger had sat in his room all night watching him sleep. Maybe I would have been the one in the hospital. I think my patron would have taken that risk. Yes, I'm sure St. Francis would have.

From under the eaves pigeons were cooing and throughout the city steeple bells began to strike six o'clock, first one, then another. *What was the Nursie's line? 'Now afore God, I am so vexéd.'* It was the hour of the Angelus, and Blaine, sitting in that wing-back chair, humbled and ashamed, begged God Almighty to have mercy on him.

CHAPTER 10

Across the street Bob slept a troubled sleep.

He thrashed on his narrow bed, cursing at the demons that haunted. He tossed and turned among the corpses in the jungle while his fingers clawed again through bamboo. He cringed before the saggy breasted Old Hag, her breath foul. He flailed out at Death, then cowered again under the Hag's blood-shot gaze. He ran delirious and naked through the midnight forest, rotten leaves underfoot.

He endured again that far country until a woman in a starched house dress found him cowering in a clump of bushes. She reached out her hand and led him quietly back to his room, where she tucked him into his bed. With a sweep of her arm over him, she said, "Flee, demons. Your claim here is not yet firm. In his father's own arms, with me standing at his side, he was baptized. You cannot boast yet, so return now to the shadows of the past."

He heard a scurrying sound, like rats in a wall, and opened

his eyes. His room was illumined with a supernatural light and there were joyous swallows flitting against the clear blue sky. Through the walls, transparent now, opened vistas of flowery meadows. His mother was standing over him, radiant in light. He gazed into the love in her eyes and his chin quivered. "Am I going to die a horrible death?" he asked.

"You fear, my child, the threats of this world?"

"Yes," he said.

She sat on the bed and took his hand in hers.

He continued on in voice that trembled with sobs. "I never told you about it, but there's someone who once threw the gladioluses I brought him in the hospital. He screamed curses at me. He swore he'd get even, but it wasn't my fault. And he's here now."

"But I am here with you, too," she said, and bent and kissed his forehead.

"I don't want to die like that. I know I've got to do it sometime, but I want it to be with family around me, maybe grandkids, too. Not some horrible agony in a cage."

"Solemnly, Bobby," she said, "at the appointed time you can pass from this world peacefully, and more than peacefully."

"Not if he has his way 'bout it."

"But if you so choose, at the appointed time there can be a benediction on your lips and love in your heart."

"Love?" he asked. "Why does He make love so very, very hard?"

"It's not," she said. "It's as easy as the air you breathe. It is but you who make it hard."

"What do you mean?" he asked.

"Do you remember Della, the waitress you once described as cabbage-faced, the one you gave that little puppy to? In her simple way she offered you a simple love. If you had reached out to her and touched, love unbounded would have been yours."

"Della? But she was overweight, and plain and not too smart. She wasn't my type."

"But from her you would have received, full measure and overflowing, love and devotion and family—all those things you dream of, my son."

"But I need a woman of soft breasts and flowing hair to cling to me and I to her. A beautiful woman, a woman I can be proud of saying, 'And this is my wife.'"

"Before the appointed time, you must learn that unto which you aspire."

"And what is that?" he asked.

"That you must learn. And when you do, you will enter into joy."

He snickered. "There's not much of that in this world. He made everything too hard. But in spite of that, I'll survive," he said. "And no way am I going to run scared from a damn eunuch!"

"But you contend and vie and struggle on your own, and will not listen to a Man who once said, 'Consider the lilies.' There was no yelling, no bombast in His voice. He never jumped up and down in a pulpit like Rev. Negley. Look at the flowers behind me, Bobby, look how beautiful they are. They too are His children. But you have rejected all that."

"Yes. If He won't even help a dog have puppies, what good is He?"

"Oh, my son!" she said. "Solemnly I tell you, your days ahead will have a heaping-full of trials and tribulation. Yet, for your good and with a mother's love, I pray to the Father that troubles descend upon you, Bobby. For you are proud and it is only by enduring trial and tribulation that you will come to know what love is, and call it by name, and enter into its joy.

"It is love you long for, and love, my son, you must attain. Troubles will come, but do not despair." She stroked his hair. "They come to edge you on toward love, and toward recognizing its homeliness and its peaceful joy." She stood up and the light surrounding her began to fade.

"I shall pray, my beloved, as you could as well," she said. "The Black Brethren continue to pray for you at every service."

"Who?" he asked.

"The Church of the Black Brethren and little Isaac are praying."

"That's nice of them, if there's anyone to hear."

"Oh, my dear little Bobby. But for now you need your rest. So sleep, beloved....Sleep, my child." Her fingers coursed lightly down his cheek. He entered a deep slumber.

At the licking of Quasi's long sandpapery tongue he awoke. Without opening his eyes he put his arm around his dog. Strangely, the room smelled of flowers and ironing boards. He was wondering if it were evening or morning as he raised his head and twisted around to look from the dark room out the window. There, in the east, the sky was dim with the pastels of sunrise.

His pillow was on the floor, the olive drab blanket twisted into a ball. He was still dressed and realized he hadn't tended Quasi since the previous morning. He sat up, the change in position making his head first dizzy. Then, filling again with blood, it began to throb. He walked with Quasi down the stairs and back up, each step jarring the contents of his skull, but he knew his dog was thankful for being let out, and thankful for the heaping portion he fed him.

As he ate, Bob took his towel, soap and toothbrush from the top of the unpainted plywood closet and went down the hall to the common bathroom. The mirror reflected hair darkened with blood, dark blood crusted in his nostrils and on his neck. There was a gash over his left eye, a black and blue on his left cheekbone. His lips were puffy. In spite of all that, he didn't look as bad, he admitted, as his head felt. It was as if someone had split his skull, emptied the contents into a skillet and scrambled it like eggs. The headache made his stomach heave in nausea.

He took off his denim jacket and tee-shirt, and undid his jeans. Dried blood glued the jeans to his thigh and he had to peel them off. The gash there began to ooze a little blood. His scrotum was tender and bruised.

The stream of water from the shower made his gashes burn, and when he held his head under the cascade, a loud racket boomed in his skull.

Back in his room he dressed for work and put a small pot of water on the hot-plate. As it heated he sat at the table with a cigarette. Quasi dropped his white tug-of-war sock—one tied into a knot—at his feet. As he picked it up mallets pounded anvils in his skull. He tossed it across the room. Quasi retrieved it, waited, sat, then put a paw against his leg. "Not now, boy," he said, and Quasi lay down with his head on his sneakers.

After a cup of instant coffee and a second cigarette he left for work ten minutes earlier than usual, each step on the pavement jolted and joggled his head. *Maybe I ought to go to a hospital instead, but that's expensive and where would I find another job?* He walked the slow blocks to the empty house lot that was the dropoff/pickup site.

Jeers and profanities about whitey greeted him as he approached. Six black men already stood on the bed of the truck while the owner of King Roofing waited beside it. Mr. King called to him to hurry up, which prompted him to jog half a dozen steps. Then his hand went to his head and he resumed his plod.

He said he was sorry he was late.

Mr. King, a tall black man with gray at the temples and one tooth of gold, said, "Just what in tarnation's happened to you!"

"I guess it was a fight," Bob said, "but you should see the other guy." He forced a chuckle.

"Well, you ain't climbing no ladders today," Mr. King said.

"I'll just do the ground clean-up then, if that's okay."

"Nope," Mr. King said.

Somebody from the truck bed said he ain't gonna carry no fuckin' shingles up. In chorus they all said they weren't either.

Without turning around Mr. King said, "You will if I

damn well tell you to! And you, Newell, get yourself home and get mended up." He climbed into the truck, closed the door.

Bob, stepping onto the running board, pleaded, "But I'll be okay once the blood gets flowing."

Mr. King didn't answer, but squirmed in the seat, took a roll of bills from a front pants pocket, folded a ten and shoved it under the neck of Bob's tee-shirt. "Get yourself some aspirin and get to bed. And a prayer won't hurt none neither." He started the engine. "And don't be slow and late come Monday."

Bob stepped off the running board. As the truck lurched into gear, the six black men on the bed—holding tightly onto the wooden slats of the sides—talked shit over who was and who wasn't going to do Bob's job: carrying up bails of shingles, rolls of tar paper and buckets of molten asphalt.

He stood in the lot, watching the truck's exhaust cloud in the morning chill. As he returned to his room, public benches beckoned to him like the Sirens calling Odysseus. *Come, rest a bit.* From Homer he knew the dangers that lurked on those benches. *Better not. In my condition I couldn't fend off Bronc's thugs.* Once home, he slept in his narrow bed until early afternoon.

After four cups of instant coffee and twice that number of cigarettes, he decided to take the risk. He needed his truck to start twice in a row, once here, once getting back from the country. With Quasi on the seat beside him, he followed an Interstate out of the city, then turned to follow a State road for a while. Finally he parked.

The sign on the barbed wire fence, NO TRESPASSING,

forbade any to enter, but he lifted Quasi through the wires and squeezed through them himself because he could not imagine that any landowner would really be upset if he should one day learn that, one afternoon, the last day of February, a man parked along the road and he and his dog wandered quietly through his meadows and woods.

From Quasi's inquisitive snoopings quails took flight, startling the dog. He chased a rabbit through brown weeds while Bob followed a little brook, along whose sides there was still green growth. He picked a sprig of watercress, the bending splitting his skull. As the prickly flavor spread over his tongue he noticed a brick chimney to his right and went over to it.

Only the chimney still stood, jutting two stories into the blue sky, the bricks blackened with fire. Gone now, the farmhouse had once stood on the sure foundation of granite. Behind the ruins were stunted apple trees, four rows of them, now gnarled with neglect.

A blue jay crossed the sky and perched on the blackened chimney where he screeched at the intruders below. Bob wondered if the ruinous fire had been by lightning bolt or accident, or if the Union Forces had pillaged their home, then burned it, driving them hence, mere vagabonds. *A home is a precious thing, not easily replaced. How well I know.*

He remembered he had once intended for the Marine Corps to replace the home his Pa had snatched from him. But curses and a swearing of vengeance drove him from the Corps. That hairy-chested, streetwise punk from the slums of Detroit, had never belonged in the Corps in the first place. The only reason Bronc was there was that a judge had given him a choice of the Corps or prison. And there Sir Charlie and American doctors did what the legal system could not. Through the use of bamboo and then knife Bronc lost his manhood. *Perhaps there's a justice in this universe after all, and little boys and girls can sleep a little safer—the sex-crazed punk!*

He sat on a granite slab and remembered Bronc had arrived in country the same day as Tanner, who came to them from the suburbs of Baltimore. Tanner was like the rest of them. He had freely enlisted, just as Bob and the others had enlisted.

Sgt. Hollinger put Tanner under Frog's wing, and Bronc under Bob's, to teach them workable ways of coping—ways they had learned from experience, ways that did not always mesh with what Drill Instructors taught and training manuals expounded.

At first something of a friendship flourished in the bush between Bob and Bronc, until—on an R&R together in Saigon...

Bronc arrived back at the motel room with a little girl, maybe four or five years old. Bob laid the Western he was reading down on the bed and swung his legs over the side. "What's the matter?" he asked. "Is she lost?"

"Wise up, dude!" Bronc said. "We'll take turns with her."

"No, fucking way!" Bob said, standing up from the bed. He pulled himself to his full height.

"Suit yourself, man. But I'm paying for half this room. So

watch the fuckin' or fuckin' leave."

"You're not touching her!" Bob said.

"But she's cherry and just a gook! I done paid her old man for it! He don't care."

Bob strode the few feet across the room to him. The little dark haired girl—her arm in Bronc's clutch—struggled toward the door. Bob smacked a hand down on Bronc's shoulder and held a finger in his face. "She's leaving, Private, still cherry."

"Busted cherry, Newell! 'cause I'm gettin' me some!"

Three hundred dollars each, a hundred dollars a month for three months taken from his pay. That's what the damage to the room cost, but she left, still cherry.

As he sat on the timeless granite of what once had been a home, another incident of the same ilk presented itself. In his capacity as fire-team leader and assistant squad leader Bob was making the rounds of the pillboxes to relieve the men one by one so that they could go up to the mess tent for pie and coffee.—Firebase Henrietta was known for its excellent mess.—When he came to the second pillbox, with the moon casting his shadow onto the sandbags below, two of his men were having at it.

Bronc was standing, hands on both hips, Tanner on his knees before him. His head was moving back and forth. Bronc looked up at Bob and smugly grinned, putting finger to lips in sign of hush. When Tanner noticed him, he tried to pull away, but Bronc grasped the back of his head with both hands and forced his face flush to the pubic hair. Tanner choked and gagged, his eyes—fearful white orbs in the darkness—fixed on Bob.

Bronc, looking up out of the pillbox, said, "I've got a good cocksucker here. Real deep throat and he needs it. You can use it next."

Bob, saying nothing, turned away to give his men a few minutes of privacy. He went to sandbags, propped his M16 against them, took off his steel pot and sat. Although it was against regulation to smoke after dark, he took a cigarette from a plastic case. He twisted around as he lit it in order to block from slant-eyed observers the glare from the lighter. He cupped the glow in the palm of his hand to block that as well. The smoke he blew lingered in the heavy damp air.

The hills before him were clothed in darkness. A moon-glow, hovering on the trees, imbued them with transcendent beauty. It was almost incomprehensible to him that among those fertile hills, in those beautiful trees, Death lurked, but he knew she did. Somewhere, behind some tree, or perhaps in the branches, lurked the saggy-breasted Old Hag. Some said she had yellow teeth; others said no teeth. Regardless, she stalked him, stalked all of them, and one day—recumbent on rotted leaves, legs spread, the odor foul—she would welcome them all into an orgy of death. Even as he sat on the sandbags in the quiet of the night, he knew stringy-haired Death sneered at them, fantasizing over the splattering of entrails and the moans of her orgy.

To the east a shooting star blazed silently in the sky, and he gazed at ten thousand stars so silent and so far away. *They were closer, I think, those same stars, when Rusty and I lived on*

Bullrush Creek.

He crushed his cigarette on a sandbag and stood up because that was enough time for his men to finish what they had begun. They had finished, and Bronc was eager for his coffee and pie. Bob took his place at the lookout, his rifle pointed into the darkness.

Tanner, now dutifully at the lookout, said nothing, but in silence would sneak glances at him out of the corner of his eye, then look away. Bob scanned the sky for perhaps a second shooting star until—with a stammer and still not daring to look at him but looking out into the darkness—Tanner said, "Uh, you aren't going to, uh…"

"Forget it, Tanner," Bob said. "Things like that sometimes happen out here, so far from home. You're not the first, so forget about it." He gazed at the moon-glow on the trees.

Tanner was silent, gazing into the darkness. "But aren't you required by the UCMJ…"

Bob interrupted him. "Do you want a Dishonorable Discharge, Marine?! You'll get it! And you'll go waltzing on home and just leave us here. Is that what you want?"

"No," Tanner said.

"Well then, uh…" He searched for a neutral subject. "Do you think the White Sox have a chance at the pennant this year?"

"No way." It was Bronc's voice, behind them. He was coming down the ladder. "It'll be the Tigers."

"Okay, your turn," Bob said to Tanner.

"Get either the cherry or apple," Bronc said. "They're both good." That remark pleased Bob, for it indicated no rift, from Bronc anyway, in the harmony of the squad. He figured there would be no rift from Tanner. Maybe, he supposed, this had been their relationship since their arrival in country.

As Bob remembered, sitting on that large granite block, Quasi chased a squirrel up the oak tree in what had once been the front yard. With excitement in his eyes and tongue panting he circled the tree. *Once children had climbed with the squirrels in that tree, and this was a happy home.*

With almost three consecutive tours of Nam under him, he had decided to make the Corps his home. By now he would have had some real rank, a cushy peace-time job and good pay. But his own failure and Bronc's response to that failure drove him from it. Again—while he sat on granite and while Quasi sniffed out scents—he admitted to himself he had not lived up to the confidence placed in him by being assigned to point. And through his negligence or distraction or whatever, he had been responsible for handing the men over to the slant-eyed. He had failed them, failed his self-appointed commission to keep his buddies safe. It was his fault they were taken POW. And although it was he who eventually escaped, bringing the Regulars and rescue, that did not nullify his responsibility for the torture and depravation the men had endured for days or weeks.

It was not his fault, though—on this he drew the line— that in his absence Sir Charlie had bound Bronc spreadeagle and had used bamboo rods against his balls. It wasn't his fault the doctors couldn't save them. To stave off gangrene they had to cut off his testicles, his pride and joy, the apple of his eye with which he tormented little girls and punished lonely men.

Had he not visited Bronc in the hospital, had Bronc not thrown the gladioluses against the wall, swearing vengeance, he probably would have stayed in uniform, humbled, but bedecked with a second medal for heroism for his escape and return with the Regulars.

But Bronc was right. Bob's escape did not redeem his initial failure on point.

He remembered he left Bronc's hospital bed to search out Sgt. Hollinger, finding him in the day room. He told his squad leader he had changed his mind and was not going to re-up. Then as they walked through the hospital gardens, Bob confessed to him his guilt and wept in front of him.

The twenty-six-year-old's arm went around his shoulders and he tried to comfort the tall twenty-two year old with sage words about nobody being invincible. Bob would not be consoled. "No, I'm leaving the Corps," he said.

"But where will you go, Bob?"

"The States."

"It's a big place. Where?" Sgt. Hollinger asked.

"I don't know. I'll find a place. I'll make a home."

"But you've got a home and a future right here with us."

"No. My mind's made up."

On the Sergeant's orders he went to see the Chaplain, who talked to him gently about feelings of guilt. His First Sergeant,

Company Commander, Battalion and even Regiment Commander each sent orders to him to report before them. Each, in turn, tried to talk him out of leaving: *If you stay, yours will be a most illustrious career.*

For a while it had been something of a home for him, the Corps, where he felt needed and wanted. They were good men and on that granite slab he missed them. He wondered which of them had returned from the Vietnamization alive. Doc Preston had. He wondered if Doc ever convinced his wife to let him trade their station wagon in on a Camaro. Had Melendez, a whiz at chess, become a Grand Master? Had Smythe established his empire in real estate?

Bronc already has a limo and bodyguards. And what do I have but Quasi and a dream in my heart? A simple, humble dream, the dream of Everyman. Yet with that ball-less eunuch and his thugs plotting, stalking me, I probably won't live long enough to attain it. And along with me in an unmarked grave—unmourned by the wife—will lie my children who never were.

CHAPTER 11

The next morning, Saturday, Blaine Shirer sat in a chair at Bob's green painted table. His eyes lusted over Bob who was at the sink rinsing a brown earthenware mug. Parallel cords of muscle flanked his spine, jeans snug, feet bare.

Bob carried two mugs of instant coffee to the table and set them on the edge. "I hope you drink it black," he said. "I don't have any milk or sugar."

Blaine nodded. *That hair on your chest, man!* he thought as things bestirred in his slacks.

Bob, leaning over the table, straightened into a stack the papers strewn there. A paperback *Webster's* went onto the top of them.

Blaine opened the red and white box he had brought to reveal an assortment of donuts: glazed, jelly-filled, crullers, chocolate covered.

"So tell me," Bob said, picking up his mug decorated with swallows, "what the hell are you doing here?"

In the seconds before Blaine responded, he thought, *Well I should have stayed the other night as my Christian duty, but I'll make up for not staying by sucking you off. God, you're handsome. Blaine! there you go again. Try to see him as a person, not Manhood.* "Well, uh," he said, "I like donuts on Saturdays and the coffee canister was, uh…" The incredulous frown on Bob's face made him pause, and start over again. "No, I was wondering how you were doing. You don't look as bad as I thought you would."

"Are you really the one helped me home? Dead weight is awful heavy, and, no offense, but you don't look too damn fit and strong."

"You walked by yourself. I was just there to kinda lean on. It's terrible what's going on in the neighborhood. What with the druggies and the gangs of punks, the burglaries are up. And there's a lot of random violence, so it's unsafe for everyone."

"So, you've got it all figured out! It was some random thing, huh?!"

Bob's tightly wound hostility was not lost on Blaine. He wondered why he should direct it against him.

"Well, you're wrong!" Bob went on. "It was planned, right down to Bud verifying my name for them. And it's not over yet. That was just the foreplay and I'm scared."

"You don't look like a man who's used to running scared from anybody. Here," he said, gesturing to the box, "have a donut." Blaine recalled the delay from his knock, the subtle creaks across the floorboards, Bob's hushed, furtive, *Who's there?* Then a scuffing on the floor. He glanced at the chair Bob had again wedged tightly against the door.

"Well I am. A man's nuts are pretty precious to him—aren't they, Blaine? And I have no desire to pretend I'm not and end up in an unmarked grave because of it." He reached for his Winstons.

Blaine, silent, watched closely as Bob lit the cigarette with a plastic lighter, then held it Marine-style—between thumb and the first two fingers and cupping the glow in his palm. "You were in the Corps, weren't you? And it's somebody you served with in Nam, isn't it?" he asked.

Bob exhaled a lungful with force and studied Blaine. "And how the hell do you know that?"

He shrugged, shook his head. "I guess I just sensed it," he said.

"Well, you hit it bull's-eye. His name's Bronc, a fuckin' punk. And he's got e-lab-or-ate plans for me," Bob said.

"Like what?"

"How the hell would you like it to be scrunched up in a bamboo cage?" he said, demonstrating the position by curling his back, his arms in front of him.

"You're kidding," Blaine said.

"I'm not kidding and he's not kidding. And there'll be drugs and cold turkey in that cage. But he'll drop me off at a hospital if I cut off my balls for him. Yeah, sure he will! He's a son-of-a-bitch, and he's got a grudge." He went on to tell Blaine about it, of Bronc's choice of the Corps or prison, and of their initial friendship. He told him of the little girl in the motel room. He piled incidence on incidence, talking on and on.

Blaine sat enmeshed, listening to every word. *Blaine, he's not Manhood itself, but every word is manly and he's lived a man's life. Flesh, blood, heart and soul a man, not Manhood. A man.*

"Then we were taken prisoner, all of us, the whole squad while I was on point. We were beaten, tortured, then put in these little bamboo cages on stilts. We were in a circle in a clearing. We couldn't talk, communicate. Any attempt got a rifle butt slammed into your skull. I don't know how long we were there—days, weeks, I don't know. It's a blur. But I finally dug through the ropes holding the bamboo together with my fingernails." He held his hands out to show Blaine the tips of his fingers, now malformed.

"I don't remember anything except running through the forest. I must have been half-crazed, delirious or something. I don't know how long I wandered, ran. That's a blur, too. The Regulars found me whistling and walking naked along some road, and the next day we went back—they knew where there was a bowl with an opening to the east, and with a stream cascading down the rocks on the north. Stealthily we surrounded the place at night. Throats were cut, the men gotten out, then the air strike came and the whole camp exploded in orange and black flames. A man covered in flames and running in flames, doesn't get very far, Blaine, not very far at all.

"Anyway, Charlie had taken my escape out on the squad. Bronc's balls had been beaten till they were coconuts. The docs tried to save them but there was gangrene and in the end they had to cut 'em off. And to his way of thinking it's my fault, all of it my fault. I told the squad leader I wasn't going to re-up."

On that he fell silent. Blaine had listened, transfixed, to the spontaneous litany for twenty minutes or more, and now watched as Bob's fingers traced the initials carved into the table by previous occupants.

Histories, Blaine thought, *indelible histories, the accumulated weight of his days.* "Well, uh…" he said. *Say nothing, Blaine! Anything you say would be sacrilege to the man, his pain and his dignity.*

Bob reached again for his cigarettes. "Sorry for dumping on you like that. I don't know why I'm telling you all that shit. It's not your problem."

"It's okay," he said, "you needed to talk it out. I'm just glad I was here to listen. I'll bet when you told your girlfriend she was real upset."

"I *knew* you'd get around to that subject. There is no girlfriend, but I've told Quasi." He patted on his thigh. "Come on over here, boy." The gray dog lifted his head from the pillow on the neatly made bed. After a great stretching, he jumped to the floor and hobbled to him. "You've heard about it more than once, haven't you, boy?" he said, scratching him behind the ears. He broke a piece from a donut and held it down to him. "By now he could probably recite the whole saga."

"That's what I figured," Blaine said. "But you've got to lay it aside now, Bob. Going over it any more isn't going to help."

"Well, let's see somebody toy with your balls, your life, and you not think about it!"

"But any more won't help."

Bob took from the box the donut he had broken, bit it, and gave another piece to Quasi. "That's what they told us at the

VA when me and Doc went for counseling: Acknowledge it, own it, but put it in its historical perspective. It was then, it is not now."

"That's what you've gotta do."

"But it is here, man! It's here and now! Stalking me on the streets *now*!"

"We've got to get you out of this room," Blaine said. "What do you say we go somewhere?"

"What I've got to do is get the fuck out of this town! But how? My truck needs work, and what would I live on till I found something?" he said and took a bite of the donut.

"How about the zoo?" Blaine asked. "We Atlantans are right proud of it, one of the world's finest. Have you seen it?"

"Animals? I love animals," he said. "And it was animals, especially birds—where they were singing, where they weren't—that I paid a lot of attention to while I was on point. And not even once, for almost three full tours while I was up there, did we ever meet ambush. The Lieutenants put me up there lots—Yeah, we went through several Louis's—Not even once was a single man injured....Until that day. I guess I just wasn't listening to the birds closely enough."

Blaine noticed Bob's mug. While the one he was sipping from was a solid brown, Bob's had swallows painted on it. "So, what about the zoo?"

"How much does it cost, though?"

"It's my idea, my invite, and I've got some extra bucks. We might even stop somewhere and have lunch—on me," Blaine said.

The way Bob looked directly into his eyes—a piercing, probing look—made Blaine uncomfortable. He wondered what the meaning behind it was: the way his left eyebrow raised and the right corner of his lips lifted.

"The zoo and animals would be fine. Give me a minute to change," he said, stood up and walked over to paw through a cardboard box of tee-shirts.

God, you're handsome. If I had known, I'd have been back sooner, but how could I have, with that blood covering you. He gazed at his strong bare back, his height. He watched as Bob took a fresh pair of jeans from the plywood closet. *Yeah, strip for me. There could be some bucks in it for ya.*

Bob had clothes and tennis shoes in his arms as he turned his head—that same half-smile, almost a sneer, on his face—and said, "I'll be back." He left the room.

He wondered if Bob suspected he was gay. He hadn't made any untoward comments to him, though, hadn't even complimented him on his good looks. And he had made it clear that he had come out of concern for his well being. He hoped he didn't suspect, for he would like to get to know the guy, maybe become friends. That was more important than just sex. He took a bite of a lemon-filled donut, its flavor tart. *But maybe we could be both friends and fuck-buddies. Go out once a week to a movie or dinner or something, then get him drunk at some bar. Come back here, not my place!...Maybe I should have brought beer over instead of donuts.*

Bob had changed into tight, faded jeans and white tee-shirt. "How is it outside? Will I need a jacket or anything?"

"You might want to take something with you, just in case," Blaine said. He tried to judge how big Bob was, but he wore himself up and to the side, not hanging down the leg, making appraisal difficult.

He took a denim jacket from the make-shift closet. Blaine watched him put it on. It looked like the same jacket Bob was wearing when he found him on the sidewalk. On the back were two smeared hand prints. He thought about mentioning it, but checked himself, for maybe the guy had nothing else to wear.

Bob bent to rub Quasi's belly, who was again on the bed. "Okay, you stay now, and you be good, and you watch the house." He stood upright and said he was all set.

Blaine felt unusually short, at five-feet-four, as he stood up and headed to the door.

As they went down the ratty stairs, Bob said in lighthearted voice, "Quasi keeps after me about getting a couple more dogs. He says it's just not fair. He says I have one job and he has three. He has to stay, and be good, and watch the house. He says with three they could each have one job. One could stay, one be good, and one watch the house."

"Are you really thinking about getting a couple more dogs?"

"Someday, but I can barely support myself and Quasi now. But one day I will. As a kid I had an Irish Setter, Rusty. And my kids—whenever that day comes about—should have the joys and responsibilities of growing up with a dog."

They drove Blaine's new, specially ordered, red MG. "Great car, guy," Bob said. "But there are no jobs in this city. The only thing I could find was roofer, and my truck doesn't even start right. Sometimes it does, sometimes it doesn't. But I'm working on something. I found out some magazines pay real good for short stories. I've got three almost done. I'm not putting all my eggs in one basket, you see. When I have all three done, I'll send 'em out to three different places, and then maybe I'll be able to get a Trans-Am or Camaro or something."

"Have you been published?" Blaine asked.

"Just a couple poems in a veteran's magazine. But, hell, I've read a lot and have been through a lot. Did you know the library has a shelf full of books on how to write a story?"

"It's an awful difficult line to break into," Blaine said.

"I'll do it. I've got to. Doors are slammed in your face when you don't have some bucks in back of you."

Haughty llamas chewed their cuds, indifferent to those who watched. Lions yawned in their leisure, while Mickey Mouse and Pluto sold brightly colored balloons to children who ran with them.

At a railing Bob and Blaine tossed peanuts to the elephants, their trunks moving—graceful, serpentine—to pick them from the ground. A little one stood close to his mother's side. At a distance, in the shade of trees, zebras swished flies away with their tails. Blaine stared at two bare chested workmen shoveling dung into a cart. Sexy.

Bob tapped him with his elbow. "Hey, the elephants are this way," he said, gesturing with his head.

"The shorter guy must work out," Blaine said. "Look at the lats."

"The what?" Bob asked.

"Lats, *Latissimi dorsi*. Latin for 'the widest muscles of the back.' These," he said touching Bob's back.

"You don't have to work out for those, just do a man's job."

"One of my friends, Carl—he's a former student and now the coach at a high school, and yeah, I'm a teacher—has been Mr. Atlanta three years in a row. The contest is coming up in about a week. It'd be great if he makes it again, but he's getting older, too, and there's a lot of fine young stuff coming up. It would be unprecedented for anyone to retain the crown four consecutive years. I hope he does."

Antelopes grazed peacefully as if they were still on the Serengeti. Polar bears basked on white painted rocks, rams butted horns.

On the way home they stopped at Jacques Patisserie and Cafe on Peachtree Street. The *maitre d'* showed them to a sidewalk table with an umbrella. Bob looked at the menu and promptly closed it.

"Do you know what you want already?" Blaine asked.

"Man," Bob said with a chuckle in his voice, "the thing's all in French. If I picked out something, I could end up with liver and onions or even something worse, like snails or innards. No, I'll let you pick out something kinda American for me."

Everybody was out that warm March afternoon walking their dogs, gray-haired men walking old Labradors, coiffured women carrying lap dogs. A young bearded father came along with a blond little girl in lime-green dress on one side and a groomed Irish Setter on the other. "I had a dog as a kid, Rusty, an Irish Setter. Maybe I already told you that," Bob said. "And she was every bit as beautiful."

"I wasn't allowed pets," Blaine said. "Mother claimed

she was allergic to dog and cat hair. It's funny, though, she now has six Siamese."

A uniformed nanny came down the sidewalk. In her black hand was the white hand of a little boy, and behind them there waddled a yellow duck on green ribbon. Both men said it was cute.

Two bodybuilders—with their gray sweatpants snug and hiding nothing, shirtless, with their chest carried before them like shields and both with identical Dobermans on leash passed by. Blaine followed them with his eyes.

"You see queers everywhere these days," Bob said.

Oh, God, he suspects! Blaine thought, and stammered, "Yeah, uh, I know."

"And it's okay with me, if that's what they choose. Just don't make a move in on me, okay, Blaine?"

Blaine's heart pounded. He felt his face turn hot. "I don't know, uh..."

Bob interrupted. "You're not a bad guy, you know. Thanks for getting me out of that room. And thanks for lunch too, I think..." He smiled broadly and assumed hillbilly talk. "...as long as you ain't gone and ordered none of them there Frenchy snails."

Blaine chuckled, Bob joining in with him. They were still snickering as the waiter put a silver pot of coffee on the table. He put salads before them and between them placed a wicker basket lined with a cloth napkin. Blaine took a croissant, then pushed the basket toward Bob, asking if he had tried croissants before.

He was pouring coffee into his cup. "What are they again?" he asked.

Blaine said, "Croissant."

"Kru-sent," Bob repeated, taking one.

"No, Croi-, croissant."

He tried pronouncing it again, with slim improvement, which amused Blaine, but took one, broke it just as Blaine had, and tried it.

"It is good," he said. "Warm, light, buttery. It reminds me of a biscuit, no, not the usual type, but the ones with all the little layers. Maybe a biscuit has more flavor than a krusent, but the texture's kinda alike. And there was this big black cook in Nam when we were in garrison who made two types of biscuits every Sunday. He gave the normal kind to most everybody, but to the southern boys he liked he gave the special ones, the ones with all the little layers. And in Ft. Walton there was this restaurant, The Twin Oaks, that made biscuits all light and layered. My Pa took me there for my birthday once."

"Then you're from Ft. Walton?" he asked.

"No," Bob said, a simple short syllable. He sipped from his coffee and was silent.

In the silence Blaine surmised the dog he had mentioned, Rusty, had been the highpoint of his childhood, and surmised as well that there was something that lurked in his childhood or teens he did not want to speak about.

The waiter brought their entrees, Petite Filet Mignon with parsleyed potatoes.

"Well, that's different, huh?" Bob said, "Wrapping the tiny little steaks in bacon. But what's that green stuff?"

"Parsley. Most places use just plain parsley butter, but here they use *Maitre d'* Butter. It makes a world of difference.

Don't worry, Bob, you'll like it."

He did like it, which pleased Blaine. As they were leaving Bob tried to leave the tip. "Absolutely not," Blaine said, "it was my invite in the first place, and it's on me."

In the car again, Blaine asked why, if the horror stories about Nam were true, had he planned on re-upping. "That's what it's called, isn't it? Re-up?"

"Yeah," Bob said. "Well, I guess I felt I was needed and had a purpose there. And besides, I didn't have much back here to come home to."

"Oh," Blaine responded. His brows creased with only partial comprehension, though he did not pry for further explanation. *We'll have to part pretty soon, and unless I think up something for later on, it'll be difficult knocking on his door again.*

"Bob," he said breaking the silence, "if you want, I could throw something together for dinner later on. You could bring your stories over and I'll read 'em and comment on 'em for you."

"Are you really a teacher?" he asked.

"Sure I am, high school English, St. Jerome's Catholic High."

"Then who said this, 'Our remedies oft in ourselves do lie, / Which we ascribe to heaven'?"

"Helena in *All's Well That Ends Well.* I teach drama, too, and we produce two of Shakespeare's plays every year. Last December we did *The True and Pitiful Tragedy of Romeo and Juliette.* We've started work on this spring's production, *Richard III.*"

"The hunchback! Then I guess you could have real insight. But you've got to be honest with me and say what you really think, and not just tell me how wonderful they are, that I'm going to be the next Hemingway or Steinbeck. You have to offer real criticism and real advice. Okay?"

"Sure I will," he said, pulling to the curb on Hyacinth Street.

"Okay," Bob said, "but where do you live?"

Blaine pointed two houses down across the street.

"Right across from me almost?!" he asked.

He nodded his jawless head. "The brownstone, with the swans, right there, second floor."

"But you're not going to pull anything funny on me, are you?"

"Just dinner and the stories, I promise."

"Okay, sure. I'd like that."

They set the time, five o'clock, and parted. Blaine pretended to be locking his car with the key as he watched tall handsome Bob vanish into the black yawn of the entrance.

CHAPTER 12

Tapping a white painted swan on the head, then grabbing the banister Blaine swung himself in arcs up the stairs. From room to room he paced. Not only did he have to appraise where to start straightening, but he also had to determine how much could and couldn't be done before Bob arrived. He changed the paper in his cockatiel's cage, put in fresh seed and water. In the kitchen he washed two glasses, a spoon and his coffee mug. In the bedroom he hung his dry cleaning, stuffed his dirty clothes into the hamper, then changed the sheets on the bed, first putting on black and white striped sheets, but changing his mind and putting on silver satin sheets instead.

In the living room he sat in the antique wing-back chair and on a small pad of paper planned the dinner. He scratched out item after item and changed the list until he had it right: ham, rice, sliced tomatoes, peas, croissants, chocolate cake. It still wasn't right. He scratched out croissant and wrote biscuit. From his menu he made a shopping list: canned Danish ham, Sarah Lee cake, Pillsbury biscuits. He stared at the word Pillsbury and scratched it out. He picked up the phone and dialed a familiar number.

"The Shirer residence."

"Rose, this is Blaine. How are you?" he said.

"Right fine. And how are you?"

"Fine. Tell me, Rose, would it be any problem for you to make biscuits for the house there tonight and make a dozen or so extra for me to pick up and cook here? I mean would it work doing it like that? Would they rise?"

"Well don't you sound sparklin' today, honey. And sure it would, but aren't you coming for supper?"

There was a noise on the line.

"Oh, that's right," Blaine said. "I forgot—Rai's coming with his nurse. But something's come up. Uh, Rose?"

"Yes?"

"I've just met a super, super guy."

"You have? Well that's just great," Rose said.

Blaine's voice raced. "Yeah. He's tall, handsome, with the palest blue eyes, my age or maybe a year or two younger. He's a veteran, a former Marine, and I think a southern boy, too, but he doesn't have an accent, so I'm not sure. But he's down to earth and kinda humble, Rose. He's trying to become a writer, nothing published yet, but he's trying."

"Well, it sounds like y'all have lots in common, honey. I still got that little poem you wrote about me, *My Sugar Cookie*. Got it stuck right on the mirror in my room."

"You do?" Blaine asked, a childish joy in his voice.

"Sure do."

"Well, Rose, will you tell Mother I called and offered regrets about tonight and I'll park on the street and sneak to the back door for the biscuits."

"I'll take it, Rose," somebody else on the line said. It was his mother. "And just what are you doing sneaking into your own home?"

"Oh, Mother. What are you doing listening in?" he asked.

Rose said she had to run. "But you take care of yourself now, honey," she said and hung up.

"Well it is my home," Mrs. Shirer said, "my son and my housekeeper. So I might have just a little right."

"Uh, well, Mother? I won't be coming for supper tonight, but I'll stop by sometime this week to see you and Father. I'll call first, of course."

"Blaine, I haven't received Dr. Holzhauer's statement. You're still going for your sessions, aren't you?"

Blaine stammered, "Uh, I'm having them sent here. I, I think I should pay for it."

"You aren't draining your trust fund, are you? You know that's got to last you. You aren't touching it, are you?"

"No, Mother, I'm letting it accrue."

"Oh, is that so? Well then, explain the mathematics of it all, please. On a teacher's pay you can afford $160 a *week* for the sessions? Six hundred and forty a month on a teacher's pay?"

Blaine didn't answer.

"Well that says a lot," Mrs. Shirer said. "And you know how important those sessions are."

"Mother, there's really nothing wrong with me!"

Mrs. Shirer forced a demeaning laugh. "Nothing wrong?

Well, who's 'this super, super guy'?" she asked, mimicking his words. "'And he's got the pal-est blue eyes.' Now we've been through it, Blaine, we've been through it and you've agreed to go. Once before you quit when you were on that religious kick of yours, and you see how long that lasted. You know we're just trying to help you."

He could feel his heart pounding. "Yes, Mother. Somehow I picked that up. But will you just tell Rose I'll be by for the biscuits about four?"

"And this 'super, super guy' you're having over is more important than your own family?"

"Mo-ther!"

"How long has it been since you've seen your brother? He's coming with his nurse, you know."

"I went up Saturday. I saw him a week ago."

"Oh, you did?" she said.

"Yes. And he's not too happy Lena's off in Europe and you two never bother driving up."

"That's not fair. You know how busy your father and I have been."

"Oh, I forgot. Country clubs and fund raisers and the Inauguration. Well, I'm not coming tonight but you can tell Rai I'll drive up and see him next weekend. I love you, Mother. Goodbye."

He hung up. Gradually his pulse rate slackened and he began to listen to the silence. Slowly the silence engulfed him, and he felt little and small in that chair. It was almost alive, that silence, and breathing, a silence huge that filled to the high corners of the room. Even from the crib it had been there, always there, that silence — stalking him, watching.

That cold, impersonal silence. Sapping his blood, his joy.

He glanced at his shopping list, and wanted to throw it away. He wanted to go out to prowl the parks. He wished Bob had a phone so he could call and cancel. Maybe he could find a construction worker, or better yet a whole carload of them, drunk and abusive. Or maybe a carload of long-haired punks.

A blue cockatiel— jabbering *Pretty-bird, Pretty-bird, I-love-you*—strutted proudly across the huge expanse of the oriental rug. Blaine called to Napoleon, lowered a finger to the floor and waited patiently. Napoleon perched on his finger and he raised him to his shoulder where he sat clucking contentedly. Blaine scratched through the feathers of his neck with a single finger.

At the supermarket he plodded though aisles, then drove to the grand white pillared mansion with circular drive. He parked on the street out front and walked around to the back door. *This is where I grew up, Mother. It's a fine house, but was never a home.*

Rose was concerned that his spirits had plummeted so low. It was nothing, he said.

Parking again on the cobblestones of Hyacinth Street, he sat in his car, wishing there were some way to get out of the engagement. Those two brothers he had had around Thanksgiving would be fun again.

Unnoticed in his window, he watched Bob walking toward him on the opposite sidewalk. In his arm he carried a brown bag from which protruded the red and white checkerboard pattern of a bag of dog food. Quasi, hobbling three-legged beside him on a leash, kept looking up at him and wagging his tail. Together they went up the walk past brown weeds and entered the darkness of the building. Once he had signed a petition to have that eyesore of a building razed. To Bob, though, it was home. A storm shutter hung askew at a window that was his.

He picked up the cookie sheet of unbaked biscuits, his eyes scanning Rose's note. Under the baking instructions she had written: *Never mind your mother. You know what's best for you. And honey, I say it's time, high time. Love, Rose.*

Inside, he set the Sarah-Lee cake to thaw on the counter. He preheated the oven, put the peas and rice into pans. Four years ago he had been happy, he remembered, for he shared his life and this same apartment with one who had loved him — or he said he did. It was the one and only relationship Blaine had ever had. Terry. Captain Terry DuLac of the United States Air Force.

He wished the interference, the attempted blackmail, had never occurred. He wished a student, Tony, had never been assigned to his class, had never turned in what was supposed to be an essay test. Tony had been the first to complete the test and had placed on Blaine's desk a piece of paper with sparse writing for an essay and already graded in red pencil.

A+

We gotta do some thing about my grades.

At the end of the school day Tony presented himself, as instructed, before Blaine in his classroom.

"Hi, Teach. I'm glad to see you, too!" From his hip pocket Tony took photographs and plopped them on Blaine's desk:

Blaine and Terry leaving a known gay bar arm in arm.

Blaine and Terry kissing in the parking lot beside Blaine's sports car.

On the reverse he had written:

Blaine Shirer, St. Jerome Catholic High School.

Terry DuLac, Captain, United States Air Force.

"How'd you find out his name?" Blaine asked.

Tony, moving close to Blaine's chair, rubbed himself. "I can find out *an-y-thing* I want 'cause fags just go crazy over this thing and you can too, Teach. Nobody needs to know— it'll be a secret love affair between you and my cock. And my old man will be proud of me and my grades."

Blaine leaned back in his chair, scooted it back from such close proximity. "I don't think so! Take your paper. Here's a pen. Sit and write your essay." Blaine stood up.

"I could fuckin' flatten you!"

"Do it and you'll find out how much you like being cooped up in juvenile detention!"

"Don't mess with me, Teach. I know people. Rough people!"

"That's it! We're going to the Principal's office."

"The pictures are going too!"

"Take 'em!"

Blaine left the Principal's office and went to his parish Church to pray. That evening he told Terry about the incident. There was a smashing of things in the apartment, screaming and a ransacking for Blaine's checkbook. The next day Blaine found he had depleted his bank account. On a phone call Terry told him he had requested an immediate transfer. And no, he wouldn't be back.

Blaine understood. While Terry's schoolmates had their varsity teams and their dating and hanging out, Terry had made pizzas, but had gone on to make something of himself— Captain in the United States Air Force. Captain Terry couldn't allow some punk to strip him of his commission. And the money he stole didn't matter. Terry did.

Alone, with the help of the Principal and the Archbishop, Blaine managed to weather the storm okay.

Yet for years following he avoided the places he and Terry had frequented together lest he be forced to confess to this friend or to that acquaintance, that his lover had left him. Even Carl seldom heard from him in those years.

He was going to give it all up, become a monk, and dedicate his life to prayer and God. For two years he prayed at home, attended daily Mass and fought off desires. He applied, but no religious order would have him. For years he continued to sit at tables for one, tables set apart from the others, lest he should hear the ignorant mock his homeliness—his slightness, his frizzy hair, his jawlessness.

As he stood in the kitchen slicing tomatoes in preparation for Bob's arrival, he admitted four years was a long time. Maybe it was long enough. And maybe it was time, or, as Rose had said, high time!

With the finest he had—his grandmother's silver, Limoges and her Waterford—he set the table. Then with twenty minutes to spare, with a lump in his throat and a hope in his heart, he walked three blocks to a florist for a single yellow rose for that table.

Maybe God will permit me to love again, love and be loved. Maybe He will. And maybe this is the time.

Bob arrived promptly at five with his stories and two quarts of beer.

FROM THE JOURNAL

What makes me do the things I do? It was nice having a friend for an afternoon, even a friend almost funny-looking and gay. And I had suspected all along, from when I first peeked out the crack in my door and saw a frizzy-haired wonder standing there. Nobody wears cardigans anymore. He said he was just concerned about me and had brought donuts. Yeah, sure. Men don't treat other men like that, maybe a brother or buddy would, but not a stranger. He had set a fancy table in his fancy apartment. That kind always have bucks. The biscuits, I must admit, were the best I ever had, the bourbon the smoothest.

I watched *Madam X* on the VCR while he read the stories in another room. I guess it was the bourbon, it went down too easy. Blaine liked my stories, though. He guessed the order in which I'd written them, and really liked MIA but not its title. He liked the titles for the other stories, Not Rusty Too and A Sip of Water. But he hated MIA, said it was a throw-away title, that it never should have risen to the top of my list of possibilities. But he said the story itself was good, suggesting I end it not with Mr. and Mrs. Simmonds at the Congressional hearing, but with the swarms of ants carrying Simmonds away, bit by bit, into the lush green of the forest. A beautiful and haunting image, he called it. I'll think about ending it there as he suggested. But talking about the story (the male bonding over the black crevice, his exact words) is what led up to—I guess *confrontation* is the best word.

He asked if I had felt as close to another Marine as Simmonds had with Redman, if I too had contemplated suicide over a buddy's death. I told him no, it was just a story that came to me and that I had to write. But he kept asking well why did I write that story—a love story, a variation of *Romeo and Juliet*, as he called it—and not some other. I told him I just made it up. He asked again if I had bonded with a Marine or had thought of the warmth of that bond. I told him not to try and analyze me—it was just a story, okay! I got up and refilled my glass in the kitchen.

When I got back he was on his hands and knees picking up peanuts from the floor and I stood there watching him. I want to say it was all his fault, he shouldn't have tried it, he shouldn't have made a pass at me.

But then I didn't have to keep standing there, legs spread, enticing him on, I guess. And there he was, on his knees, looking up at me. Slowly he began crawling across the floor toward me. I didn't move. Then there was this hand on my foot, then calf, and, his eyes all big, a reaching up to my zipper. Even then I could have laughed it off, walked over to the windows or bookcases, or something. I didn't.

I had even warned him at lunch not to try it, so he shouldn't have, but then I didn't have to shove him flat on the floor, bending down into his face and screaming about mother-fucking sick, conniving faggots. I snatched up my stories and knocked over a lamp as I left. I did that on purpose.

I strode down the center of the street, went up, threw the stories on the table and gulped down a beer. Then I was outside again, headed toward the park where Quasi and I sometimes go.

I went to a clump of bushes that had been hollowed out by years of use as a lover's nest. In the full moonlight I stood next to it as dark shapes loitered here and there in the park. I had the glow of a cigarette in hand and kept rubbing myself until a pudgy shape took the bait and started to approach.

I slipped into the bushes and the man sidled in after me. Without a word he touched my thigh, rubbing his hand up and down. As he did, I undid my belt buckle. He slipped down to his knees and fingers touched the snap of my jeans.

I grabbed him by the collar, yanked him up. My fist was all clenched and arm cocked, but the light of a street lamp glistened off his glasses. His eyes, under them, were magnified and huge. He was an old man and his mouth was twisted with fear. I shoved him backward into the bushes and screamed at him, my curses shattering the quiet of the night.

Then I tore out of those bushes toward the swings, and sat on one and began to swing, swinging back and forth with my eyes closed. I heard the queers running away from me, out of the bushes and the park. They sought the relative safety of street and street lamp and left the park to me.

I remember I hoped the old man's backward plunge into the bushes hadn't hurt him. He should be ashamed of himself, but he didn't deserve to be hurt—not by me, not by anyone. How'd I like it if some young stud beat up my Pa in some park?

And swinging in the dark, kicking my feet out and back like a child, and feeling the cold against my face, I began to cry. I don't know why, but there I was, swinging and crying at the same time, the tears cold on my cheeks.

I wish Blaine hadn't tried it. It was nice, yesterday afternoon, having a friend, or I thought he was a friend until he showed me it was a scheme he had connived up to use me and get what he wanted.

It was a nice afternoon, though. The zoo. The animals, lunch.

Spilt milk now. I'll go on. Maybe things weren't so bad with Carmen after all. But then again, they were. I'm not somebody's amusement—not hers, not Blaine's.

I'll survive.

And one day—not days like these, so damp and cold—but one day a woman's breasts will fill with milk and with me by her side, our infant son or daughter will put mouth to nipple and suckle.

It'll be in our back yard, a clear spring afternoon, the two of us sitting on the settee I had rigged up as a swing and hung from our oak tree. Birds will be chirping. A butterfly or two. As our child suckles, she'll put her arm around me, draw me close, and offer to me her other breast and her love.

CHAPTER 13

Bob laid his pen on the large spiral notebook that was his journal, fixed a cup of coffee and carried it over to the window. Sunday morning had come in wet and cold. There was a sheen on the pavement where pigeons pecked unperturbed by the constant drizzle. But children and pedestrians were huddling within closed doors today, keeping off the streets, though a blue jay squawked in the bare limbs of an oak and a squirrel ran up its trunk. *I'll never see a swallow from this window,* he thought. *The sky isn't expansive enough to contain their joy....Well, better get on with it. A little rain never stopped us in the Corps, and it's not stopping me now.*

He took off his tattered robe, put on a flannel shirt, windbreaker and floppy camouflage jungle hat. Outside, he placed *Automotive Repair Made Simple* on the fender and covered it with a piece of clear plastic. Puddles collected on his floppy hat and whenever he moved his head water trickled down his collar, or onto the shoulders of his wind breaker, but he had to get his truck fixed so that it would start every time. His escape away from this god-forsaken city depended on it.

But he was leaving, he told himself, because there were no decent jobs to be had in this falsely heralded mecca. It had nothing to do with Bronc, the punk, the eunuch. For three days now there had been no further evidence of him or his threats, so Bronc wasn't really going to do anything. He only wanted him to run scared. Well, he was now aware of that game, and Bronc had better keep his distance, bodyguards or no bodyguards. No way was he about to run from a ball-less druggie. He was leaving for only one reason—a reason Linda had demonstrated by driving off in a shiny new Camaro. Without a decent paying job, he could still get himself laid, but without a decent job no woman would consider him suitable for anything other than a roll in the hay. He needed a better job. Everything he envisioned for his future depended on it.

In the cold gray drizzle he would poke under the hood, then turn to the book to compare the diagram with what he actually found. He would bend again over the engine, then reread a portion of the text, wiping the raindrops from the plastic so he could. Around noon he decided the problem had to be the distributor cap, which he removed and put into his pocket. Come midweek he would get a new one from his pay.

Back in his room he wrote his weekly brief letter to Mrs. Sloan, omitting any mention of Linda. He ate a bologna sandwich, stuffed dirty clothes in his duffle bag and on his way to the Laundromat dropped the letter into a mail box.

On the wet streets traffic was slight, the sidewalks empty. He figured he wouldn't have to wait to use the washing machines. He passed Bud's Place Cold Beer, telling himself he'd never spend a dime there again. The rain was coming in heavier drops now, but the Laundromat was just ahead, just past the storefront church.

As he had suspected, the Laundromat sat largely unused that cold, wet Sunday. Only one man was there, checking the dryers for any clothes ready for removal. Helping him fold his laundry was a kid about nine years old, obviously his son. With an uplifting of the head and a smile the man greeted Bob, who nodded in response.

Bob put his clothes into three washers, started them, then sat in an orange plastic chair which was chained to the wall. He thumbed through a July copy of *Time* magazine, now and then sneaking a glance at the kid, remembering that the laundry was one of his chores when he was that age. "Cute kid," he said to the man.

"Yeah, thanks," the man replied. He wore a blue down vest over a crisp white shirt, professionally starched by a laundry. He came over to Bob, standing over him, his eyes sinking deep into Bob's. He extended his hand and they shook. "I'm Rick," he said. Bob told him his full name, first and last. Rick still clutched Bob's hand, the handshake too long, as he said, "I get him from his mother every other weekend."

With steady backward pull Bob extracted his hand from the man's grasp. "That's better than nothing I guess," he said.

"I've noticed you around the neighborhood..."

I'm sure you have, Bob thought.

"...and wanted to find some excuse to strike up a

conversation with y'all, but that'd be kinda pushy, wouldn't it?" He chuckled.

"It'd be free speech, I guess," Bob said.

"That's quite a shiner you've got there, guy. How'd you get it?"

"Settling a debt. At least I hope it's settled."

"But why don't you come over sometime, not this weekend, but maybe during the week or next weekend — I'll be free then."

"And why would I do that?"

"Oh, we could watch TV together, or find something more exciting," Rick said.

"Well guy, thanks for the invite, but I don't think so."

"I'll just jot down my phone number in case you change your mind one of these dark and stormy nights." He gave a little chuckle, then moved to a washing machine where he took a pen from the pocket of his shirt and fumbled through the contents of his wallet for something to write on.

"Dad," the kid said, "we're missing another sock."

"That's all right, they're replaceable," he said. He handed Bob an old cash register printout and whispered, "Call me," then went over to the folding table. "Nice, neat job, Rick," he said. "So, let's load this stuff up and head on down to McDonald's."

"Burger King's better," the kid said.

"Okay, Captain, whatever you say."

Bob watched them leave, watched the man turn his head to him and wink. *Has the whole world gone queer?* He knew it existed, had seen it firsthand in the Corps, but had never imagined there were so many of them. He loaded his clothes from the washers to dryers, sat again in the orange chair and watched them tumble.

Even his own Pa, the man out of whose love, passions and sinews he had been fashioned, was queer. Or had turned that way. For years, he remembered, they had trekked throughout the Southeast in a relentless search for a woman who wanted him, or he would settle for earning a mite better living. Then came Macon and beer, and skintight jeans and pointy western boots. And hitchhikers spending the night in pajama parties. His Pa always grinned when he called them pajama parties. Then he met a dark, hairy guy with sloping brow, Grady, and weeks later his Pa snatched home from Bobby's life and was gone, but not entirely, for Bob had searched for him. It probably would have been better, he conceded, had he searched but not found.

After his discharge from the Corps, after living with Doc and his wife, after his employment by the Manville Corporation and his enrollment in the University of Colorado, he had ended a wonderful vacation of backpacking in the Alaskan wilds with a foolhardy search.

On the trail he had met Laura, a forest ranger. They hiked in the same direction and for convenience sake had made a common camp. As wind swooshed in the fir trees above, as wolves howled in the distance, and as his bare back moistened with sweat, she moaned under him and dug fingernails into his back. In the morning around the little fire, over oatmeal and instant coffee, she mentioned that Bob reminded her of somebody she had met—his height, his hair, good looks. Especially his eyes—pale as faded denim. "You don't see eyes like yours every day."

"Do you remember his name?"

"Haven't the slightest, Bob. Sorry. But he was a prospector, had made a strike. Copper, I think. He was going to sell the rights to American Mines and move to San Francisco."

"Did he have an accent?" Bob asked.

"Oh yes! Heavy southern drawl."

"Did he have anybody with him?"

"Yeah, with a bigger drawl than him."

"Do you remember what that guy looked like?"

"What are you getting at, Bob? Why all the questions?"

"Just answer me. Please! It might be important!"

"Well, the guy with him was dark haired, hadn't shaved in days, and had a sloping brow."

"Like a Neanderthal?"

"Exactly."

Me and Grady been talking about Alaska. There're fortunes being made up there, boy. "You said San Francisco, Laura?"

"Yes, but why?"

He didn't answer her, but folded his sleeping bag, collapsed his tent, and bounded down the trail. He got in his jeep—only two years old, but paid for and his—drove it and sold it at the first place he came to, Pioneer Used Cars. He got not a quarter of its worth, but he didn't care, because the salesman there offered to drive him to the airport.

It was dusk when the jet landed in San Francisco, and dark when the cabbie let him out where he had asked to go: "Uh, you know, to the, uh, the queer district." With backpack hoisted to his shoulder he spied a policeman, went to him and asked where a bus station was. He followed the directions, deposited his backpack in a locker and was out on the sidewalks again, asking this pedestrian and that if he knew a Robert Newell, who looked like him, but eighteen years older. He asked a policeman and several bums in alleys. He asked bartenders and men in queer barrooms. At last a bartender directed him to The Silver Spike.

He followed the directions up the hill and to the right until the sign he sought, The Silver Spike, beckoned him to cross the street. The sign was of wood, hand-carved and painted. Under the fancy scroll, in smaller, plain letters, were the words, R. NEWELL, Proprietor. Louvered shutters blocked off the plate glass window.

As he reached for the doorknob, his resolve faltered. *Do I dare disturb his life after all these years? Hasn't there already been too much water?*

A sudden voice behind him spoke: "Well, are you going in or not?"

"Yeah, sure I am," he said and entered.

This place was more crowded than the others, more smoky, noisy and festive. Multi-colored Tiffany style lamps hung over the bar along the right wall. There were a dozen tables, half of them taken. A brightly colored jukebox was against the far wall with a small dance floor near it. On it two men, both shirtless, danced together in the darkness, a strobe light's sudden bursts freezing their motions. It was as if they were dancing in a lightning storm or writhing together in hell.

Bob moved to the ell of the bar. He was pressing to it

between men and raising his hand to get the bartender's attention when a somber pock-marked guy on his right pushed his glass forward and left. Bob took the stool and ordered a bourbon.

Throughout the room men pressed and laughed and drank and talked. Many here wore black leather vests over bare chests, others cowboy hats and fancy shirts. A few wore everyday clothes. Midway along the bar a chubby guy in pullover shirt and feather boa entertained a grouping with comic imitations of Mae West. But no, his Pa was not among them.

Down the bar a balding man and a long-haired kid who looked like a surfer began arguing with the bartender. He took from the kid's hand something that looked like a driver's license, held it under the lights under the bar, handed it back and shook his head no. Finally he poured them a draft and a shot, and a plain Coke. As he rang up the charge, the balding man poured the shot into the kid's Coke.

Against the wall opposite the bar stood a bodybuilder, posing with arms folded across his chest, his muscles flexed and oiled. He wore skin tight jeans and leather straps that crisscrossed his chest, straps accented with silver studs to blade the light and catch the eye. He looked like a gladiator in *Ben-Hur* or *Spartacus*. *Probably the bouncer,* Bob thought.

And there he was, standing a head over the crowd, his Pa. He wasn't there a moment ago. He wondered where he had come from. He appeared to be no more than in his mid-thirties. *When you were in the Corps, Pa, and stationed here, and before you met Mom, an artist once paid you three-hundred dollars to get you to pose naked, huh Pa? What were you then, seventeen, eighteen? But you're still handsome and look like you always looked. I'm glad you're not wearing a black leather vest or those leather straps. The light blue work-shirt looks good on you, always did. I wish you'd button it up some, but the way the hair forms a line going down your abdomen...well, I'm the same way.*

A customer was introducing somebody to him. They shook and a moment later his Pa's head tossed backward in laughter, which, abating, left a lingering smile, wide and inviting. And there he was, his own father, the man who, with a shuddering of the loins, had engendered from his own body all that was to become Bob.

The bartender took his Pa's glass to fill it. Ice and coke went into it, not a drop of booze. The drunkenness that had hung around him in the months before he vanished, the drunkenness that had left crushed beer cans on the kitchen table and on the floor beside the sofa was gone. And there he was, both of them breathing the same air, both surrounded by the beat of the jukebox, a beat strong and joyous, a beat incessant like the heartbeat of ten thousand men.

Someone at a table stood up on a chair to announce an orgy to be held in celebration of somebody's birthday. All were invited. The rubber sheets had already been spread on the living room floor, the bottles of poppers set out and cans of Crisco. The joints had all been rolled. Everybody was invited to the festivities.

A dozen or so began moving to the door. The tall bodybuilder in leather straps went over to his Pa, who looked at his watch, nodding.

Bob looked at his watch, 10:15. He downed his drink, pushed his glass forward, and glanced again in his Pa's direction. This time he met his Pa's steady gaze. Bob smiled an unsure smile and lifted his palm from the bar in a little wave.

His Pa's mouth fell open in gape. His mouth closed, his Adam's apple rose and fell, then a hand went slowly to the side of his face as his head bowed.

The bodybuilder leaned toward him to speak in his ear. His Pa, still with hand on face, shook his head.

Quite a shock, huh? Bob thought. *But I understand. It's been a long time. But you'll be down here in a minute or two, huh, Pa?*

With drink after drink he waited for that minute, for his Pa's approach. In that minute the ashtray began to overflow with half-smoked cigarettes.

In that minute the young, long-haired kid would dance on the floor, dance with the mirror, dance alone with the beat. From drunken men would come wolf whistles and commands for the kid to strip. The balding man would stand near the floor, jerking his head to the side and obviously telling the kid to cut it out. His Pa would smile politely at the entertainments of the chubby Mae West. And one song on the jukebox gave way to another in that minute, and Bob drank and waited.

And in his heart he imagined his Pa approaching him through the crunch of men.

He imagined his Pa's arm going around his shoulder and his Pa saying to him, *Come, Bobby, let us walk together. And they went out of the gloom and smoke and noise through a door. And the door opened onto a sunlit meadow where swallows darted and butterflies flitted on the breeze. And watching quietly over it all were the oak and long-leaf pine of his childhood. And his Pa said, I shall show you wonders and marvels. Look, son, do you see? The elfin world of tree-houses and summer thunderstorms, and marshmallows toasted by campfire. A world of sand castles built of the white sands of the Gulf of Mexico. A world of the selfless devotion of dogs. Heed unto my words now, Bobby—Remember these things and forget all the rest, even me. And if you do, my son, you will be happy in your strength and your gristle. And you will be content with your days. Forget me, Bobby, and goodbye. May the good Lord watch over you in my stead. And having spoken thus, his Pa vanished and with him the door through which they had come. And Bobby was alone in that meadow which now stretched out an unbounded expanse. It was a void without landmark or points that define, an emptiness stretching from horizon to horizon, and the oak and long-leaf pine were no longer to be seen.*

Someone squeezed his arm. He looked around and it was the bodybuilder with the studded black straps. A ring pierced his left tit. He had dark hair. "I'm supposed to tell you your dad wants to see you in the back room," he said.

Bob looked to where his Pa had been standing and noticed a door next to the jukebox was closing. He hadn't noticed that door before because it was painted the same off white as the walls.

"Thank you," he said with a smile. He squeezed the man's arm, a huge overwrought slab of beef, which, under his touch, tightened into a solid striated rock.

The bodybuilder's brows arched, a corner of his lips lifted.

Through the crunch of men Bob sidled, excusing himself to this one and that, making his way along the bar. At last. At long last.

He opened the door.

His Pa was sitting on the desk. Behind him was a filing

cabinet and metal shelving with liquor bottles neatly lined on them. On the top shelf was Grandma's clock. He was glad his Pa still had it.

Joy parted Bob's lips.

"Close the door, Bobby," his Pa said.

A motion of his leg slammed it shut and he rushed to his Pa, bending forward to hug him on the desk. He threw his arms around him, his eyes blurring. "Been a long time, huh, Pa?" he said.

His Pa's arms went around him loosely and a hand hesitantly consented to pat his back. "Whacha doing here, boy?" he asked.

Hugging him tightly, Bob said, "Good seeing you, Pa! Damn good!"

His Pa placed hands on Bob's shoulders and leaned back to separate them. "You shouldn't have bothered. Best leaving it like it is. How'd you find me?"

Bob wiped the runniness of his nose with the back of a hand and stammered as a kid would, "Well, uh, I was on vacation from my job, uh, and backpacking and I, uh, met this…"

"You look good," his Pa interrupted. "Tanned, healthy, not all scrawny like you were back then, so I figured you were working. It's good having a job that gives you a vacation so you can go off backpacking. But really, you shouldn't have bothered. You've done okay on your own and we can't go back and change what's been."

"Good seeing you, Pa!"

"Whacha doing here, boy?"

"I just thought we'd do some catching up, and start fresh,

all over again."

"What for?" his Pa asked.

"Because that's how it's supposed to be."

"Lots of things in this world ain't how they s'pposed to be."

"But that doesn't mean..." His words trailed off, for the coolness of his reception struck him for the first time.

"No, Bobby. It was best then and best now. And why ain't you married?"

"Well I will when I find one," he said.

"Boy, I want you to marry and settle down and be happy, really happy. Not with no damn make-believe happiness of booze and drugs and cheap sex. But a woman who loves you and kids who depend on you. So find her, Bobby. I don't want you following after me in no ways."

"You don't look like you're doing too shabby. You've got a good business and all. Your place here is the busiest..."

"If your mother hadn't died on us, things would have been lots different. And for years I wondered what you did, how you managed when you got back from YMCA camp."

"I just took Rusty down to the big oak on Bullrush Creek and we lived there, Pa. I had to lie about my address at school, though, and had to forge your signature on report cards and all," he said, smiling, "but we did okay."

His Pa looked at him sadly.

"Honest, it was okay," Bob said.

"You lived under a tree and did okay. That's your mother in you. I don't know what the fancy words for it are, but you've got spunk, gristle. I figured you'd do okay. But think about it, Bobby. Think about it hard: I ran off and let my son live in the woods with his dog. Think about what I did to you!" His Pa, silent, gazed at him unblinkingly, then said, standing at the same time, "Come on, I've got somebody I want you to meet." His Pa went out, past him.

A sorrow began to well within Bobby like a wave approaching the shore and like a beaten dog he slowly trailed his Pa back into the noise and smoke of the bar.

The bodybuilder was grasping the back of his Pa's head, forcing their mouths closer.

Bobby's eyes flitted here and there. He shoved his hands into pockets. *You really don't have to do that right in front of me, now do you?*

His Pa turned to him and with an arm around the bodybuilder's waist introduced him as Mark. "And we're going to a birthday party in a little bit. There'll be dozens of men, all in their birthday suits, all rolling on the floor. Want to join us, boy?"

Mark, smiling at Bob, luxuriated a hand up and down the muscled contours of his abs. His Pa put his hand on top of Mark's to course along with it. "Want to feel?" Mark asked Bob, who didn't answer.

"Pa," he said, "can't we go somewhere—I've come a long way—just you and me?"

"And what the hell for?!" his Pa said. "Just seeing ya makes me hurt inside. And that's exactly what I want for you, boy—having you sit in the parlor with your wife or your kids or in-laws, and you're sitting there with your hands between your legs and your head down, ashamed of your Pa, your runaway Pa, your faggot Pa! No, boy! Your Pa's dead, just tell 'em that."

"But you're not!" he said.

"Just tell 'em I am! But, uh, uh...me and Mark are going to a birthday party. Wanna go to a birthday party? You're handsome as sin, Bobby, and I promise you'll be *real* popular. You'll have four on ya at the same time and others waiting to take their turns—a cock in your ass, a cock down your throat, some guy's mouth sucking you off and somebody else's tongue licking your balls."

Bob studied the crumpled pack of cigarettes on the floor.

Pa continued, "And a good time was had by all! Wanna be a good time for 'em? Do your duty for 'em? See how many men you can satisfy and have 'em come back begging for seconds? They'll come back for you, boy. And a good time was had by all!"

He shook his head.

"But you heard him," his Pa said. "The rubber sheets are all spread. Poppers and Crisco and joints. It's all set. Wanna go?"

Bob, looking at the floor, again shook his head.

"Well, the drinks are on me tonight."

"And that's it? After my coming..."

"That's it!" his Pa said. He turned and hugged Mark.

Bob gazed at his Pa's back, at the veins and sinews of Mark's arms. Mark, looking at him, mouthed the words, "Come on, go."

He turned and poked along the bar, through the men. Back on his stool, his fingers tore pieces from the napkin under his drink. The pieces were rolled and flicked across the bar. He ordered doubles from the bartender, "And they're on him!" He guzzled drink after drink, getting himself drunk. His fingers turned swizzle sticks in his hand, snapping them. The pile of broken swizzle sticks grew and the room and men began to spin. Even when he closed his eyes, colors and anger and hurt swirled.

He stood up on the rungs of the barstool, and there was a calling of his Pa's name above the crowd. There came a hush over the men, only the ululations of a single guitar on jukebox. And there was a hurling—with all the strength of arm and shoulder—of a glass across the room. Bottles in back of the bar shattered, shards flying, glistening in the air, tinkling onto the floor.

The mouth of the crowd gaped open to the sound of a great inhalation. Then there was yelling and commotion among them, and from Bob a striding to the door. Behind him was a calling for the police and a voice he knew saying, "No! For Christ's sake, just let him go!"

Across the street he paused to lean against the wall. As it sagged and swayed behind him, he waited for his Pa to follow him out, to call his name up and down the street. He waited as the wind scuttled newspapers past him.

His Pa did not follow him out.

He went down the street, steadying himself with a hand on the walls, until he came to an open doorway. He entered, and sat alone at a table. A barmaid brought him a bourbon and he stared into the amber liquid. A middle-aged woman—her hairdo falling apart and lipstick smeared—stood over him, leering down. "Have a seat," he said. She did and began to rub his thigh.

He awoke the next morning in a pink and blue bedroom overlooking the darker blue of the Pacific. While the woman still slept, he dressed, finding his shirt under the grand piano, and called a cab. He took the address from an envelope beside the telephone. And he returned from his vacation to Denver, to his job and the groundwork of his days. Gradually he let slip, one by one, his enrollment in the University, his job, his apartment. Then began his downward spiral from which he had not yet recovered.

He watched the clothes tumble in the dryer and lit a cigarette.

CHAPTER 14

'Water, water, everywhere, and all the boards did shrink,' Bob said quoting Coleridge at his window Monday, Tuesday and Wednesday. The continuous rain prohibited any roofing work in Atlanta, stopped him from replacing his distributor cap, the old one on top of the refrigerator. It kept him in Atlanta, still a pawn in Bronc's game, still a pawn in Carter's depression. By Wednesday the lack of work had so depleted his funds that all he had to eat that day was two poached eggs on bread and his last can of beans.

Yet even so, he had used the idle days to work on something productively. *A good man never gets caught with his options down, Bobby.* It was his Pa's voice, from childhood.

And by Wednesday, he had three short stories all typed up and double spaced, and although he had found the keys on the cheap typewriter at the library all scrambled and not arranged alphabetically, he had managed. As he walked in the light rain from the library toward home and Quasi, he hoped an editor would see the worth of his stories. He could use a big check.

Clear skies in Atlanta finally allowed roofing work to begin again on Thursday. It had been a solid week since he had worked—since the day he had encountered Bronc in a barroom—and in that time the throbbing in his head had abated to a dull ache and his wounds had healed. He was ready and eager.

Throughout the morning he hoisted rolls of tar paper to his shoulder and carried them up a rickety, swaying, three story ladder. He carried up hundred pound bails of shingles and buckets of molten tar that smelled of the fires of hell and cleared his sinuses. He had to be careful with the tar for a single drop would cling to the skin and blister. Years ago angry mobs had used it to tar and feather those they judged offensive—swindlers, uppity blacks or the unnatural. In the clear, cool morning he wondered how anyone, covered in it from head to feet, could ever remove it without taking with it a layer of skin. In practice, he realized, to the one tarred and feathered, the task of removing it would be equivalent to flaying himself alive. His people, white southern folk, had much to repent of. But even so it was still hard to shrug off the insults from the guys he worked with.

As he climbed up with a bucket of asphalt, the ladder under him began to jiggle and sway grossly. He clung to it, motionless, his body flush. The swaying increased and he looked up to see black work boots, one on each upright, pistoning back and forth. Four of the men he worked with, three on one side, one on the other, were looking down at him. White eyes were agleam in black faces, white teeth bountiful in grins. *Let go of the bucket, you fool,* he told himself, but didn't. He clung to the ladder and the bucket.

Then came a voice from below. "Cut the crap!" It was Mr. King's voice. The four who were watching vanished onto the roof. The ladder stopped swaying. "Jeffrey, get your ass down here!"

Bob, his heart pounding, started climbing up again—he only had a score of rungs to go—but Jeffery started coming down. "Wait a minute!" Bob hollered.

"Move your white ass, Newell!" Jeffery spewed, above him.

Bob descended the ladder with the bucket of tar.

Mr. King was waiting on the ground, hands on both hips. "Take a break, Newell," he snapped.

He stepped aside. His hand was shaking as he tried to light one of his three remaining cigarettes.

Jeffery stepped down from the last rung, went to Mr. King and said, "What's up?"

"Grab your lunch bag and get the hell out of here," Mr. King said. "And you're not coming back."

"Shit, man! Just a joke!" Jeffery said.

Mr. King didn't answer, but dug in his front pants pocket, peeled a ten, looked at it, and added a five to it. That was more than half a day's pay. He held it out to Jeffery.

"You don't mean that, bro," Jeffery said, not taking the money.

Bob approached them. "Mr. King," he said, "he wouldn't have pushed it over—I know that."

"You stay out of this, Newell!" Mr. King said, then to Jeffery said, "Just a joke, huh? Well, my workman's comp is already sky high. And he served his country honorably, got himself a little college, and he's a damn harder worker than you ever thought of being! And how do you stack up against that? So you get your black ass out of here! Don't come back."

Jeffery snatched the money from Mr. King's hand. "Whacha takin' honkey's side for, Amos?"

"Go!" Mr. King said.

Jeffery looked at Bob, rubbed his crotch, shot him a bird, then sauntered off, loose-limbed, as if out on the town. He kicked a soda can from his path.

"Mr. King," Bob said, "a man's job…"

"Smoke your cigarette," he interrupted, "then get the tar up there. They're waiting for it."

"Okay," Bob said.

"And at lunch I need to see you."

"Okay," he said, apprehension tightening his throat.

He smoked the cigarette. *He's going to let me go too. It's not my fault, but I just don't fit in. But he's not going to do it all loud and in front of everybody. He's not a bad boss. Maybe he'll let me work out the rest of the day and tomorrow too.* He crushed the cigarette under his sneaker, then climbed the ladder.

This time, for the first time ever, one of the guys reached down to take the bucket from him, saying, "Come all the way up here a minute." Another, for the first time ever, helped him onto the roof with outstretched hand. The city stretched out below him and he gazed down at the tops of oak trees.

"You stuck up for him, huh?" Ishmael said. He wore his hair in a huge Afro.

"Not really. Mr. King wouldn't let me get…"

"But you tried," Bill said.

"Doesn't matter now. I think I just got myself fired come lunch-time."

"Always been just us nigger-boys up here," Kyle chimed in. "Go get yerself some honkey job, man."

"Yeah, well...he's watching, so I'd better get back down to work." He climbed down and throughout the morning filled buckets and carried them up. *And just where am I supposed to find a honkey job, Kyle? You just don't get it. I'm a Vietnam vet so they stamp me REJECT.*

At noon Mr. King called out, "Lunch!" and Bob presented himself before him.

"Jump in the truck. Gotta talk to ya," Mr. King said.

Bob got in, closed the door, but instead of talking, Mr. King started the engine and drove. *You may as well get it over with,* he thought. They drove to a house in a black section of town and pulled the truck into the driveway. "Want you to meet Mrs. King," Mr. King said in explanation. The house was of brick, the white trim neatly painted. A chain-link fence surrounded it.

At the front door he was introduced to Mrs. King, who wore glasses and whose salt and pepper hair was covered with a hair net, a proper and dignified woman. "I hope you like meatloaf, Bob," she said.

"You know," he laughed, "I thought I was going to get fired, not fed."

"That's silly," she said, "I've heard good things about you. Come." She led the way into the dining room, small but attractive with hutch, oak table set with three place-mats and real china. On one wall hung a tapestry of *The Last Supper.*

Mr. King shooed a yellow tiger cat from his chair at the

head of the table and sat. Bob sat and looked out the window in front of him. From the adjacent house came the scales of someone practicing the trumpet.

"Come summer I'm thinking of expanding the business," Mr. King said and paused as Mrs. King brought dishes from the kitchen. When everything was on the table, Mrs. King sat.

"We always say grace, Bob," she said and bowed her head. Bob bowed his head as well.

"Father," she said, "for this food and for all your bountiful gifts we give you thanks. But most of all we thank you for Jesus. His continued presence in the world and the absolute surety of His promises are what make this life worth living. For Him we give you thanks, Father. Amen."

"Amen," Mr. King said.

"Well, help yourself," she said to Bob, "and there's plenty, so don't be bashful."

He nodded and as he put a serving of green beans on his plate, Mr. King said, "So, come summer I'm thinking about buying another truck and equipment, and hiring more men. There'll be two job sites going all the time. But all this is conditional, Bob."

"On what?" he asked, the rich tang of mashed potatoes flooding his tongue.

"You've got to stay with me and be foreman for me."

His mouth gaped open, but he closed it and swallowed.

"Now I'll pay you six dollars an hour, and..."

That's almost twice my wage!

"Charles," Mrs. King spoke up, "I thought we figured it out to be seven."

"Seven dollars an hour," Mr. King corrected himself,

"plus five percent of the price of each job. But you've got to see to it your crew does quality work—I've worked hard building a name and we can't let that slip. And you've got to see to it you keep the cost of materials within the estimate."

Joy overwhelmed him and he was smiling broadly, deep dimples on each cheek. Yet even so, he was not naive. "But, uh, the guys won't…"

"We've thought about that, too," Mr. King said. "That's another reason why we gotta wait till summer. If Martin Luther hadn't died…"

"…and taken with him," Mrs. King continued, "a uniting dream of different peoples at peace…"

"…we wouldn't have all the problems we have now," Mr. King said.

"He was a prophet," she said.

"But waiting till summer," he said, "and you keeping doing what you're doing and how you're doing it, the guys will come around. They might squawk out loud and bellyache a little bit at first, but they'll really see the reasons for it. You'll keep the crew—the guys you're working with now— and I'll put together a new one."

"Well sure," Bob said. "Sure, if you think it'll work."

"But for the time being we'll have to keep it quiet about expanding and all," Mr. King cautioned.

"Of course," he said with both eyebrows raised, his grin from ear to ear.

After the cherry pie, there was a second grace, this time holding hands. With head bowed, Bob thought it may be hypocritical of him to bow his head, but it wasn't hypocritical to hold their hands.

With joy in his heart he worked that afternoon, more tar, shingles, metal flashing. Perhaps now, at last, his break had come. About three o'clock the men finished the job and Mr. King climbed the ladder to inspect the work. He was pleased. At the dropoff/pickup site he gave each man an extra five dollars.

At day's end not only did he have thirty dollars in his pocket but his gait toward home was brisk. He ran ahead, grabbed a light pole, and swung himself in an arc around it. Twice he hop-scotched on boards children had chalked onto the sidewalk.

He stopped at a supermarket and stood in line with a whole carton of cigarettes for himself and a box of rawhide chews for Quasi. *The little guy likes them and they're good for his teeth. He should probably have one or two a day, not just on special occasions.*

On the sidewalk again he figured that come summer—just three months away—he could rent a little house with a fenced-in yard for the little guy. And perhaps he could get another Jeep like the one he had sold years ago in Alaska. And dating. Come summer he could afford to date again. Maybe he'd fall in love, raise a family. It wasn't such a bad city after all.

CHAPTER 15

On the corner of Hyacinth Street children were playing jump rope. They were beautiful little girls, all four of them in the pleated plaid skirts and white blouses of a parochial school. "Do you mind if I try?" Bob asked.

"Sure, go ahead," they said.

The girl jumping ducked out and he ducked in, the brown package in his arm. Faster and faster the girls twirled and faster and faster he jumped, until at last he ducked out. "Wow!" he said.

"That was pretty good for an old guy," one of the girls said.

"Thanks," he said, chuckling and continuing on his way. He entered the dark yawn of his building and leapt up the stairs three at a time. As he fumbled in his pocket for his keys, he called Quasi. He swung his door open wide and gasped.

In the doorway, his breathing stilled, he beheld chaos.

The green chair vomited up its cotton, gashes in its fabric.

His mattress puked out yellow foam. Covering the floor were his books, the covers ripped from some of them. His clothes had been torn and flung about.

Slowly, hesitant to make a sound, he entered the silence of the room. Books and papers slid and crunched under his feet. He placed the bag gingerly on the floor. His green table had been knocked over, the chairs smashed against it, the broken pieces lying in heaps. His refrigerator had been overturned.

He stood among the debris, his gaze on the single smear of catsup. It was like blood, streaking across the books on the floor and up onto his bed.

Yellow egg yolks drooled down the walls. His discharge over his bed was darkened in the center.

He moved to it. It had been taken down, its center section charred black with a lighter, then rehung. Bronc.

His eyes snapped to the door and fixed there as he waited for him to appear, grinning a crazed grin, and dressed not in a suit but in fatigues. Expectancy stilled his mind. He scarcely breathed.

With his eyes fixed on the door, he stood there, waiting. No thoughts filled his mind, he just waited until the name, "Quasi?" came softly from him. Still immobile, still looking toward the door, "Quasi?" came from him again, louder.

The name came from him a third time, and he was down on his hand and knees. His neck twisted to look under the bed. Then his arms and hands pawed though the debris of books, papers, clothes. He crawled about, searching, scattering. "Quasi!" he called. "It's okay, boy, come!" He crawled, pawed, scattered, searched.

He stood up. His eyes coursed over the destruction till

they fixed on the refrigerator. He jerked it upright. The metal racks clanked within.

Quasi was not inside. He was nowhere. His dog was gone.

Grief welled within him. Looking, he stepped over the streak of catsup, on slices of bread, on the torn typed pages of his stories, he moved slowly toward the plywood closet that still stood.

There against the wall, under the window, lay gray fur.

He approached and knelt. Quasi was still. He who asked so little, was so appreciative, and gave so much was still. "Quasi?" he said, a meek quality in his voice.

There, beside him, half-buried by the torn cover of a book, lay a hypodermic needle. *How dare he!* bellowed in his mind.

He reached over to stroke gray fur. Gently his hand moved over him from head to shoulder, to rump. His vision began to blur as he stroked his dog, but then he felt—or thought he felt—a motion, a breath, under his touch. He held his hand still on Quasi's chest, and stopped breathing himself to feel it better.

And there was a shallow, slow breath.

He cradled Quasi up in his arms, standing as he did. The little guy's head flopped toward the floor and he lifted it to his shoulder. "Please, God!" he said and he moved toward the door.

Then he was dashing down the stairs. He flung the truck door open and eased Quasi onto the seat. He slammed the door and ran around to the driver's side, climbing in and slamming the door behind him. He inserted the key. *God, if You exist, this time let it start!* He turned the key and turned it again and it gave not a sound, not a rumble, not a squeak. *It can't with the damn distributor cap off!* His fist struck the steering wheel, and struck it again. *God damn, mother fuckin' shit! Fuckin' hell!*

But he noticed a red MG was parked ahead. He scurried out from behind the wheel, threw open the passenger door and with Quasi again in his arms, ran across the street, up stairs. He banged and pounded on Blaine's door, hands and feet, the thuds echoing in the stairwell, heavy, insistent thuds. "Blaine! Blaine!" he screamed. He pounded and his fist began to ache.

The door opened. "Oh my God!" jawless Blaine said. "Let me get my keys."

As the shiny red MG zoomed and zigzagged through rush hour traffic, Bob cradled Quasi. "Come on, boy. You've got to hang in there for me now. We'll have lots more good times together, you and me—I promise. Just hang in there. Do it for me!" he said.

They parked and Bob followed Blaine into the veterinarian's. He was standing at the receptionist's window. "Is it your bird?" a woman's voice asked him.

"No, it's a friend's dog," Blaine said.

Bob stood beside him now, gray fur limp in his arms. "Go right on back, Mr. Shirer. Second door on the left. I'll tell one of the doctors."

"See if Jim is available," Blaine said.

"Who?" she asked.

"Dr. Nadler," he said.

"Sure," she said.

They went down a short hall and entered the second door on the left. He placed Quasi on the stainless steel table and stood there, helpless. From the lobby they heard her voice again. "I'm sorry, everybody, but we've had an emergency. There may be a little delay."

A young man with closely trimmed black beard and white smock came into the examining room. "Hi, Blaine," he said, immediately beginning to examine Quasi. "What happened?"

Bob spoke up. "I don't really know. I think it's drugs."

"Why do you think that?" Dr. Nadler asked, prying open Quasi's eyes. An assistant came and stood in the doorway. The doctor asked him for a flashlight and shined it into the eyes.

"There was a needle on the floor beside him," Bob said.

"Did you bring it with you?" he asked, putting a stethoscope to Quasi's chest.

"No."

"You should have," he said. "He's scarcely breathing. Mark, get the oxygen and Narcan. And call Dr. Stevens back in." He looked at Bob now, for the first time. "What happened to his hind leg?" he asked.

"I don't know. He was like that when I got him, but he's a wonderful dog. It doesn't bother him. He can sorta play Frisbee as long as I keep it low and everything."

"Well, you gentlemen had better go now. We'll do everything possible. I can't offer any guarantees or even very much hope for that matter, but we'll do what can be done. Do you have any idea what type of drug it may have been?"

Bob shook his head. "Whatever people inject with needles, I guess."

"Okay," Dr. Nadler said. "Go on now."

Bob nodded.

Blaine said, "I'll call."

"Sure," the doctor said.

As they went through the lobby, Blaine paused at the receptionist and said, "I'll call, Alice."

She nodded. "Oh, Dr. Stevens will be here in ten minutes."

"Good," Blaine said, and they left.

Once outside Bob asked, "Who's Dr. Stevens?"

"The senior vet."

"It's that bad, then, huh?"

"They're good doctors, Bob."

"Yeah," he said. They drove, in silence. Bob wondered what he would do without Quasi. He wondered how he had managed before Quasi had entered his life. The little guy was family, all of it. Not a championship dog, but a wonderful, gentle, loving dog.

He looked at Blaine, the frizzy hair, the receding jaw. This was the guy he had shoved onto the floor and had screamed curses at. And here he was helping him. He needed to find a way of thanking him. "I don't know about you," he said, "but I'm hungry. How about stopping at McDonald's or something?"

"Uh," Blaine said, squirming in his seat to feel his hip pockets. "No, I didn't bring my wallet with me."

"You don't need it," Bob said. "You bought lunch for me the other day, and I've got some money on me."

"Okay," Blaine said, "I was wondering where I was going to go for supper anyway."

Over their Big Macs and fries, Bob told him of the defilement he'd found in his room. He spoke of his fears.

"How do you know it's Bronc?" Blaine asked.

"Who else would have bothered to burn my discharge, huh? I've got to get the hell out of this town. Someway I will."

Back in his room, he sorted out the chaos. The spiral notebooks that comprised his journal went into this stack, his torn stories there, unharmed books back in the boxes, book covers here, books missing covers there. Torn clothes he tossed into a pile by the door. Fortunately, Bronc and his thugs had not bothered with his backpack under the bed or his one suitcase containing his best clothes. He walked to the supermarket and with his remaining funds bought tape and glue.

Back home again, he Scotch-taped together the typed pages of his stories and taped the appropriate covers onto books. He glued together his kitchen chairs, using torn tee-shirts as vises. He stuffed white cotton back into the easy chair. He turned his mattress over.

It was past midnight when he carried two large garbage bags of debris—including his blackened discharge—out to the Dumpster. He slept alone in the narrow bed that night with boxes piled in front of the door as security.

The next morning, while Mr. King explained the finer points of properly applying flashing around chimneys, he kept wondering how his little friend was doing. Funny, he didn't know where the vet's was, or what it was called. At noon he asked Mr. King for a lift to wherever the best pawn shops were. There he purchased a chrome .38 caliber and bought a box of shells. If Bronc showed again, he would be ready for him. He then checked the yellow pages under veterinarians for Stevens but found none. The only thing he knew was it was something Animal Hospital. He would have to knock on Blaine's door again and impose. In return, he might have to let the gay guy get what he wanted. It wouldn't be the first time a pervert had propositioned him, but it would be the first time he obliged. But if it required that to get his dog back, he would.

At day's end he stopped at the supermarket for a quart of beer and drank it dry next to the carts lined up outside. Fortified, he walked the blocks to Hyacinth Street.

As he turned the corner he spied—past the brown weeds—Blaine's frizzy hair. He was sitting on the steps to his own building. "Did you call?" he shouted and began jogging toward him. He tossed the bag with the empty bottle into some bushes.

"Yeah, I did," he called back and stood.

"Well?" he said, standing now on the walk. Blaine, on the steps, was eye level.

"It was heroin, a massive dose, should have killed him. No guarantees, but things look good at this point. They think he'll make it. "

"Thank God!" he said, his head inclining.

"But Bob," Blaine said tenderly, "they're worried about the effects of the hypoxia. He was scarcely breathing for some time. There could be neurological damage."

"What?"

"Brain damage," Blaine said.

"There won't be. No way." He looked directly at Blaine. "What's the vet's called? There's no Stevens in the phone book."

"It's Assisi Veterinary Hospital. If things go well, we can pick him up Tuesday or Wednesday."

"Assisi," Bob repeated aloud. Funny, he thought, he's not holding anything back, but maybe he's expecting an offer. "I appreciate your help, guy, and so if you really want, uh…" This was hard, and the words stuck in his throat. "Uh, you know, want to do the, uh, gay stuff on me…"

"No," Blaine said.

You're not a bad guy after all, ain't cha? he thought.

"Just the other day I told you I wouldn't make a pass at you," Blaine said, "but I did. I'm sorry. But will you join me for dinner tonight?"

With dimples emerging on his cheeks he moved forward to give a jovial punch at Blaine's shoulder. "With all your help with Quasi it should be the other way around," he said. "My rent's due today, though, and it rained almost all week. So I won't have much extra till I get paid again on Monday."

"I don't care about that," Blaine said. "But will you meet me at a restaurant about eight?"

"Sure," he said.

"Good. It's not awful far. You see, I have to have supper with my family tonight, but we always eat at 6:00. I'll just eat a little and save my appetite for dinner with you."

"Where is this place?"

Blaine gave directions and they parted.

Bob figured if dinner was his way of apologizing for the pass, he'd be taking him somewhere nice, so once upstairs, he took his maroon suede jacket and gray slacks from the suitcase under the bed. They would be okay after hanging for a few hours, but his dress shirts were horribly wrinkled. He wished he had an iron.

He thought about inquiring if one of the other tenants in the building had an iron, but decided there was slim chance of that. He took the .38 from his pant leg, where the muzzle had been wedged down into his sneaker, and put it on the refrigerator. He then walked to a secondhand store where, for fifty cents, he bought a long-sleeve white shirt, freshly starched.

Back home he showered in the bathroom down the hall and dressed in his room. By way of gratitude he had attempted to offer sexual favors to Blaine. *So you've had your chance and you refused it. I won't offer it again.* He hoped the issue would not come up.

CHAPTER 16

Bob had surmised correctly. Even the door to the Maison Richelieu proclaimed money, but then gay guys always had the bucks. The door was of stained glass and carved wood, the stained glass depicting a female nude, the ocean and sea gulls overhead. The door itself was of oak, hand-carved into vines, leaves and flowers.

On the sidewalk he re-tucked his shirt tail, adjusted the tie, and combed his hair with spread fingers. He entered. A crystal chandelier hung in the foyer which was crowded with potted plants and cut flowers. Though he had been expecting a nice place, the elegance awed him and he stammered a little as he asked the tuxedoed *maitre d'* if Mr. Blaine Shirer had arrived yet. The *maitre d'*, who spoke with a French accent, escorted him to a table and held the chair for him.

As he sat he asked, "How's your family?"

"Same," Blaine said. "Mother gave me the same line. You look sharp. Nice jacket. Suede looks good on you. And the color's good on you, too."

Immediately a tuxedoed waiter had a bar cart at the table. Bob ordered a Grandad and water.

The waiter pushed the cart away. "To tell you the truth, it's really all I had to wear," Bob said. "It was a present from an ex-girlfriend of mine, Carmen. She picked it out." He swizzled the drink and tasted it. It was strong. The tables throughout the room had white cloths and real flowers on each one—not one or two in a bud vase, but an identical arrangement of roses and carnations and baby's breath on each one. At every table were elegantly dressed people. Bob knew the pearls and the diamonds had to be real. All the customers were middle-aged or older, except for a large table of twelve, six young men and six young women. He presumed it was a wedding rehearsal dinner.

On a raised dais in the corner a string quartet, sitting behind golden music stands, played soft beautiful music. Behind them was a gilded harp that no one played.

"Bob," Blaine said, "the menu is in French, so I hope you don't mind, but I've already ordered for us."

"Meatloaf and mashed potatoes." He hit the table with his fist. "That's what I'm hungry for."

"Bob!" Blaine said, a pleading in his voice.

"Just kidding," he said. "But isn't this going to cost a fortune?"

"A person's got to splurge sometime, doesn't he?"

"What's the occasion?" he asked. "Is it your birthday or something?"

"No. I just wanted a really fine meal. The chef here is the Michelangelo of chefs. He and my brother were negotiating about opening a place as fifty-fifty partners. Talent on one side, finances on the other. They already had the location picked out when the curse struck."

"Then you are rich," Bob said.

"No, not me. My family is. And Raiford is a corporate attorney, or was. He's done real well. I'm just a school teacher. I'm not rich."

Three tuxedoed waiters descended on the table to busy themselves. While one filled the water glasses, another placed the first course before them, and the third opened a bottle of wine. Bob looked at the plate before him. The steam arising from it was scented with lemon and garlic. The bottom was spread with something pale green, chopped up real small, in some type of sauce, with three large white mushroom caps filled with something, topped with crumbs and broiled a golden brown.

"You're supposed to eat this?" Bob said. "It's as beautiful to look at as those covers on cooking magazines."

"He's the Michelangelo of chefs. And I assure you it tastes even better than it looks."

It did. "What is it?" Bob asked.

"Translated it would be something like escargot in mushroom caps on coulis of leeks with cream, garlic and lemon."

"Um," Bob grunted, swallowed and said, "Really good. What's the chewy thing inside the mushroom?"

"Escargot," Blaine said.

"What's that?"

Blaine wiped his lips with his napkin to hide his smile as he answered, "Snails."

Bob looked at him in disbelief. "You're kidding."

"Uh-un," Blaine said, taking another bite.

Bob pushed his plate forward.

A different wine accompanied each of the courses that followed, each beautiful and delicious. Though Bob was curious, he did not dare ask what anything placed before him was. Leisurely they finished each bottle of wine, and talked, before the next course arrived.

"...out of the city tomorrow," Blaine was saying. "I was thinking about maybe going to the lake, do a little fishing this weekend. Would you like to go?"

"Sure," he said, his words becoming slurred. "There's more country in me than city. I just wish Quasi could go, but he's in good hands, I guess...But, oh! I don't have a fishing license."

"Doesn't matter," Blaine said. "If you get fined, uh, um, well, my Mother will cover it."

At 9:30 the string quartet finished playing and stood up taking their music from the golden stands.

"Oh, the place closes early, huh?" Bob asked, with words now thick.

"No," Blaine said, the alcohol lengthening his drawl. "Conservatory students. They gotta study and practice."

Two busboys removed the music stands and chairs and the centered the gilded harp on the dais. A tall woman in her late thirties—striking in a pale blue evening gown, and with straight long blond hair flowing down to her waist—crossed the room to it. She positioned her stool, sat a moment looking over the guests, then closed her eyes and began to play, slender fingers gliding gracefully over the strings.

"There she is!" Bob said in liquored words, "my future wife."

"Her name's Brigit. Her daughter's in my tenth grade class. But she's married, Bob."

"Not her necessarily, but somebody like her. A beautiful woman, feminine," he said and gazed at her.

Waiters would approach her to whisper in her ear and place bills into a large brandy snifter. She would nod, smile angelically, and blend one ballad into the next. Blaine requested the *Meditation from Thais*, sliding a twenty dollar bill into the waiter's hand for her.

Late, over their chocolate soufflé, Blaine said, "On the way to the lake, we'll have to stop and visit Raiford for a spell. That'd be okay, huh? But there's a nice cabin and it'll be just the two of us on the lake."

Bob said in heavily slurred words, "But you've gotta promise me somethin' there."

"Don't fret. I'm not going to try and get ya."

"Naw, not that, we done been through all that," he said with a gesture as if shooing a fly in the air. "But you gotta promise we'll get a shit-load of worms."

"Why?"

"And you gotta promise you'll bring a cookbook, a big, fat, fancy French cookbook."

"I'm not the greatest cook there," Blaine said, almost falling out of the chair.

"That's why ya got the book, 'cause awful seeing yous going hungry 'n all. And this way, when yous don't end up catching nothin', yous find some big highfalutin name and has yerselfs a big mess of them Frenchy worms just a-wiggling on yers plate."

Blaine chuckled, covering his mouth with his napkin, trying to control it, but to no avail, for the chuckles broke out into laughter, which proved contagious, and both of them, drunk, guffawed uproariously as they exchanged repartee for repartee. Distinguished patrons looked silently at them from under raised brows, and the penguin at the desk began to look nervous and fidgety. That only fueled their good time.

As they parted drunken ways on Hyacinth Street, Bob called to him to remember that big falutin Frenchy cookbook, then stumbled up the stairs to his room.

CHAPTER 17

On the drive to the lake they zoomed in a red MG along the Interstate at seventy miles per hour, fifteen over the posted fifty-five. Blaine recalled that after his last visit with his brother, as he was heading back to the city, he had stopped in the rest areas, had loitered in the bushes and there, on his knees, had satisfied three men — a trucker and a soldier returning from leave to Ft. Bennington in one rest area and a punk who rode a motorcycle in another. Today, he told himself, he had no need to prowl, for Bob not only was with him, but wanted to be with him. He glanced over at his friend, noting how the morning light made the fine stubble on his face visible as individual hairs. He hadn't shaved this morning.

As they parked in the visitor's lot at Seven Oaks Nursing Home, Blaine said, "I'd appreciate it if you'd go in to meet my brother."

"No, I wouldn't feel right. He probably doesn't want everybody going in and gawking at him. From what you've said he sounds pretty sick."

"He likes company, though. It makes him feel he still has a significance in the world and is still a part of things."

"No. I'll wait outside here. I'll take a walk around the grounds or something, smoke a cigarette."

"Okay," Blaine said and followed a flagstone path to the entrance. As he walked the corridor to room 226, he passed a couple black housekeepers beside a cart of mops, brooms and cleansers. The women fell silent, their dark eyes upon him, and once a little ways past, he heard their stifled chuckles and whispered mockings. He knew his appearance had generated their merriment. It hurt but he was accustomed to it. He looked straight ahead, and with head held high, continued on through corridor that smelled of Lysol. He reached the last room in the hall, number 226, and knocked.

A handsome black orderly in white smock opened the door. The sleeves of the smock were rolled tight around biceps. "We've just finished up here," he said in a Bostonian accent. "Come on in."

Hot, Blaine thought, watching him go. *I haven't had dark meat in months. Up real close blacks have a scent all their own, a pungent mustiness with a hint of honey...But there I go again! Seeing men as one dimensional, as Manhood itself. I have to stop that and really try to see them as complex as I am. As sexy as they are, they are still real people. I must start to see through their sexy flesh all the way into their hearts. I've got to keep working on that. The old ways have tentacles.*

He entered his brother's room, which was as attractive as possible for a room that housed a hospital bed. The furniture was of polished mahogany, and there were two wing-back chairs. A window opened to the east, and on the south sliding glass doors opened onto a small flagstone lanai. Raiford was lying among white sheets gazing up at a television mounted on the wall. Severe weight loss marred, but did not completely obscure, his brother's former good looks. His cheek bones protruded sharply and dark circles lay under his eyes. Yet he still had the attractive cleft on his chin. His dark reddish-brown wavy hair now had streaks of gray in it. He needed a haircut. He was freshly shaven, though, with a bit of white foam at the ear.

They greeted one another and Blaine sat in a wing-back chair, richly upholstered in gold and white stripes. Five or six copies of The Journal of the American Bar Association were neatly stacked on the night stand. On the television a game show flickered.

After preliminaries during which Blaine apologized about not coming up last Saturday, they spoke about the management of Raiford's bone cancer.

"This machine here is a God-send," Raiford said. He was referring to the rectangular machine attached to an IV pole. A glass bottle hung on the pole and clear tubing ran from it into the machine. Clear tubing then ran from the machine into Raiford's arm. In his left hand he held a beige button that was connected to the machine. "It's called PCA Pump, that's a Patient Controlled Analgesic Pump. It's newly on the market and it's wonderful. All I've got to do is press this button here and I get a dose of morphine. The doctors set the machine for the size dose and how often it'll dispense it, but whenever I need it, it's there. The pain is hideous, brother. It's like a thousand rats gnawing on your bones. They're inside you so there's no way to get away from them. But right now, with this machine, they've got the dose of morphine just right. It deadens the pain but doesn't zonk me out as well."

"I guess that's why Grandfather was always sleeping or screaming. They zonked him out with some drug so he wouldn't feel the pain."

Raiford nodded. "Yeah, the pump's brand-new."

Silence cast her pall over them until Raiford resumed his complaints about the pain. "I've been thinking about you a lot this past week, and I pray to God Almighty that the family scourge skips over you like it did Father. I could put up with being sick, if it weren't for the pain. It's unbearable."

Blaine nodded.

"I really appreciate your driving all the way up here like you do," Raiford went on. "You're the only one that seems to care I'm dying."

"Bull! With your doctors, the finest money can buy, and with the advancements being made every day, you'll beat this thing."

"Wake! Up!" Raiford said, his words so slow, so ponderous they bespoke an acceptance of finality. "This is no longer Duke University Medical Center, Blaine. This is no longer the Mayo Clinic. It's Seven Oaks *Nursing Home.*"

Blaine could think of nothing to say. He looked out the windows at Spanish moss wavering on the limbs.

"I wish now we had been closer," Raiford said. "We were really never much of brothers, too many years separating us. But still you're the only one who comes. Lena and little Stephen thought this was a wonderful time for an extended visit with her parents in London. And except for that first weekend, and once besides, Mother and Father can't be bothered."

"Well, you know how busy they are with the election just past, the fund-raisers and all that. And of course the Inauguration came up. And there's the rectifying of accounts and jockeying for position and influence and all."

"Yeah!" Raiford said, anger in his voice, "I know."

There were cheers on the television: A young black family had won the round and twenty-six hundred dollars.

"Good," Raiford said. "I was rooting for them. He's just a cook in some restaurant."

"Gees, you haven't changed your politics too, have you?"

"Reagan never should have won. And I bet Nancy's claws are long and sharp. And his vice president hit it on the head about the voodoo economics. Watch and see. The rich are going to line their pockets and food will be taken from the mouths of the poor to provide it. It's a dark time for the country."

"If Mother and Father heard you say that," Blaine said with a chuckle, "they'd go shrieking out of the room to a phone and call a psychiatrist."

Raiford smiled at the image. "Monsignor Neff comes weekly or so—you know formerly of St. Paul's—and the Archbishop has come twice. Every day Monsignor sends a priest over to visit and read to me. This past week he read from the Psalter, something about 'Happy the man who feeds the poor.' Think about it. That's right. I think everybody's going to be more than a little shocked at my new will. But it's ironclad—I'm still a sharp attorney—just let them try to break it."

"Little Stephen's taken care of, though, isn't he?" Blaine asked.

"Of course," Raiford said. "Through college and the rest of his life. But when he passes away many years hence, his Trust is merged back into the one I've established for the Catholic Relief, to feed and clothe the poor *in perpetuum*. And Lena will be comfortable as long as she remains *my widow*. She won't be able to live quite so high and mighty as we did in the days before the curse, but she'll be fine. When you begin to look at ultimate things, you reevaluate. And I've had a lot of time just lying here to do so."

Blaine nodded.

"And you!" he said, then was silent, with those horrible sunken eyes fixed on him.

The intensity of those words, that hollow stare and the ensuing silence made Blaine squirm. "What about me?" he finally asked.

"You're not responsible for being the way you are. That's what. Maybe if we'd been closer as brothers, but I don't know if that would have made any difference. But my thinking has changed. I want you to drop the psychiatric sessions. I want you to find a good man and settle down."

"I've already dropped the sessions. That was easy and long overdue. But for a person with my looks it's not so easy to find somebody."

"But that's what you need," Raiford said, "somebody to love you, completely, for the first time in your life. And...I guess you should know sometime. Dad would have been okay, but you never should have told Mother you had written a letter to the Holy Father asking his help in gaining entry into an Order. The very next day Mother wrote one to the Pope too. I read a copy. She came across all sweetness and maternal and expectant that just a little longer with your sessions, and you'd be rehabilitated and would give her grandchildren. Oh, it was a masterpiece, phony as hell, but impassioned, eloquent and ever so loving. Father's chauffeur flew to Rome and hand-delivered it to the Vatican, so it got there before yours. Blaine, you never stood a chance of a fair hearing, not one in hell, Brother. Money talks, even in the Church."

"No she didn't," Blaine said. "She wouldn't. She knew what I went through when Terry left me, the heartache and despair. She knew I was giving it all up, everything, and that I had decided to become a monk or a brother. I was determined to dedicate my life to the service of God and man. But Rai, I never expected that every Order I petitioned—the Augustinians, the Carmelites, the Franciscans, the Passionists, the Benedictines—would all refuse me because of the psychiatric sessions and my former sins. But then I never expected the Pope to just wash his hands when I asked his help in gaining admission."

"Blaine, open your eyes. Admit it," Raiford said. "Our *loving* parents live for themselves. They are enmeshed in their own lives, totally and completely. Always have been. And your taking Orders would have been a pimple on their perfect facade, just as much a pimple as your being gay, just as much a pimple as Reagan's ballet dancing son is to him. Even your being a lowly school teacher."

"But that's what I'm good at and what I like to do," he protested.

"I know that but to them, in their world of money, power,

and prestige, that a son of theirs teaches school is an embarrassment. I've seen it, Blaine. Whenever somebody at the Club inquires about you, they soft-shoe it to another subject. Being unmarried at thirty-three, or teaching school, or taking Orders doesn't fit into their world. You've had a rough time of it, starting with your birth, Brother, so late in Mother's life. But now I see the whole picture. When you approach the crevasse you reflect on things. And I have made a U-turn in my thinking. Whatever you want for your life, I want it for you, Blaine. And on top of that, I want you to find the right man and settle down."

"You're not the first to tell me that," Blaine said. "The afternoon the blackmail thing came up, I went to the church and was kneeling in the pew and Father Tomé came to lock up and saw me there. I guess he could tell I was troubled. He asked if I wished to confess and I nodded. And Raiford? For the first time in my life I dared confess my grievous sins.

"'And I accuse myself, before God and before you, Father, of ho-mo-sex-u-al acts,' I said. I folded my arms across my chest and sunk down. I feared Father Tomé would strike me."

"Why Blaine," Father Tomé asked, "have you never confessed this before?" The Father's question was rhetorical and he did not pause for an answer. "My son, the Church recognizes the complex interplay of psychological factors that so incline a person. Neither the Church nor God condemns such an inclination. But the Church is adamant that it is serious and grave sin to give rein to such an inclination in sexual acts.

"There! I've told you what I'm told I must tell you. The official stance.

"Now I'll tell you what the Lord tells me in *my* heart. Please don't misunderstand what I'm going to tell you. I speak of the recollections from my life before I entered the Seminary. I take my prayer life, my celibacy and my pastoral duties seriously. But this is what God tells me.

"He is not concerned with our sexual lives. He blessed us with sexuality to bring us joy. He really doesn't care one way or the other. Straight, gay—He doesn't care. What He cares about is that we love one another. That suffices and that alone leads to Him.

"So what I'm saying is just follow your conscience, Blaine. Use your heart to select your friends, the places..."

Blaine interrupted. "But what about Canon Law?"

"That is but a flea compared to the love that flows to us from our Father...Jesus called him Daddy, Blaine. Try substituting that in your own prayer life. See if that makes a difference."

Head still bowed, Blaine began to sob.

"Blaine, that's enough. In the future you need not confess to me any homosexual acts, just let those acts be swaddled in love. No random sex, Blaine."

Blaine sobbed in earnest.

"But if you fail and it is random, my son, remember that it is but a flea and not nearly as great as the love we receive from our Lord. He gives us space to be ourselves. Let that sink in."

Through his sobs Blaine said, "Father, I'm worried," and

told him of Tony's photos and his blackmail. In jumbled fashion he spoke of his love for Terry, Captain Terry DuLac, and how lucky he was to have him. He spoke of his years of psychological sessions and of his parents' coldness. He spoke of his sorrow for having smeared the school in scandal with this blackmail thing. He spoke of his fear of losing his career or losing Terry, or losing both.

"Blaine, that's enough," Father Tomé said. "Confession is not the place for worldly concerns. Things will work themselves out one way or another. And I'm going to tell you right now that, from this point on, you are in my prayers that Daddy grant you a male companion you can share your life with, chastely or not. The choice is yours. His love is boundless. Let yours be as well."

"That's what he said, Rai, 'a male companion you can share your life with, chastely or not.' And then he raised his hand over my head, said the prayer of absolution and I thanked him. And do you know what the penance he gave me was? 'Go out and do something special, something you'd really enjoy.' Imagine! But you know and I know, Raiford, it's not easy for somebody like me to find somebody."

A nurse had pushed the medicine cart into the doorway and stood beside it.

"Start looking with your heart, Brother," Raiford said, "and not just your eyes, and you'll find him. He's out there, the right man, somewhere, though maybe he doesn't know it yet. Most likely he probably won't be a Sylvester Stallone or a

Redford or that new guy, Selleck. But find him, Blaine, and live together happy."

The nurse waited patiently at the doorway as Blaine stood up. "You were exaggerating a little bit, weren't you? Like about Mother's letter? She knew how much I wanted admission to an Order. She only said she'd write one, right? But never did, right?"

"I read a copy and Father's chauffeur hand-delivered it."

"But by now I would have professed permanent vows," Blaine said.

"I know," Raiford said with manly tenderness. "I hope I haven't laid too much on you. I didn't mean to upset you, Snaggletooth."

Blaine smiled. "You haven't called me that in years."

"I love you, Brother. Thanks for coming."

"I'll be back next Saturday," he said.

"It's the high point of my week, a touch of normalcy, to have my brother visit me."

Blaine nodded and waved a goodbye. Raiford lifted his hand from the white sheets to wave in return.

Outside he found Bob sitting on a bench under swaying moss. Within half an hour they were at the lake, and in another fifteen minutes they had purchased bread, bologna, mayonnaise, sodas and a bucket of worms. They rented a rowboat and fishing rods.

The air held the crispness of winter mingled with the earthy scent of spring. The lake, surrounded by hills, forest and meadows, was six miles long, and at its widest point a mile. In the cloudless blue sky swallows darted. At times two bald eagles perched at their nest high in a dead pine, at times soared majestically aloft. As kingfishers dove along the shore for minnows, the two men sat peacefully on seats of the rowboat, facing one another. Red and white bobbers floated on the clear water.

Into the comfortable silence, Bob said, "Do you support the Save the Naugha Foundation?"

"Well, no I don't," Blaine said. "What is it?"

"Oh, you don't know? I'd have thought your being a teacher and all, you would keep up with these things!"

"Well what is it?" Blaine said.

"I don't know a lot about it myself. But this black Cub Scout, about fourteen, maybe fifteen, came to my door a few weeks ago. You could tell he was from a real poor family because his uniform just came down to his calves and didn't stretch down to his wrists. Anyway, he was collecting for a foundation, Save the Naughas. They're these cute little animals with pointy little noses and brown eyes, and with these tiny ears and all furry. And they're gentle animals, peaceful little things.

"And it's just terrible how they're being slaughtered, clubbed, trapped, poisoned, the little dears. They're being massacred, Blaine! It's a genocide—that's what he called it— all for the sake of corporate greed and rich people's portfolios.

"I gave him four dollars when I heard about it. We've got to do something to stop the slaughter. You don't have anything in your house made out of Naugahyde, do you?"

Blaine began to chuckle, trying to stifle it, his spread fingers going to his face. His attempt to stifle it made him cough, then he abandoned the effort and gave himself over to belly-laughs.

"So, what's so damn funny about it!" Bob challenged.

"Nauga-hyde," he managed to say between his laughs. "You were duped!"

"What do you mean!"

"Synthetic....Naugahyde is plastic!" he forced out. "Four dollars!...Save the Naughas!... You're so innocent!... Everybody, save the Naughas!"

Bob turned red, embarrassed by his credulity, but then saw the humor in it and joined Blaine in laughter at himself.

At day's end, they paddled back to the public campground to return the boat. Then, standing on the dock, both of them were smiling and holding to the camera the day's catch— Bob's three small perch, and Blaine's two fine trout.

"Do you want to clean them?" Blaine asked.

"That's okay, I'll let you," Bob said.

Along the shore a black family was fishing, all five of them with cane poles and red and white bobbers.

Bob waited on the dock and watched frizzy-haired Blaine give the fish and the bucket of worms to the appreciative father. *You're really a nice guy*, he thought. He watched them talk a moment.

Back in the shiny MG they drove along a dirt road through a hickory and pine forest. On the way Bob asked Blaine about his hair, maybe straightening it.

"I tried that, but I had a terrible reaction to the straightening solution. Burned my scalp real bad, hair all fell out and I was in the hospital for three days. Something I just have to live with."

"I hope you don't object to my having mentioned it," Bob said.

"No, I don't. It had to come up sometime. Things like that are things people share when they are beginning to get comfortable with each other."

They parked at the Shirer cabin. It was nestled among the trees on the shore, the outside fashioned of stone, with green moss growing on sections of it. The interior, though, was bright with indirect lighting shining onto the ceiling and polished hardwood floors. The kitchen could have come from the pages of a magazine, with dried flowers in earthenware crocks and even a dishwasher. The cabin was by no means the rustic affair he had expected.

While Blaine tended to things in the kitchen and the bedrooms, Bob gathered kindling from the surrounding trees. He wished Quasi were there to enjoy this with him. *He would have liked the experience of the rowboat, too.*

A short way from the cabin the forest opened into what had apparently once been a farmer's field, sloping gently upward from the stand of trees at the shore. Bob put his armful of branches and twigs down to walk the slope upward.

The weeds came knee high on Bob and were brown and brittle, though at their bases they were greening with new growth. Here and there, on plants that hugged the ground and were difficult to see, were tiny flowers. He knelt on one knee to inspect them. The flowers were white and star-shaped, the leaves a deep green and the stems had a tinge of crimson. He picked a single flower, so tiny that dozens could have fit onto his thumbnail. Across its snowy unblemished whiteness a tiny insect was moving, the tiniest he had ever seen. Never had he imagined an insect so small. He laid the flower and insect on the ground next to the plant on which it had grown, then stood up and gazed toward the deep blue of the lake. Beyond it, the sun was touching the tips of the trees on the opposite shore. He sat down among the weeds and watched the sky blaze forth into colors.

A couple feet from him a spider, spinning a web, dangled from a thread. It would be an ephemeral web, for a gust of wind would move the weeds and destroy his labor. Overhead a blue jay bisected the sky, while high over the lake two eagles soared effortlessly.

All of it was beautiful, so very beautiful. Words, ancient words—words ingrained in his memory from the years when he endured Reverend Negley's bombasts—came to him. They were, though, not the Pastor's harsh words of constraint, but words gentle and loving, words spoken slowly, softly. *Consider the lilies how they grow: they toil not, they spin not; and yet I say unto you, that Solomon in all his glory was not arrayed like one of these.*

How he wished at that moment to pray. How he wished there was a God to hear a prayer, but he knew there wasn't. Years ago, while yet a teen, he had sworn never, ever to pray again. Yet, even though there was no God and prayers did no good, yet, even so, the world was beautiful. And the world, in its own right, was arrayed in glory.

As the sky began to darken into gloom, below him on the right three deer came from the woods. One of them was only half as big as the others. They bent their heads to the ground and ate.

Back at the cabin, he used the kindling he had gathered to start a fire in the fireplace while Blaine busied himself in the kitchen. After a supper of four TV dinners from the freezer—Salisbury steak—they sat on the rug before the crackling fire with glasses of red wine.

"I love the country, Blaine," Bob said. "Unfortunately there are no jobs to be had in little towns. When I was a kid, I lived in the woods with my dog. We dragged this big box a Frigidaire had come in down to Bullrush Creek and covered it with plastic. I adorned it with pictures of animals. My collection of them was one of my treasures, I guess. In the second or third grade my teacher had assigned collecting animal pictures as a project. But even after the project was over and she assigned grades—I got an A—I kept on collecting them for years. I kept them in a shoe box labeled MY ZOO. I got 'em from magazines and newspapers and all. Oh, I had warthogs sniffing and lions yawning—like we saw at the zoo?—and squirrels nibbling acorns between their hands, and narwhals, and falcon—Is it falcon or falcons?"

"Falcons."

"And falcons, armadillos and robins. I had everything. My picture of a spider was just a diagram labeling the body parts. I got it from one of those school science magazines, you know? I used pine resin to glue some of them to my Frigidaire box, both inside and out. Every inch of it was covered, like the Sistine Chapel, I guess. And we lived there on the creek, Rusty and me."

"It sounds like a lovely summer vacation," Blaine said.

Bob looked at him. "It was no vacation. It was permanent, or was going to be."

"Permanent?!" Blaine said.

"It was to be our home, Rusty's and mine. We fixed it with all the comforts, a metal grate for the campfire to cook things on, an easy chair, a metal cabinet to keep things dry in and a kerosine lamp so I could get my homework done."

"But why'd you run away from home?"

"I didn't, but we made ourselves a home, Rusty and me. Just before my thirteenth birthday my Pa left and abandoned us."

"Oh, my God!"

"Three times me and Rusty set out to find him, but the furthest we ever got was forty miles. Three times we returned to the oak on Bullrush Creek. But we did okay—went to school and then bagged groceries in the afternoon. We had everything we needed, except Pa. Looking back, I can see what led up to it—the struggling to make ends meet, the trail of beer cans, the lure of Alaskan gold. And he was lonely and really handsome, and somebody came alone who didn't care about his finances. Anyway, it's a long story and I'm not going to bore you with the details. It'd make a big book. But I know it was hard for him to leave. He wrote me a goodbye note. I found it when I got back from a week at YMCA camp. To earn the money I needed for the camp, I had worked awful hard, cutting lawns, raking, weeding—you know, the things kids do. It was a wonderful week at camp, but when I got back there were only a few stray coat hangers in Pa's closet, this note and Rusty tied to the long-leaf pine out back. And forty dollars. He left me forty dollars."

"I'm sorry, Bob."

"Hey," he said and shrugged.

"Where was this?" Blaine asked.

"Macon."

"Macon, Georgia? Well, that's not far. Would you like to go there sometime?"

"Yes, there's something I've got to check on there sometime," he said and stood up.

Blaine watched him go to the table, get the bottle of wine and return to the floor in front of the fire. *You're a man of dignity and strength, there guy,* he thought.

He poured red wine into Blaine's glass, then his, and as the fire crackled before them, they argued in jest over whether Bob's three small perch or Blaine's two fine trout proved the better fisherman. They laughed again at Bob's credulity in supporting Save the Naughas. Blaine explained the obligatory intervention of the supernatural at the end of Shakespeare's so-called Romance plays. "Those are his late plays, complex things which jumble together tragedy, comedy and supernatural intervention. But, Bob, isn't that how we experience our days? A jumble of its elements?" He went on to say that he had never attempted to direct one of those, but was thinking of staging either *Pericles* or *The Winter's Tale* come fall.

It was late when Bob retired to what was to be his room for the night. He paused at the door and turned. *You're one hell of a man,* Blaine thought, *what with that stature and healthy good looks. And your heart, guy! Don't think there's ever been a bigger one.*

"Blaine?" Bob said.

"Yeah?"

"Goodnight, buddy," he said.

Never before had he used that term of endearment. "Goodnight," Blaine said, and, smiling, added, "Buddy!"

Bob's door closed, and Blaine sat before the fire, weeping quietly and giving thanks for what he had been granted.

CHAPTER 18

Sunday morning at the lake came in wet and with a warm southerly wind. Bob rose unusually late, about ten, and joined Blaine at the table for coffee and toaster waffles. They talked until early afternoon, when the wind died down, leaving a light drizzle.

"I guess we're not going to get any fishing done today," Blaine said, "so I'm wondering if we should head on back to the city. There's something I really should do. My friend Carl—the one I've mentioned? Well, the contest is this afternoon. I've attended the last three, so I should probably attend this one too."

"Okay," Bob said, "and I'll be able to call the vet's about Quasi."

"You probably won't get anybody, just the answering service."

"But I might," Bob said.

"Carl was a student of mine years ago, varsity everything,

class president and his work as stage manager made for a great *Macbeth*. He's a high school coach now. I hope he retains his Mr. Atlanta title for another year. We're not all limp-wristed, you see."

"He's gay?" Bob asked.

"Yes, but I didn't know it back then. I don't think he knew it either, but God had fashioned him that way. Would you go with me to the contest this afternoon?"

Bob looked at him, homely, ever so homely. He imagined himself in the audience, a solitary man in a sea of humanity whose masculinity was suspect. The queers would wolf-whistle at the contestants and shout propositions at them. It would at least be funny. "Sure, I'll go," he said.

Once back in the city, Bob called the veterinarian's from a pay phone, getting only the answering service. Then he witnessed his first bodybuilding contest. As Blaine went backstage to congratulate Carl on his victory, Bob stood out in front of the auditorium to smoke a cigarette. His projection about who would make up the audience had been unfounded. Among the hundreds, there had been only five or six men whose masculinity was suspect. The audience looked like bodybuilders themselves, or coaches, or collegiate wrestlers. He assumed the women and children in the audience had been the families of the contestants.

He found it amusing that, for all these years, he had always hesitated to even thumb through a muscle magazine in a supermarket lest someone in the aisle look at him askance. *Where'd I ever get that idea? Or why should I care what strangers think?...But I do.* He glanced up and down the street to make sure nobody was watching, then, pumping his right arm up and down a few times, he lifted it sharply and felt his biceps through the flannel shirt. A man's body developed to its potential, he conceded, was an awesome thing. Maybe he'd start working out, get a little bigger, though not as big as what he'd seen, just a little bigger. Muscles like that—oiled and lit with dramatic lighting—were beautiful on the stage or sculpted in marble, but on the street they would be freakish, or at least on him they would be freakish. Yet it had been a new experience to witness firsthand what was possible. He was glad he had come, although he knew he would never write Mrs. Sloan about it. And he knew he would never mention it to any woman when he could afford to start dating again. Women thought differently. No woman would ever understand a man's interest or enthusiasm for bodybuilding. She would see it as a flaw in the masculine personality and would forever question how deep that flaw went. Women could be concerned with their bodies. Men were supposed to just have them.

There was the sound of hinges squeaking. He turned around and slight, frizzy-haired Blaine was coming out of the heavy glass doors. Bob greeted him with an upward tilt of the head.

"I've got to go have a victory drink with Carl," he said. "You want to go home, don't you? You don't want to go, do you?"

"Sure, I'll go," he said.

"Are you sure? I mean, I've got to tell you Graffiti's is a gay bar. Are you sure you want to?"

"I'll go. I've been in gay bars before. It's not like I was born yesterday."

"Great!" Blaine said. "I've told Carl all about you. Come on."

🌺

They walked to the parking garage, then drove out of downtown, away from the lofty office buildings, banks, merchants and governmental buildings. A light drizzle, more of a mist than a drizzle, fell onto the windshield, and Blaine set the wipers to one sweep every few seconds. *Never imagined he'd go. I'll get to show him off. Eat your heart out, girls!...Sure hope Carl approves.*

"Are the drinks real expensive at this place?" Bob asked.

"Not today," Blaine said. "It's Sunday T-dance and beer bust, with live DJ and all. There's a five dollar cover charge, but once you get in, it's free beer till 8:00. All the beer a man can drink."

"What a deal," Bob said. "Straight places don't have bargains like that."

"We're knocking the competition dead and still making money. No one can drink five dollars' worth of draft beer. And at Eight the prices go up and we start selling booze."

"What do you mean? 'We start selling booze and we're knocking the competition dead.' I thought you're just a school teacher. Are you the owner or something?"

Oh, God! Blaine thought. *How do I get out of this one?*

"Well are ya?!" Bob asked again.

"Of course not," he said. "I, uh, just have a few shares. Not much." He hated to lie so blatantly, but he figured Bob's reaction would not be affable if he knew he had directed his attorney to invest a hundred fifty thousand dollars of his trust in the venture. Bob was struggling hard just to maintain, doing the dirty work of roofer, struggling harder than he ever had to, or would ever have to in the future. He could quit teaching tomorrow and live off the interest from his grandmother's trust—never touching the principal—and live very well in the fashion of a minor princeling. Not everybody was blessed with the proverbial spoon, and those who were so blessed needed to walk humbly among those who struggled.

Out of downtown now, they drove a street in a residential district where black children rode bicycles even in the late afternoon drizzle. They tried to enter Graffiti's parking lot, but a uniformed security guard waved them off, saying, "Full." They found a place to park on the street several blocks away.

Blaine had second thoughts about taking Bob to a gay bar. As he was backing into the spot, he said, "If you want to, you can change your mind and I'll take you home. It's going to be all gays in there."

"If anybody propositions me, I can say No! pretty damn powerfully. But won't there be a few women?"

"Dykes usually hang out in dyke bars," Blaine said.

"No," he said, shaking his head, "real women."

"You're out of luck there, guy."

"Well, that's okay," he said. "I can't afford to date now anyway. I'd just be teasing myself."

Blaine nodded. *And just wait till they see you. They'll be just a-drooling, but they had better keep their clutches off.*

As they walked back along the cracked sidewalk, dogs—chained into yards—barked at them. From a block away came the muffled beat of drums, like tom-toms in some primitive rite. There was a line of men under an awning awaiting entrance and Bob and Blaine took their place at the end of it, Bob towering over heads. As they queued slowly forward, Blaine noticed single men brazenly staring at Bob. He noticed men in pairs each sneaking furtive glances at him. *Eat your heart out, Mary—he's with me!*

How he wished he had a jaw like Bob's, a chin like his. The plastic surgeons he had consulted had agreed that his receding jaw could have been corrected in childhood, while the bones still had the potential for growth; but now with the complications of teeth and bite, none of them could offer any acceptable assurances of favorable outcome. He was doomed to the life of a jawless wonder. And he wouldn't mind being a little taller. Oh, he didn't have to have Bob's stature, but a little taller, a little more manly. But in spite of his appearance, he at least had a good heart, was kind and helped people. It was wonderful Bob seemed to like him and wanted to spend some time with him. *If only Carl approves!*

Blaine paid the admission for the two of them and they entered the turnstile.

The place had a teeming aliveness within, though it was an aliveness sensed, not seen, for the place was black. At first the only thing visible was the eccentric graffiti painted on the walls. With black lights illuminating, quirky letters glowed in carnival colors. They seemed to hover in the darkness:

You're on Duke's turf!
Biceps and pecs.
Scotty, be careful! — Raven's watching.
Hot stuff here.

Just too much, Mary.

Over the dance floor, a dozen mirrored globes flashed and sparkled and reflected multi-colored lights from one to another and cast orbs of insubstantial color onto the sea of men below. The colors flitted on the crowd, from one to another, like festive fireflies.

The men dancing emerged from the darkness. A few were bare-chested, others in sweatpants and tank tops, some in jeans, tee-shirt and jacket, others in pleated slacks and fancy sweaters. It was an eclectic crowd, gyrating to the disco beat, pressing three deep up to the bar. Behind the dance floor was a raised stage and next to that a glassed-in booth for the DJ.

Blaine stood on tiptoe, put a hand on Bob's shoulder, and said, "This is the main disco and show bar. There're three other bars in the place—a Western bar, a leather bar, and a romance bar. The others don't open till eight when the prices go up and they start serving booze as well."

"The graffiti on the walls is fun. It's kinda like it's just floating in the air," Bob said, raising his voice to make it heard over the boom of the music.

Blaine nodded. "I'll squeeze up and get us some beer," he said and left Bob to sidle and excuse himself through the men.

At the bar Blaine was waiting to get the bartender's eye when someone tapped his left shoulder. He looked and said, "Oh, hi, Kevin."

Kevin was bare-chested, with thick neck and shoulders like melons. The black hair on his chest was long and silky. On two previous occasions Blaine had paid him to spend the night with him—He liked muscles on a man.

"Where'd you pick him up?" Kevin asked, with a motion of his head toward Bob.

"He's a friend," Blaine said.

"So, I've got new competition in town, huh?"

"I told you he's just a friend."

"Yeah, sure he is," Kevin said.

Blaine, irritated by the insinuation, turned again to catch the bartender's eye. As he waited, a pleased satisfaction came over him. *Let Kevin think what he will. It doesn't matter what a hustler thinks, because Bob's with me. Tall, handsome Bob is my date for the night!*

Blaine got two drafts in plastic cups, and with the music relaxing into a soft Streisand number, sidled back through the men. He handed him a draft.

"I don't like standing in the middle of the floor," Bob said. "It's like being on display."

"Would you like a table?" he asked.

"I never sit at a table in a barroom. We'll squeeze up to the bar. It'll take a minute or two," he said, "but we'll get a spot. Everybody can kindly shift up and down a little bit to accommodate us."

"Okay. I've got to go see somebody. I won't be long, though, and I'll look for you there," Blaine said and skirted around the dance floor which was crowded with men dancing cheek to cheek. *Captain Terry and I used to dance like that. Perhaps we were dancing in one another's arms while Tony stalked us outside with a camera. Or maybe he had been inside, seen us, and went home for the camera. Some places don't check ID's very often. It wasn't here, though. We only opened the place six months ago.*

Through those dancing he approached a table of two women near the DJ booth. One of them, Sofonda Peters, wolf-whistled and called to Blaine, "Where'd you find him?" Sofonda was a sleek, black drag-queen, dressed this evening in a blue sequined gown. On a recent trip to Washington, DC, Blaine had discovered her in a bar and had offered her the position of chief performer, show director and emcee for Graffiti's shows. Also at the table was Summer Raine, one of Sofonda's proteges. She was a white guy, dressed in black velvet, pearls and blond wig.

"Find who?" Blaine asked in mock incomprehension as he stood at their table.

"You know who!" Sofonda said. "The sexy blond in the flannel shirt." She patted a hand briskly over her heart, rolling her eyes upward and pretending to swoon.

"Oh, him," Blaine said, taking a seat and turning to locate Bob at the bar. "We've been seeing each other three or four days now. His name's Bob."

Sofonda reached over and squeezed Blaine's cheeks sharply inward. "You devil you!"

"That's what I mean by *stud!*" Summer Raine chimed in.

They all looked at Bob—Blaine smiling broadly. Bob—who was watching them and standing now at the bar—stretched, his hand arching upward to his head. His fingers then coursed slowly through his hair to the nape of the neck. He stood there, holding the back of his neck, with his head tilted upward. One corner of his lips lifted in a sexy smile.

"Je-sus Christ!" Summer said.

"He's giving me a hard-on, Blaine," Sofonda said.

"Sofonda, he's straight! We're just friends. He's probably thinking you two are the real thing."

"What a waste!" Sofonda said.

"Not for me, it's not," Summer said. "That's exactly how I like 'em, straight. Or they say they're straight and you hear this line about them not getting nothin' from their girl friend and they just need a little help with their hard-on. Or that's what they tell you anyway."

"Carl won again," Blaine said, changing the subject.

"Did he really?" Sofonda asked. "Is he coming?"

"Yes." He looked at his watch. "He'll be here within the hour."

"That calls for a celebration!" Sofonda said.

"That's what I was hoping you'd say."

"I'll throw a celebration together he'll remember!"

"Just make it fun. He's worked hard for this."

"Blaine!" Sofonda said in mock theatrics. "Leave it to the party queen and it'll be funfunfunfunfun!"

He thanked her, stood, and worked his way along the edge of the dance floor back to Bob.

Once beside him, he said, "I see you got a place at the bar."

"You lied! There are women here!" Bob said. "Who are they?"

"I knew that's what you were thinking," he said, suppressing a smile. "They're not, they're drag queens. The one in sequins is a friend of mine and the emcee for the shows. I asked her for a favor for Carl. Her real name is Jim, but here she goes by Sofonda Peters."

"By what?" Bob asked.

"So-fonda Peters," Blaine repeated.

Bob laughed, the laugh becoming a belly laugh. The men standing around them turned and smiled at his amusement. "And what's the other one called?" Bob asked in his merriment, "Ima Queer?"

As their laughs subsided into snickers, someone came up behind Blaine and nudged him, saying, "Well you're here now! 'Bout time." Blaine turned.

His name was Chuck Stryker, a male stripper. He wore skin-tight leather pants and instead of a shirt a black leather harness. His blond hair descended below his shoulders. Blaine had first seen him and The Men of Power while on a recent National Education Association convention in Chicago. Blaine had entertained Chuck in his hotel suite and later had called Mark about them. Mark, the major investor in Graffiti's, flew up the next day, saw them and offered them a contract.

"I've got it all set with the others," Chuck said. "You'll get what you deserve and then some. It'll be a heavy scene, fuck-boy! Kevin and Gene won't join in—they're lovers, but the others will play."

"Well, Chuck," Blaine said in lowered voice lest Bob hear, "I don't think so. I'm with somebody tonight."

"What the shit!" Chuck said, his voice flaring. "You said the next time you came in, so I set it up. And you're here now and now you're fuckin' weaseling out?" He stepped toward him.

"I just asked you about it," Blaine said, easing a few inches backward, "nothing was definite."

"I did a lot of fuckin' work setting it all up. So just go and pay me my share now, piggie! Pay me fuckin' now!" He held a hand palm up.

Blaine felt a hand from behind, Bob's, go onto his chest. It pressed him to move behind as Bob stepped forward. Standing between Blaine and Chuck, he towered over both. "Whatever this is about, it's over!" he said to Chuck.

Chuck snorted and smiled a lopsided smile up at him.

A panic seized Blaine. *Oh, God!* he thought, *you're going to find out I buy sex and never want to see me again.* "Bob," he said, "it's okay, I can take care of it."

"Stay out of this!" Bob said to him.

"You may be tall," Chuck said, "but a little slut like him ain't no *one man's* turf. And I'm a better lay than you ever dreamt of being."

"Bob?" Blaine said, a pleading in his voice.

"Me and your sweetie had a deal," Chuck went on, "a contract for services and he's weaseling out."

"I'm pretty sure the deal's off," Bob said.

"Can't the little rich piggie talk for himself?"

"Sure he can," Bob said, "but he's telling you the deal's off and that's the end of it."

"Fuckin' asshole!" Chuck said.

Blaine watched as Bob grabbed Chuck's leather harness and jerked him upward and toward him. "Look, I don't know who you think you are, prancing around here half naked, but you'd better cool it, understand?" He released Chuck's harness, pushing him away at the same time.

"But he's rich enough…"

"If you have any fuckin' thing more to say," Bob said,

"we'll go outside, just you and me. And you say it to me up right close and personal!"

Chuck glared at him, lower teeth bared. Bob glared back, his hands clenching into fists.

Chuck turned away, muttering as he went, "Asshole."

Blaine, his lips trembling, put his hand on Bob's arm. "I don't know how to thank you," he said. "You could have gotten hurt."

Bob mussed the frizzy hair. Blaine noticed men adjacent were watching.

"No," Bob said in lowered voice, bending down to Blaine's ear. "It's something I read in a novel once. I've never been in a barroom fight my entire life. It's something I picked up from that book." He snickered and went on: "Did you notice how I was the first one to make a move, picking him up by those straps? Well, the first guy to show aggression takes the other guy off guard. And the first guy who throws a punch, an unexpected punch, wins—always. So I knew from the start nothing would come of it because I was going to move first." Again he chuckled, and stood up, away from his ear. "So I guess I'm not quite the hero you think I am."

"To me you are," Blaine said, looking up at him now.

He shrugged.

You're wonderful, Blaine thought. *You don't know it, but I could fall in love with you.*

As they drank their beers, men began to come up to them and he introduced many to Bob. Some were true friends, like Russ, a florist who was trying to grow a beard, and like John and Jon, neighbors the next street over. Acquaintances came up to Blaine as well—men he had seen, but not spoken to, in months. Tonight they came up to speak, and with each introduction his pride grew. *Imagine, with Bob beside me they're envious! Of me, homely me!*

CHAPTER 19

They were on their third draft beer when the music stopped mid-song. The crowd hushed and stilled. Into the expectant silence a fanfare suddenly blared forth—trumpets and drums—and a roving spotlight began to search the crowd. Throughout the room men turned their faces here and there, looking. While the roving spotlight still searched, a smaller one illumined Sofonda on the stage. The fanfare stopped.

In blue gown aglitter with sparkles she announced in triumphant voice: "Graffiti's is proud to congratulate!...One of our own!...Retaining his crown!...For the fourth consecutive year!...Mr. Atlanta!...Our own!...Carl!...Gagen!"

The crowd burst into applause and whistles and the roving spot fixed on muscled Carl. He was just coming in the turnstile, his hand replacing his wallet in his jeans. The bright light on him took him by surprise. Standing there in red tank top, with his closely cropped blond hair, his deep tan and shoulders that stretched four feet wide, he began to grin. He raised his arm in a little wave, the muscles of his arm and shoulder etched into deep shadows by light. But then a younger man—dark-haired and in black tank-top—grasped his wrist and lifted his arm upward. As the crowd continued to applaud, Carl thrust both arms upward in triumph.

Sofonda Peters appeared before them and with Carl on one side of her and his young dark-haired lover on the other she sashayed them to a table, now covered in white cloth.

A bartender was standing there with a magnum of champagne. The cork popped, the champagne spewed, the disco music resumed, and the crowd resumed its chatter and dancing.

Blaine nudged Bob's arm. "We'll be expected at the table," he said, and they went over to it where they stood holding stemmed glasses which the bartender filled. After Sofonda's toast, Carl put his glass down, came to Blaine and pointed a finger in his face. "You're responsible for all this, aren't you?" he said.

"Me? Not me!" he protested.

Carl, not responding, put huge arms around him, picked him up and twirled him around. "Thanks, little guy," Carl said. Blaine, smiling broadly and with his legs flying outward, hugged closely to his neck.

Back on his feet, a little unsteady and his hand going to his head, he said, "I've got somebody here I want you to meet," and introduced Bob to him.

"You definitely deserved the title," Bob said. "You were the best." He offered his hand.

As they shook, Blaine noticed that Carl's eyes darted

suspiciously between them. He knew he wouldn't have to wait long before the inquisition began.

Following etiquette, Carl introduced his lover, Steve, to Bob. He was an athletic man, eighteen, maybe nineteen, the one who had lifted Carl's arm while under the spotlight.

"Have you been coaching long?" Bob asked Carl.

"Ever since I graduated," he said, and they sat. Besides Steve and Carl and Blaine and Bob, besides Sofonda and Summer, also at the table were Russ, John and Jon, and a couple men, friends of Sofonda's that Blaine did not know.

Carl leaned to Blaine's ear and said, "He's a hot looking man. I hope the deal's not too expensive."

"I knew you were thinking that. He's just a friend."

"You two aren't having sex?" Carl asked over the throb of the music.

"He's straight, Carl," Blaine said. He was glad the loudness of the music would prevent Bob from overhearing.

"Well, if he's straight, what's he doing with you and what's he doing here? He's not just telling you that now so that when it comes down to brass tacks, he can up the ante, is he?"

"I really think he's straight," Blaine said, "and I wish you'd give him half a chance."

"Okay," Carl said. "I'm sorry. I'm just sorta protective of you."

"I just wish you'd trust my judgment now and then."

"Well, around Thanksgiving your judgment got you beat up and thrown into a dumpster."

"That was different, that was just a sex thing."

"And this isn't?"

"Sure, I'd love to get him, but not in bushes or an alley or something like that, but on soft sheets and make love to him. But it won't happen, he's straight."

"So, besides looking like something on a calendar, what do you see in him?"

"I like him. We spent the weekend together at the lake. There's a strength to him and a heart. When you were twelve years old, what if your parents had abandoned you? Would you have continued to go to school, get a part-time job, and make a home for yourself in a pasteboard box in the woods? That's what he did, and provided for himself and his dog."

"He did that?" Carl asked.

"Yes," Blaine said. "And in Vietnam…"

"He's a vet?" Carl interrupted.

"Yes. And he was taken Prisoner of War, him and the whole squad or platoon or something, I forget. But he clawed through the bamboo cage and escaped and brought rescue for all of them. There's somebody from back then who's stalking him now here in Atlanta and beat him up. That's how we met. I found him lying on the sidewalk. And he's got a dog, a mongrel, three legs. He saw him shivering in a snowdrift and felt sorry for him and adopted him. How many men would do that?"

"He only had three legs when he adopted him?"

"Yes. Like I said, he's got a heart. He's just working as a roofer, doesn't have any money, but his truck — a pickup truck that doesn't even start — has brand new Michelin radials all around. I asked him about the tires and he just said a Church in Indiana gave them to him in gratitude. But he wouldn't tell me gratitude for what. I'm asking you to give him half a chance."

"Carl," Sofonda said from across the table, interrupting. "Why don't you put on an exhibition for us, show us girls what real work and real dedication can achieve."

"I've already done that," he said. "And if anybody were interested they could have come to the contest."

Blaine said, "But you know you can't budge a gay guy from a barstool. Show 'em something."

Carl looked at those seated at the table, all nodding. Blaine noticed Bob was nodding too.

"Okay," Carl said, digging in the pocket of his jeans. He handed Steve a set of keys. "Will you go home and get the same posing strap and the Tchaikovsky tape? And the cables. No, bring two sets of cables, and we'll end the routine like we practice it at home."

Steve agreed and took Russ, the florist, with him.

Sofonda began huddling with Summer Raine, then went to the DJ booth, then backstage. She returned to the table visibly upset. "Blaine! You've got to do something with those strippers. They won't take part. The poor dears don't want to expose themselves to comparison with Carl's development. But that's okay, we'll get a show together. I'll get them from the audience. But I want you to talk to Mark about them for me." Again she huddled with Summer, then both went out among the crowd.

While men writhed and gyrated on the dance floor, a bartender opened another magnum of champagne for the table. "Carl's lover seems awful young," Bob said into Blaine's ear.

Blaine nodded. "He looks younger than he is. He's

nineteen. They met at the gym and Carl's putting him through junior college so he can make something of himself. But he's not applying himself and isn't doing well. Carl's disappointed. Everybody's got talents, Bob, just not necessarily academic talents. He's good at all the sports, plays them all and Carl claims he's a natural at bodybuilding."

Bob nodded and turned to watch those dancing.

Blaine wondered if Bob were offended by the bar. He wondered if Bob had noticed the men in the corner kissing and groping one another. He wondered if Bob approved of Carl, a mature man, with a nineteen year old kid.

Steve and Russ returned, and Carl left the table for backstage. When the disco song ended the DJ did not merge it into another, it simply ended. There were sighs of disappointment from those who had been dancing. They left the dance floor for their tables or back to the bar.

In silence a spotlight went onto Sofonda now up on the stage with a microphone. "For your pleasure!" she announced. "And in recognition of one of our own!...Graffiti's is proud to present a Special Show!...Will the bartenders please get the smelling salts ready!" The crowd laughed. She laid the microphone down on the edge of the stage, and to a slinky, striptease-like number, lip-synched and gestured and danced sluttily. Men went up to her and pressed bills into her hand or down her sequined bosom. She kissed each on the cheek. Summer then lip-synched to a romantic Streisand number and men tipped her as well. When the applause died down, Sofonda announced in triumphant voice: "Graffiti's is proud to have with us!...The crowned Mr. Atlanta!... Renowned for his muscles!" She put the microphone close to her lips and whispered, patting her heart, "And believe me, dears, they're real, all man!" She pretended to swoon and the audience laughed. "Mr!...Atlanta!"

The DJ started the high-spirited *So Many Men*, and this customer and that—men she had spoken to among the clientele—either sauntered or strutted up to and across the stage. It was much like a fashion show. Several of them stripped off their shirts. Each one was applauded and took a place flanking center stage. Once assembled, the men started dancing together, but when the words were reached, *and with muscles too*, the music ended. The men simultaneously stopped and knelt with hands stretched out to center stage.

Into the silence soft, romantic orchestral music—strings and woodwinds—wafted down. On a stage absolutely still, the curtain behind slowly opened. And there Carl stood, pumped, in full biceps pose, oiled and nearly naked. The crowd went wild. From pose to pose the ovations rang out as Carl radiated a joy and vitality of being. There was no hint of arrogance or exhibitionism. With energy and verve Carl eased effortlessly from one pose to the next, his muscles rippling with each change.

It was as if Bob were watching a dance, for one man alone, exploring the possibilities of what a man could be. It was a dance of self-sufficiency and joy. But then, just as he had at the contest, Carl paused. He was facing the audience with his head bowed, arms limp at his sides, muscles limp. He seemed exhausted or confused. While violins swooped and soared, Carl stood motionless. The audience began whispering, just as they had at the contest. But then Carl slowly looked toward the ceiling—his eyes widening, the muscles of his neck awesome—and one arm started reaching up, toward something, then the other arm. With a pain and longing on his face, his arms hugged someone imaginary to him, the muscles of his shoulders, arms and torso etched sharply with shadow.

And you shall renew your strength on wings of eagles, Bob thought. It was strange that ancient words, words memorized in childhood, should come back to haunt.

Then Carl captured, in place of the previous self-sufficiency, something else. He captured from pose to pose what Bob saw as a yearning or a longing for another. The routine ended as it had in the contest, with Carl on one knee, the other stretched in back of him, the muscles as perfect as if in marble. His right arm—the muscles gleaming—reached with beckoning fingers toward something still just out of grasp. But here, unlike at the contest, a young man, dark-haired, muscled, and in black tank-top—his lover Steve—came onto stage, stretching out his hand. Fingers touched fingers. The touch lifted Carl from kneeling to his feet. They hugged.

The crowd went wild, and Bob could not imagine how Carl's smile could possibly be wider. He thought he saw tears in his eyes as well.

Above the whistles and cheers came Sofonda's voice:

"The City's Mr. Atlanta!...But our own dear friend!...One of us!...Carl!...Ga-gen!"

While the room still burst with applause and whistles, the

DJ put on a high-spirited number and the dance floor immediately filled.

Bob stood up and excused himself to the rest room.

It was a large, well-lit, nicely tiled rest room, with enclosed toilets and four urinals. The urinals were unlike any he had ever seen: A rectangular piece of polished stainless steel had been affixed—crotch high—to it, in order to reflect upward what a man held in his hand. He rolled his eyes.

As he stood at the urinal, a man took the one adjacent. He pulled the front of his sweatpants down and said, "You must be new in town, huh?" He was a shirtless, muscular guy with thick neck, and long silky black hair on his chest. Bob thought maybe Blaine had introduced them.

"Been here a few months," he said.

The guy, his eyes fastened on Bob's cock, said, "Why haven't I seen you before?"

"I don't get out much." He shook the remaining drops off.

"How big is it hard?" the guy asked. "I've got eight inches here when it's up."

Bob looked him in the eye, tucking himself away at the same time. "Well, I've got you beat, and wouldn't you just love to find out." He turned to leave.

"Wait a minute," the guy said. Bob paused. "How much do you charge? I get thirty bucks for a wham-bang, and sixty for the night. What about you?"

"What *the hell* do you mean, 'What about me?!'"

"Well, you're with that teacher—he pays."

The muscles of Bob's jaw were pulsing as he turned away. He strode to the table, stood behind Blaine's chair and snapped, "Are you ready?"

Blaine said he was. They said their goodnights, and they left.

As they drove toward Hyacinth Street, Bob gazed out the side window into the darkness. *It doesn't matter if he's paid somebody now and then. I too have been indiscrete at times. Look how long I sold myself to Carmen. It won't be me who casts a stone.*

"Well, Bob," Blaine asked. "Did you have a good time?"

"Yeah, it was okay," he said. "I don't think your friend Carl likes me — he didn't have two words to say."

"You're just being paranoid. It was noisy there. He likes you fine."

"He's awesome, his build, that is. And the young kid he's with, he's good-looking too. What is it that makes a man like other men? How'd you get that way, Blaine? What was your first time doing it?"

"I'm starved," he replied. "What about you?"

"No, I'm fine," he said. The car's headlights shined off the wet pavement and caught the eyes of a 'possum, making them glow red in the darkness. Her snout was pinkish, hairless, and behind her stood three little ones. Bob turned in the seat to see if she would cross the street or not. "But really," he said, turning back around, "how'd it come about, your first time?"

"You won't think it pretty, Bob."

"Do you?" he asked.

"Well? I'm mixed on that."

"What happened?"

He saw Blaine bite his lip. "Well...It wasn't my first time, but it was early on. I'll tell you about that time because it was more significant then. And still is now. It kinda shaped me.

"It was in high school. Matter of fact, the very high school Carl teaches at. I had always gone to private schools, but I begged and pleaded and pouted till I got permission to attend public high. It was in the locker room. It's a big school and they have three shower rooms, one set in back of the other. You know, you have to go through one set of showers to get to the others farther back. I was in the last shower room that day, and the whole class was showering after PE. And I was there and Sonny—he was a real jock—called to me. I went over to him and said, Yeah? He grabbed his cock and balls in his fist, smiled a crooked smile and put his hand on my shoulder. His hand got heavier and heavier. I sank down to my knees and he rubbed his cock in my face. He called to Mike and Jim that they had a real cocksucker there. They came over, all naked and wet, and stood over me as I took Sonny into my mouth. He kept telling me to watch the teeth, and kept calling me faggot, scum. He got hard in my mouth. And a whole bunch of guys gathered around us, and I kept choking and gagging on Sonny, and all of the guys kept calling me names. A lot of 'em jerked off on my hair and shoulders. That was the first time.

"Then every day after PE it was the same. After I had undressed, Sonny or one of the other guys would come over to me, put his arm around my shoulder, and walk me back to the third shower room. I think they had some way of deciding who would get first options on me. They would say nice things on the way back, like how I was a real pal to help 'em out, and how they really appreciated it. And I was a pal and I went back willingly. But when I started on one of them, they would start calling me names. I never got any time at all to shower.

"But then somebody must have whispered in coach's ear. He came back and found me there on my knees. My parents pulled me out of that school. They sent me back to the academy and sent me to see Dr. Holzhauer."

Bob, shocked, didn't know what to say, or if he should say anything. He sat with his hands folded between his knees, his eyes out the window. Finally he said, "Wow, you poor guy. All that abuse, those bullies."

"No," Blaine said. "I don't see it like that. Those guys liked me, liked what I did for them. They couldn't admit it to each other because they had their manly status to protect — young as it was! —but they liked me and thought of me as their friend who would help them out with stuff."

"Hard stuff."

"Yeah. Calling me names was just protecting their status. It wasn't about me. They were men being men."

He looked at the parked cars, at the oak trees skeletal and dark, Spanish moss hanging on some of them. *Twisted.*

He looked at the dark two-story houses they passed by and wondered about the intimate secrets that lived and breathed and wandered through their rooms. Intimate secrets, secrets hidden from the eyes of the world, from gossiping tongues. He wondered about his Pa, if he had found happiness in turning toward men.

"But is it possible," he said into the silence, "for a man to fall in love with another man? Isn't it just a sex thing?"

"I loved Terry," Blaine said. "And I'm sure Carl loves Steve. And there's John and Jon —they've been together six years."

"Oh," he said and remembered his months at Boot Camp on Parris Island. He had reveled in the comradeship, the vying to excel, the crisp haircuts and sharp salutes, the uninhibited maleness displayed proudly in shower stalls. In Nam he had never once longed for a woman, never once paid a whore, for the men he lived with in society—served with through danger, laughed with in leisure—were enough.

"I'm amazed there're so many gays in this city," he said.

"By ten or eleven tonight, Graffiti's will be so crowded you wouldn't be able to turn around. And besides that, we have over two dozen gay bars here."

"How can they work, staying out so late?" he asked.

"I can't figure that one out either," Blaine said. The light drizzle became a rain now, heavy drops hitting the windshield.

Blaine parked in front of his brownstone on Hyacinth Street, turned out the lights and started to get out. "Well, we're here," he said.

Bob did not move, did not reach for the handle.

Blaine—not speaking, not prying, as silent as Bob was—gazed at him. There was the pattering of the rain on the canvas top. The light from a street lamp, coming through the windshield, glinted on Bob's eyes, so deep-set. And here, in this light, his eyes were colorless, a pale shade of gray.

"Do you hear it?" Bob asked.

"The sirens?"

"No. Listen close...In the distance. An owl...And now geese are fending against some intruder....I've got a connectedness, I guess. But don't ask me connectedness to what." He chuckled. "I couldn't name it. If I call it Existence, that gets all spooky like God." He moved his hands like a child making a ghost. "Just a connectedness to things, I guess, Blaine. The natural world."

Blaine watched him listen to the patter of rain and to whatever he heard in his natural world. *I could fall in love with you!*

"Buddy," Bob said, breaking the silence, "instead of my going home, how about it if I spent the night?"

Disbelief opened his mouth. "No, Bob!" he said. "That could mess it up! And in just a few days we've started to have a really good friendship. And I don't want anything to mess this up! Ever!"

"Blaine," he said softly, "I want to."

"Well if you're horny, ol' buddy, and need a blow job, just go to any park, you won't have any trouble finding one."

"But it's raining," he said and gave a little chuckle. He averted his gaze to the floorboard.

Your hair, wavy, sexy, the type my fingers would love to entwine. Your profile so strong, intelligent. Blaine's heart pounded. Although last night at the lake he had fallen asleep longing for Bob's arms around him, he had never thought such a moment, a moment such as this, would ever actually come.

Slowly Bob lifted his head and looked directly at him. The street lamp illumined one side of his face, the other in deep shadow. "Blaine...it's not just a sex thing," he said. "I want to hold...and be held."

Blaine continued to gaze at him. How many of the

thousands he had stalked in parks, rest rooms, truck stops, how many of those had been attracted to him as well? How many had actually wanted him—slight, squirrel-faced him? But this man did, this handsome man, this man so different from men. His eyes misted. His receding chin trembled as his hand reached over toward Bob's, resting atop his thigh. His hand descended to rest lightly upon it, that other hand so much larger than his, stronger.

"Okay?" Bob asked.

He nodded.

Inside Blaine made preparations in the bedroom as Bob showered. He turned the lamp on the night stand on low. He folded the spread down, exposing silver satin sheets. *Except for you, only Captain Terry came to this bed freely. All the others I had to pay.* He undressed, draping his clothes over the straight back of a Shaker chair. He heard the shower stop and, naked by the bed, anxious and uncertain, with his heart throbbing in his ears, he waited.

Bright light from the bathroom suddenly flooded into the room, silhouetting his friend. A towel was tied at his waist. From across the room, motionless, they looked at one another, until Bob reached to his left and turned out the bathroom light. It was silent except for the plunks of raindrops against the window.

With the warmth of Persian wool under his feet, Blaine moved toward him. He reached his hand out and Bob's hand—slowly, hesitantly, little by little—rose from his side.

Fingers touched, hands clasped.

Blaine led him, like a lamb on leash, across the room to the bed. He squeezed his strong hand, then walked around the antique footlocker to the opposite side. He turned out the lamp, the room dark now except for the meager light entering from the living room. Bob loosened the towel which fell to the floor, and lay down, his feet on top of the spread.

Blaine crawled on the bed and scooted across it to lie next to him—hips grazing hips, his head at Bob's shoulder. He was still slightly damp from the shower and scented with expensive English soap. He raised his hand to hover over the single line of hair at Bob's abdomen, lightly, feather-like, not touching the skin. Then the hand was moving upward, over the chest, where a single strand of hair would now and then touch his hand in the darkness. His fingertips grazed his nipple, and hovered there, grazing it, then descended to flesh and pressed down, the softness of the skin veiling the striated firmness of muscle beneath.

He scooted up in the bed, turning onto his side and looked at his friend. One by one he pecked tiny kisses—kisses light as a butterfly's breath—on his forehead, eyelids, lips.

Bob returned one tiny kiss, then set his lips in a line. Blaine kissed those lips time and again, and worked his tongue through them. Bob allowed his mouth to open and Blaine's tongue moved deep inside his mouth. Tongue contended against tongue and Bob's breathing quickened. A firm hand went against the back of Blaine's head. It forced mouths closer, joining them together. The other arm encircled him, squeezed him tight and hoisted him on top, naked small body on naked manly body.

They hugged, Bob pressing him down tight, his hand coursing over his slight back. They kissed and began to moan. With hands on the sheets Blaine pressed himself up and sat up on his haunches straddling him. How he wished Bob would open his eyes and look at him. He scooted back to position himself over Bob's loins. Bob kept his eyes closed.

He forced his weight down a shaft as large as a baby's arm, and a searing pain coursed through him, severing him in two. It was a pain blinding in its whiteness. He gasped deep spasmic lungfuls. Gradually the pain eased into a warm fullness and the whiteness darkened into blackness. His hips moved up and down, and under him Manhood Itself thrust upward, piston-like, to meet thrust with thrust. Around him, as the room filled with moans—deep ones, and lighter airy ones—time ceased, thoughts ceased, distinctions crumbled away. Not even the distinction of you versus me arose to intervene or interpret the moment. It was the primordial moment, a moment stretching out to infinity, a moment that stretched to eternity and interstellar blackness. And around him planets spun, stars twinkled and galaxies—timeless and silent—revolved.

The universe now thrust roughly to him. And Manhood, Existence, groaned louder and louder, till, against the blackness of the sky, a galaxy convulsed and quivered and exploded, a violence scattering fire, throughout the universe. Another, lesser galaxy, exploded as well. And there was a collapsing down, down from the heights and the heavens, down, floating downward, silent, floating through time, downward, together in darkness.

Still quaking with spasms, he jerked and twitched on Bob

who also quaked. He was slippery with sweat.

Both hearts were pounding fiercely. He could feel Bob's heart beat through his own chest. *Tom-toms, primordial tom-toms.* He hugged the man he loved as the pace of the beat slackened. He gingerly rolled off, his hand still on Bob's chest. He snuggled his face into Bob's side. He was safe here, forever safe in the shelter of his wings.

"Wow!" he said.

Bob said nothing.

I'm safe here, forever safe in the shelter of his wings, he thought as he drifted into sleep. He slept soundly that night…

Bob not at all.

CHAPTER 20

While it was still dark and Blaine still slept, Bob climbed out of bed, dressed and left. He got thirty dollars from his room—the emergency money he kept hidden between the label and the metal of a can of asparagus—then walked the chill, dank streets to a park over a mile away, to a place where Blaine wouldn't find him. It was a large park with a lake with tennis courts at one end of it and a playground with monkey bars at the other. Joggers would run the encompassing sidewalk. He sat on a bench, a cold wetness seeping through his jeans, and watched as low-slung clouds turned gray with sunrise.

On his own shoulders, by his own volition—It had been his own idea, his proposition!—he bore the sins of his father, those disgusting, unmanly sins, sins gross and mocked and disparaged by real men. *So, I'm not a better man than you after all. Huh, Pa! I thought I was. But it's done. I did it and only time will separate me from that sin. Weeks will go by and months on a calendar and the disgrace will fade.*

Indiscretions are more tolerable for those with faith. Now would be a good time to get some, Bobby. But nope! Not me! Catholics have their priests and the confessional. Fundamentalists have remorse, although they never have assurance their self-incriminations have lasted long enough. But eventually they are assured their sin will eventually be bleached white as snow. Maybe there's a Chlorox commercial there! He chuckled.

I myself have no such assurance. Because if God won't answer a child's prayer then there is no merciful God. So there's no one to forgive my indiscretions, no one to forgive my animal lusts.

And how far that lust is from my dream of love. I guess it's the dream of Everyman — my dream of wife and hearth and children.

I need Quasi with me! Right now. Not tomorrow, not the next day, but now! This very moment!

He continued to sit. At the water's edge before him, four ducks awoke in the gray diffuse light, stretching and preening themselves. Two gray ground doves searched in the wet grass for their seeds and bugs. Joggers in sweat clothes — with hoods pulled over their heads against the lightest of drizzles — began their circuitous route around the lake. The only place in Atlanta he had seen swallows was here. Swallows prized open spaces and the park here was large enough and the expanse of sky welcoming enough to contain their joy. He hoped to see swallows this day. With the weather inclement, there would be no roofing work. About that he was glad.

With steps heavy he walked the blocks to the diner where Linda worked — the woman he had dated until a red Camaro had whisked her away. *No way do I want to see her, ever. It would be awkward for her. Me too for that matter. But it's not her shift and it'll be dry there. Besides, its walls will shield me from*

Bronc's thugs.

At the counter he loitered over his coffee and cigarettes, watching the clock on the wall. At eight he asked the waitress for a phone book and looked up the address of Assisi Animal Hospital. At nine he asked her what bus would take him that way.

He went back to his room to get Quasi's leash then caught the bus.

There were three people in the waiting room at the veterinarian's, two with cats, one with a Labradore. He went up to the window and said to the young woman, "I'm here to pick up my dog."

"Oh, uh...Mr. Newell," she said.

"Yeah," he said. "But how'd you remember that?"

"I guess you made an impression," she said, blushing a little. She had straight brown hair pulled back into a pony tail. Fair complexion. Nordic.

"I'll take that as a compliment," he said, smiling and raising one eyebrow. He needed to be especially nice because he had a favor to ask. He tried to remember her name but couldn't.

She said, "I just hung up from talking with Mr. Shirer a few minutes ago. I called him to say you could pick Quasi up this afternoon, after two o'clock. Mr. Shirer is staying home from school today. He's not feeling well."

"I can't wait until this afternoon. I need my dog now," he said.

"Dr. Nadler did say this afternoon. I'll have to check with him first."

"And as a personal favor, would you ask him about my

making weekly payments."

"I was just doing up the bill. Here it is," she said and handed it to him.

He looked at it. "That's all?! Fifteen dollars? For what?" he said and counted off on his fingers: "Thursday, Friday, Saturday, Sunday—four days board? And the medicine and the doctor's time and whatever else you did? Fifteen dollars?"

"That's all of it," she said.

He reached for his wallet in his hip pocket. "Well here." He handed her a twenty. *Wow! I don't have to grovel and plead about payments!* "Here."

She took the bill and the money from him, stamped the multiple copies PAID IN FULL, CASH, and handed a yellow copy back to him, along with a five. "Let me go speak to Dr. Nadler for you," she said and left.

As he replaced his wallet in his hip pocket, he questioned the bill. But if Dr. Nadler was a friend of Blaine's, he was probably a queer too, and maybe the small bill was his way of making a pass. *He'll probably come out with her and Quasi and want to chat a bit.*

She returned with the bearded doctor who led Quasi out on leash.

"Quasi!" Bob said and knelt on the floor as Quasi squirmed like a puppy, climbed on him and licked his face. "Aren't you a good boy! Daddy's good boy!"

Above them the receptionist said, "Mr. Shirer is really a good friend, isn't he?"

"Good seeing you too, boy!" He ignored her remark, but pondered it. *That question coming right after I paid the bill? Too small a bill! That's it, HE paid it, leaving me a pittance to protect my pride. That ilk always seek to ensnare with their money. Conniving queers!* "You're fine now, boy. Now aren't you?" He replaced the hospital's lead with his own and stood. "What was the whole bill?" he asked.

Dr. Nadler responded, "Sharon tells me the bill is settled. It's a closed matter. But if you ever need our services again, Mr. Newell, we'll be more than happy to ac-<u>com</u>-modate you. He is a good dog."

Accommodate me? He checked a demeaning response, but said, "Yes, he is. Thank you for helping us. If you would pass me a card I'll put it in my wallet." Sharon reached over to the counter and gave him one.

"Thanks again," he said and left. *Connivers!*

On wet leaves and sidewalks they walked the forty blocks back to Hyacinth Street, skirting puddles along the way. Quasi heeled perfectly and sat promptly at street crossings. He remembered adopting him from a snowdrift back in November. The little guy had certainly become a blessing in his life and he wondered if—on that day he had adopted him from a snowdrift—if on that particular day he had had any inkling of just how much of a blessing Quasi would prove to be.

Back home he found an envelope on the floor inside his door. It was thick, beige paper—expensive. Leaving it unopened, he tore it in half lengthwise and let it drop from his fingers into the kitchen trash.

He dried Quasi with a towel, fed him, and as his little friend curled up on his pillow, pawed through the box with the spiral notebooks. He was looking for the one with the yellow cover. That's the one he was filling up in Billings, Montana. He found it and sat in the easy chair—the green overstuffed chair, with white cotton visible through the gashes that Bronc had made. He flipped through his journal until he found the date in November. The first of that entry was about driving through the storm for the German shepherd puppy, about seeing something gray struggling through drifts toward the light from the diner, about Della's joy in receiving the gift of the puppy. And he continued to read.

Right now I have a three-legged mutt pressing close to the wall, his fearful white eyes on me. I've fed him, but he's still scared. I wonder how long he's scavenged in trash, had people shoo him away. 'Get lost!' But I know about dogs. He'll come around and be a good dog.

It's funny how some things keep lingering on in the mind. Some things just take hold and keep coming back—don't know why. But there was this guy at Edna's, just drifting through, waylaid by the storm, he said, unless there were any jobs hereabouts. He had served one tour in Nam, not a Marine, but almost as good, a Ranger. His name was Zane. Zane Carlson, with eyes the most beautiful brown I've ever seen, eyes dark and vibrant like polished chestnuts.

I told him he should speak to Mr. Burke at the counter there—he's a rancher and rich. Zane went up and they chatted a while as I watched from the corner of my eye. In this world you can't let it be known you're interested in another man's business. He apparently got a job, though, for he smiled and waved at me from across the room. I nodded a manly single nod.

But then at the register Mr. Burke snatched the check from his hand and announced for the whole world to hear, 'You're working for me now and your keep's part of it.'

Your keep's part of it! —like he was an animal or something!

All along the counter men turned their heads for a look-see. He had purposefully made Zane look bad before them. I wanted to go up and say, But Mr. Burke, you're already rich, what do you need more Brownie points for? But I didn't, I just sat there feeling bad for the guy. As they left he looked at me with a hurt, questioning look on his face.

I wish I had never pointed the big rich man out. If Burke hadn't been there, I couldn't have.

Maybe I would have invited him to join me at my table, eat lunch with me.

And maybe I would have invited him here to the apartment to wait out the storm —he's a vet, he served honorably. And he could have used the spare bedroom as he looked for work.

Come supper time I could have fixed us a couple salads, broiled a couple steaks. We could have broken hunks off a loaf of French bread, and washed it down with a six-pack. Tomorrow I could have borrowed another set of cross country skis —I've never had a chance to use mine. And as we drove past the miles of ranch land to the foothills, we could have joked and kidded each other on the way, like brothers do.

Once there, the fir and spruce would be arched and snow-covered, like a story-book illustration. And there, in the wilderness, the two of us, a Ranger and a Marine, it'd be quiet.

His stomach knotted. As he sat in the easy chair with Quasi on the bed, he reread those last lines: *And there, in the wilderness, the two of us, a Ranger and a Marine, it'd be quiet.* And he saw it, saw for the first time something Carmen had seen. *'Romantic. Two man tent and all.'* He stared at the page, his eyes wide, and heard Carmen's voice. *'It's no big deal,'* she had said. *'Tonia and I have been—shall I say friends?—for years.'*

There on the page, in his own handwriting, his own words incriminated him. The sins of his father lurked inside him. He hurled the yellow notebook against the wall. "No fuckin' way!" he yelled aloud.

Quasi lifted his head from the pillow to look at him. "It will not be!" he bellowed.

This city is dangerous for me. I'm not like you, Blaine! But with so many gays, it makes it seem almost acceptable, fashionable and fun, the in-thing to do. Even my Pa, with his invite to a party so I could do my duty by satisfying nameless men, their lusts and their cocks. But I'm a better man than you, Pa!

And now there's Bronc out there somewhere, seeking revenge, skulking in the shadows, lurking in wait. It will not be, none of it. Not perverted games, Blaine. Not Bronc's games. None of it!

I have to get away from the demons in this city.

Unseen, perched atop the unpainted plywood closet, the ancient Hag slapped her thigh in merriment. Her saggy breasts jiggled and dribble slimed down her chin. In her interminable existence she found amusement in distress and especially relished the stench of death, especially the long, protracted, agonizing waiting for death.

Bob caught a putrid whiff as if of a backed-up sewer and

curled his lips. He ran a finger across his nose. He had smelled that foulness before, in Nam. It arose from abdomens blasted asunder by grenades.

CHAPTER 21

In the weeks that followed he avoided Blaine. Even a wave from across the street he would not return. Whenever he found a note—either on his return from work, or later in the evening as he watched it being slid under his door—he would toss it into the trash unopened. He worked his job, tended Quasi, read his paperbacks and at dusk would jog the sidewalks. He went to no movies, purchased no burger and fries. He couldn't. He was saving his money to fix his truck and have enough to get the hell out of Atlanta. His future lay elsewhere, maybe Florida.

One afternoon he found a bundle of letters in the mailbox. The addresses on them were in his own handwriting. These were the letters he had written to Mrs. Sloan. Under the RETURN TO SENDER, the word, Deceased, was circled in red. He cried that night.

The next evening, Friday, he was reading in his overstuffed chair when there was a knock at his door.

With his hand on the baseball bat he had purchased for a dollar, he opened it. "And what the hell do you want?" he said.

"I've got a favor to ask," Blaine said.

"Ask somebody of your own kind."

"Would you listen to me just a minute?"

"What?"

"I've got a funeral to go to."

"Whose?" he asked, his voice softening a bit.

"My brother's. Raiford's," Blaine said.

Bob was silent as he considered the trauma of that on him. He noticed his eyes were bloodshot. "Uh?...Do you want to come in?"

"Can I?"

"Sure," he said. As Blaine crossed to the green painted table, Bob asked, "Want a cup of coffee?"

"That'd be great." Quasi jumped from the bed to sit by Blaine's chair. "I see you're all fine now, little guy." He bent and scratched him behind the ears.

Bob put two cups of instant coffee on the table and sat.

"Even when you know it's coming," Blaine said, his gaze on his hands, "it doesn't make it hurt any less."

And Bob listened as Blaine explored his grief and rehearsed memories of his brother. He listened as Blaine regretted that none of his family, except him, had bothered to visit him in the nursing home.

Bob listened and tried to understand. About midnight he asked, "Would you like me to go to the funeral with you?"

"You mean you would?"

"Yeah," he said. "But we can never, ever..."

"I agree," Blaine said. "See, it did mess things up."

"Let's never mention it again. And you didn't tell anybody, go bragging about it, did you?" Bob asked, his brows lowered in an unfeigned need to know.

"No. No one."

"Not even Sofonda or Carl? Nobody?" he asked.

"No one. I swear."

"Okay," he said and reached across the table to squeeze Blaine's hand. Under their hands were the carved initials, hearts, and profanities of previous occupants. "I'll have to get something to wear. When's the funeral?"

"It's Monday, but you don't have to get anything special. It's your being there that matters. I didn't want to go alone."

"No one should have to," Bob said. "You *did* love your brother, didn't you?"

"Yeah. We got real close near the end. I just wish we'd taken the time for each other years and years ago."

"I understand," he said.

"But I've got to warn you about Mother. She probably won't be very nice to you if you're a friend of mine."

"I've only got to see her once, then never again. So if she's curt or anything, I'll just ignore it. Don't worry, I won't embarrass you."

"I wasn't worried about you embarrassing me," he said with frail smile. "But she's good at hurting people's feelings. I don't want her to hurt you. You protected me at Graffiti's and I want to protect you."

"Whatever she dishes, I'll just consider the source and take on the cheek and turn the other one. I promise."

"Okay," Blaine said, stood up and said his thanks and

goodnights. Bob closed the door behind him. *Poor guy, with a family like that. How is it Tolstoy opens* Anna Karenina? *'Happy families are all alike; unhappy families are unhappy each in its own way,' or something like that. Families are often more cruel than worst enemies. You can run from enemies, but the heart has umbilicals that tie you to family, even when the hurts inflicted are calculated and planned. The poor guy. But I'll do what I can to help you through your grief, Blaine. I'll offer a shoulder, an ear, a little of my time. But that's it. You need to find the stud service you're looking for, and I need to realize the dream in my heart.*

He undressed, climbed naked into bed and slept while Quasi curled against his legs.

At nine the next morning, Saturday, he knocked on Blaine's door and they spent the morning together in the apartment. At noon they parted, Blaine to attend to familial obligations. While he was away, Bob and Quasi walked to a florist where he purchased a small sympathy arrangement and left it on his doorstep. He then played Fetch the Stick with Quasi in the little park a block away. The sky was blue, the air temperate. He took Quasi home and changed into gray sweatpants.

Shirtless, he jogged the sidewalks of the city, until sweat began to trickle down his torso and darkened the sweatpants. As his tennis shoes hit the pavement, he accelerated his pace and thrust his arms upward in triumph, for this, pure physical exertion, was to him was an innocent joy. The body and its pleasures were not to be despised, but were given to be reveled in, as children revel in their games.

His lungs filled and emptied and he remembered that under Rev. Negley's roof the body and joy had been despised as contrary to The Teachings. The high school had even exempted him from PT classes because the Pastor objected to the locker rooms: "Do you know what goes on in those locker rooms? There's nakedness there, Bobby, and profane talk, and young men flaunting sizes, and flicking buttocks with rolled towels! And do you think that praises the Lord! No! Let the heathen wallow in their frivolities, we have the Lord's work to do." Upon graduation the Pastor shipped him off to Bible College in Birmingham, and he went, seemingly obedient yet actually he was only biding his time until his eighteenth birthday should arrive.

On that day, September 23, he did not go to his Old Testament class. Instead, he presented himself before the Marine Corps recruiter. There he filled out forms, took tests, and passed the physical at a doctor's office across town. Then, in the afternoon, standing with a bunch of other guys, he raised his right hand before a uniformed officer and an American flag and swore to defend the Constitution against all enemies foreign and domestic.

In a twinkling of the eye, while a shiver ran up and down his spine, a grin came over his face and the sparkle returned to his eyes—the sparkle that years of enduring Rev. Negley's bombasts and prohibitions had leached from them. And in that twinkling of an eye, he was a Marine, just as his Pa had been before him, and there was nothing in all this world Rev. Negley could do about it.

For three months he and his platoon had crawled through mud, grunted and shimmied up ropes and over fences. They detonated Claymores, rappelled off platforms, and charged straw dummies with fixed bayonets. Although they yawned through classes on water purification and on the care of personal gear, they vied with one another to excel in firing the M16, the bazooka, and the M60 Machine Gun. In the evenings, with muscles dog-tired, they scrubbed the squad-bay, using toothbrushes on the wire coils their mattresses lay on. They polished even the drain covers in the shower room with Brass-O.

Every morning at five A.M. they had run through the fog-shrouded streets of Parris Island in perfect formation, all the while singing and chanting. Again in the afternoon they ran in formation. And now on the sidewalks and cobblestones of Atlanta, as sweat matted his hair and exertion pounded his heart, he heard a chorus of young men. They were singing double-time cadences, and he was again running in perfect formation with those young men, was one with them, wherever they were running. And he was one with the sky, the clouds, his body. His mind, his heart and his sinews were one and the same. There was no conflict between the several parts of him. There were no several parts: *Hear, O Israel, the Lord your God is one. And I, too, am one!*

An approaching car started honking and wolf-whistles came from it. It was a car with four men in it, one of them leaning out of the rear window. He clenched his teeth, ignoring the fags, but then thought better of it and raised his hand in wave. It could be they were friends of Blaine's and he did not want to give offense.

He walked back home, smoked a cigarette, showered, and looked out the window. A red MG was again parked on the street, so he again knocked on Blaine's door. They talked, watched television, snacked. Blaine—not much of a cook—

called out for pizza that evening. On Sunday he called out once for burgers, then later for shrimp fettuccini. Bob was true to his word and spent time with him, as he had said, except for the hours they slept.

At nine A.M. Monday Bob, in his gray slacks, white shirt and tie, was outside the League of Mercy Thrift Store, waiting for it to open. There, among the racks, he found a black three piece suit. Apparently it had never been worn, for the tags were still attached. It was nice material. New, he surmised, it would have cost over three hundred dollars. He tried it on, and surprisingly, it fit his six-foot-two frame. He wore it to the cash register, paid six dollars for it, and asked the clerk to remove the tags for him. He wore it out of the store, his gray slacks in a bag.

At eleven he scrunched into Blaine's car as they drove to the Cathedral. "I know you Catholics have all types of gesturing and kneeling and all, and I hope I don't embarrass you."

"Don't worry about it. Sure, we genuflect, and cross and kneel and all types of things. We incense and asperse and bow. And when you know the significance of each of them, it does add to a person's sense of humility in approaching the Eternal. But that is something we do for ourselves to remind us. God doesn't ask any of those things. He only asks the gift of the human heart."

"Well, I'll just do whatever you do," Bob said.

"Sure," Blaine said.

As they went down the long aisle, Bob lagged a little behind. When Blaine genuflected and entered the first pew, Bob genuflected and started to sidle into the pew as well. An usher in gray suit stopped him with hand on his shoulder. "Are you family?" he asked.

An erect gray-haired woman who was sitting in that front pew — in black gown, black pearls and with black lace covering her face — spoke up. "He certainly is not!"

"I'm sorry," the usher said to him, "you will have to sit elsewhere."

Bob nodded and moved into the second pew to sit directly behind Blaine, who was kneeling, so he knelt as well. When Blaine sat, Bob sat.

The Mass, celebrated by the Archbishop, stretched out a long time. He was pleased Blaine was maintaining his composure. They were all standing when the Archbishop said in a voice slow and dignified, "By your power you bring us to birth...By your providence you rule our lives... By your command you free us at last from sin as we return to the dust from which we came."

With that, Blaine began to sob, his shoulders jerking and his hands going to cover his face. Bob reached to his shoulder, to comfort him with a hand. Moments later the organ was playing majestically and the whole congregation was singing "Holy, Holy, Holy" — everyone except Mrs. Shirer. Instead she glared at Bob with haughty eyes and said in a loud whisper. "Get your hands off him!" Bob glared back at her and kept his hand on his friend's shoulder until they all knelt.

Following the Mass, they processed in cavalcade to the grave site. Though the service there was brief, it drained the last of Blaine's strength and Bob had to drive the MG, following his directions, to his parents' for the reception.

At a grand white-pillared mansion with circular drive a

parking attendant took the car.

Once in the foyer—parquet floors and circular staircase—Blaine told Bob he had to join the family in the library for the reading, but he'd be back out soon.

Bob followed those arriving into a spacious room. All the furniture had been removed, and the carpet had not a single indentation where furniture had been. He figured the carpet had been replaced over the weekend. A table at least thirty feet long had been set up. White pleated linen covered it and, swagging downward were garlands of evergreens from which black velvet ribbons hung. On the table were platters and chaffing dishes and ornate silver candelabras. Three women in black and white dresses were lighting the candles. Behind the table and to the right were two walls of French doors. The doors on the right overlooked the pool, while the one behind overlooked the gardens. The azaleas were brilliant in a uniform pink. In them a mockingbird repeated its medley of calls, throwing its chest out and with head high—obviously so very pleased with himself. A black waiter in tuxedo inquired Bob's preference in beverage.

He noticed the room was filling up, the women in black, the men in black suits or dark gray. The Archbishop arrived, plump and ruddy complected and still in flowing white robes, although without the high hat he had worn into and out of the cathedral. Three young men in black cassocks attended him, two of them the most handsome men Bob had ever seen, too handsome even to be actors, because no one would ever believe such good-looks actually existed in the world. An audience would never believe any role such an actor might play.

He thought he recognized a distinguished gray-haired man from somewhere and asked the black waiter—bringing him his bourbon and water—who he was. "Why, that's the Governor, sir."

He was certainly standing among the stratosphere of society. These were the shakers and movers, these the power and the money. He was glad he had taken the time that morning to purchase the black suit.

The room buzzed now with conversation, sparkled with diamonds, was scented with fine perfumes and colognes. Here and there tuxedoed waiters moved about. *It's a lovely cocktail party, Mrs. Shirer,* he imagined himself saying, because in this gathering the one single nod toward anything even vaguely suggestive of grief was the absence of music. Had there been music, he was sure this event would have received its due recognition in the annals of society as the perfect cocktail party. It was all so proper. Several times he caught the Archbishop's handsome attendants staring at him through coiffures and suits from across the room. Almost everything was proper.

He wondered where Blaine's friends were. Not one of them was here, neither Carl, nor Russ, nor Sofonda. Nor had any of them been at the church or the cemetery. He questioned how deep their friendship ran, and that made him both disappointed with them and sad for Blaine.

A commotion and voices toward the front of the house drew attention. Throughout the room faces turned to watch a young woman in black veil stomping her feet, flailing her arms and cursing. Then she, dragging a little tow-haired boy behind her, went barging out the front door. Bob assumed that was

Lena, Raiford Shirer's wife, who had been in London while her husband lay in a nursing home.

Bob watched Blaine go over to stand with a plump elderly man with weak chin and not much taller than Blaine. The man put his hand on Blaine's shoulder, and Blaine covered his hand with his own. That man had been in the front pew, so Bob figured that was Mr. Shirer.

Mrs. Shirer—still in black veil, pearls and gown—was talking to two men, the younger holding a briefcase. She was raising her fingers one by one as she talked. The older of them kept nodding.

When she went to join Blaine and her husband, the older one dictated to the younger one who had been holding the briefcase. He wrote on a pad held in his hand and then the two headed for the door. *Attorneys,* Bob thought. *The will must not have pleased very many of them.*

Mrs. Shirer took her husband's arm, and, all composure, they started through the room to receive condolences. Blaine followed a little behind. They paused at the Archbishop, over whose plump face came a look of consternation as Mrs. Shirer, standing erect, talked. When the Shirers continued on, the Archbishop's gaze followed after them, his lips pursing. His attendants studied their master's face.

Above the hum of conversation the Shirers received condolences from this one and that. Slowly they approached where Bob was standing, the palms of his hands cold and wet. Repeatedly he wiped them on his slacks in preparation.

"Mother and Father," Blaine said, "I'd like you to meet Robert Newell...Mr. Robert Newell, this is my mother and father, Mr. and Mrs. Shirer."

Bob cleared his throat. "Mr. and Mrs. Shirer, I am terribly sorry at the loss of your son," he said, extending his hand.

Mrs. Shirer turned from Bob and lowered haughty eyes onto Blaine. "How dare you drag your perverted white trash into this home!" she said, and, on her husband's arm continued on.

Blaine looked at Bob, who smiled sheepishly and shrugged.

Blaine's mouth opened, twisted. Pain furled his brow and tears pooled in his eyes. "Mo-ther!" he bellowed.

"Blaine, it's okay," Bob said, reaching his hand out to grasp Blaine's arm.

"Mo-ther!" he shouted again and rushed after her to pull on her skirt.

The room hushed, faces turned. In the silence Bob beckoned in rising tones, "Blaine?"

Mrs. Shirer stopped and turned her eyes on her son.

All eyes watched. All ears listened.

"And just WHO the HELL do you think YOU are!"

Mrs. Shirer smiled condescendingly. "Mrs. Alicia Clement Shirer."

"So grand! So high and mighty!" Blaine shouted.

She turned away, but Blaine moved in front of her.

"Blaine?" Bob called again, to no avail.

Throughout the room mourners watched and listened as accusation met accusation. They watched as bandages were ripped from wounds, as bits of skeletons were unearthed before their eyes.

Outside, waiting for Blaine's car to be brought around, Bob tried to comfort his friend. "She didn't mean what she said, guy. She's just upset and is under a lot of strain. And don't worry about me. I've been called a lot worse than white trash." His attempts, though, did nothing to still his sobs.

As he drove, Blaine rested his head on his arm and wept bitterly. Though Bob tried, there was no comforting him. *There's got to be a word for a woman like that, but bitch is too broad and means too many different things. Wouldn't even walk, all three of them, side by side, but made Blaine tag behind like some stray dog. I don't know how he's put up with it all his years. I'd have been long gone. No way would I put up with conscious and calculated abuse. No wonder none of his friends dared to support him with their presence.*

Bob parked on Hyacinth Street and they got out. "Come upstairs with me, please," Blaine said.

"You've got to deal with this. The hardest part is over, and I was there for you through the whole thing. I was there when you needed somebody."

"I know."

"But it's best we now go our separate ways."

"I don't want to be alone," he said, his chin quivering.

"I've done what I said I'd do, Blaine. There is nothing more I can do. It's time to say goodbye, with no hard feelings on either side."

"You mean p-p-permanently?" Blaine stuttered.

"Yes," he said.

"It's because w-we're from different worlds, huh?" The words were garbled with stifled sobs.

Bob nodded. "I don't fit into your worlds, Blaine. Not the money world, not the queer world. But you're not a bad guy. I don't dislike you and I wish you all the best. Good luck," he said and turned.

CHAPTER 21

At the black yawn into his building he glanced back. Blaine was still standing in the street watching him.

Bob entered his building.

CHAPTER 22

When Bob got home from work on Tuesday, he put Quasi's leash on him and they went down the stairs for their evening walk. As Quasi did his business in the weeds, Bob noticed Blaine's MG. *I've met my obligation—exactly what I said I'd do—but still I ought to go check on him. In Nam I said goodbye to many good men, my own fingers closing the eyes of some of them. That casts a light on the ultimate things and I'd hate for him to do anything foolish. Don't you agree, Quasi? He's not that strong of a guy, now is he? Let's go check.* From the weeds of the front yard he and Quasi crossed the street.

Blaine's cockatiel, Napoleon, greeted Quasi with high, horrible squawkings which forced Blaine to put the bird in his cage and to darken it with the night-covering.

Once the bird was tended to, they went into the kitchen where Blaine slid aside stacks of test papers. They snacked on Oreo cookies, Bob dunking his in milk, Blaine breaking his in half, and Quasi gobbling his in one bite.

"There's a production of *Equus* this Friday," Blaine said. "I'd like to go see it. It's not a professional production, a junior college thing. But Ellen is the drama teacher. She's a friend of mine. Would you go with me?"

"To tell you the truth," Bob said, "I thought I'd find you a little more upset, what with the funeral and all."

"I'm sad but I have a perspective on things you don't share, Bob. Raiford may not have lived all his days according to the Gospel, but he died in accordance with it. And because of him, as long as this country lasts — its laws and its financial institutions — the hungry will be fed and the naked clothed. Raiford died well and is now in a far better place."

"Yeah, I know," he said, his tone sarcastic. "That bit about the first last and the last first. Pipe-dreams, nothing but a pipe-dream."

"Bob!" Blaine's voice flared. "You don't have to share my beliefs, that's your choice. But don't ever disparage them."

Bob dunked a cookie into the milk. *I know better than to mock what another clings to. That was shabby of me.* "I'm sorry," he said.

Blaine nodded. "So will you go to *Equus* with me?" He broke a cookie in half.

"Okay," he said, "I'll go. I've seen the first part of it before. Carmen chartered a plane and a bunch of us flew to Denver to see it. At intermission, though, she pronounced it sick — I can understand that, she bred Morgans — and so we all left and went out for drinks and dancing instead."

"Did you like the part you saw?"

"Yeah, it was kinda interesting."

"It's gotten rave reviews," Blaine said. "I'm looking forward to it, even a junior college production."

"I wouldn't mind seeing how it ends," he said.

The ending of it—witnessed on a Friday evening—left Bob emotionally drained and fingering the elements of his own childhood. They walked out of the theater and drove from the college campus in silence.

At a Pizza Hut they ordered a pitcher of beer and a large pizza. "Magnificent art!" Blaine said. "Shaffer weaves a night dream of power and beauty, so unlike the drab and stuttering world we inhabit. A dream world of strange music, poetry and forbidden loves. Even the costumes for the haunting chorus of horses—see-through metallic horse heads on sensuous, magnificent torsos, male and female. Brilliant, Bob."

"Yeah," he said, "I liked it."

"And Dysart's opening line—'With one particular horse, called Nugget, he embraces'—scans beautifully into Shakespearean pentameter, iambs and dactyls. I wonder why he didn't write the whole thing as such...Uh...Breaking it with prose for the parents, maybe."

Their pizza came, a large one with the works, but with anchovies on only half of it. Blaine liked 'those salty, slimy minnows.' And over it they discussed the play's psychological elements, the commingling of sexuality, religion and guilt.

"And did you notice the artistry of live performance? It could never be successfully remade as a movie, because film's bluntness would destroy it. But as theater, it captures a quality of myth. And I'm sure it was Shaffer's intention that as live performance the audience should enter into that myth, and should themselves sense that their own eyes, staring at Alan from the darkness, also condemn him, also haunt him."

"Well, I kinda felt sorry for him," Bob said, "what with that childhood he had and all."

"Absolutely. But Alan made the choice to take the icepick and blind innocent horses, a whole stable-full of them. And that act now deranges him. But was it a choice of free will? or was it, at the time, the only option he had? To blind the accusatory eyes. It's theater of substance and brilliance. Shaffer's a genius."

"I bet you could write something just as good, Blaine. You've been through a lot of shit."

"I'm good at analyzing and teaching, and I love to teach. I'm not creative, though. Oh, I've dabbled with a little poetry. That's all. But you've got a natural talent for writing, Bob, and I bet you have a thousand stories inside you, bursting to be told. You need to start writing again."

"I wish I hadn't dropped out of school. I was doing good at the University of Colorado," he said.

"Why did you?"

He responded with a single word, "Reasons," and in silence recalled his foolishness in selling his jeep, his flight to California only to end up smashing bottles behind a bar. "I wanted to be a teacher."

"You're kidding!" Blaine said. "Maybe you should think about going back."

"Yeah, sure. On what? But someday maybe," he said.

It was late when they arrived at Graffiti's, where eccentric letters glowed on the walls in neon colors, where lights glinted from revolving globes overhead. The place was three-quarters filled with men. The 11:30 show was on, with Sofonda lip-synching and dancing with a feather boa. They went to the table by the DJ booth, joining Carl and Russ. "Where's Steve?" Blaine asked, as both men took seats.

"He's supposed to be writing a term paper," Carl said, his arms bulging with muscles, with veins on top of the muscles. "But he's probably watching TV, either that, or working out some more."

A waiter came to the table and they ordered a bourbon and water and a gin and tonic. Sofonda's routine ended. When the applause and cat whistles began to wane, she announced into the microphone: "For the first time ever!...On this stage!...Graffiti's!...Destined to be a star of stars!...A new-found talent!...An entertainer *par excellence!*...The incomparable, Tu-tu Much!"

As the music started there was motion behind the curtains, which suddenly opened, taking the man there by surprise. He was a barrel chested man with black beard who had donned a blonde wig, house dress, sweater and heels. And there he was with a shopping cart and in drag as a bag-lady. Across the stage he lip-synched and gestured. Repeatedly his hose slipped down hairy legs. The audience loved the spoof and many went up to tip him. Bob stilled his laughter long enough to go up onto the stage as well and there pressed a dollar bill into a bra padded with crumpled newspapers.

Back at the table, he heard Blaine shout over the din into his ear, "You gave it to a good cause. His name's Matt, a friend. He's an environmental engineer with the Highway Department, and all the tips are going to St. Vincent de Paul. Clever, huh?"

The show had ended with Matt's number, and the dance floor had filled. Blaine excused himself to the rest room and Carl—in turquoise tank top with shoulder straps as narrow as strings, and shoulders seemingly four feet wide—slid over to take the chair Blaine had vacated.

"You don't know it, but I owe you an apology," Carl said. "I didn't trust you and was suspicious of you at first. You know, the little guy's vulnerable and I'm sorta protective of him. But I hear you went with him to the funeral and just shrugged it off when Mrs. Shirer was, uh...well was just Mrs. Shirer. I'm glad you took the time to go. And I'm sorry you had to endure that bitch's mouth. Her husband should have taken her out to the woodshed and thrashed her soundly years ago, but most of the money is hers. I'm sorry you had to find out about her like that. I could have forewarned you."

"But getting back to what you started with...What did I ever do to make you not trust me?" Bob asked.

"Nothing. Not a thing. It's just Blaine. He needs somebody too damn desperately. It makes him vulnerable. It's good to know he's got you."

Bob's brows creased as he pondered what Carl meant by *he's got you*. He didn't know what Blaine may have been saying. He wondered if he should clarify matters.

"Oh," Carl said, "I realize you're straight, and you two are just friends, but that's almost as good." He leaned toward Bob and hugged him, pulling him close, strong arms pulling him to muscled chest, his scent that of Ivory soap. There was a tiny razor cut under his ear. *Kinda awkward you hugging me here in public like this but I appreciate your acceptance.*

They separated and Carl leaned back in the chair. Bob looked at his deep tan, his glinting eyes and those muscles. In spite of himself, he felt a stirring in his jeans, a hardening.

"Welcome to the family," Carl said.

"Thanks," he said. He raised one eyebrow and lowered the other as he pondered what Carl meant: The family of friends? or the family of gays? *Regardless, it doesn't matter. Whatever Blaine may have said or whatever Carl may think, no person's private thoughts have ever, since the beginning of the world, changed the facts. I'm not gay and my getting a hard-on was nothing. It happens numerous times a day and often I don't even know why. And with him it was just the natural response of the male animal to proximity. It was nothing.*

"When I can afford to join a gym," Bob said, "would you come down some day and give me some pointers? I'm doing push-ups and sit-ups now and you're really awesome."

"Awesome?" Carl chuckled. "Thanks, but let me clue you in about drag. Drag comes in three flavors, Bob. There's dresses, there's leather and there's muscle. But honest, Bob, under this drag here…" He fanned hands down his torso then did a mini-pose. "…it's just me underneath. Plain ol' me."

Bob chuckled just as Carl had moments prior. "I wouldn't mind having a little bit of that drag on me!"

Both men were laughing when Blaine returned from the rest room, saying, "If you don't mind, could we go?"

"What's wrong?" Bob asked.

"Don't know. For some reason my stomach's queasy, that's all."

"Well, it's probably all those salty, slimy minnows."

"There's nothing wrong with anchovies!" he said.

"Ain't nothing wrong with them there Frenchy worms there, neither," he said, chuckling.

They said their good nights and once in the MG Bob asked, "Is Carl's development natural or does he use steroids?"

"What difference does it make? It still takes a tremendous amount of work. The steroids by themselves don't do it. They just help. And nobody can achieve a musculature like his with the amount of testosterone the body produces by itself. And besides, they all use steroids, so it's not like he's cheating. But please, if anybody ever asks you, tell 'em it's natural. Carl doesn't want it known he uses them."

"Okay," he said. He gazed out the side window. He wondered if Carl believed he was straight. But that didn't matter. It was his acceptance that mattered. And Blaine's. It had been many years, since the Corps, that he had felt himself accepted, that sense of belonging, of being liked and wanted.

CHAPTER 23

As soon as Bob arose each morning, he went to the window to check the weather and to note the progress of the greening. Toward Easter, there was an explosion of growth. He had managed to get his truck fixed so that it started each time and now drove back and forth to work.

Once or twice a week he and Blaine would see a movie or theatrical performance. He was even prodded into going to something as wimpy as a ballet: "But Bob, the Bolshoi's doing it, the world's best." Funny, it wasn't wimpy—the men absolutely masculine and the women soft and feminine. When the curtain fell on *Swan Lake*, Bob was on his feet with all the rest, joining his bravos with all the rest, tears in his eyes. Another Friday they went to a roller-derby, the Amazons versus the Dominatrix, where muscular women in scant attire snarled at one another, pulled hair and yanked off halters. Loads of fun.

But most evenings he and Blaine would watch television

and snack, Quasi lying on the oriental rug, Napoleon eyeing the dog with haughty indifference from Blaine's shoulder—a red pencil in his hand and stack of essays to grade on the end-table. About ten Bob and Quasi would cross the street to their room where he would read a few chapters, then make an entry into his journal before retiring.

On the Saturday before Easter Sunday, Bob did his laundry, then went over to Blaine's about noon. This day black cloth draped the crucifix that hung in the living room. Black cloth draped the one in the dining room, in the kitchen.

"Sure, go ahead," Blaine said, "fix yourself anything you want. But I'm not eating anything today and I'm only going to drink water."

From his years of living under Rev. Negley's roof he knew what Holy Saturday signified. "No, well, uh," he stammered, thinking, *I admire your devotion.* "Anyway, I'm not really hungry, and uh, you've got things to do today, so I guess I'll see you tomorrow," he said.

Blaine walked him to the door. "Thanks, buddy," he said.

"Sure," he said, and left Blaine alone with his prayers, remorse and petitions. This was an important day for those who believed, the climax of the Triduum, those three days preceding Easter. And it was a climax all the more poignant for it was celebrated with no service, no song. It was the day Jesus lay in the grave. It was a day of mourning and silence. Well he knew what Holy Saturday signified, but it was based on nothing but a myth.

He crossed the street back to his room and propped himself up in bed. He began a new novel but from the squiggles on the page no sounds arose, no scents, no images:

By the half-light of a suspensor lamp, dimmed and hanging near the floor, the awakened boy could see a bulky female shape at his door, standing one step ahead of his mother. The old woman was a witch shadow—hair like matted spiderwebs, hooded…

The words lay ink on page. He put the Herbert novel down and started to straighten the place up, but decided that could wait.

He sat at his green table with his journal before him, but could think of nothing of significance to write.

He looked at Quasi's leash and thought about taking him for a walk, but that could wait until evening. Restless, he dressed in his gray slacks and pull-over shirt of horizontal lavender and white stripes, then he drove his truck toward town where they had the better cocktail lounges.

He parked on the street and entered one, McAfee's. From a barstool he ordered a Grandad and water, paying two-fifty for it. He tasted it once, then again, and called, "Bartender, come over here."

The young man in long sleeved white shirt and tie came to stand before him. "Yes, sir?"

"This ain't Old Grandad, buddy. This is bitter," he said. "I ordered Old Grandad."

"That's what I poured you," he said.

"Then why's it bitter?"

"Here," the bartender said, exasperation in his voice. He took Bob's glass, sloshed the liquid and ice into a sink, then filled a clean glass with ice. He bent to take a fresh bottle of Grandad from the cupboard, opened it and free-poured into the glass. He topped it with a splash and set it before him.

"Thank you," Bob said. The bartender gave a single nod.

He tasted it. It too was bitter and puckered his mouth, but he drank it, pretending to watch the golf tournament on the television. Actually his eye was on the three women sitting at the ell of the bar. *If I'm none the worse for wear, one of you three will be coming down here to chat in a bit. It'll probably be the older, more experienced one in the middle. She'll do for a lay, but the one with the tight sweater with all the colored triangles would be a better catch. Young stuff, but legal.* As he waited for one of them to find a reason to come down to chat, he drank his bourbon, watched the tournament, and sneaked glances at them. They would look at him then mutter among themselves. The drink was going down easily now and he ordered another.

As the bartender took his glass and began to fix a fresh one, the woman in the tight sweater came over. "This seat isn't taken, is it?" she asked, sitting.

"No. What are you drinking?"

"Bloody Marys."

"Bartender?" he said with a sideward tilt of his head toward the woman. The bartender nodded.

She had curly brown hair and lightly applied makeup, about twenty-two. Under her geometric patterned sweater, her breasts, unrestrained by a bra, were full. Her white jeans, he noticed as she sat, were skin-tight.

"Are those your real eyes or is it contacts?" she asked.

"I don't wear contacts! Don't need to, 20/20. And I've got my Pa's eyes. Same for both."

She swiveled on her stool and called to her companions, "Real." Then, to Bob, she said, "They'd be great in a close-up. That's what Jovita was saying. Oh, I'm sorry, but you probably *already* know my name. All three of us noticed you were studying me from the corner of your eye."

"No, I don't think I recognize you."

The bartender placed the two drinks before them and Bob paid him.

"Think," she said. "I'm an actress. You've probably seen me."

He looked at her, shrugged and shook his head. "I'm sorry. You're pretty and all, but uh…sorry."

"But I've made dozens of films. The Arcade is always showing at least one of them. They're showing one of my best now, *Sailors in Port.*"

He knew what the Arcade was, a triple-X theater where sexual fantasies consummated on the screen.

"I'm Rachel. I'm a star!" she said.

"Rachel!" he exclaimed, "Well, of course! The camera doesn't do you justice, you're more tantalizing here, with clothes on."

"You don't think I'm beautiful naked?"

"Well sure you are. But I never imagined I'd meet you in person, right here beside me. And the way you get into it, Wow! Takes a man's breath away!" He reached over and stroked her, a lingering stroke from the side of her face, down her arm—but with fingers extended to brush the breasts. Finally he rested his hand on her thigh and gently massaged it.

"We're filming again tomorrow afternoon. Something original, and it was my idea. I'm going to be kidnapped, held for ransom, you see, and repeatedly raped. Something like that Patty whoever it was, you know, a few years back. But I like it and want to stay with the kidnappers, just like that Patty whoever. At first, you see, I'm their sex slave, but in time they become my sex slaves.

"Jovita said it was deep, something a philosopher would come up with. Pretty good, huh? and it was my idea! But we still need a few good-looking extras. And if you're half as sexy naked, you could earn a couple hundred dollars on the set tomorrow," she said.

"Huh," Bob said, swizzling his drink. "Really? All that, huh? For just letting people watch me do what comes natural?"

"You got it!"

"Wow!" he said, his eyes undressing her.

"If you're good at it, you could make yourself a hell of a lot of money. And even more if you worked as an escort on the side. We all do. Jovita down there can tell you about it.

"Maybe she'll let you have an audition this afternoon with me. She'll watch us, and will tell you what to do. Now you're awful sexy and I'm sure you're really good at it, but Jovita's got a wild imagination and it turns out better like that. She's nice, too, almost like a mother to me, and has taught me everything I know."

Down the bar the older woman, her face made up and without wrinkles—the one he had assumed would be the one to approach him—was looking directly at them, nodding her head.

He smiled at her, pretending an interest and stood up. He squeezed Rachel's arm and, leaving his almost-full bourbon on the bar, went down to her.

"Pretty, isn't she?" Jovita, the older woman, said.

"Yeah," he said, "but she's got one flaw."

"It's just a white-head she squeezed, it'll be gone tomorrow. If you're interested, there's a woman flying in tonight from Brussels who likes young, tall studs. Are you game for some big bucks?"

"Well, I ain't no escort, madam, and her flaw is she ever got mixed up with a bitch *like you!*" He turned and headed for the door.

Behind him came Jovita's voice, "Preacher's son!"

He was fairly pleased with himself as he walked the sidewalk toward his truck. He certainly needed to earn several hundred. Even two hundred just once would help, but not like that. And imagine, he could still go to a barroom, order a drink, and before he had finished it some woman would still find a way to sit next to him, her juices flowing. But it wasn't that type of woman he wanted. He wanted a woman to be his wife—his best friend, his lover in the secrecy of their bedroom and the mother to their children. *Perhaps someday.*

As he climbed into the truck, he figured maybe he was being foolish about all this. It would be easy money, probably a couple hundred tonight, a couple hundred for the filming, and maybe perform an escort's duties once or twice in the coming week. That would be probably six to eight hundred dollars. On that he could afford to get out of the city, go somewhere else. But then summer would be here soon and he'd get the new position with Mr. King. And it had been many weeks now since there was any sign or hint of Bronc. His life had been disrupted by him twice, but only twice, the meeting in the barroom and then the destruction of his apartment. Perhaps he had grown tired of the game or had moved to another territory, or better yet, had been arrested.

As he parked on Hyacinth Street he noticed Blaine's car had not been moved. He hoped the guy's guilt and remorse for his sins would not plunge him into despair. As Carl had said, he was vulnerable and before God's accusatory finger, there was no telling what he might do this Holy Saturday. He hoped it wouldn't be anything drastic or injurious. Or terminal. He wanted to knock again on his door, but the man was entitled to his spiritual life. And penance this Holy Saturday was what he chose for himself.

Bob napped in his room for an hour, then for the first time ever took Quasi jogging with him, a slower jog. He managed just fine on three legs and seemed to enjoy it. *For that matter, as long as we're together the little guy seems happy whatever we do. Guess he sees us as a pack...Maybe I do, too.*

After supper in his room, he picked up Herbert's *Dune* that he had tried to start earlier. And now the words transformed into images and evoked emotions.

> *Within the shadows of his bed, Paul held his eyes open to mere slits. Two bird-bright ovals—the eyes of the old woman—seemed to expand and glow as they stared into his.*

As he read, he kept sensing that something was wrong. No, something was missing. The room was too quiet, the city. In mid-paragraph he suddenly looked up from the page. He knew what was missing. It was the lack of church bells that day. Not once the whole day, Holy Saturday, had the bells sounded. He realized he had grown immune to hearing their frequent pealings through the normal day. But this day, by their absence, he noticed.

With the novel in his lap, he listened to the unnatural silence until far off in the distance one single bell started pealing. He looked at his watch, seven P.M. He put the book on the floor and went to the window and opened it. Cool air spilled into the room, flowed over his bare abdomen. Gazing into the twilight, he listened. Another bell, blocks away, began to strike. He listened closely. Each strike sounded gravelly and coarse at first, but then as he listened, the pitch rose higher and higher, ascending upward from the gravel, seemingly a never ending arpeggio, until at the very top the pitch hovered, wavering softly, almost inaudible. It was, he supposed, like the chatterings of angels. And though he did not believe, he was comforted by the rightness of the pealing of bells.

Another one, somewhere to his right, started to peal. Throughout the city bells were now sounding from every quarter. How he wished he could believe and join with so many in celebrating what, if true, would be so wonderful—the ultimate assurance of ultimate victory.

He knew from experience, though, that belief was empty and belief would do no good. It was a harsh world, but he would make it through on his own strength and with his eyes wide open, with realism, and not the opium of fairytales. He returned to the overstuffed chair and the visions of Herbert.

CHAPTER 24

"I finally caught you," Blaine said on the telephone.

"Yeah, busy," Carl said. "There are a thousand meetings at the end of the school year, you know that," Carl said. "But only two more weeks."

"I have only one week, and that's just exams," Blaine said. "But I may not be going to St. Thomas this summer."

"I thought you had your reservations."

"I do, but I may be canceling them."

"Why?"

"Well, you know the guy that Bob's scared of?"

"Somebody he served with, right?"

"Yeah. He drove home from work yesterday and took care of his dog, then walked down to the store for something and when he got back he had four flats—his Michelin radials, you know—still whistling air. So he dashes upstairs, kicks open the door, and there, sitting on the bed, is this bamboo cage. He tells me his dog was inside it. I saw it, a tiny thing. I can't imagine how a person could live in it. He's scared, and has moved in here with me. He's not going to rent that room anymore. We're going to be roommates."

"When did all this happen?" Carl asked.

"Yesterday. He only had one suitcase, and boxes of books and clothes. I'm waiting for St. Vincent de Paul to get here and clear out the junk from the spare bedroom."

Carl said nothing and there was silence on the line, the silence pregnant with a demand that he explain.

"Four years is a long time, now Carl!" he said, his voice emphatic. "If I had your looks and your muscles, it wouldn't be a problem, but I don't."

"But there are young guys out there who need some financial help—like my Steve. You can afford it better than I can, share bed, provide board and pocket money, and send him to school. And even if it doesn't last too long, you'll know perhaps you made a positive difference in the guy's life. And it's nice having the sex right there in the house. It'll keep you out of the parks. You can't afford to be arrested."

"I haven't been out cruising for eight or nine weeks, since I met him. And I want…"

Carl interrupted. "And you two aren't having sex?"

"No. And I want to finagle a way to get him to go back to school. He wants to be a teacher, elementary level, but he should study writing. He's got the talent. That's one reason why I called, to ask you to put on your thinking cap about how to get him back in school. He's a proud man, Carl. He wouldn't take charity from me, and if he even knew about my trust fund, it'd put a barrier between us."

"But you say he's got the talent?"

"Let me read you something. Now I may have to cut this short. It's Friday and they sometimes get done earlier on Fridays, so if I suddenly break off, that's why. Let me ask you something first. Did you save any of your school assignments?"

"No."

"Well, this guy did. I'll read it. It's on lined paper, of course, and has an A-minus in red pencil and two words circled. In the corner is Bobby Newell, 6th grade, Mrs. McCullough, March 7, 1963. The date makes him twelve years old, so that's just before his father abandoned him. It's called *Rusty's Prayer*, and I'll put in the inflections to make it sound like a dog's voice.

God? Excuse me, God. I know you're busy and all because so many people always ask you for stuff. And I know I'm only a dog and not too high up in your order of things, but won't you listen to me for just a minute?

God?

Are you there, God?

Rrruff!

Oh! I didn't mean to scare you. And uh, thanks. I know I'm only a dog so I promise I won't take up lots of your time.

First off, I want to thank you for making me and giving me my Bobby. He's awful nice. He squats down sometimes and hugs me. Thanks for him, God.

But the reason I'm bothering you is to ask a favor. I know I'm just a dog and all, but could I ask a tiny little something for myself? If you're not too busy, that is.

Oh, what's that big word again?

In-, infinite? I'm sorry, but dogs don't understand big words. But I sure hope you like being it, in-, infinite.

But uh, would it be okay, could you work it out somehow, to let me have some itsy-bitsy part of life everlasting? Just a crumb or something of it? I promise I won't make no trouble. But could I come to heaven too? Could I just lie at Bobby's feet forever and gaze up at him? He says I've got pretty eyes when I look at him. I just want to know he's happy.

I promise I won't make no trouble, God. I'll just lie there all quiet and still. I won't bark and won't chase no angels neither. I'll just lie there and look up at him.

I'm only a dog, but could you do that for me? When the time comes, that is? If it's not too much of a bother?

Well, I'll let you go now. I know you're busy and, in-, in-finite and all. But God, you did make me, thanks for that. And thanks for listening too. Bye now.

Blaine finished reading and there was again silence on the line. In that silence he saw Bob in heaven standing with a group of angels, Rusty sitting at his feet. As Bob turns the page of the hymn book, Rusty lifts her head and howls in duet with him. The angels don't seem to mind, for they just look at each other and smile.

"A kid wrote that?" Carl asked.

"Yeah," he said.

"And you said he's written stories?"

"Three. The first one he wrote is called *Not Rusty Too,* about a boy orphaned by car accident running away to prevent the State from taking his dog from him as well. Then there's a story about a whore plagued by religious guilt and financial need, giving herself without charge to a half-deranged vet haunted by the jungle. That one's called *A Sip of Water.* I assume the title comes from the act of kindness shown to Jesus as he collapses under the weight of the cross. That's potentially good material, but without training his skill isn't yet up to telling such a profound story.

"But his best has the worst title, *MIA.* It's about a Marine Corporal, Simmonds, who despairs over the death of so many and then even his buddy, Redman. While on patrol he slips away from the squad and, alone in the forest, strips off his uniform, flinging it away. Naked and crazed, like Nebuchadnezzar, he crouches on all fours and paws through dead leaves for toadstools. Then, thinking of Redman and the good times they shared, he crams toadstools in his mouth. The bitter taste makes him choke, but he forces himself to swallow. His stomach heaves, his body spasms, and swarms of ants carry him away, bit by bit, into the verdant, quiet green of the forest. He ends it with Mr. and Mrs. Simmonds appearing before a Congressional Committee, holding a picture of their son, and begging them to do everything possible to find out what happened to him. The reader knows, though, that if they ever found out about the atrocities witnessed, the deprivations suffered and his ultimate madness, it would destroy them. They don't need to know."

"Except for the dog one," Carl said, "those aren't the stories you usually read in magazines."

"That's what I mean. They aren't copycat. They are original, authentic fiction. He's got talent. So how do we get him back in school?"

"I'll think about it for you. It'd be easiest if you could just tell him about your resources and that you'll cover all the expenses. Maybe you could stipulate that he do things around the house for pocket money like I do with Steve."

"Carl, he's a grown man, not a kid!"

"But you're going to get yourself hurt. If he's straight some chick's going to come along and take him away from you."

"I know. I've thought about that. But for now it's wonderful."

CHAPTER 25

Getting home an hour early, Blaine parked on Hyacinth Street. High horrible squawks greeted him. He flung the stack of test papers back onto the passenger seat and, all arms and legs, dashed up to his apartment. His door was open.

"What the hell you doing!" he screamed. Three men identically dressed were in his apartment. He darted to the telephone, his eyes on them, dialed 911. Napoleon, hung by the feet in a window, continued to flap his wings and squawk. He quickly memorized descriptions. All three in camouflage. One man was tall. One dark, Italian looking. The third one had a scar on his forehead. On all three, black rifles slung across their backs.

With quick strides the tall man approached him. One hand grabbed the telephone, the other plunked solidly on his shoulder. He replaced the telephone and said, "Why don't you have a seat, little faggy-pooh."

With his arm gripped as if by a vise, he was walked to an

antique straight backed chair and shoved into it. "Don't just stand there, Tony!" the man said. "Get something to tie him with!"

Bob's tormentors!

The third man was now kneeling on hands and knees at the credenza, the gleam of a knife in hand. He jabbed the blade forward. There was a growl and a single bark. "Fuckin' mutt bit me!"

The Italian man darted back out of his bedroom with a fistful of neckties, then vanished behind him.

Blaine's arms were pulled behind the chair.

The man with the knife stood up. He looked at Blaine. There was an orange scar on his forehead, the veins at his neck pulsing. *Bronc!* Bob had mentioned the scar.

Pain from his wrists shot through Blaine, so tightly he was being tied. Already his fingers were going numb, prickly.

"Get over here, Spider," Bronc said.

"Okay, boss!" the tall man said, still compressing his hand to keep Blaine in the chair. "Do you have him?" he said to the man binding him.

"Good 'nuf."

Spider went over to Bronc. "Grab the other end of this thing," he said referring to the credenza. Quasi dashed across the floor to slither under the sofa. "Fuckin' little shit!" Bronc said.

The Italian man came from behind him, knelt and with imported silk ties now bound his ankles to the chair. Blaine looked down at the dark hair, the now-broad shoulders. He had gotten a glimpse of him and recognized him. It was Tony, the former student whose pictures and threats had stripped him of the companionship of Captain Terry DuLac.

"What the hell you doing, Tony?!" Blaine demanded.

"See, Bronc, he does remember me."

"Yeah, yeah," he said, then to Spider, "Let's toss it over."

Tony stood up and sneered down at his former teacher. He was darkly handsome in the military uniform, twenty-two or - three, with white teeth and dark good looks.

"You and that priest caused me all types of trouble, even got me grounded for a month. And for what? for asking ya to grade me easy? And once I got your attention with the pictures, I tried to be nice about it, saying you could swing on my cock once or twice a week if you wanted."

"That's not how it works!"

"But what big fuckin' difference would a few A's have made to you!"

Blaine glared at him. To his right there was the sound of furniture overturned.

Tony rubbed his crotch. "Bronc, do you mind I show this cocksucker what he passed up?"

"Do whatcha want," came Bronc's voice.

Tony unbuttoned his camouflage pants.

Blaine turned his head, trying not to look, but from the corner of his eye saw him pull himself out, and Blaine slowly turned his head to stare. Huge uncut cock. Flaccid, wrinkled. Heavy balls. Dark Italian hair.

"Okay squirrel-face," he demanded, "do me!"

Blaine clenched his jaws and glared up at him.

Tony grabbed the back of his neck, pulled him. His head was ground into crotch, the soft cock twisting over his cheeks, nose, eyes. And he smelled the scent of him. *Ah! That earthy, musky, luscious, manly scent! Nothing in all the world is as intoxicating or as real!* His tongue poked through his lips, to taste it as it moved across his face. He opened his mouth, caught it as it moved and sucked it in, warm softness filling his mouth. He bent forward until his lips were against pubic hair. It began to engorge.

"See what you missed there Teach? And I was young then too!"

He began to suck and to move his head back and forth. Hardening, it pressed to the back of his mouth. He couldn't take it all. Tony yanked his head flush, forcing it down his throat. "Deep, squirrel-face! Deep!" He gagged and needed to cough, but couldn't. He couldn't breath. His stomach heaved. His face turned hot and he felt the veins popping out on his face.

With eyes wide, he saw Bronc and Spider standing behind Tony. They were sneering at him, the black barrels of their rifles poking into the air.

"Could have had it back then!" Tony said. "Better than chicks, guys! Queers let you do more! Very vers-a-tile! And when I'm done, I'm going to beat the shit out of ya!"

"You'll get the chance!" Bronc said. "The fag fucked things up coming home early. Now we gotta take both of 'em!...Spider, window! Be on look-out!"

With two hands on his head, Tony pumped his head back and forth. Blaine gasped for air on each backward pump. "Fuckin' rich bitch! Scum! Fag!" he said.

As Tony's cock plunged into and out of his throat, Blaine's own erection pressed now against his slacks. *I need this, deserve it!*

He coughed, but Tony stilled the cough by shoving himself deep down the throat and again holding it there. Again he couldn't breathe.

Abuse, Tony! Blaine thought. *Be a man! Rougher!* Yet even so, another part of him, a better part, kept alert for the sound of Bob's approach. They could do with him as they wished— he wanted them to, the three of them. *Take it wherever you need to take it!*—but he would not allow them to harm the man he loved.

"Spider," Tony called, "you're missing out. He's good. No teeth, nothing. Bronc, can I untie him and fuck him?"

"Later!...Where the hell that damn mutt go?! He didn't get out, did he?!"

"Hear that, Teach? I'm gonna fuck you in the woods while your sweetie's in a cage watching and floating on cloud nine."

In pleasure Blaine moaned under the man. Whatever it took, he would please him, satisfy Manhood. Yet he heard what was possibly a sound on the stairs. He strained to hear it more clearly. It was footsteps. *Bob's!*

He coughed, pulled away. "Run, Bob! Run! Run!"

Bronc looked at Blaine, the door, then yelled, "After 'im!"

Tony remained stationary, slapping and backhanding Blaine, whose head was tossed this way and that.

"Now, Tony!" Bronc shouted. And three uniformed men, M16's unslung, dashed to the door, scurried down the stairs.

Blaine heard shouts and the sound of running in both directions down the street. He heard women screaming and calling out for their children. Napoleon still squawked, making hearing difficult. There was the sound of tires screeching away, then that of someone bounding up the stairs.

"Oh, my God!" Bob said, charging into the apartment. "You didn't really believe me till now, didcha?" His lower teeth bared in anger, he went to the telephone and picked it up.

"Untie me first!" Blaine shouted. "They're gone, so untie me first!"

He flung the telephone against the wall, went to him, knelt behind the antique wooden chair. "You get your own legs." He strode over to the bird, and fending off bites and pecks untied his legs. Squawking, Napoleon flapped around the room, hitting the walls. "Where's Quasi?" he asked and spied his dog peeking at him from the bedroom. He dashed back to the telephone, and bent to pick the receiver from the floor.

"Don't, Bob!" Blaine said.

"Don't?!" he flared.

"Please don't," he said, massaging sore wrists. *How can I explain this and make you understand?*

"Look at the mess! Look at you! All tied up and you say *Don't?!*"

"I'm not tied up now and please don't call 'em. And where'd you find to hide out there?"

"And why not?!" He slammed the phone on its hook. The bell inside rang with the brutality. "And I hid in the bushes by the landing."

"Well first, what proof do we have?"

"Look at the place. It's a wreck," he said, coming to him. He knelt before him. "I'm sorry this had to happen to you.

It's because of me. He's dangerous. Do you believe me now?"

"I've always believed you. But we can't call the cops."

"And why the hell not! It's not just *me* anymore, *buddy!*"

"Because they've got to have my name on one of their lists. Why do you think I've never called them whenever I've gotten beat up? We don't have the same rights—Not you, Bob, I mean gays don't. Sure the officers will oblige and they will come. But when they assess things, they'll just snap their little pads closed, look at each other, and smile. Then one of them will say something casual and understanding, something like, 'Well you boys have all the fun you want at home here tonight. But do us and yourselves a favor. Stay out of the fuckin' parks!'"

"Bull-shit!" Bob said.

"It's not bull-shit. Gays don't have the same rights or the same protection as other people. And I'm not being paranoid, it's true. And I have my career to worry about. And if you do call, you'll get your name placed on that list of theirs right alongside mine. The faggot list. Extra scrutiny."

Supper was silent, leftovers. Chinese. The evening in front of the television was tense, until Blaine said, "Bob, I'm flying to Sarasota in the morning. I've thought about it for a long time and months ago, long before I met you, I sent a resume to the public school system there. But then Rai got a lot worse and I didn't pursue it. But I'm flying down tomorrow, see if I can get an interview, and if I'm offered a job, I'm taking it."

"What will your parents say about that?" he asked.

"The same thing they've always said whenever I've wanted anything. They'll oppose it, or Mother will. But let 'em—I've heard it all before. But I'm a grown man, so I don't intend to ask their permission, I'll just tell them what I'm doing once it's all set."

Blaine had thought Bob's response to the plan would be one of happiness, one of problems resolving. Instead, he was silent, a single finger tracing the weave of the fabric on the sofa's arm.

"I wouldn't mind getting the hell out of this town while I still can," he said.

"That's what I mean, both of us."

"That's not what you said."

"I thought it went without saying!"

Bob stood up and mussed his hair. "Would you like some cookies and milk?" he asked.

"No, but you go ahead. I'm calling the airlines."

He flew from Atlanta on a 7:30 A.M. flight. At 6:30 that evening he picked up the telephone in his motel room and called his own number.

"Hello?" Bob answered.

"I've been offered a contract, tenth grade! And Florida has a Master Teacher program. I'll probably qualify for it in a year. And Sarasota's a beautiful town, Bob. There're art galleries and museums and colleges. Beautiful," he said.

"Have you been out to the Gulf of Mexico yet?" Bob

asked.

"Haven't had time. I'm staying over the weekend to look at apartments for us."

"Nothing too expensive, please," he said.

"Of course not," he said. "I need for you to call the principal for me. Have him let you in my classroom and send me everything from my desk. It'll take a big box. And the papers in my car too. Ship it all to me air-express. And use my car while I'm gone. I'll finish the final grades here and will special-delivery it back to you just in case I'm not home by the time I've got to have everything turned in."

"Then you're staying there a while?" he asked.

"No longer than I have to. I have to find us a place to ship the furniture to, and see about the utilities, and open banking accounts, and just those things that need tending. I'll be back as soon as I can."

"Okay," Bob said, "but stay out of trouble."

"You too," he said. They said their goodbyes and hung up.

In the days he was gone, Bob purchased retreads to replace his radials and said goodbye to Mr. King. He explained a little bit about Bronc in order to make credible to him why he needed to leave. He recommended Kyle. "He'll make you a good foreman."

"The plans we talked about a while back," Mr. King said, "are off for right now, Bob. You see, Mrs. King has had a diagnosis from the doctor. I've been meaning to tell you, but didn't know how."

"I'm sorry, Mr. King," Bob said.

Mr. King gazed directly into his eyes, then lowered the gaze and said, "Thanks. But, can I advance you a little something to help out with the moving?"

"I've got a buddy, and he's covering the cost and I'll pay him back when we get situated."

"Then you don't have any family?" Mr. King asked.

"No," Bob said.

When Blaine returned, they dined with friends every single evening. They were taken to restaurants, or feasted at somebody's home on a meal that had been labored over. No invitation came from the Shirers. On three nights there were farewell parties, the various apartments wall to wall with men.

The flurry of closure filled their days.

On the second Friday in June all that came to an end when a moving van parked on the street. Bob and Blaine, Quasi and Napoleon watched workmen carry the furniture and the boxes they had packed down the stairs.

The next day about noon an old pickup truck began to follow a red MG down the Interstate. They were headed to Florida to make a new beginning, their only scheduled stop— only seventy-five miles and at Bob's request—Macon. Of no concern to them whatsoever was the fact that the Florida Legislature had recently re-enacted the death penalty. They had never even commented on that, although they had mentioned Florida's excellent health care system, just in case.

From the Journal

He's as anxious to get there as I am, but I didn't even have to argue about stopping here—he just said sure if I needed to. He's a good guy, already asleep over there, three blankets piled on him. I don't know how anybody could sleep that warm. I'm glad the results he got a few days ago from his last batch of tests were all negative. I would hate for the family curse to strike.

I left him in the room here while I drove out to pay respects.

The years have not been gracious to our secret place, Rusty's and mine. A shopping center parking lot extends nearly to the oak itself. A bulldozer has razed up to the southwesterly portion of the creek and yellow stakes now mark out the area. There are still cattails, though, and squirrels still scamper and chatter in the oak limbs. It was there that—while Pa was still around—Rusty and I would skinny dip together, or fetch sticks, or stalk frogs, or lying in the grass, dream of growing up.

It was there that we lived in a box a Frigidaire had come in and that I covered with plastic. As time passed we gathered amenities around the creek—a grate for the campfire, a white metal cabinet to keep things dry in, a brand new kerosine lamp so I could get my homework done and a one-armed easy chair. Good memories.

After school and work, I would feed her and heat up a hotdog or can of pork and beans or something for myself, and we would watch the woodpecker who lived in a hole in a dead pine across the pond. He would always bob his head up and down in the fading light. We were sure—Rusty and I—that that was the woodpecker's way of telling us goodnight.

It was there, the Christmas after Pa left, that Reverend Negley and white clad women came to baptize, and found me and took me in.

It was there I prayed the last prayer I ever prayed—That no one should ever dare cut the oak, that squirrels should forever scamper among its limbs, that sunlight flicker forever among its leaves. That the oak should forever protect Rusty's rest.

And the oak does stand, and over the spot where she lies there are leaves and twigs, and the dance of sunlight through limbs.

When I got back to the room, Blaine and I went out looking for a Kentucky Fried Chicken. As we drove around, I had him turn and pointed out The Church of the Living and Crucified Christ. The front door was open and there was a mop bucket beside it. I told Blaine somebody else was now doing my job. He wanted to have a look inside and stopped. I stayed put in the passenger seat while he went up alone to see it.

He came back a little pale and I asked him what the matter was. He asked what used to be behind the pulpit. I told him a wooden cross.

He said it's now a mural, a horrible thing in blacks and blues and an ugly dirty green. Jesus's eyes are red. A city lies destroyed, charred and burned, smoke still rising from it. Skeletons lie here and there. And in the foreground are white clad people kneeling and stretching forth their arms toward the center of the mural where an atomic mushroom cloud rises. And descending on it—as if it were the clouds of the Second Coming—is an angry Christ, his eyes harsh and horrible. Over the whole thing, he said, are words painted in yellow, "Let your fire descend, O Lord, yet save your people." He said he'd never heard those words, that that wasn't Scripture, but he would ask a priest about it to make sure.

I told him it didn't amaze me, and how Rev. Negley was never ordained, but had ordained himself, or as he put it, ordained not by human hands but of the Holy Spirit.

Blaine said he sounded like a kook.

I told him he wasn't much of a man, that most men have a little bit of human understanding, a little compassion for another's sorrow. He asked what I meant, but I couldn't bring myself to tell him. Just things, I said.

To even think about it hurts.

But Rusty's okay, my girl, my Most Beautiful, sleeping peacefully and undisturbed, with songbirds overhead.

We should arrive in Sarasota tomorrow evening between 9 and 10. We could get there earlier but he's got to go to Mass. I asked why he couldn't miss just one Sunday, but he said he couldn't. I wish he would forego it, get us to our new beginning sooner. But friendships require a little give and take, a little sacrifice now and then. And it is good having a friend.

Chapter 26

Sarasota, Florida.

As they inspected the apartment Blaine had rented at about 10:00 Sunday night, Bob said, "The dining room's really super, how it juts out like that, with glass walls on three sides, with the oak limbs so close you can almost touch 'em. It's almost like being in a tree-house."

"I was thinking maybe a glass table or one of Italian marble would look nice," Blaine said.

"Yeah. And the way both bedrooms have doors that open into a common bathroom, that's nice too. But how much is it?"

"Four hundred a month."

"That's all?!" Bob said. "Well, my half will save me, uh, sixty dollars a month from what I was paying for that dumpy room!"

"Will it?" There was surprise in Blaine's voice.

"That's right. I was paying sixty-five dollars a week."

If you think this place is nice, Blaine thought, *you should see the one I preferred. I would have taken it had you not been with me—guard house, manicured grounds, brownstone, right on the water, private dock.* "Well, which bedroom do you want?"

"I'll take the one up front."

"You can have the bigger one if you want," Blaine said.

"Naw, you take it. The one up front has bookshelves and I'll even be able to unpack my books. I've never been able to do that."

"Okay, if you're sure," Blaine said. He was pleased that—after he had signed the lease—he had contracted with a carpenter to build bookshelves from floor to ceiling on two walls in that room. The carpenter had tried to schedule it for the first of next month, but a tip of five hundred dollars had convinced him he certainly could do the job then and finish it in just a matter of days.

The moving van arrived Monday at nine. They spent all day arranging, unpacking, rearranging, grocery shopping and some more rearranging. Quasi supervised and sniffed everything afresh in each new location.

Tuesday and Wednesday they drove around in the MG to orient themselves to the area. Both days they drove out to the Gulf of Mexico where Blaine sat on a towel in the sand, watching Bob's strong body cut through the green water with sure strokes. Both days they walked up and down the beach collecting sea shells.

On Thursday morning Blaine stood on the landing at the front door. As Bob walked to his truck, Blaine called down to him, "Good luck in finding something!" Bob raised his hand in acknowledgment. Blaine continued to watch as he headed forth and recalled Bob's words from months previous about the habitat of swallows. *You won't find them in forests, Blaine. They like meadows and fields and open spaces.* "And they like parking lots, too, Bob. They're following you."

While he was away the first mail arrived at the apartment. It was notification by Franklin Templeton that they had received the transfer of Blaine's trust fund, and that they would manage it as he had directed. Upon receipt of the letter he immediately drove to their office. There he had an attorney draft him a new will leaving his entire estate—38.44 million dollars—to a Mr. Robert Newell, same address.

When Bob returned in the afternoon, there was cause for celebration. He had landed a job with the Jim Walter Corporation in the division that makes pre-fab homes. Blaine took him out for dinner at a Red Lobster.

In those first weeks there arose a natural separation of household responsibilities. It arose without hassle, or even much discussion, for Bob took pride in their home and wanted to keep it presentable. Saturday, almost singlehandedly, he did the vacuuming and dusting and waxing and the other chores that go with keeping a place nice. Throughout the week he did most of the cooking too. Blaine wasn't good at it, and besides, he dirtied every dish and utensil in his attempts, which made cleanup for Bob laborious and that in spite of the fact they had a dishwasher. So Blaine let Bob do the household chores and the cooking, while he assumed the tasks of cleaning up the kitchen in the evening and doing the weekly shopping and laundry.

After supper Bob would either go to the little gym in the complex, or would make a slow jog along the trails with Quasi. He would then join Blaine and Napoleon in front of the television until about ten when he would say goodnight and retire to his room. His light would stay on for at least an hour. Over morning coffee he would sometimes speak about the novel he was reading.

Only one time—on a Friday after work—did Bob join his coworkers at Mario's, where wives and girlfriends waited for them. Instead he would meet Blaine at the Herculeneum Italian Cafe for a start-of-the-weekend beer and pizza. They would order a large one, with the works, but with "those salty, slimy minnows" on only half of it. Quarters would be dropped into the jukebox, and the waitress would be teased, and they would laugh and talk, never running out of things to talk about.

With Bob off at work, with no friends in a new city, and no longer with any need to seek out anonymous men, Blaine found time dragged. To fill it he worked on writing an introduction to Shakespeare's *Romeo and Juliet* for his upcoming classes. That done, he decided to write a synopsis of the action, which turned out to be a prose retelling. Then he decided to annotate the text with footnotes. All of it was geared to high school students. To help them visualize the action, he made many drawings, cartoon style—a newly found talent. When he had it done he spent a week typing it on mimeograph paper (the play's text included), made 130 copies, xeroxed the drawings and inserted them into the appropriate spots. He gave a copy to Bob, asking for his comments.

Days went by without hearing a word from him about it, until one night, around midnight, Bob—reemerging from his room into the living room—waved the stapled pages in his hand. "For the first time ever, Shakespeare makes sense to me. What a beautiful story! I could have strangled that monk. You have got to send this to a publisher. Many students will be forever grateful to you, Mr. Shirer. Really. What a story, what words Shakespeare has! And uh, do you mind if I keep this copy? Do you have enough?"

The next day while Bob was at work, Blaine typed a cover letter to William Morrow Publishers, went to the post office and mailed off the packet. Back home, he started work on *Julius Caesar*.

One Thursday he had done the laundry in the room on the first floor and had carried the basket into Bob's room. Usually he left his portion folded in stacks on the bed, but this day he decided to put it away for him. As he was doing so, he noticed a cigar box in the top drawer. He took it out, and sitting on the bed, dared to open it.

A smile came over his face, for there, on the very top, was the snapshot taken on the lake in Georgia, the two of them holding to the camera the day's catch—Bob's three small perch and Blaine's two fine trout. *You kept it, guy. That's so sweet!* Reverently he laid it on the bed and took a glossy, white-covered magazine, *Ares*, from the box. A paper clip was on page thirty-five where there was a poem by Robert Newell. He flipped to the title page: *Ares, the American Experience of War*, published by a firm in San Diego he had never heard of. He turned back to page thirty-five to read Bob's poem, *Eulogy*.

> *A fatigued warrior*
> *stands post*
> *over sleeping comrades*

and hums in his heart.

But then a reddening
in the mud
and fragmentary
silence.

Backseat conquests,
beer cans in the sand,
scribblings on scattered
restroom walls.

These the marks
he leaves,
his achievements,
insignias.

Beer cans in the sand.

Talent. Bob had a natural talent, though probably not poetic talent. But there was some merit here. Poems short as this one usually annoyed him, but this one didn't. Short poems usually presented but one image, and such was best left to painting, not language, which in its fluidity demanded progression of thought and emotion, not a stagnant picture. But here, short as it was—he counted the words, forty-eight—Bob had captured a man's whole life, a teenager's, no doubt, maybe a draftee. The poem used the word *fragmentary* both as a grenade and as a description of a silence broken with moans, and also there was double meaning with the word *fatigued*. Sensitivity to words. But more importantly the poem evoked empathy for a wasted life. Any writer whose works have stood the test of time had compassion, evoked empathy. *And Bob has a natural empathy. He needs to develop his talent, though his—most definitely—is not a poetic talent, but a narrative one.*

He placed the magazine next to the snapshot and picked up military ribbons, one by one, studying them, caressing them with his fingers. Whatever they signified, whatever achievements they proclaimed, he didn't know, but never before had he realized how sacred to him were his years of military service. Here, in the palm of his hand were the relics of a lifetime, relics that were to him precious.

He put them on the bed and took a folded piece of paper from the box. The paper was cheap, coarse, elementary paper, brittle now with age. He unfolded it and gazed at a child's pencil drawing of a man, whose eyes were shaded with crayon the palest blue, "Pa," written under it.

Last in the box, previously hidden by the drawing, were his dog-tags. On shiny metal a name was embossed—a sacred name—and a number. He raised them to his lips, kissed them, and reverently draped them around his neck. Reverently, he tucked them under his shirt.

That evening as they sat in front of the television snacking on popcorn, Blaine turned to Bob and said, "I've been thinking about your stories and your God-given talent with the written word. It would be a shame to waste that. You need to go back to school and start writing again."

"No, what I need is to find a good woman and raise a family."

"But maybe you'll find her there, a student."

"That's why I started with University of Colorado, why I enrolled in the first place. I got tired of the easy women you meet in bars and wanted to find a good one and settle down. That's not a very good reason to go to college, I guess, but I did good, all A's and B's," he said and put a handful of popcorn in his mouth.

"You owe it to yourself to go back," Blaine said. "Study creative writing, Bob. You may owe it not only to yourself but to the world as well."

"I can't afford it," he said.

"This apartment isn't as much as what I was paying for the one in Atlanta. We just won't go out to eat quite as often. We could get by okay on just my teacher's salary for a few years, and they've got a brand new college here, New College. Everything I hear about it is good. The new trimester will be starting in a couple of months, so why don't you apply, see if you get accepted. It's kinda late to apply, but it is also a brand new school. And, besides, an application isn't a commitment that you *have* to go, but see if they'll let you in."

"You really do believe in me, don't you?" he said.

He nodded. "It'd just be for a couple years."

"A degree is four years," he said.

"Sure, if you wanted. But you don't need a degree to write, just something to say and the skill to say it well."

"To be a teacher you need a degree," Bob said. "Once I started at the university and found out I could do it, I got to thinking and decided I wanted to be a teacher, so I changed from Core studies to the College of Education. I began fantasizing about going to work every day to a room full of kids, teaching 'em. You know I love kids. But I've been meaning to ask you something. What would you say if I asked you about us adopting a child?"

The question astonished him. "Well, uh..." he stammered. "I'd say you'd make a fine father."

"No, I said us. Would you help me raise him or her?"

"Sure I would."

"Thanks!" Bob said, his cheeks deeply dimpled.

"But uh, we've got to think about this now," Blaine said. "There are lots of implications here, like....Well, first off, before you make any inquiries, we'd better move and get apartments side by side."

"I thought you just said you'd help me!"

"I will. But if the State ever found out I was gay, do you think they'd put a child in our home?"

"You aren't turned on by kids, are you?"

"No, no! Never-never-never! But then I'm not turned on by anybody anymore. That's something from my past. But if the State knew about that past, they would never put a child with us. And so first thing, we'd have to move into adjacent apartments, or maybe get a big house that we could divide."

"How'd we ever afford a big house?" Bob said, disparagement in his voice.

Blaine gazed into his eyes, so pale blue, then lowered his gaze. *Oh God, I wish I had been forthright with you from the start. Do you want a mansion? We can have a mansion if you want, buddy. You want a Corvette? Yours. Maybe a Porshe instead? No problem. But now there's no way to tell you. Just today while you slaved away at work, I just lounged around the house here, worked at my desk a little on* Julius Caesar *and now I'm several thousand dollars richer. Bob, I make at least three thousand dollars a day. Every day. Hurrah for me, right?! And you don't really have to work, either, but how can I tell you that now?!* "Well, uh, my *Romeo and Juliet* submission," he said. "I might get a little advance if they like it. That might be a thousand or so."

"Well, having a kid a big house would definitely be better. We could fence in the back yard, have a sandbox, and swings and all…"

CHAPTER 27

There was much to think about as the weeks rolled onward in their comfortable pattern.

Saturday evenings Bob would go out on a date or just out for a few, while Blaine went to one of the three local gay bars, or, on occasion, to one of the more than two dozen gay bars in Tampa. Now and then, especially when Blaine would be driving so far, Bob went with him, which pleased Blaine—to bask in his physical glory and be the source of envy to many.

Sunday was the day they did something together. Blaine would arise early, go to Mass, then read the paper and drink his coffee until Bob arose about ten. At first the white sands and the warm green waters of the Gulf of Mexico drew them to it every week. As time passed, the other summer attractions of the area exerted an equally strong pull: a Minor League game, the Ringling Museum, horseback riding, the Asolo Theater, pick-your-own tomatoes, or corn or beans. Sunday was a day full and together.

One morning in the first week of the school year, Blaine had failed to set his alarm clock and was frantic about being late for school. Bob, having already showered, was naked and shaving at the common lavatory. As his razor removed the white foam, he noticed in the mirror that Blaine's hand yanked the towel behind the curtain to dry. His modesty amused him. *You can sure tell you weren't in the Marines, but then you have reasons deeper than a little shyness, huh?*

The curtain opened and the mirror reflected a slight Blaine with beige towel tightly secured around the waist. As he was rushing out of the bathroom, something around his neck glinted to catch Bob's eye. He snapped around. "Wait a second!"

"What, Bob?" he said, pausing. "I don't have time!"

"What are those?" he asked.

"What's what?!" There was annoyance in his voice.

"Around your neck."

"They're…they're dog-tags," he said, turning again.

"Wait!" he shouted. "*Whose* dog tags?"

Bob approached and, towering over him, reached out, lifted the shiny metal and read his own name. "What the fuck you doing with my tags!"

"I, uh…" Blaine stammered.

"Yeah, I really like that! Snooping in my things and now my tags are around some faggot's neck!"

"Bob, I gotta go! I'll see you tonight!" he said and slammed the door to his room behind him.

The muscles of Bob's jaws pulsed, his lower teeth bared. "You'd better be-*lieve* you'll see me tonight!" he shouted.

All through the morning he furiously moved two-by-fours

across the saw's blade. In anger he joined rafters together. Twice his foreman told him told him to slow down, he'd give himself a coronary. Singlehandedly he carried thirty-foot A's across the room.

In the afternoon he began to realize, though, that it did no real harm that another man thought enough of him that he wanted to wear his dog-tags. Any real harm? *Actually it's kinda nice Blaine thinks that much of me. Sweet guy! I'll find a way to apologize.*

On the way home he stopped at a Danish Bakery and purchased a dozen croissants.

When he went in the front door, he saw Blaine sitting in the wing-back chair facing him. He had dragged it across the room to confront the door. There was apprehension on his face, maybe fear.

"Hi, buddy," Bob said.

Blaine did not answer.

"Got you something here. Thought you might like some." He went to him and opened the white box. "They'll be good with dinner."

Looking down into the box, Blaine smiled his jawless smile. "I'm glad you're not still mad because I got some mail today," he said. "William Morrow liked my *Romeo and Juliet*. They're going to publish it if I agree to do ten of Shakespeare's plays. They sent me a contract."

"That's great," Bob said, punching his shoulder. "How much more work do you have to go on *Julius Caesar?* I can't wait to read it, then just eight more."

"Two or three weeks, nights and some on the weekends and it'll be done."

"I'm proud of you, buddy," he said. "And students throughout the country will be grateful to you. Come on, you can have the kru-sents in the morning. I'm taking you out for dinner."

"We can go Dutch."

"Bull! You deserve it and I'm taking *you* out. Where do you want to go?"

"The Herculeneum would be nice."

"No way," Bob said. "I said dinner, not pizza. I'll think of someplace. Let's get ready."

The dog tags were not mentioned that night over Bob's shrimp cocktail and Blaine's escargot, which Bob made sport of. Nor were they mentioned over their entrees of boiled Maine lobster. The tags were never mentioned in the days that rolled on and Blaine continued to wear them.

As Christmas approached Blaine mentioned getting a tree. "No," Bob said. "Let's go to a nursery and get something we can plant outside afterwards."

"But where would we plant it?"

"They're plenty of woods and fields around. There's no sense in killing it. Have you ever read Hans Christian Andersen's *The Little Fir Tree*?"

"No," Blaine said.

"I've got it in my room. I'll get it for you." He did, Blaine read it and was moved by the story of the little tree's pride in being selected, its joy in having people sing songs around it, its sorrow in being cast into the attic, then, come spring, being burned in the yard.

They purchased a five-foot cypress in a large pot from the discount table. Since it looked rather like a western sage bush, the ones that roll and tumble in the wind, it would never have won an award from *Better Homes*. But they didn't care, for it was their tree, the one they selected together and decorated together. On a Sunday in January they planted it together in a swampy area on the other side of Bradenton—leaving on it the popcorn and cranberries for the wild critters to enjoy.

In June they spent a week's vacation in St. Thomas. On their return they found notification in the mailbox that *Julius Caesar* and *Macbeth* were scheduled for publication. There was also a request that *A Mid-Summer's Night Dream* be next.

That same week Bob was promoted to foreman and he decided it was time to trade in his old pickup truck, which was painted now and kept well-tuned. With Blaine's co-signature he bought a new Jeep, similar to the one he had sold in Alaska.

In those months they always found something to celebrate and they filled Sundays with a togetherness—the State Fair in Tampa, the Renaissance Festival in Clearwater, or trying their darnedest to windsurf, or a Bucs game or a performance at the Asolo, or something, always something. Between them there flourished an abundant joy. Things seemed to be going well for them in a simple, uneventful way, although Blaine started to take aspirin for what he thought was a tinge of arthritis.

The last week of July and the first week of August 1982, they took their second vacation together, this time along the Appalachian Trail in Maine. They hiked the verdant woods, climbed mountains more ancient and more gentle than the Rockies, drank from clear mountain streams. They slept under the stars, though on three nights the chill prompted them to sleep in Bob's two-man tent. Only Blaine's fervent prayers those nights kept him from turning to the man he loved. For two weeks and two hundred miles they dwelt in the wilderness.

It pleased Bob that Blaine enjoyed it as much as he said: "The sheer beauty of the world, Bob. The sense of accomplishment and self-sufficiency I got. And the peace of it all. A peace almost tangible. It took a little prodding, yes, I know, but I'm indebted to you for introducing me to it. I never imagined! I can only say, Wow! What an experience! To tell you the truth, for me it was almost a spiritual experience, Bob. A peace present and tangible!"

"The spiritual *is* tangible, Blaine. The spiritual world is the natural world."

"Well, I would like to do it again, or maybe hike the whole thing. Two thousand miles, isn't it?"

"How'd we ever be able to afford that? It'd take four or five months."

"Oh, I don't know. Maybe something will come up."

"Well, better send in for the Irish Sweepstakes, there ol' buddy."

The only mishap they experienced in the Maine woods was Bob chipped a tooth on a pebble in a box of raisins.

Back in Sarasota, as he sat in his dentist's waiting room, Bob started talking with a woman with a polka dot bandanna with straight dark hair streaming below her shoulders. Her name was Lola, an activist in the cause of animal rights. That Saturday he went with her to a Save the Manatee rally and slept that weekend in her condo. He learned she had been an advertising agency executive who simply dropped out when she received an inheritance. Her taste in clothes was gypsy-like—stripes and polka-dots and bright colors. The next weekend he demonstrated with her and hundreds of others against the University of South Florida's policy of buying dogs from the SPCA to use in their medical research.

Afternoons he would go directly from work to her condo, spending both the evening and night. Two or three times a week he would return home about eleven to sleep there. He made a point, though, of meeting Blaine at the Herculeneum after work on Fridays for their pitcher of beer and pizza. One Friday Blaine told him that of course he didn't mind tending Quasi and he was getting pretty good with the vacuum cleaner too.

That Sunday afternoon Bob and Lola sat in the shade of a tree as the horses they had been riding grazed on a knoll. Bees buzzed between the wild daisies and the clover. A family of crows caught the bugs roused by horse hooves. "I love 'em," Bob said gently. "And crows are unjustly vilified. Probably the vilifiers—if that's a real word—are people who have never really looked at them. People have got to learn to look at things themselves and see for themselves. Crows are lovely, intelligent birds who live in extended families, not flocks, families, related by blood. And look there. Some would say those are just common barn swallows, kinda drab. But just look at them, their joy, how they swoop and soar, dart and…and almost turn summersaults in their zeal. Without the flight of birds, Lola, the world would be a depressing place. Unthinkable."

"Agreed. A question for you," she said. "Do you want a

boy or a girl first?"

"It doesn't matter," he answered. "Whatever we're lucky enough to get, I guess."

"Now these things take planning. Now think about it. If the boy comes first, and then the girl, well then the girl has an older brother to look out for her. But if the girl comes first, and then the boy, then you have an older sister with a younger brother, and that's no good. So we should have a boy first and then a girl."

"That sounds fine, I think, but how are you going to direct a male sperm first and then a female sperm? It can't be done, so let's just be happy with whatever we're fortunate enough to get."

"But with the new medical technologies…"

"Lola!" he interrupted, "there are some things out of our control, and there's nothing wrong with that. The world has gotten on just fine without letting parents decide, so we can too. Let's just hope, when the time comes, whatever we're lucky enough to get will be healthy. And let's hope we'll be able to provide a loving home and maybe some brothers and sisters, and a little guidance too."

"Brothers and sisters? How many children do you want?" she said.

"As many as we're capable of loving and providing for."

"And just how many's that?"

"Oh, I don't know. At least three, maybe four."

"Bob, I'm a woman, not a breeder! You'll be damn lucky with two," she said, her voice bristling.

He looked at her—her long dark hair, her dark eyes.

"I'm not a breeder!" she said again.

"I am very well aware of that, Lola," he said softly, lovingly. "Don't think I'm not. But I know what it is to grow up alone in this world, without brothers and sisters. It's not the prettiest thing. So if it happens, it happens, but let's don't willingly choose a lifetime of isolation for a solitary child."

"That sounds just like a man," she said. "You don't have to go through it."

"But that's how the world is ordered, Lola, and neither you nor I can do anything about it. But when a mother takes into her arms her newborn, the pain and travail are forgotten, become as naught, in her overwhelming joy at the new life, the new beginning."

"You men know all about it, don't you!"

"We probably know more than you think," he said softly.

"Sounds like preacher babble to me," she said.

He shrugged.

Meanwhile Blaine was meeting Carl at the Tampa International Airport, for that day, September 23, 1982, was Bob's birthday and he had made special arrangements.

As they walked the long corridor, Blaine said, "I know it's been too long. When Steve left you, you should have come down. You probably could have used some change in scenery."

"But if I had, I wouldn't have met Peter, here," Carl said, his muscles bulging under a loose silk shirt.

Blaine looked at Carl's companion, Peter, a man with fair complexion and dark hair, a recent graduate from Duke

University Medical School. "How many more years of residency do you have?" Blaine asked.

"Two more, then I'll set up practice."

"What are you making your specialty?"

"Internal Medicine for now. From that you can branch out to a lot of 'em."

"We met at Graffiti's," Carl broke in. "Matter of fact it was the exact same night that Steve told me he was getting married to a woman and was leaving."

"What are they living on?" Blaine asked.

"She works as a receptionist in a law firm. And Steve has come a long way—another year and you'll see his picture on all the bodybuilding magazines. I'm still supplying him with the juice, but I didn't attend the wedding. No way would I go."

"It was time, though," Peter said, "for both of them to move on. And we've got a good, mature relationship, Blaine—Carl and me."

"Yeah," Carl said. "It's a lot less strain not having to play lover *and* daddy."

"Well, sometimes you play Daddy," Peter said coyly.

Carl put his arm around Peter's shoulders in a quick hug as they continued to walk the corridor. "Does Bob know anything about his birthday party?"

"No. And party isn't the right word. A caterer is doing dinner and the cake. It'll just be six of us: you two, Bob and Lola, me and Kathy, a teacher in my school. For appearance's sake I invited her to play the part of my fiancée."

"Why are you pretending? It's your home," Carl said.

"It is *our* home. But I don't know if Bob has told Lola

about me. It could be embarrassing for him to have to admit he's lived a couple of years with a queer. Lola might question that, so to protect Bob I asked Kathy. And for Lola, too, I guess, to have another woman there."

"This must be difficult for you," Peter said, "having to watch the man you love leave."

He nodded. "*Difficult* is too gentle a word for it."

The caterer, Bon Appétit, did a magnificent job with the table-side preparation of the Caesar salad, with the Lobster Thermadore and lemon mousse. Blaine tipped the waiters a hundred dollars each.

After dinner the six of them gathered in the living room, where Blaine had Bob sit in the chair of honor, the wing-back chair. Lola sat on the floor at his feet. There he was presented with his cake and gifts. Lola gave him a gold USMC pendant on gold chain, the pendant studded with the red, white and blue of rubies, diamonds and sapphires. Carl and Peter gave him a trial membership in American Fitness. Blaine presented him with a custom made black leather jacket.

As he stood up to try it on, Kathy said, "It makes you look a little like Fabian." They all agreed.

About eleven, Lola said, "Let's dance till dawn, Bob. What do you say?"

"Sure, if you want," he said. He lifted his bourbon, finished it, and said his goodnights and thank you's to Peter and Carl and Kathy. He hugged Blaine for all the trouble he had gone through. "It's the best birthday I ever had. Thanks, buddy," he said.

Blaine stood at the door watching them leave down the stairs. Tears blurred his vision and his chin trembled in spite of himself. He closed the door, braced his head against it, and broke into sobs.

Carl went to him and gently walked him to the wing-back chair and had him sit. He knelt beside it. "But you knew it had to happen sooner or later," he said. "It had to, with his being straight."

"But I love him! I love him, Carl," he said between his sobs.

Kathy, on the sofa, spoke up: "It's just changing, not ending, Blaine. He'll still be around. He's still your friend."

"But I don't want it to change. I love him. Can't you understand I'm in love with the guy?!"

Peter stood up and, holding his Drambuie on the rocks, came to him and put a hand on his shoulder. "You might have to prove that love of yours, Blaine, by letting him go with your blessings."

"I've been telling myself that, but I don't want to."

Carl spoke up: "Why don't we all go out for a few drinks?"

"I want to go out and suck cock—a dozen or two."

"Blaine!" Carl said.

"Well, I do. Big, fat, juicy cocks!" he said.

Outside, as Bob was starting his new Jeep, he said, "It was nice—Wasn't it?—that Carl flew down. And isn't his development awesome?"

"Freakish, if you ask me."

"Lola, it takes an awful lot of work."

"Yeah," she said, gazing out the window into the night.

"It was a nice meal, I'm sure it cost Blaine something. And this jacket here. I'll never tell him, but I don't like black leather, not on me. On other people it may be fine, but not on me. I'll be taking it off as soon as we stop. Where do you want to go dancing?"

"I don't. Take me home."

He looked at her and said okay.

She continued to gaze out the window. "And how do you know people like that?" she asked.

"Well, they're still people, and damn fine people."

"But what's your interest in them?"

"And just what do you mean by that?" he asked.

She smiled, inclined her head, and looked at him from under her brows.

"Cut it out. You know better."

"Do I?" she asked.

He grabbed her wrist, pulled her hand to his crotch. "Rub it," he said.

She tried to pull her hand away. He tightened his grip. "I said fuckin' rub it."

She did and he began to engorge. He released her wrist and both of her hands went over to it.

One afternoon in October they sat on the beach on a blanket

Lola had brought—a purple blanket with meandering waves of beige. As the sun sank low over the waters, waves lapped at the sands with muffled sounds and scented the air with salt. Around them a flock of black and white sandpipers, about two dozen, kept close together as they moved in unison here and there. Bob's head was resting on her lap, while the USMC pendant glistened among the hair on his chest in gold, red, white and blue. He was gazing upward, past full breasts—constrained with a peach-colored bikini—to a single sea gull seemingly stationary in the cloudless sky. He noticed how Lola's hair, so black, glistened with blue, silver, red.

She ran her fingers through his hair, saying, "There's something you should know."

"Don't bother—I've seen the Lady Clairol in the bathroom," he said, chuckling.

"You cad, you!" She smoothed one of his eyebrows. "But several years ago things just weren't right, what with my working for a paycheck at the agency and the policy at the complex I'm in, and so...so I had to have an abortion."

He stopped breathing as he considered that. His brows creased and he sat up. His face twisted with incomprehension. "You what?" he said.

"I had an abortion," she said. "The timing was all wrong. It just wasn't right."

He was looking at her lips as they moved, the lips he had kissed so many times. His eyes lowered to her breasts, full, straining to burst free of her bikini top. *While I was still a stranger,* he thought, *you would offer me those breasts, but deny them to your own child?* Superimposed over those breasts he saw a baby, bloody and still—umbilical still attached, ripped untimely from the womb.

He shook his head, slapped his cheeks. The phantom baby vanished.

He looked into her face and again her dark hair was moving in the sea breeze. Again her lips were moving as she spoke, but only bits and pieces entered into his awareness:

come a long way...

right to determine...

you men...

the timing.

As she sought to explain the logical rationale behind it, he kept seeing what his heart showed him. Before her face lay a baby bloodied and blue and still. It would have been a boy. Never would he learn to catch a football, never learn to drive a car.

He stood up, brushing the sand from his legs.

"Sit back down and listen to me," she said. "Please!"

His pulse was pounding, throbbing. Every fiber of his being wanted to strike her, but he controlled himself. With his voice constrained into a gentleness, he said, "Lola, you need to find yourself another husband, not me." He turned and started down the beach.

"Bob! Bob!" she called behind him, but he walked, at first slouched, but as he went he straightened upright and carried himself with military bearing.

Then later, as the expanse of white sand between them lengthened, his shoulders began again to stoop. His head inclined. "Bob!" came her voice behind him. *How I wish I had that child.*

He walked, yet coming from behind was the thudding of

running feet. He stopped, stood and watched her approach.

Breathing heavily, she grabbed his arm and raised a finger as if lecturing: "Now Bob, women have had enough of you men…"

He shoved her hand from his arm. "Shut up and listen to me! First, the Constitution gives you every right to do as you wish."

"Cor-rect!" she said.

"Second, as a person you have the right to do as you wish."

"Also correct. My body!"

"That is not the issue, Lola. You forget that I have a right and *also a responsibility* to select the mother of my children. *Our* children, but they're not going to be yours, baby!"

She slapped him.

He stood silent a moment, immobile. There was the gentle crash of little waves onto the shore, the screech of seagulls. He lifted the pendant over his head. Gently he spoke. "Take this back" —placing the pendant of gold and precious stones in her hand— "I don't need it. And my children deserve a mother whose heart overflows with love and not a heart fixated on herself. Good luck, Lola. And *Ciao*." He turned and began to walk.

Duped. I was duped! So vocal in her concern about animals, yet brutal to a helpless child. Over the life of a child her pampered convenience is more important. That's bullshit! Absolute! Bullshit! Might be legal but it's wrong. Speak of hardness of heart?! What type of mother has a hard heart? Not the mother I need for our children.

Although he had on him the seven or eight dollars a cab

would cost, he had to walk, needed to. He did not go up to the highway to call a cab. He went along the beach, shirtless, barefoot, thinking. Sure, in high school he had heard of medieval marriages of convenience, but had he ever heard of any society, anywhere, that sanctioned murders of convenience?

As he crossed the bridge over the intercoastal waterway, a baby boy, bloodied and dead, went before him. He stretched tiny arms back toward him, calling to him, *Daddy! Daddy!* How could the angels in heaven explain to that newborn and make him understand that no, the infant had done nothing wrong, it was just that another had judged the timing to be inconvenient.

I could provide for that infant, guide him.

Traffic passed him by as he walked onward four miles to home.

He let himself in and discovered Blaine had the kitchen strewn with every dish, pot and utensil. Napoleon was sitting on his shoulder and Quasi on the floor watching him. A cookbook was open to meatballs and spaghetti sauce. Bob went to the refrigerator and popped open a beer.

"Where're your shoes?" Blaine asked.

"On the beach, I guess," he said.

"Oh," Blaine said.

Back at the counter he noticed that Blaine had a shoebox of seashells on the dining room table. Blaine had named their dining room the Treehouse, the name harking back to Bob's first comment on seeing it. And that box of shells. They had collected those together. *You were going through them and remembering. Weren't you, guy?*

"Come over here, boy," he said to Quasi, who hobbled to him, his tail wagging, and his tongue drooping from the side of his mouth. He lifted the beer to his lips, drank, then squatted to pet his dog. "I'll take you jogging after dinner tonight, okay?"

"He's already been out for a walk," Blaine said. "So I take it you'll be home for dinner tonight?"

"Well, he can go out again. And yeah, I'll be here from now on, if you don't mind."

"Mind?! Of course not. But, uh..." he said, but cut the question short.

"It's off," he said, standing. *The only good thing,* he thought but did not say, *is she told me about it now, rather than three weeks from now when it would have been too late: What type of wife or mother would a murderess make, buddy? So self-absorbed and selfish. So well-known among animal activists, yet she herself doesn't have a single pet, not a dog, not a cat, not a bird, not even a fish.* He watched as Blaine, silent and unquestioning, resumed his amateur attempts to roll meatballs.

He walked to the sink, washed his hands, and with them still wet went over to him. He took a small quantity of meat, and quickly rolled a ball. "You've got to do them fast and with your hands wet. That way you don't give the fat in them a chance to melt."

"I wish the cookbook had told me that. I've been trying to roll them for at least ten minutes. And that's all I got. What? Seven of 'em?" He went to the sink.

"We'll get them done in no time," Bob said.

Together they stood at the counter and rolled meatballs,

silent.

When the bowl was nearly empty, Bob said, "I just decided she would make neither a good wife, nor mother. That's all."

"But something must have made you start thinking that."

Bob considered if he should tell him, and knew Blaine—so devout in his faith—would condemn her. He wasn't going to murder her with his tongue. "Just things about her past made me reevaluate. That's all."

"I see you gave her back the Marine Corps pendant."

"Yeah." He took the last bit of meat from the bowl to roll it.

Blaine looked up at him. "Bob? I'm sorry," he said.

"Aw. Lots of fish! I'm just glad the rings she had me put on lay-away are still there. I'll be able to get my money back, or at least most of it."

"They're certainly magnificent rings."

"Out of my league. I never should have agreed to those rings and only those rings. I'm just a working man. I should have seen her selfish side then. Convenience and comfort are the priorities in her life, and all else and everyone else be damned. That's not what my children deserve in a mother. I'm just glad I saw it now."

After an excellent supper of spaghetti and meatballs, he jogged the trails with Quasi for the first time in a month. Then he and Blaine saw the Rambo movie, then went to Sergeant's, one of the three gay bars. There, on a barstool, as men mingled and chatted, Bob mused if he would ever find love.

"There are good women out there, Bob," Blaine said. "Just don't push it."

"Do you remember you called her a blithe spirit when you first met her? Well, blithe spirits aren't substantial enough to make a good mother. I wouldn't take a blithe spirit to wife."

"Bob, you're still young. If you had a child now, you'll just be in your late forties when high school graduation time comes around. You don't need to push it."

"Yeah," he said.

CHAPTER 28

On a Sunday morning three weeks later a pounding on his door awakened Bob. "Come on! Get up!" Blaine said from behind that door. "We've gotta get to Sanibel Island!"

"What?" Bob said in the voice of sleep. He wiped his eyes and sat up in the bed. He pressed the pillow behind him. "Come on in."

Blaine, dressed in sweater and slacks, entered. "There's this school of whales, Bob. And they've beached themselves during the night. I just heard it on the radio coming from church. Come on! Let's go!"

For two hours Bob drove his new Jeep and while still miles away circling helicopters pinpointed the location. Once there they joined others already in the labor. They poured water on the whales from buckets. They pushed and tugged, tried to dig sand away from under them.

Many came, some took pictures, some joined in for a while and left. A dozen or so labored unflaggingly, Bob and Blaine among them. Throughout the morning Bob gradually learned names: Carol, a redhead, and Sandy, a chubby blond beautician; Josh, a lifeguard who was an inch taller than Bob and just as handsome, though a few years younger and with a much deeper tan. He had one of those rare, natural physiques in which every muscle of his abdomen stood out clearly defined, although he told Bob, "No, I never work out. Don't have to."

In mid-afternoon, a dozen newspaper and radio and television reporters arrived. Blaine waded over to where Bob was digging sand from under a whale. "Look who's here," he said.

He looked up to the beach and saw Lola—in slacks, silk blouse and wide straw hat—coming down from the road. He watched with shovel in hand as she began to give interviews. Smiling lopsidedly, he looked at Blaine and said. "Only words, buddy. She's great with the words," he said. "But she ain't got no heart. Come on, we've got things to do." They resumed the labor with shovel and hands digging away sand.

"We're getting nowhere," Blaine said. "You've got to organize this, Bob."

"What do you mean?"

"Why don't you and Josh get everybody to work on just one whale and just assign five kids to douse the other five with water. If we all work on just one at a time, we might get somewhere."

"Okay," he said, "I'll see what Josh says."

He waded over to speak to Josh, and together they organized the effort.

After an hour the two dozen who labored managed to free

a whale. Cheers went up along the beach while those in the water hugged one another indiscriminately. Arms went around shoulders. Groups gathered in mutual hug. With joy they saw her swim out into the Gulf, about fifty yards, and pause there, flapping her tail onto the water, apparently in signal. *Maybe the others will listen*, Bob thought. She loitered there, meandering back and forth. *She's waiting for them to heed.*

Suddenly she was charging the beach, two tons of strength and life.

With frantic splashings arms and legs scurried out of the way as she again beached herself on the sandbar. There was a hollow thud.

White sea foam loitered around her and slowly dispersed.

With stunned expressions people looked at other people, then at her, at the other whales, then back into uncomprehending human eyes. Those who had labored so hard started going to the shore, and those on the shore began to leave.

Slowly Bob walked over to her, stood gazing into her eye, then knelt on the sandbar, resting his head on her. "Look," he said, "we will get you *all* out. You won't be all alone out there. We'll free all of you. But we have to do it one at a time. Can't you under-fuckin'-stand that?!"

"Bob," Blaine said from behind him, "I'm exhausted and chilled to the bones. I'm going up to the beach to rest a bit."

He nodded. As Blaine left the water, with renewed vigor — as if making up for his absence — he commenced his efforts anew. He noticed that less than ten remained in the water. He now labored with Carol, Sandy, Josh and a few others. He noticed Blaine sitting on the beach, a blanket around his shoulders and another man, husky, sitting on the sand beside him. Ten minutes later they were nowhere to be seen. He continued to labor, his skin now a bright red with sunburn.

A line of black thunderheads over the Gulf hid any sunset that evening. The thunderheads were headed toward them, fierce fall thunderstorms. Yet the tide was coming in now, bringing with it hope among those few left that it would assist their efforts. The tide also brought in purple, jelly-like, man-o-wars whose tentacles stung legs, arms, torsos and whose arrival drove from the water all but Bob.

As darkness descended, he alone continued to labor. He drove his Jeep onto the sand and used his headlights to illumine them. But then the rain came, the wind and the thunder. Heavy drops were cold on top of his sunburn. The rain gave way to hail, which finally drove him to abandon the attempt. He huddled behind the steering wheel as chunks of ice danced on the hood and as jagged lightning bolts angrily lit the sky, the water, and the whales.

There were still whales beached there on sandbars, still six of them, though one of them, the largest—they had decided hours previous—was already dead. The efforts of the day had done no good. The surf crashed around them now as they lay there unaided. Lightning bolts streaked the sky. The hail again gave way to a heavy battering rain, which, in the headlights, formed a slanted curtain between him and them. *The storm, the waves and the tide have come to aid you. Take advantage of it. Do it! Do it now!* He leaned forward that he might witness them do for themselves what they had tried to do all day.

He strained to see them do it.

He needed to see them do it.

The thunder boomed. The waves crashed on the sandbars, crashed against the whales and onto the beach.

He got out of the Jeep, the heavy cold rain bulleting him, then sheeting off him. He walked until warm waves crashed first against his leg, then his chest, then only his legs again. He knelt on the sandbar and plunked his head against a whale's. He tried to encircle her with his arms. Time and again the water surged against him, splashing into his eyes, making them burn, the taste of salt in his mouth.

Then he stood in the darkness and the storm to gaze into the large unblinking eye. Illumined by the headlights from the beach, the eye gazed back at him.

He looked at the other dark forms as lightning blazed forth. Now and then white sea foam surrounded them.

He went up to the beach. The labor of the day had been in vain.

He was haunted by their eyes, which watched him from the darkness of the highway as he drove the hundred ten miles, the first of it in fierce storm. He could not identify, though, what it was about their eyes that so troubled him.

He arrived home a little before midnight to find Blaine sitting at their Tree-house table in his Chinese robe of blue and white, Napoleon on his shoulder. Papers and thick hardbound books, one of them *The Complete Plays*, were strewn on the glass table. It had not stormed here, the light from the dining room lighting up the oak trees just outside the windows. They greeted one another and Bob crossed the living room to the kitchen, where he opened the refrigerator.

"I got a ride home with Allan," Blaine said. "I'm sorry, but I was just exhausted."

"Who's he?" he asked putting a package of cheese slices and a jar of mayonnaise on the counter.

"You know, the waiter at Red Lobster. He didn't come up to the apartment, though—he needed to get ready for work."

Blaine's rationale puzzled him, the rationale that needed to tell him whether somebody had or had not come up to the apartment. That didn't need to be spoken. He looked at Blaine closely. Even from the kitchen he could see a dark red hickey on his neck, the first he had ever seen there. He didn't mention it. He fixed himself a cheese sandwich, ate it standing in the kitchen, then poured a glass of milk and took a package of chocolate chip cookies from the cupboard.

As he sat at the table, dunking cookies in milk, he asked, "How's *King Lear* coming along?"

"Fine. I'm approaching it from the standpoint of the essence of personal dignity. I think it's one of Shakespeare's best. I just wish I had directed this one. I'd have better insight having done that degree of scrutiny. Some scholars poo-poo it with its impetus arising from Lear being willingly hoodwinked by the degree of flattery or lack thereof. But Bob? That's academia for ya! Never a dull moment!"

He chuckled, then laughed aloud.

"Oh, the whales were the lead story on the eleven o'clock news. Lola was interviewed in her straw hat, and you could see you and me in the background."

He nodded as a cookie disintegrated slowly in his mouth.

"Would you mind rubbing some Calamine on my back? It's awful sore with sunburn, and the man-o-wars don't help anything either. I can get the front, just the back."

"Sure I will," he said.

Bob got the bottle from the bathroom and stood there as Blaine's hands rubbed the pink lotion gently, caressingly, in circles on his back. It was cool just as the rain had been, and Blaine's hands were warm, as the surf had been. "Back at the University of Colorado," Bob said, "I had this professor who taught that whales, as warm-blooded mammals, had once been land-dwellers, who, for some reason, had returned to the sea about the same time dinosaurs became extinct."

"Yes," Blaine said, his hands tracing pink circles on Bob's back. "That's the accepted theory."

"Well, it may be farfetched, but is it possible that the whales' beaching was an attempt to again live on land?"

"Wow! I never heard that," Blaine said and knelt to apply the lotion to the back of his legs.

"And did we, the well-meaning rescuers, actually interfere with their evolving—to again dwell on land? Could it be, Blaine, that they are evolving further? Is that their destiny?

"And their eyes. Those are not the eyes of some dumb brute. They tried to communicate with me with their eyes. I'm certain of it. You know the recordings Jacques Costeau sometimes has on his show? Well, what if those songs are not just a strange melody, but a fully developed language? He thinks so. Perhaps whales have a language in which, in poetry and song, they capture their watery world with ballads about freedom and the high seas, and lullabies about domestic scenes, the little ones swimming close to their mother's side, and dirges about harpoons and ships and being hunted."

"Bob. We need to seriously put our heads together and work out some way for you to go back to school...Turn around and I'll get the front for you," he said.

"That's okay. I can do it. Thanks."

Blaine capped the bottle and handed it to him. He took it without turning around and headed across the living room to the hall that led to the bedrooms.

At it he paused and turned around, aware he was fully erect, his boxer style suit standing out as if a child's arm were under it. "Well, I guess we did our best today," he said.

"We tried," Blaine said.

"Yeah, we tried. Goodnight, buddy."

"...Goodnight, buddy," Blaine said.

He went down the hall, closed the door behind him. He spread a large towel on his bed and took his journal from the nightstand drawer. With his back against the headboard and a pillow pressed behind him, he lay on the bed and made an entry, slowly, laboriously, thinking, then writing, then thinking.

Whether whales have a language or not is beside the point. I know they tried to communicate with me with their eyes — sad, knowing, loving eyes. They have, from my observation, at least two concepts, that of self and that of others. And since they tried to communicate from self to others, then they have other concepts they wish to communicate. And so they are intelligent, sentient and conscious.

The implications of that are staggering.

For what if we humans are not the only sentient beings on this earth? What if science should one day prove that whales are fully conscious and sentient beings, with their own world, a world vastly different from ours? Just imagine how that would change mankind's exalted place in this universe.

Perhaps, for that matter, perhaps all God's creatures are conscious, each in its own way. And if that is so, it makes mankind's place in this world so very much smaller. And it makes our responsibilities in it so very much larger. Such is a humbling thought, and a fearsome one, lest we be held accountable for our ignorance and our arrogance.

What nursery rhymes do whales teach their young? What epics do the old ones sing? What tales could a spider weave? What psalms a flower? Perhaps the glories of the world are of such a magnitude that eye hath not seen, nor ear heard, nor the mind imagined its true glories. Perhaps the very stones cry out in praise.

If I could pray, I would pray just such a prayer, that such be true.

The next evening, Monday, he started reading again his worn copy of *Moby Dick*—this time paying close attention to the extended digressions concerning whales.

Two weeks later as they were wandering a mall, he happened upon a recording of whale songs. Now and then on a Saturday evening, when Blaine was going out and Bob just wanted to stay home, he would turn out all the lights and lie on the floor with Quasi beside him. In the dark he listened to that recording and tried his darnedest to understand the songs whales sing.

In mid-November each of them took three vacation days and

added them to a weekend in order to fly up for the dedication of the Vietnam Memorial in Washington, DC. The black scar in the city of white marble awed them, and the names, the endless names, faceless and anonymous names. Bob located a dozen of his buddies: Robert W. Pitts, from Dallas, who played short-stop with them. Juan Melendez, a whiz at chess. LCpl Stemmle, Lt Loomis.

They spent that afternoon in the quiet dignity of Arlington National Cemetery. "Did I ever tell you," Bob said as they waited for the Changing of the Guard at the Tomb of the Unknown Soldier, "that I was on one of the Marine Corps posters?"

"No," Blaine said. "Do you still have it?"

"I did have one, but it got damaged in Nam. It was of me and a couple other guys at Present Arms—that's saluting. One of the recruitment things, you know?"

"I'm sure they've got it in their archives somewhere," Blaine said. "Why don't we see about getting a copy?"

"Do you think they keep those things?"

"I'm sure going to find out," he said.

That evening they dined in the restaurant President Reagan sometimes frequented. They were there as Eric's guests—a student of Blaine's from his first year teaching and now an attorney. Tom, his lover, had recently left him.

The next day they visited the National Gallery, where Blaine explained the symbolism in late medieval painting— things such as the depiction of a dog symbolized fidelity, a mirror signified vanity and a finger raised heavenward meant the Presence of God. Bob was fascinated with the Gallery and by the transition from medieval stiffness to the realism of

Renaissance painting. Though he never fully understood what Blaine meant by the term foreshortening, he appreciated the advent of perspective in the works, and he appreciated how the traditional symbolic depictions continued on with renewed vigor. In masterpiece after masterpiece, Bob pointed out to Blaine the raised finger, their symbol for the Presence of God.

Then it was two days at the Smithsonian, where twice it was only closing time that pried Bob away from the displays of natural history.

That Christmas they again strung popcorn and cranberries and again garlanded a potted cypress. This time they added pine cones and red silk poinsettias, and white doves fashioned of feathers. On Christmas morning Blaine discovered Santa Claus had brought him an IBM computer.

"I just figured it'd make your Shakespeare series easier to do," Bob said. "And if you take this thing here and slide it slowly over a page, it'll copy the words into the machine. That way you won't have to type out the entire play. Or that's what they tell me anyway."

Bob received a state-of-the-art stereo system, an electric typewriter, a ream of paper, John Gardner's *The Art of Fiction*, and a framed Marine Corps recruitment poster.

Over Christmas morning coffee and Danish, Bob said, "If it's not too hard to learn, would you show me how the computer works. And if you don't mind, may I use it for term papers and all?"

"Then you'll go back to school!" Blaine shouted.

"I'm thinking about it, buddy," he said.

"Excellent! I couldn't be happier! And read the Gardner.

It's good. In it he explains that fiction is the only art or science in the world whose subject matter is human emotion, emotion both great and small."

And things continued to go well for them, in a quiet, settled way, as between them there flourished a friendship that equated to love. They never ran out of things to celebrate—Bob receiving a raise, a report of no cavities at a dental checkup, Blaine having a Letter to the Editor actually printed, both of them mastering the sport of windsurfing. Even the purchasing of new carpeting for the living room called for a celebration.

CHAPTER 29

"Hello, Mr. Shirer. I am Dr. Michael Levy. Dr. West has sent me your lab results, your bone scan and the pathologist's report on the bone marrow. Won't you please have a seat?"

They shook hands. "It's not good, is it?" Blaine asked as he sat. Behind the desk were many framed documents.

"No, Mr. Shirer, it's not good. But your mental attitude will go a long way in helping you cope with this. How old was your brother when he was diagnosed with bone cancer?"

"Forty-four."

"And you are..." Dr. Levy said, flipping through pages in a manilla folder.

"Thirty-six."

"And your grandfather?"

"I don't know exactly," Blaine said. "In his late sixties."

Dr. Levy made notations. "I've been in contact with colleagues at Duke University concerning your brother's case. I will need his complete medical record. As you are leaving today, will you please sign the consent for the release of those records?"

He nodded. "How long do I have?"

"No one can tell you that. It depends on how aggressive the cancer is. And there are several chemotherapy treatments we can try and radiation as well. But everybody responds differently. How well you will respond, no one can foretell. And yours, Mr. Shirer, is a genetically transmitted disease. The cancer has been dormant in your genes your entire life, and now something has triggered it. If we knew what, we could possibly figure out a way to counteract it. But medicine is many years away from figuring that out. The best we can do is seek to kill the affected cells, but in the process we will also kill healthy cells."

"You don't sound very encouraging," Blaine said and forced a smile onto his jawless face.

"Would you rather I paint you a rosy picture?" Dr. Levy asked.

"No," Blaine said, dejection in his voice.

"Your attitude, Mr. Shirer, is vitally important. You have a disease process going on in your body. But you are neither a leper, nor an outcast. You are still the same person with the same personality, interests and heart. The disease affects only your body, Mr. Shirer, not your soul. Are you a man of faith?"

"Yes."

"Good. Lean on that faith now. Take care of yourself. Sleep well, eat well, get some exercise. Enjoy the good things. Share everything I've told you with your wife."

"I'm not married."

Dr. Levy pursed his lips, and flipped to the first page in the folder. Silent, his dark eyes gazed at Blaine from under dark brows. "Are you a homosexual?"

"Yes."

Dr. Levy took a deep breath and held it. "There are a couple additional blood tests I'd like to run. One's an ELISA, the other the Western Blot. Of course you have heard of the epidemic in the gay community. Well, the CDC has a new name for it, AIDS. Maybe that's the trigger for your cancer. Let's find out."

"Okay."

Dr. Levy made a notation in the folder but paused midway and looked up. "But uh, aren't you a teacher?" he asked.

"Yes. High school English."

"Well, on second thought, we don't want those tests. With the hysteria among the public, there's no telling what the legislature will do and those tests are diagnostic. Instead, let's just get the T-cell Subsets. That alone will give us a pretty good idea without being diagnostic. And we'll have the results from that within a couple days instead of waiting two weeks or more."

"Okay," Blaine said, looking at his hands in his lap.

"I know your diagnosis is a severe blow to you, Mr. Shirer. Do you have somebody special in you life?"

"Yes."

"Well, share it with him. Tell him everything I've told you. Two shoulders carrying a burden make it lighter. And I promise I'll do everything in my power to work with you in overcoming this. And if that's not enough, I'll refer you to where they are conducting experimental treatments—Duke University and the Mayo Clinic. And your attitude, Mr.

Shirer, once again your attitude. When the shock has worn off, cultivate a positive, hopeful attitude. Lean on your faith and your friend. Take good care of yourself and enjoy the good things." He went on to say a nurse would be in to draw a blood specimen and to have him sign a release for his brother's records. He was to make an appointment for the first of the week at which time, after the doctor had reviewed Raiford's record and had studied thoroughly all of Blaine's tests, they would discuss treatments.

"Can I call in a couple days to find out about the AIDS?" he asked.

"Of course, but ask to speak to me directly."

"Okay. Thanks, Doctor."

"Sure."

The next evening he took Bob out for dinner, with the intent of telling him in a public place. Though the drinks were strong, the dinner good, and the chocolate mousse delicious, he could not bring himself—lest it upset Bob too much—to inform him.

On Thursday he called Dr. Levy, who told him that the T-cell Subsets were completely normal, that there was no reversal of ratio, that he did not have AIDS in addition to his cancer.

On Friday after their beer and pizza, he went to a mall where he bought three hundred dollars worth of vitamins. He lined them up on the kitchen counter, and told Bob he could have some if he wanted.

In the weeks that followed, he accompanied Bob to the gym in the complex. Bob showed him how to use the equipment and explained what muscle groups were affected.

Several times a week he would attempt to jog with Bob and Quasi, though his first time trying he only got two blocks. Within the month, though, he was jogging a mile and a quarter, and saying he enjoyed it. Bob told him he was pleased that his interests had broadened to include the physical.

Around the first of May he was nominated Teacher of the Year and Bob went with him to the banquet at the Hilton in his honor. For appearance's sake, Blaine technically went alone, with Bob escorting Kathy, though they did manage to sit side by side on the dais.

The next day the newspaper dedicated a two page spread to Blaine, his educational philosophy and his Shakespeare series. They printed two of his Shakespeare drawings, and a page each from his introduction and his prose retelling. They reproduced two pages of Julius Caesar with his footnotes.

Accompanying the long article was a sidebar in which testimonials by some of his students were presented. He had inspired several to become teachers themselves. A couple wanted to become writers. Blaine was proud of those, but most proud of what two of his students in a slow group had to say:

"Why can't we have more like him? He's a teacher, man. He knows what's important to us and don't talk down."

"Can't skip no more. Might miss somethin' 'portant. And hell, even watched *Midsummer's Night Dream* on PBS last night. It's funny as hell, man."

Toward the middle of May, as his cancer worsened, he would dress mornings to give Bob the impression he was going to work, but then either return to bed, or to Dr. Levy's for another dose of chemotherapy. In the last week of May he managed to get to school only one day.

That same afternoon he drove out to the Department of Education where he offered his resignation to the superintendent, who refused to accept it, and directed his secretary to put him on extended leave of absence.

All this he kept secret from Bob, as if by doing so he were protecting him. On June the sixth, though, he called Bob's work number, waited for him to be summoned and informed him that he had been hospitalized.

Within twenty minutes Bob was at the hospital and in his room. In his blue and white silk robe Blaine was sitting up in an easy chair and reading a magazine. "Oh my God!" Bob said. "I thought something horrible had happened. What are you here for?"

"Have a seat. There's something I've been meaning to tell you, but didn't know how."

"It's not AIDS, is it?" he said, sitting.

"No. You know my brother died of bone cancer…"

"Oh my God, no!" he said, jumping to his feet.

Blaine nodded and his jawless chin trembled, but he stilled it.

"Well has the doctor been in yet! What does he say? Is he certain?"

"Bob, I've been seeing an oncologist for months. And please sit down."

He did.

"The reason I'm here is for pain control and a different

type of chemotherapy. The pain is horrible, like…It's like a sadist has gotten inside me and pours Drano into the marrow of my bones where it burns and bubbles and froths. And he's inside me and so there's nowhere to run. It's horrible. I started out with Vicodin, then went to Tylenol #3. I've just had a dose of Roxanol, a fast-acting oral morphine. And they want to start me on MS Contin, which is a sustained release morphine."

"And so the vitamins and the health kick, that was all part of this, wasn't it?"

"Yeah," Blaine said.

"Why the hell didn't you tell me then?"

"I didn't want to upset you."

"Bullshit! That's bullshit!" he yelled, and buried his face in his hands.

"I knew you'd take it like that," Blaine said softly.

"Well how the hell am I supposed to take it!"

"Bob, I'm in God's capable hands."

"Is your doctor the best?"

"He comes highly recommended, and if the Platinol does not give a positive result, he is referring me to Duke University Medical Center for experimental treatment."

"You ain't no fuckin' guinea pig, buddy!"

"Bob, just calm down. It's okay. 'Cast all your cares upon Him, for He cares for you.' And that's exactly what I've done."

"Well, we're going to beat this thing. Together, you and me, we're going to beat it!"

"I sure hope so. But either way, it's okay. The hardest thing is the impending loss of all those things and those people that, over the years, have been there, and that, in some way, I have used as points of reference to define myself to myself. The interactions or the presence of them—I don't know what. But when you're stripped of everything, how do you define yourself? That sense of loss, Bob!...That's what's hard. Am I making any sense at all?"

"I think I understand, like being in snowstorm without a compass and you can't see any of the landmarks. So you're lost and don't know what to do."

"I guess," Blaine said. "But I'm sure God understands our need for reference points, and has worked that out someway so that—though we may foresee the loss of self and our reference points—we don't actually experience that loss. Somehow the reference points continue. Don't ask me how, but He is a loving God and a wise One, and He understands the human heart. So He's got that worked out someway too."

Bob sat on the arm of Blaine's chair and said reassuringly, "You don't have to talk like that because we've going to beat this thing, Blaine. What's your doctor's name? I want to talk to him."

"He said he'll be here this afternoon between five and six. You can talk to him in person if you want to come back then."

"Come back?! Hell! I'm staying!"

He stayed for the rest of the morning and through the afternoon, and talked with Dr. Levy in Blaine's presence for some time. He stayed until nine o'clock when a woman's voice on loudspeaker announced the end of visiting hours and asked that, for the benefit of the patients, would all visitors please leave quietly.

Back home he jogged briefly with Quasi, then took him

back to the apartment, and alone, jogged furiously in the dark for over an hour and a half. As exhaustion overtook him, the first tears steamed down his face to mingle with the sweat.

Upstairs again, he wrote a letter to Mr. and Mrs. Shirer, informing them of their son's condition. He drove to the post office that night and mailed it, then called Carl in Atlanta.

The next day when Bob arrived at the hospital after work, he found Carl there. Together he and Bob—Carl in muscles and tank-top, and Bob in his work clothes—kept vigil at the bedside. The doctor zonked Blaine out for the intravenous administration, over eight hours, of Platinol. For days afterwards Blaine was nauseous and vomiting. After a week Carl had to return to Atlanta.

Somehow word of Blaine's admission got out, and now and then a teacher from school would visit. Twice the superintendent visited. When the newspaper ran a short article in the continuing news section about the Teacher of the Year undergoing treatment for cancer, the room was flooded with flowers, cards and students. After a few days, though, Blaine asked that the nurses not allow the students to visit for it was not appropriate for them to see him like this.

Every day Bob visited after work, and on weekends he visited twice a day, from eight until eleven in the morning, and again in the afternoon from three until eight. The Platinol did not have the desired effect, and on June 30, 1983, Bob took leave of absence, without pay, to accompany him to Duke University Medical Center.

From there they flew to the Mayo Clinic, where Bob pushed Blaine's wheelchair from the airplane to the awaiting ambulance.

They returned to Sarasota on September the first, Bob to his job, Blaine—now shriveled and emaciated—to the Terminal Care Ward in Memorial Hospital. It is a ward set up much like an Intensive Care Unit, with only curtains between the beds. But there, unlike an Intensive Care, there would be no heroics, neither resuscitation nor intubation, in the event of cardiac or respiratory arrest.

Blaine's first day there, he asked Bob to bring in his computer and papers. "I need to finish the last in the Shakespeare series. And my books, too, especially the Kittridge. You know where everything is, don't you?"

"Do you think you should be tiring yourself out with that stuff?" he asked.

"It's almost done. And they've got the pain controlled pretty good now. *Hamlet* will be the tenth in the series, and that's what the contract was for—ten plays."

"Well, I'll ask the nurses if I can."

"I'm sure they can work it out somehow!" Blaine flared. "It shouldn't be that much of a problem. Oh, you'll need to pick me up a new sketching pad, too."

Bob brought everything the next afternoon, and with the help of the nurses set up the computer, books and papers on three additional over-the-bed tables.

Within five days *Hamlet* was complete, and Bob carried everything back home. He xeroxed three copies, and mailed one to William Morrow Publishers.

Muscular Carl again flew down from Atlanta, this time accompanied by Peter, the MD. On the night of their arrival, after visiting hours, Bob took them out for a late dinner. He told them he had written to Blaine's parents twice, and asked if Carl knew whether they had received the letters. Carl said he didn't, but he himself had called Mrs. Shirer. Her response was that whenever Blaine called them and wanted to come home, they would fly him by air ambulance to Seven Oaks Nursing Home. Peter stayed only two days.

Carl stayed four days longer. As Bob was carrying Carl's suitcase down the stairs, Carl asked how much they paid in rent.

"Four hundred," Bob said, "but then there's the electric and water and renter's insurance on top of it."

"You can't really believe a place like this costs only four hundred a month!"

"That's what Blaine told me. But I suspected all alone he knocked a couple hundred off of it to make it palatable to me."

"Bob, it has to be four, five, six times that much a month."

"But he's just..." His words trailed off.

"He's rich, Bob. Filthy rich."

"He never hinted, or let on, Carl, or anything."

"He didn't want the size of his wallet to put a barrier between you. As long as I've known him, he's kept it a secret. I think I'm the only one who knows. Not even the employees at Graffiti's know he owns it, or half of it. He never wanted his wealth to be an enticement to some people or be a barrier to others. You know how people are."

❧

A couple weeks later Sofonda drove down—calling from Jacksonville for Bob to wire her money to get her transmission fixed. He did and she visited Blaine in the hospital twice, but only twice. Yet for over a week she stayed in Blaine's room, performing in the gay bars, and dragging home, night after night, a different trick. After eight days Bob told her she had to leave.

Bob continued to visit Blaine every day and on weekends twice a day. Toward the end, though, he had to force himself to the hospital. That made him feel guilty, his not wanting to go. But going gave him such feelings of helplessness, to sit there day after day, no more than a witness to the horrible wrenchings of pain. And even on better days, to sit there, searching desperately for something to say. He was ashamed of himself for not wanting to go. He should, after all Blaine had done for him.

But regardless of that, he went.

Day after day he went, forcing himself—if, for no other reason, than to keep Blaine from giving up hope.

CHAPTER 30

When the whistle at the Jim Walter Corporation blew quitting time that momentous Friday, Bob waved his crew goodbye. Then he walked around the large, deserted room checking the yellow tags attached to the saws for any that were scheduled for routine servicing. He gathered the time cards from the holder and took them into the cubical that served as his office. There he initialed each of them and locked them into the top desk drawer.

He looked at the note which lay on his desk. Untouched by his hands and unmoved from its spot for two weeks now. Again he noted how uncanny was the handwriting, each word flowingly penned in liquid ink, each letter perfectly formed and spaced, with curlicues and tendrils and embellishments. Only in display cases at the National Gallery had he ever seen such handwriting. It was the handwriting of a monk with cowl pulled over head, a monk from a simpler, unhurried age, an age filled with pealing bells, incense and candles. Only once had he read the note, a request from one of his men to talk with him privately. He had read it only once, and, his skin in goose flesh, had carefully laid it back on his desk, unanswered. The note frightened him, and he held its writer—Reggie, the new man that Human Resources had hired—with a distant awe.

There was something about Reggie that had an unearthly quality, a timelessness. His translucent, perfect complexion and piercing eyes evoked the recollection of the Italian Renaissance paintings in the National Gallery. Blaine had pointed out those artists had three subjects—portraits, mythology, and the apparition of the Divine. To Bob's eyes, Reggie could have been resurrected to life off one of those canvases.

Never once had he seen him shoo a fly or slap a mosquito. By midmorning the shirts on the crew would be drenched dark with sweat, all except Reggie's, who never seemed to break a sweat. Even at quitting time his appearance would be as fresh as if he had just stepped out of the shower. There was a strangeness to him. Bob avoided him.

Again he left Reggie's note unmoved by his fingers as he stood up to leave for the weekend. He turned off the wall unit air-conditioner, opened his door, and slid a wastebasket in front of it to keep it open for the weekend cleanup crew.

Outside, all the men had departed in their cars and vans, all except Reggie, who, in the gravel parking lot, was jumping up and down on the starter to his motorcycle. A cold shiver ran up and down Bob's spine as he crossed quickly to his Jeep. Hired three weeks previous, Reggie had initially hitchhiked to and from work, but with his first paycheck had bought a used motorcycle. He alone among the men rode a motorcycle, and he, good-naturedly, took a lot of kidding about that:

~

"Ooh, wanna be a man, huh?"

~

He took a lot of kidding from the crew about his youth and his beardless complexion.

~

"Come on, kid, how old are you really?
Fifteen, sixteen?"
"Naw, I'm nineteen."
"And me and Jim's a hundred."
"More than that between us."
"Gotta remind me, huh?"

~

His black leather jacket did not escape comment.

~

"Wow, kid, sure scares me!"

~

As Bob inserted the key into the ignition, Reggie got the cycle going, its rumble loud—like the quaking of the earth and the crashing down of buildings. He circled over to Bob's Jeep. Just feet from him, his black leather jacket glistened with stars against the night sky. As he spoke, his eyes—unblinking and glinting with an unearthly light—pierced into Bob: "I'll buy the pizza and we can talk."

"Can't," Bob shouted over the rumble of the motorcycle.

"Okay, I'll see you later," Reggie said, revved the engine, and pulled from beside the Jeep.

Ordinary, he thought, just a young kid with his first job,

trying his best, and trying to get along with the seasoned crew. He'd probably love to tell his girlfriend he shared a pizza with his boss. He watched in the rearview mirror as Reggie circled the lot toward the highway.

He had to stop for a break in the traffic. Bob studied him in the side mirror, then turned around to look. Neither Reggie nor his cycle cast a shadow. *That can't be!* He opened the door and partially got out to look. He could see no shadow.

As Reggie slowly began to ease into the traffic, he raised his hand in wave, his index finger pointing gently upward. *And the finger raised heavenward in this painting and the last three? Well, that's the symbol they used for the Presence of God.* Reggie kept his finger raised as he vanished into the traffic.

Through rush hour and start-of-the-weekend traffic Bob fought his way to Memorial Hospital. He parked and took the elevator up. The double doors to the Terminal Care Ward squeaked on their hinges behind him as he entered, passing the nursing station, nodding to a nurse as he went, and going to Blaine's bed. He was apparently asleep, which was good, for it gave him some time to assemble a mental list of things to talk about. He pulled a chair beside the bed and sat.

The rails were up, pillow and sheet soaked with sweat. Even in sleep, dark circles lined his eyes. His arms, never large to start with, had shriveled until they were now but twigs. The fine, blondish-reddish hairs on his arms had beads of moisture on them, like dew on spider-webs.

He thumbed through *The National Geographic* he had brought up from the Jeep, looking at some of the pictures: Carob beetles, Pueblo excavations, the ruins of Pompey. Then he closed it and listed for himself things to talk about. His raise. Reading Blaine's *Hamlet*. Quasi's shots next week.

Suddenly Blaine's arms jerked and his eyes shot open, face twisted. His arms, suspended in the air, started to quiver. The quivering turned to shaking, the shaking to convulsing. Bob leaned more and more forward, silent and helpless in his inability to help.

Every muscle and sinew of Blaine's neck and arms stood out, till, at last, his eyes rolled upward into his skull and he collapsed limp into the sheets.

Bob stared as Blaine now gasped for air. He stood, took a couple tissues from the box and dabbed the sweat from his forehead, an act he had done a thousand times before—at least a thousand times by now. "Are you still on a hundred milligrams of morphine, buddy?"

"God, I can't stand it anymore," Blaine said, opening his eyes and looking at him. "How much longer? Bob, how much longer?!" He sobbed.

Bob leaned over the bed, looking down. "Don't give up. Do you hear me? Just don't give up," he said.

"And give up what!" he flared. "What's left to hold…" Again pain wrenched him, twisted, convulsed.

"Nurse! Nurse!" Bob shouted into the quiet of the ward. One hastened over. "Look, look!" he said, pointing at the bubbly froth oozing out of Blaine's mouth, down his chin.

The nurse put a hand on his arm, squeezing it. "We can't give him any more yet. There is such as thing as respiratory arrest, Bob. There is nothing we can do. I'm sorry," she said.

He looked at her—her short gray hair, her eyes framed with silver frames. He bit his lip and nodded. As she returned to the desk, he took a couple tissues to cleanse the froth from his buddy's chin, but instead followed the nurse out.

"Nurse, a moment, please?" he said.

"What can I do for you, Mr. Newell?"

"There's this thing, called a, uh, a PCA Pump. Have you tried that?"

"We did. It failed. Blaine's a redhead, Mr. Newell, not flaming red, but red. And there's something with the genes of redheads that prevent opiates from having the same effect. That's why even injections have such limited efficacy on him. I'm sorry."

"Sure," Bob said and returned bedside to dab sweat from his friend's brow. At last Blaine's breathing quieted and he seemed to rest. Bob sat. A beeping started somewhere in the large room. He looked and saw the same nurse go to the IV machine four beds down.

Blaine opened his eyes, sunken, dark-circled, bloodshot, and looked at him. He raised a finger heavenward and parted his lips as if he intended to speak. Whatever thought it was, though, eluded him, and he frowned, apparently trying to remember it.

Bob cleared his throat. "Oh, the raise I was supposed to get, well I got it in today's pay. It's not that much, only seventeen dollars after taxes, but it's something, I guess."

Blaine was silent, his red eyes on him, but then his gaze slowly drifted toward the ceiling. He leaned his head back on the pillow and, with a faraway look, stared at the ceiling. "Do you see the clouds, how beautiful they are? See the funny one that looks like an elephant?"

Weeks ago a nurse had told him that it would be best that he not play along whenever Blaine hallucinated. "Blaine?" he said tenderly. "That's just the morphine, buddy. There are no windows here, so there are no clouds." Through the bed's railings he took Blaine's hand.

Blaine looked at him, incredulous, then again at the ceiling and squeezed Bob's hand. Whether he still saw clouds or not, he did not say.

"Oh, your *National Geographic* came in yesterday's mail. I put it on the bedside table for you."

He nodded. "Didn't somebody tell me it's Friday?" His words were weak. "You don't have to sit there, not on a Friday, you big lug."

"Hey, stop talking dumb, okay?" He reached his left hand through the bed rails to hold Blaine's. His right hand went to rest on his shoulder.

For some moments neither spoke, until Bob—sitting back in his chair—said, "Oh yeah, *Hamlet*." I read your *Hamlet* last night. I laid down on the sofa, with Quasi on the floor and Napoleon on the back of it, you know, and read the whole thing—introduction, retelling, text, footnotes and all. Took me until three A.M. But I understood it. I sure liked it a lot better than when we had to read it back in high school. A lot of kids, buddy, are counting on you to get out of here and help them through that stuff."

It was silent except for the same IV pump four beds down, which again beeped and beeped.

"Bob?" Blaine said, averting his eyes.

"Yes?" Bob said.

"You've got to help me," he said, his left hand sliding across the bed toward him.

He took it, small and bony. "Sure. Whatcha need,

buddy?"

As his hand clasped Bob's tightly, as his bloodshot eyes looked directly into Bob's, he raised his right hand to his temple and put the index finger against it. In the gesture of firing a pistol, he lowered his thumb, pulled the trigger. "Kill me," he said.

"What?! What did you say!"

"Please—kill—me," he repeated, each word separate.

Bob's mouth gaped open. He stood up, and busied himself with adjusting the sheets, grasping the top one, flapping it out, making it billow like a parachute, and slowly descend, then tucking it gently around shoulders and neck. A condescending smile came over his lips. "Sure, buddy. Whatever you say," he said. "Why don't you get some rest now, huh?"

"Please. Bob?"

"You don't know what the fuck you're talking about!" he flared.

"But I can't do it myself. Somebody's got to, because I can't."

"Do you think after months and months of going through this stuff with you I want to hear THAT SHIT!"

"But Bob?" he said, his voice weak. "Remember the whales? They knew, and in spite…"

"Damn the whales! You've got to beat it! *You've* GOT to!"

"But Bob?" he said, tears streaming down sunken cheeks.

"You get that sissy cop-out shit out of your head. Right now! You hear me?" He pointed a finger at him. "And you just keep fighting it, and punching it, and fighting it, till you win. I'm leaving. And you THINK about it. I'll see you tomorrow." He turned sharply to the doors.

"No. Wait. Please!" Blaine called after him, his arm lifted inches off the bed in pleading.

The double doors banged against their stoppers behind him. With his fist he hit the elevator button, glanced at the floor indicator, and as he waited immobile at the doors, legs spread, head squared on shoulders, he slowly pivoted his head to gaze back at Blaine's bed. "God damn you, Blaine Shirer! Fuck!" he said. He clenched his jaws, and stared at the elevator's closed doors. *Oh, if I could turn back time, could redeem it, could change the past and heredity. Oh, to become a kid again and wear Mickey Mouse ears, the ones Blaine and I bought last summer and wore all the grand day at Disney World. Or the day we chuckled and jabbed one another in the ribs in the House of Mirrors at the State Fair in Tampa.* He sighed, got into the elevator. *Oh, to go windsurfing again, or canoeing on one of the lakes.*

Without noticing he crossed the lobby and the parking lot. Surprisingly, he already stood at his jeep. He got in and drove.

Yes, they did have a good life, and had always found things to celebrate — paydays, Napoleon's learning a new phrase, the start of a school term, its midway point. Even something as mundane as purchasing new flatware for the kitchen called for a celebration. Together they celebrated the common and negligible milestones of one life, of the other, of the life they shared together. They celebrated, until Blaine's illness struck, anyway. He couldn't go home, not now, not the apartment they shared, used to share.

He found himself at the shopping center that housed the Herculeneum Italian Cafe where he and Blaine would meet on

Fridays while the men he worked with gathered at Mario's to start the weekend. He parked and walked toward it, knowing he would find murals painted on the walls, the eruption of Vesuvius, the Colosseum, Nero playing a violin while the city burned, Christians tied to stakes as lions gouged them and crowds cheered. Parked directly in front of the door on the sidewalk was a motorcycle.

He entered, and Reggie, munching a slice of pizza, tilted his head upward in greeting and called out, "Mr. Newell?" He was in a booth under the scene of Christians and lions, wearing the same clothes he had that day leaving work, black leather jacket and camouflage military pants. Bob went over to him and sat.

"Strange, bumping into you," Bob said, his voice lifeless and without resonance.

"I haven't been here too long," Reggie said with the joyous vitality of youth. "After work I had to go down and pick up a little something for my mom, and today was the first day I could, being payday and all."

Bob nodded, looked at his hands, folded and resting on the table. He said nothing.

A waitress came up and asked if he wanted a menu.

"No, just a draft."

"What flavor do you want?"

"Doesn't matter," he said, looked up at her and smiled. As she left he looked at his hands. He raised them, slowly turning them over, studying them.

"I want to thank you," Reggie said, "for taking me on and giving me a chance. You're a pretty good foreman, fair and all. And I've done okay so far, haven't I?"

Without looking up from his hands, he said, "Yeah, you're working out fine."

"You know, Mr. Newell, I guess I can tell you now—I lied on my application. I never had a job before, not a real full time job, I mean. And uh, I'm only sixteen, not nineteen. But uh, I lied because, well, you know. There're seven of us kids, you see, and Dad's been sick a long time and Mom's just gone in the hospital."

"Don't worry about it," Bob said.

"Thanks," Reggie said, and silent, watched as Bob stared at his knuckles, then at his palms. "Are you okay, Mr. Newell?" he asked. "Is anything wrong?"

"Wrong?" he said. "I'm just wondering what these hands might do." The tips of his fingers were still malformed from clawing out of a bamboo cage. "Hands can do a lot of things, Reggie, like building. Like destroying."

"Want some pizza? I can't eat all this, and besides I don't have lots of time."

Bob shook his head no.

Reggie finished the slice he was munching on, then said, "Whatcha think?" He took from a side pocket of his military camouflage pants a rectangular white box that he placed on the table. He wiped his hands on his pants, then took from it a deep blue and white scarf, which he flapped out and proudly displayed. "I got it for my mom."

Bob glanced at it and at the draft just then being put in front of him. *Blue and white,* Bob thought. *Blaine's robe is blue and white.*

Reggie continued, "Dr. Holtz says the operation was too late. That it's all meda...medasized, or something like that.

Anyway it means the cancer's all spread. And she gets sick to her stomach a lot and her hair's falling out from the stuff they give her. She's all self-conscious about that, you know. So I thought she'd like a scarf."

Bob nodded and, looking directly at him, said, "You're lucky to have your mom....And she's lucky to have you, Reggie....But I'm getting pretty damn fucking good at being robbed of all those tender and common things." His chin quivered.

Reggie frowned. "Mr. Newell, if you want to talk, we can."

"Thanks, Reggie," he said. He cleared his throat, straightened himself up in the chair and shrugged.

"Whenever I had something bothering me as a kid," Reggie said as he folded the scarf, "I could always go to Alex. That's my older brother. He's in the Army now. That's where I got these pants. Anyway, just by talking with him, things weren't so bad." He raised his eyebrows in coaxing.

Bob did not respond, but watched the drops of water that had formed on his mug. They were like the drops of sweat that beaded on Blaine's forehead.

As the waitress passed by the booth, Reggie asked her the time: 6:15. "Oh no, wow!" he said. The waitress asked if they wanted their checks. "Yeah, I've gotta have mine."

The waitress tallied both checks and put them on the table.

"Wish you'd finish the pizza for me," Reggie said. "I can't, you see, because I've got to go, Mr. Newell. Katie— That's one of my sisters. She's seven, my princess.—is in this little dance recital tonight and I've got to get her there early so she can practice, then stop off at the hospital and give my

Mom the scarf. And then I've gotta get back in time to watch my princess dance. You know how much stuff like that means to a kid."

Bob studied that beardless, unblemished, translucent complexion, those sky-blue eyes, the leather jacket. "Don't fool yourself, Reggie," he finally said, "not just to a kid, but to grown-ups too."

"Well, maybe," Reggie said as he picked up his check.

"Give Katie a hug for me after the recital," he said. "And remember moments like that, Reggie, those tender and common things."

"You can come too, if you want, Mr. Newell. But if you do, you've gotta promise you'll clap real long and hard. That'll make my Katie smile."

"No, I can't. But your being here's helped."

"It has?" he said, a chuckle in his voice. "But I didn't give you any advice or anything. You didn't even tell me what's bothering you."

"You'd better hurry, Reggie. Your sister's depending on you to get her there. And that is a sacred trust—that depending and that being there to be depended on. You must not fail your sister," he said, a resonant intensity in his voice.

"Yeah, I've gotta go," he said, sliding across the seat.

"And Reggie, I now know what I've got to do. Thanks."

"Okay, if you say so," Reggie said. "I'll see you when I'm supposed to, I guess. Bye, Mr. Newell."

Bob nodded and watched him leave. His wave was again with finger pointed gently heavenward. Again the back of his leather jacket glistened with light, like stars against the sky.

Bob picked up his beer, looked at it and put it down. He

listened to hear the rumble of Reggie's cycle. He paid his check at the register.

Outside he thought it strange the cycle was gone, though there had been no rumble.

He drove to the apartment to let Quasi out, telling him to hurry about his business. Then he went to his bedroom and lifted from the nightstand drawer his chrome .38 caliber. He stood at his closet wondering which of his jackets had inner pockets, and took his black leather jacket. He didn't like it, but today it seemed appropriate, and besides, Blaine had given it to him. The mirror reflected his image clothed in blackness, and that blackness catching light in its folds and reflecting it—just as Reggie's had—like stars against the sky.

In the kitchen he pawed through drawers until he found Quasi's veterinary record. He put it in plain sight on the counter. He filled Quasi's dish with food, changed the water, and checked the amount of seed in Napoleon's cage.

At the door he called Quasi, who moseyed up the stairs, glanced up at him as he passed and hobbled on toward the kitchen. He stopped midway, turned and looked quizzically at him, motionless at the door. His tail started wagging.

"No, we've not going out now, boy, but come on over here." He knelt on one knee as Quasi limped toward him. He hugged him, telling him he was a good dog and a damn good friend besides. "I'm going to miss you, boy," he said, then stood up as Quasi sat down at his feet, his dark, loving eyes upon him.

Napoleon came strutting proudly across the floor, jabbering *Pretty-bird, Have-a-good-day, Want-some-coffee, Pretty-bird, I-love-you.* He strutted over to Quasi and climbed up his back to the top of his head. Once there he spread his wings in what Blaine always called his eagle imitation. Bob smiled at the sight of the two of them. He stood. "That's right, you are a pretty bird...and Quasi's a good dog."

Standing there, he talked to them, long pauses between the thoughts. He told them people would come tonight or in the morning....The people would take them away....He told Quasi not to get his hopes up about a new family, maybe one with kids to play with. "It won't happen, boy...People only adopt pretty dogs...pretty and young....But you are a good dog....And both of you have been real good friends....Thanks, and I mean that...But there's a sacred trust, you see...A dependency...But dogs don't understand big words." The door closed quietly behind him.

At the hospital he waited at the nursing station while a priest, sitting in a chair, conversed with Blaine. Yet even in the presence of a priest pain seized him, twisted, convulsed him. The priest stood up, called for a nurse and watched as she held a cool cloth on his forehead. The pain abated; the nurse left; and the priest made signs and gestures over him, sat, talked a moment longer and also left the bedside.

Bob went to it, standing at the foot. Blaine was mumbling the Rosary, the beads held on his chest, his fingers working them.

"Hi, buddy," he said.

Blaine opened his horrible eyes. "Hi," he said.

"Hi," Bob said again.

Eyes fastened on eyes, lingered there.

"Are you going to?" he asked.

He stood there without answering.

"Bob—are—you?" The words were separate.

"Yes," he said and unzipped the leather jacket part way and took the gun from the inner pocket. He dangled it limp in front of him for Blaine to see. Its chrome glinted with the same starlight as did his jacket.

Blaine nodded and closed his eyes. "Thanks, you big lug. I was happy with you."

He put both hands on his chest, covering the Rosary, and was silent.

So long a time, the wasting away, the pain, Bob thought, *but how am I to say goodbye? What words were there that would say it?* "Uh...Think of Horatio's speech now, buddy," he said. "His saying goodbye to Hamlet. 'And flights of angels.' That one."

He sniffled once. "They were friends, remember?" he said.

Then with both arms outstretched, he aimed the gun. And, in a voice hesitant and choking on the very words, said, "And flights of angels, buddy...sing thee...to THY REST!"

The gun was discharged twice.

Blaine's head flopped to the side.

CHAPTER 31

Throughout the nursing unit persons hollered and shrieked. Bob slumped to the floor and someone pinned him there with a knee in the small of the back and his arms behind.

Five minutes later he was handcuffed.

After detectives had taken their statements and forensic photographers had snapped their pictures, he was escorted away by a uniformed officer on either side.

When the elevator opened into the lobby, Bob saw a man standing there dressed as Bob was, in black leather jacket.

Reggie's mouth fell open.

"Oh, Reggie!" he said and shrugged.

"Move out of the way, kid!" the officer on his right said.

"He's a friend!" Bob said. "Can I just have a moment!?"

The officer on his left denied his request. "No! Move it!"

Bob pulled back as both officers tugged on his arms. "Just one moment, that's all!"

"Move it!" from one. "Now!" from the other.

As they pushed and shoved, he struggled against them. Craning his head around, he called out behind him: "Reggie! Tell 'em I won't be in anymore, will ya!? And oh yeah, my dog!... Please, officers!"

"Keep moving!"

"My dog, Reggie! You don't know of anyone!....Officers!... He's an old dog, but....Of-fi-cers!"

As they shoved him through the hospital's electronic doors, Reggie's form behind him — glimpsed by Bob, unnoticed by others — seemed to dissolve into a twinkling of stars. Only wall remained where he had stood.

From Public Records

Bob's public defender, Mr. Glenn Padgett, informed him that the SPCA had placed Napoleon with an elderly couple living in an efficiency in downtown Bradenton. Quasi they put to death by lethal injection. "And just who do you think is going to adopt an old, three-legged mongrel?" Mrs. Raznian had asked.

In time the public hoopla died down and the newspapers published fewer Letters to the Editor on the matter. The public outcry was to arise two more times in addition to the uproar when the murder occurred: at the trial and at the appointed time. The case was a *cause célèbre* for special interest groups: for the Moral Majority, for gays, for groups of Vietnam veterans, for those supporting euthanasia, for those opposing the death penalty. It was not a *cause célèbre* for Bob.

In his trial Mr. Padgett tried as defense the heretofore unsuccessful principle of euthanasia, mercy killing. The prosecution, however, argued Bob had been motivated by a greed and an avarice and a lust for Blaine's trust fund. And although the judge consistently upheld the defense's objections and ordered questions and innuendoes stricken from the record, the jury—those eight women and four men—took bits and pieces of innuendo to fashion a specter: Two men—one rich and homely, Blaine, and one poor and handsome, Bob—would, alone in their apartment, writhe together, night after night, in perverted and unholy passions.

Three weeks after their verdict of guilty, another jury—again eight women and four men—sat for the penalty phase of the trial. After hearing both arguments and the judge's sage instructions, they assembled in a paneled room, took one vote, and returned to the courtroom, death on their lips.

Judge Nathaniel Carlyle lambasted the jury. He told them he regretted their decision, that Bob's guilt had never been at issue, the whole trial was over the extent of that guilt. And here they go, those eight *fine* ladies and four *outstanding* gentlemen, and reach a decision regarding life in prison or death in twelve minutes, the shortest on record. He dismissed them with the wish they would be able to sleep at night.

He turned to the Prosecutor and said he took umbrage at the prosecution's cunningness in the conduct of the trial, and, immediately following, he and his whole team were to report to the judge's chambers.

Judge Carlyle then had Bob stand. Saying he was constrained by law to follow the jury's recommendation, he delivered the sentence of death, adding, "God go with you."

While he was incarcerated, appeals were presented in his behalf, though none of them found any technical difficulties with the proceedings. The defense was adequate. The judge allowed all admissible evidence and struck from the record all inadmissible hearsay and innuendo. The judge's decision to prohibit testimony both from Mrs. Shirer and from Mr. Carl Gagen was appropriate. His instructions to the jury were full and proper.

And even though the higher courts by mandate seek the full application of justice within law, none of them overturned.

It could have been because Reagan was in the White House, or because of the pendulum's conservative swing, or because of the natural superiority of the Righteous. In any event, as grounds for appeal became exhausted, the governor signed the Death Warrant. When he did, Bob was moved, per protocol, from his cell to one in Q-wing where those about to die watch the clock.

There, in the clutches of the State, Bob watched, for weeks, the slow jerk of the second hand on the clock above the cell monitor's desk. He watched its slow jerk forward to the appointed time, and there was nothing in all this world he could do about it. It would take a miracle, and a simpler age when people believed in miracles.

To the eleventh hour public funds were used in an attempt to stay the hand. Even on the eve of the appointed time— April 4, 7:00 A.M.—two legal thrusts were simultaneously made: One, that Judge Carlyle had erred, for the testimony of Mr. Carl Gagen would have dispelled the innuendoes the prosecution had weaved; and Two, that the jury for the penalty phase had abrogated its duties because they had not deliberated the issues, but had taken one vote, voiced the word death and returned to their jobs and homes and pastimes.

Even on the eve of the appointed time, these other attempts were being made, behind Bob's back, though he no longer cared. In the clutches of the State he had given up hope.

Housed for weeks within concrete walls, without even a glimpse of the sky, he laid down his will to survive — the will that had provided a woodland home for him and his dog, the will that had delivered him and his squad from the Viet Cong, the will that had stood by him in his downward spiral as he trekked from place to place.

He laid down that will, and simply wanted to die with a tiny mite of dignity, and that was pretty hard under the arrangements that had been made for him.

CHAPTER 32

Florida State Prison, Raiford, Florida.

Shortly after supper time on his last scheduled evening, Father Joseph Schiller, a chaplain at the prison, came to visit him. Over the years of his incarceration they had become friends. Now an Episcopal priest, Father Joe had formerly been a Catholic priest, who had found himself unequal to the Church's demand for celibacy. He left the Church, married and had taken vows in the Episcopal. He now had a wife, Anna, and two daughters, Helen and Elaine, six and four. He also had a rambling farmhouse, circa 1920, that he was gradually fixing up. He wasn't a good carpenter, but was learning.

As the cell monitor unlocked Bob's cell with a key, Bob noticed Father Joe's thumb was no longer bandaged as it been for the previous two weeks. He entered the cell and Bob stood up from his bunk to go to him. They shook. "I thought you forgot about me today," he said.

"Just awful busy," Father Joe said. "I'm not on the clock

now. I just wanted to see you."

"How's Anna? The girls?" he asked.

"Fine," Father Joe said.

Bob moved the book he was reading—Whitman's *Leaves of Grass*—from his bunk to the stainless table and gestured for him to sit.

He did. "They're fine, Bob," he said, repeating himself, then added, "There was quite a ruckus yesterday though. Anna took the girls through the fields picking wildflowers. And it seems there is wild asparagus on the land. She says it's too late this year for any, but next year."

"Wild asparagus isn't really wild," Bob said. "It's the exact same plant as the cultivated." Bob sat on the bunk with him.

"That's right," Father Joe said, "you're a backpacker, so you know those things."

"Was a backpacker, Joe."

Father Joe cleared his throat. "Anyway it seems Elaine, that's the youngest, stepped on a board with a rusty nail. Anna says she doesn't know what was worse, Elaine's bawling or her own panic. The doctor gave her a tetanus shot and the nail didn't go all the way through, just punctured the skin, you know?"

"Yeah," he said, the hint of dimples on his cheeks.

"Oh, I brought you a pack of cigarettes," he said, taking them from his pocket.

"Thanks," he said, taking them. "But you don't have to bring me anymore. I'll make this my last pack."

"Oh, Bob!" Father Joe said. "Last night after the girls went to bed, I had a long talk with Anna about you. She sends her love. But even after all these years, I couldn't tell her how you had lost your faith."

"That's okay. I never told Blaine. It's too painful."

"But it would help me understand a little better," Father Joe said.

"Why do you have to understand, or dissect me or analyze? Can't you just be my friend?"

"I am. But you have rejected, uncompromisingly, something I hold precious and I would like to know why. But I won't preach. We're not clergy and laity here. We're friends. So won't you tell me?"

"Lose my faith, Joe? Tell you about it? Hmm?" he said. He grabbed the slender gold plastic strip on the pack of Winstons and pulled it off. With thumb and index finger he carefully tore the silver foil. "Lose my faith. You've used that term several times over the years. I'll tell you but let's get one thing straight from the start." Anger was beginning to flare in his voice. "I did not lose my faith. I did not misplace it. I did not waylay it! It was stolen from me with violence! Driven out of me! And good riddance!"

Father Joe leaned away from him. "Bob? I think it best we not pursue the subject. This is your last night on earth. There is some…some volcanic trauma behind what you say. Let's let it lie, for your sake. You don't need to tell me."

"No! You've asked! I won't get into all the details. Like you imply, conjuring them would tear me asunder. So," he chuckled, "I'll give you the Cliff Notes version."

He fell silent, then said, "I wonder if I could have ordered a six-pack for my last night. I didn't. Don't know if it's allowed or if they would have provided it. But I wish I could have a few cold ones right now." He laughed. "Just being honest, Joe. I like beer. Or did."

He noticed Joe's smile and his nodding. *A good compadre,* Bob thought. "Suds. That's a funny word for it. Could use it in a piece set in the '30s or '40s. Would be appropriate then, but not in a contemporary story, except for a comic character in a comic scene. It'd work then. *Bubbly* is another good one."

"I think I could get *three* cold ones sent up for you. I think that's the limit."

"No, don't bother…Getting back to what was driven out of me…I wish I still had that faith, fairytales or not….It'd be something to lean on, Joe. But hell, I've got you! Gotta warn ya, though, I'm pretty heavy."

"Lean all you want, my friend."

"Getting back to it. Again!" And again he laughed, hesitant to actually start. "Well, here goes. You know Rusty, my childhood dog? Well, we were chums, pals, roustabouts, my one true friend. And if God can't help a dog have puppies, what good is He?"

"What happened?"

"That Christmas morning when the good Reverend walked us from the creek to his house and said, 'Oh, no! The dog stays out!' Well, right then and there I should have told him, 'No, then. We're going back to our box. We're doing just fine, Rusty and me. If she's not welcomed, I'm not either.' I didn't say it, but I was just a kid then, Joe. We had everything at the creek we needed. We weren't having any problems. But then of course we had to be careful with the authorities and with the home address for the school and all. But it was okay. Really.

"Then came those years under Rev. Negley's rod and roof. They were years without sports, without friends, without dating, without pocket money for a soda. To this day I don't even know if they sold popcorn and hot dogs at the football games. Nobody ever said." He sniffled. "Those years were years of school books and Scripture, Joe, of cleaning the church, cutting the yard, of going calling in the evenings and five church services a week. I read the Scriptures at every one. And instead of the woods and meadows and fun that we had on the creek—Rusty and me—she got a fenced-in yard. The whole big world contracted down on us. Negley's *Straight and narrow*. Ha! His straight and narrow is a picture of hell! People need space, Joe. Space to be themselves. 'We are Christians, Bobby. Instead of friends, we have brothers and sisters in Christ. Instead of heathen frivolities, we have the Lord's work to do.' Ha! Bunch of subhuman bullshit."

He noticed Father Joe slid his arm forward on his thigh to glance down at his watch. "I'll speed this up some or try to," he said. "Anyway, Rusty's pregnancies were troublesome. She lost one litter when I was still with Pa and another in Negley's garage. This third time was going to be different. She depended on me, Joe, and I was going to see to it. I was in the eleventh grade when all this happened. At the end of church, I stood up, told them about my dog and asked for prayers. They all said they would pray and told me to expect a miracle.

"But I also called a vet and explained things. In exchange for doing some chores, they agreed to help her whelp. That's what it's called, Joe, whelping—a good word. I was all set to sneak out Saturday morning and take her to them. It was

Friday night—the night Jesus was in the grave—and I tiptoed in my skivvies out to the garage to be with her through the night. I spread a canvas tarp on the floor next to her box, laid down and prayed. And I saw Jesus kneeling over her and loving on her, his holy hands caressing her silky red hair. I fell asleep with that image.

"But then morning comes, and has Jesus done anything? I wake up in the earliest gray of dawn and called my girl.

"No paw plopped on my arm, no humid breath on my face. No sandpapery kiss.

"I opened my eyes and stared at the unlighted bulb overhead. I forced my gaze, inch by inch across the ceiling, down the wall.

"Blood blacked the rags of her box, traced circles on the floor. Inches from my thigh she was sprawled out, my girl, my Most Beautiful, Joe. Her hair was matted with dark blood.

"I picked her up. I cradled her in my arms, gently propping her head on my chest. Then I sat back down with her, holding her. She breathed without ebb, flow. Any breath could have been the last. 'Don't, Rusty! Please don't!' I told her.

"At last she opened her eyes and smiled at me. I knew her voice and she said, 'Thank you for everything. It's been real nice and I've had lots of fun. And I'm awful sorry, but I really do have to go now. Bye, Bobby. Bye."

"She closed her eyes and breathed twice more." Bob took a long drag from his cigarette, blew it, crushed it and lit another. He felt his chin tremble.

Father Joe put his arm around him. "What a horrible thing for a young man to endure after all those assurances of prayer."

"That's not it, Joe! That's not the end of the story! It gets worse, a fuckin' lot worse!"

"Bob, you don't have to go on. I hear it in your voice and see it in your face. It's upsetting you too much."

"You're not weaseling out! You asked for it and you're going to fuckin' hear it!...Give me a moment." He sobbed softly to himself. Joe's arm was around on his shoulder.

"Okay." He shrugged. "Stop! Hands off! I'm not queer...Anyway, there I was in my skivvies holding my dead dog, rocking back and forth, but I wasn't going to cry. You see, I had to be strong. I had things to do. And there comes this voice, 'I'm sorry, Bobby.'

"In all the years I had lived with him that was the most loving thing the Reverend had ever said to me. Oh, how I wanted to be held, Joe! I needed it. I needed to be comforted! But did he? Could he?

"HELL NO!

"The good Reverend just stands there. 'The straight and narrow, Bobby, is hemmed in on all sides by Scripture. And that dog had a hold on you, a hold strong and unwholesome and vile. It was your love for her, your attention and devotion that were keeping you back from offering to the Lord your whole burnt offering. And He is a jealous God!' On that he fell silent. A technique he used in his sermons to let things sink in, you know, and let the people apply it to their own lives.

"By strength of will I forced my sobs to quit and wiped the runniness of my nose. I looked up at him from the floor. 'Get out of here,' I said. I stood. I eased my girl gently down into her box.

"I glanced around, and the good Reverend was still there. 'Funny!' I said, 'I thought I told you to get the hell out of here!'

"He was silent as I picked up the box and whispered, 'Come on, Most Beautiful, I'll take you somewhere nice.'

"'The Prophet Isaiah, I believe in the Twenty-...'" he started to say.

"I turn and face him and say, 'You and your prophets can go pray...or you can go to hell...or you can go fuck yourselves! But just get the fuck away from me!'

"'Watch your mouth!' he says.

"I step forward until the box is flush against him and glare down from my greater height. 'Look. Look at her! Some won-der-ful Je-sus! Can't even help a dog have puppies!'

"'Fall on your knees, boy! Beg forgiveness for your blasphemy!'

"I sneer down, say nothing, and take a shovel from the wall."

He wiped his nose with the back of his hand. "I started out."

"'Bobby! This is Saturday! You have a church to mop and wax!'

"I stopped, turned around and yelled back at him, 'You, your dirty floors and your God, can all go to hell!'

"While he stood in the garage door yelling and commanding I carried my girl through the gray fog. Barefoot and in only skivvies I carried Most Beautiful through the streets of Macon and then through the woods to a place of happier memories.

"There, alone, unaided by any, Joe, with blisters and raw flesh and sweat stinging my hands, I buried my girl. Finally, on my knees, under that oak, I prayed one last and final prayer. It was the last prayer ever to pass from my soul to my lips. I prayed that the oak should forever protect the sanctity of her rest.

"Then I stood up and swore I'd never pray again.

"I bided my time. I turned eighteen. On that day I raised my right hand and swore. And I was a Marine, Joe! And I was out of there. Gone! And there was nothing in all this world the good Rev. Negley could do about it."

Father Joe was silent, an ashen look on his face. Q-wing was silent.

Bob fumbled to extract a cigarette from the pack. "Cat got your tongue?" he asked.

"Wow!" Joe said.

"Not a pretty tale, is it? Never told Blaine."

"Wow!" Father Joe said again and looked at his watch. "I called Anna and told her I'd be late. I'll have to call her again and tell her I'll be even later. Thanks for trusting me with that, Bob, but I've got to go," he said.

"Yeah," he said. He stood to accompany Joe.

In silence they waited, side by side, for the cell monitor to come from his desk. On the other side of the aisle were five cells, each cell windowless, each identically constructed, each with furnishings immobile, bolted securely to the concrete of the floor. Against the back concrete wall was a bunk and next to it a seatless commode. Several feet out stood a stainless pedestal table with a single seat attached. In one of those cells, the only other occupant of Q-wing lay on his bunk, black feet extending over the end, wool blanket pulled over his head.

Once in the aisle and as the cell monitor again locked Bob's door, Father Joe said, "Know that you will be in my fervent prayers tonight."

"Thanks, Joe," he said. "Hug the girls for me."

"Sure," he said, and, accompanied by the cell monitor, went to the electronic door. The cell monitor closed it behind him.

Bob returned to his bunk and *Leaves of Grass.*

Unknown to him, people were assembling outside the walls of Florida State Prison. They came in cars and campers in order to be there at the appointed time, April 4, 1986, 7:00 A.M. They came with their placards and their causes. The Vietnam veterans congregated together. Gay activists found the other gays. Those supporting euthanasia formed an enclave, while those opposing the death penalty mingled from group to group. Throughout the evening and night the Highway Patrol watched from their cruisers parked on a knoll and did not prohibit the bonfires.

In Tallahassee someone had a cake with pitch-black icing delivered to the Governor's Mansion, while on the steps of the State Capitol the Ecumenical Council held a candle-light vigil in his behalf. The Second Court of Appeals received a new petition.

And April the Third eased into the Fourth with Bob lying on his bunk with blanket pulled and clutched over his head. Against the darkness of his lids he watched his destiny, as he had watched it every night for four weeks, every night since the governor had signed a paper and he was transferred into Q-wing.

With blanket over head, he watched roots grow down into his coffin, watched water drip and watched white fungus grow on his flesh and his flesh liquefy into sludge. He tossed and turned, and thrashed against that destiny, flailed against it, against entering the blackness, the aloneness.

And into the blackness of his coffin a visage appeared and he again cringed before her, just as he had cringed running naked and crazed and hiding in bushes from her in Nam. Again, the Hag! She laughed so riotously her fetid breath enveloped him in a fog and there she was, like a puppeteer or a clown, dangling puppies from their umbilicals, and Oh! so much fun!

He bolted upright, screamed and ran to the iron bars. He clutched them, out of breath, tears streaming down.

"Hold it down in there!" came a voice.

And another, "You okay over there, Bobby?"

"Yes, Obie. I'm fine...just fine."

He turned to his bunk, looked at it. *No. No. I'm not going there. Not until they lay me in my coffin will I lie down again. No.*

He sat for the rest of the night on his bunk. To the humming drone of fluorescent lights in aisle he cast backward from his destiny to his past and asked himself how his life would have been changed if his mother hadn't died, if his Pa hadn't left. He could have used a little help along the way. But even so, he told himself, he had done the best he could.

How he wished this last, interminable night would pass. He just wanted to get it over with, say goodbye, and do it with a tiny mite of dignity.

The arrangements the State had made for him made that pretty hard. The fluorescent lights continued their monotonous, subhuman drone.

CHAPTER 33

At 5:05 A.M.—according to the clock over the cell monitor's desk—the Chef entered Q-wing with what Bob had requested for his last meal, and which, as a standard security precaution, the Chef himself had prepared. He entered with three cartons of milk and a plate of freshly baked Toll House cookies. Per protocol, he delivered them to Bob himself.

At 5:30 A.M. guards entered his cell with a folding chair and clippers.

Bob put his third carton of milk on the concrete floor and moved from the bunk to sit in the chair. The clippers moved over his head from nape of neck upward, then from forehead to crown. The guard then knelt before him and ran the clippers up and down his right calf. He then stood from the floor and said, "Okay, Newell, if you'll strip now, we'll take you down so you can get all that fleece washed off."

He stood, unbuttoned his striped prison shirt and took it off. He pulled his striped pants down, bent, and as he was taking them off, picked up a small clump of hair from the floor, pressing it, hidden, between thumb and two fingers. He stood and looked at the guard.

"Everything, Newell," he said.

He took off his jockey shorts.

"Okay, Johnson, let us out," the guard said.

Johnson, the cell monitor, bent to unlock the door.

Shaved bald, naked and barefoot, with a uniformed guard clutching an arm on each side, he was walked toward the showers.

"Like your haircut, Newell. On you!" the guard on his left said.

"Cut it out, Bolls," the other guard said, the one who had shaved him.

"Yes, SIR!" Bolls said and chuckled.

He was directed to use the second shower head on the same side as the sinks and was handed a small bar of soap.

As he went to it, Bolls said, "But you can't fuckin' jerk it. We got eyeballs on ya."

"You're fuckin' crude!" the other guard said.

With the lock of hair still pressed between thumb and two fingers, he stood out of water's way as he turned it on and adjusted the temperature. Bending his head and feeling the warmth as it streamed from crown, to cheeks and chin, feeling its caressing line as it streamed down his back, he held his arm down and out of the water's path. He opened his fingers and looked at the light brown lock of hair he had picked from the floor. Even in the light from the fluorescent bulbs overhead, and even at arm's distance away, individual strands of hair bladed the light differently. Some were golden, some reddish, some silver, some pale blue.

He lowered his arm further, till water began to stream down it. The hair, wet now, was darker and of one hue and took on a shininess. The locket dammed the steady push of the water, but then it loosed its grip and fell to the small white tiles. The water nudged it, in fits and starts, toward the drain. Then it circled and circled.

The sudden rattle of a buzzer, like that of a tambourine, startled him and he looked up, straining to hear who wished entry to Q-wing, where no one entered without purpose. Over the splash and pelting of water he heard footsteps in the aisle. He listened. He watched steam cloud around him.

"It's the Chaplain, Newell," the guard said. "The Monitor will let him in your cell. He'll wait for you there. Go ahead."

"Which one is it?" he asked.

"Rev. Schiller."

My friend! I didn't ask him to come. It's too early. He starts work at nine. But he bothered!

Quickly now he lathered and washed. He was rinsing when the buzzer rattled again. He stared at a single white tile on the floor. "Who's that?" he asked.

There were black lines between the tiles.

"The Warden," the guard said.

The water pelted against his shaved head.

"Yeah, Newell," Bolls called to him. "I hear you like readin'. Well, he's going to read ya something will burn your brain right out."

"That's enough!" the other guard said.

"Shit, he's just a faggot and a crispy critter. Hey, Crispy, hurry the fuck up! Wanna watch ya burn."

Mr. Thorpe, the Warden, barged into the room. "I heard that, Bolls!"

"But..."

"But nothing! You're relieved of duties, and don't hold your breath till I convene a review board! You might starve in the meantime. Now, go find Mr. Evans and tell him to send a replacement."

Bob was standing in the doorway, fog from the shower around him.

"But..." Bolls said.

"But nothing. I run a professional establishment here, and won't have garbage like you around. Get out of here."

"Yes, sir," Bolls said and left.

Mr. Thorpe looked at Bob—naked, the shower room behind—then his eyes lowered uneasily to the floor. Mr. Thorpe was a tall, distinguished, once-lithe man, though now he had a paunch. There was gray at his temples and his widow's peak. He was dressed in a three-piece dark blue suit that had small strips of a pale blue in it. His shirt was white, with dark blue tie. He raised his eyes from the floor to look again at Bob. "It's not supposed to be like that, Bob," he said. "I'm sorry."

He shrugged. "You're not responsible for everything that goes on around here, Mr. Thorpe."

"Please tell the politicians that."

The guard handed him a towel which he wrapped around his waist.

Mr. Thorpe fingered his Meerschaum pipe, looking uneasily at it. "I'll see you back in the cell," he said.

Bob nodded. When he was gone, he started to dry, but noticed something he had not seen minutes ago when the guards had escorted him in. A gray suit was hanging from a hook above the bench. He moved to it, and, the towel dangling in one hand, took the cloth, a medium shade of gray, between his fingers and felt it. It was thin and cheap. One eyebrow lowered and the other raised. "Do I have to wear this?" he asked the guard, not looking at him.

"Uh, I guess you can refuse to. The previous nine have all worn it, but I guess the choice is yours."

Considering it, he looked at the guard, into his eyes. His eyes were a deep green. He looked back at the cloth. "You know, for years I struggled hard as I drifted from place to place, trying to find work. I ate mostly beans. Baked beans on a couple slices of bread makes a nice sandwich, especially if you have some onion. But not once in all those years did I ever accept charity. Not even a pork chop or a bowl of soup."

"Would you like me to get you a fresh set of stripes?"

"Is this what they measured me for last week?"

"Yes. It's brand new."

"I didn't know why they were measuring me."

"Would you rather have stripes?" the guard asked again.

"Uh, no. I don't want to look like a bum in there. I understand people are coming to watch....I'll wear it."

Still damp, he dressed in the white shirt, the slacks, the jacket. There was no tie, no belt. Gray dress socks were provided, no shoes.

Once dressed he asked, "What time is it?"

"It's about half past six."

"No, exactly."

The guard looked at his watch. "It's thirty-two minutes past six. We're right on schedule."

"Just ten more minutes, then," Bob said.

"No, it's not supposed to happen till seven."

"But sunrise is supposed to be at six forty-two. In ten minutes the sun will be up, so the birds are already rousing. I know it may sound dumb, but I didn't want to die in the dark. I don't know why—It really doesn't make any difference. That's where I'm going, the darkness.—I just didn't want to leave this world in the dark."

"I understand," he guard said. "Are you ready?"

He nodded.

CHAPTER 34

As they left the shower room, he saw the door to his cell was wide open, something he had never seen before. In it Mr. Thorpe was standing by the pedestal table, studying the chess pieces there. Father Joe was standing farther back, near the foot of his bunk and next to the Jim Beam box. He was dressed this day in black cassock, with buttons from neck to floor. His right hand held the silver cross that hung by chain from his neck. Both of them watched as he approached.

The guard stopped at the door and Bob entered alone. Behind him the door clinked solidly, metal on metal. Mr. Thorpe smiled a sad smile.

"Hi, again," Bob said with a nod to Mr. Thorpe, passing him and going to Father Joe, extending his hand and shaking. "I'm glad you're here. But I'm sorry you had to get up so early," he said.

"Of course I'd be here. And about last night, I need to apologize for my failure to…"

"What?! Apology? For what?!" Bob flared. He tightened his clasp of Joe's hand. "You listened. You responded. You said, 'Wow!' You said 'Wow!' twice. Two times. What else could you say?"

Father Joe looked sadly at Bob then at Mr. Thorpe. "He's my friend, Warden."

"I can see that."

"Bob, I really would have been here earlier," Joe said, his hand still clasping Bob's, "but it was hard getting past all the demonstrators." With his free hand he grabbed the Warden's hand and moved Bob's hand toward the Warden's that he might clasp both of them together. "We're in this together. You're not alone, Bob."

As they shook, Bob gazed into Joe's deep blue eyes, at the tiny crow's feet around them, at the sincerity there—till someone shrieked and Bob flinched and hands were released.

He looked. Across the aisle in a cell closer to the entrance, Obie Swingle had jolted from his sleep, wiping his forehead with the back of his hand. He swung his legs to sit on the bunk, his tee-shirt darkened with sweat. He was the only other occupant of Q-wing, a huge black man, who weeks ago had told Bob his nightmares were spawned by the man-made foam they put in his pillows.

~

"They's s'possed to be feathers in dem and they go and take out my feathers. Why they do that to me, Bobby?"

~

Obie looked at Bob, gave the thumbs-up, and called, "Y'all hang in there, Bobby, now ya hear?"

"Yeah, you too, Obie," he called back.

As Mr. Thorpe continued to look at Obie, Father Joe asked, "What's he in for?"

"A rampage that left behind eight corpses," Bob said. "But he should be in a hospital."

"Do you think he would be receptive if I saw him?" Father Joe asked.

"You can take him a pack of cigarettes anyway. Maybe," he said.

Mr. Thorpe, looking at Obie, pursed his lips and poked a finger absently into his pipe. Then he looked back at the chess set on the pedestal table and said, "Whose move is it?"

"Mine," Bob said. "White."

"Well, then, Black's already lost."

"See what I told you about that pawn?" Bob said. "But don't feel bad. We've played twice and Mr. Thorpe beat me both times."

"Bob," Mr. Thorpe said, "I have something here I have to read to you." He reached into his inner jacket pocket.

"I know. And I have to stand, don't I?" he said as his gaze fixed on the folded bundle of papers emerging into view.

"Yes, please."

As both Bob and Father Joe moved into a position side by side in front of the bunk, Mr. Thorpe took a position directly before them, unfolded the thick sheaf of papers, glanced at it, up at Bob, then to the document. "Warrant of Execution," he said. He looked again at Bob, cleared his throat and began to read in a voice perfunctory and moderately fast:

Whereas Robert Newell did on the 18th Day of November, 1983, murder Blaine Shirer;

And whereas on 17 May 1984 Robert Newell was found guilty of Murder in the First Degree, and was sentenced to death on 7 June 1984, and was re-sentenced to death on 10 July 1984;

And whereas on 10 October 1984 the 2nd Court of Appeals refused jurisdiction;

And whereas on 12 December 1985 the Florida Supreme Court upheld the…"

"Uh?" Bob interrupted.

"Yes? What is it?" Mr. Thorpe said.

"Uh…" *An error! It should be 21 December. But maybe it wasn't on the paper. Maybe Mr. Thorpe just read it wrong.* "Uh? I'm sorry," he said. "I guess my mind wandered. Would you mind starting over again, Mr. Thorpe?"

Mr. Thorpe's lips set into a line and he exhaled audibly. "Warrant of Execution," he said, and as he read it again, read it faster:

Whereas Robert Newell did on the 18th Day of November, 1983, murder Blaine Shirer;

And whereas on 17 May 1984 Robert Newell was found guilty of Murder in the First Degree, and was sentenced to death on 7 June 1984, and was re-sentenced to death on 10 July 1984;

And whereas on 10 October 1984 the 2nd Court of Appeals refused jurisdiction;

And whereas on 12 December 1985 the Florida Supreme Court upheld the sentence of death…"

Again Bob interrupted. "Uh, excuse me?" he said.

"Now what is it?" Mr. Thorpe asked, irritation in his

voice.

There was a typographical error. "Uh..." he said. He hesitated. "Uh?..." *Should I mention it? Would it do any good? If I do, wouldn't that just postpone things a little while? Wouldn't that just make a secretary retype it, and make the governor re-sign it? Would it change anything whatsoever? Wouldn't mentioning it only force me to endure again the slow creep of minutes, creeping again, grain by grain, to yet another final minute? No, I won't willingly endure this again—this pain of watching the slow inevitable approach of the appointed time, and watching it with nothing whatsoever in all this universe I can do about it.* "Uh?..." he said.

Mr. Thorpe grimaced and resumed the reading:

And whereas on 12 December 1985 the Florida Supreme Court upheld the sentence of death imposed on Robert Newell; and certiori to the U.S. Supreme Court was denied on 18 January 1986;

Whereas it has been determined executive clemency, as authorized by Article IV, 8A, the Florida Constitution, is not appropriate;

Now, hereto, I, BOB GRISMAN, as Governor of the State of Florida, do hereby issue this Warrant, directing the Superintendent...

Mr. Thorpe paused, cleared his throat. When he started to read again, he pronounced every syllable, he weighed each word. He transformed it into poetry, weighted and majestic:

> *do hereby issue this*
> *Warrant*

> *directing the Superintendent of*
> *Florida State Prison*
> *to cause the sentence of*
> *death*

Mr. Thorpe cleared his throat.

> *to be executed upon*
> *Robert Newell*
> *on some day of the week*
> *beginning noon*
> *Thursday*
> *the Twenty-eighth*

All meaning was lost in the rhythm of that ponderous and majestic flow, till the chanting stopped. "Signed, Bob Grisman, Governor. Attested, George J. Fielding, Secretary of State."

Bob backed up two feet and plunked onto the bunk. In the silence he averted his eyes to shoes, the table's pedestal, clumps of hair on the floor, his journal visible behind Father Joe's cassock. He averted his eyes to anywhere, lest he look into the eyes of those studying him.

And into that silence—a silence primordial, filling Q-wing from concrete floor to concrete ceiling, a silence cold and clammy—he needed to speak. His words were at first hesitant and stammering, but as he continued his pace accelerated until it became, at last, a breathless torrent: "Well, uh, though it did have, uh, some m-music to it, S-Shakespeare or somebody would have d-done it better, so I don't think Grisman's going to win the O'Henry Award for that though it might make a TV movie as long as the script writers flesh it out some making that Bob guy and that Blaine guy real flesh and blood people but then film's easier because with all that money..."

"Bob?" Father Joe tried to interrupt.

"...you have actors and sets and music and special effects while in books..."

"Bob?"

"...you have only ink and paper and everything's in the words and the willingness of the reader to see those words not as words but as pictures and meanings with associations and innuendoes which take on..."

"Bob? Bob!" Father Joe said, bending over him, and putting hands on his shoulders.

"...meaning from surrounding..." he said as his gaze fastened on Father Joe's face.

Bob turned away, shielded his eyes with both hands and his chest jerked in quick spasms.

"Now, Bob!" Father Joe said, "Now in your moment of weakness! Admit you've done wrong!"

"He asked me to," he answered between his sobs.

Joe grabbed his shoulders, shook them. "Admit you've done wrong. Beg His forgiveness. Beg!"

Bob pounded the bunk with both fists. "Don't you have somebody else you can go *comfort*, holy Father!" He sniffled once.

Father Joe pulled back a little. "I'm your friend," he said, a stunned gentleness in his voice. He squatted before him. "You are scared, scared shitless, Bob. You can at least admit that. And I didn't sleep at all last night, worrying about something. I have always had an obligation to you, but I'm afraid I haven't lived up to that obligation very well. I've let our friendship interfere with my office and my obligations. But it's not too late—you need not die. Beg His forgiveness, for there is more rejoicing…"

"That's enough, now, Joe!" he said, straightening his back. "I figured you would. You're going to be a man of the cloth today, now aren't you? But that's not what I need. In a little bit I'm going to be climbing into my coffin, Joe, and I just need a friend to hold my hand while I do it. Just a friend."

"Bob, you've got one," Father Joe said. He reached into the pocket of the cassock and handed him a handkerchief.

He blew his nose twice.

"It's okay to be scared," Father Joe said, gently, still kneeling before him. "But I do have my obligations, and they're not just for sometimes and with some people."

"I know that," he said. "I've been wondering when you were going to start. And it's okay if you push me a little, just not too hard. Just a little. Don't louse things up now. Okay, Joe?"

Father Joe nodded and stood up.

Mr. Thorpe, still standing in the spot from which he had read the Warrant, said, "Reverend, last night at home, the house was awful lonely, what with Marguerite gone to her reward and Tom off at school. I put on a record, one of Schumann's symphonies, and while Lacy slept beside my chair, I did something that when I began correctional work thirty-two years ago, I swore I would never, ever, ever do. I read the transcript of his trial.

"And based on that, and on his help with the Manning affair, and what I've seen of him the last couple years—and, yes, Bob, our talks and our chess games—I am now going to make a statement, and you can quote me, Reverend."

"Mr. Thorpe, please," Bob said. "Whatever it is, I don't want to hear it."

"It's favorable."

"No offense, but I don't fuckin' care! And I really don't want to hear it."

Mr. Thorpe pushed a finger into his pipe.

"Uh," Bob said in explanation, "it's hard enough as it is."

Mr. Thorpe ran a thumb around his pipe. "Of course. I'm sorry."

Q-wing was quiet, the three of them motionless, except for the eyes. The eyes of each probed first these eyes, those eyes, these.

"Would you like me to leave for a bit," Mr. Thorpe asked, "so you and Rev. Schiller can talk?"

Bob's eyes, seeking Father Joe's, lingered there. He was considering that, until a man's voice came over the loudspeaker: "An order from the Warden: All guards are to remain at their stations and on duty. There will be no exceptions. The Highway Patrol has arrived outside the walls in full riot gear. Again, all guards are to remain on post and on duty. This is a direct order from Warden Thorpe. No exceptions."

The buzzer sounded, summoning the cell monitor to the electronic door. He admitted two guards into Q-wing, guards Bob had never seen before. Behind them came the assistant Superintendent, Mr. Evans, a short slim man with straight blond hair, parted and combed to the side.

Bob looked through bars to the bold-faced clock over the

cell monitor's desk. It was 6:46. "What's the weather like?" he asked.

"It rained last night," Father Joe said.

"Oh no, it did?" he said, a child-like disappointment in his voice.

"Yeah, but this morning as I left home, the stars were out. And by the time I got here it was getting light. Not a cloud in the sky. As the Highway Patrol escorted me past the protesters, there was this bird darting around my car. You know, up some, then back the other side and around again. Three or four times. It was weird, something I've never seen before, and then she flies over the prison and just keeps circling there, up, down, around. Like waiting for something. A swallow, I think it was. I'd say it's going to be a nice day."

"Good," Bob said, standing up. "Well, Gentlemen, shall we?" he asked.

Mr. Thorpe looked at Father Joe, then at his watch and called, "Okay, Johnson. Let them in."

The cell monitor came from his desk and unlocked the door. Three men entered: Mr. Evans and the two unfamiliar guards, both of whom carried a wooden shank around which was wrapped a chain. Each chain terminated in a single handcuff. Father Joe stepped aside as the guards stood on Bob's right and left. Bob looked at the guards—one with full dark beard, the other with pockmarks left by youthful acne. They grasped opposite arms, fastened the handcuffs on wrists, and, pulling on the shank, crossed his arms in front of his chest.

He glanced down at his arms, fashioned like some Egyptian mummy. "Are these things really necessary, Mr.

Thorpe?"

Mr. Thorpe put his pipe in his mouth, thinking. "That's a procedure, that, in good conscience, I can't overrule."

Bob nodded.

Mr. Evans spoke to Mr. Thorpe: "It's getting ugly out there. The fags and the church folk are no real problem. It's the veterans, they're mad as hell. But this place is tight as a drum, just let 'em try and storm it."

"There will be no shooting, Mr. Evans. Absolutely none," Mr. Thorpe said. "I trust you have made that clear."

"Yes, sir. Your orders were attached to each time card yesterday."

"Good," he said, then looked at the cell monitor outside the cell, and said, "Okay, Johnson."

As the cell monitor bent to unlock the cell again, Bob glanced back at his cell. There wasn't much to dispose of. "Oh, Joe? When you go home tonight will you take the cookies. I didn't eat too many. Maybe your daughters would like them?"

"Yes, Bob," Father Joe said.

"Will you tell them they're from me, too?"

"Yes," he said.

"Oh, the chess set, take that too. And the Jim Beam box. That's my journal. I call it *My Works and Days*, just spiral notebooks, but would you take it for me? There's a stack of stories I wrote in it, too. Yeah? Me. Blaine was always pushing me to go back to school, study creative writing. Pushing is the wrong word. That's what I called it back then but now I see it differently. He wasn't pushing, Joe. He was nurturing me, as a mother nurtures a child. In one of the stories I have a character say about another, 'He could have used a little nurturing along the way.' But don't bother reading them. They're probably no good. Just take the whole box and put it somewhere safe and dry, maybe an attic or something. Okay? I just don't want the guards to throw it in the trash when they come to clean out the cell. You'll do that for me too, won't you?"

"I'll take it," Father Joe said.

Mr. Thorpe spoke up, "Are you all set now?"

He nodded and they moved into the aisle and there positioned themselves: Father Joe first, then Bob in his gray suit, shaved, handcuffed and flanked by the two guards, then Mr. Thorpe and Mr. Evans. They waited as Father Joe took a long piece of purple cloth, a stole, kissed it, and draped it around his neck. Father Joe then bowed his head in silent prayer.

As the procession started forth, Obie Swingle was snatching at something imaginary in the air, flies maybe. He noticed them, stood up, and grasping the bars of his cell with huge black knuckles, said, "Y'all hang in there now, Bobby, ya hear?

"Sure, Obie. And you take care."

"You too. Will y'all be back, Bobby?"

"Only if you believe in miracles," he said.

"I do! I do!" Obie called back.

The electronic door opened and closed behind them.

CHAPTER 35

Through beige painted corridors that Bob had never seen before they made their way. Time and again an electronic door opened and closed.

Finally Father Joe stopped beside a real door, one with a knob, one painted black and posted, POSITIVELY NO ADMITTANCE.

As Mr. Evans moved past them to unlock the door with a key, Father Joe asked, "Are you okay?"

"A little nervous," he said. "Stage fright, I guess."

Mr. Thorpe checked his watch. "We've got a couple minutes yet."

"You know, guys," Bob said, "if I wanted, I could put a stop to all this right now."

Mr. Thorpe, bristling, shot alerting glances to Mr. Evans, the guards, Father Joe.

"No, Mr. Thorpe," he said, "nothing like that. But uh, there is something that I guess renders all these, these proceedings null and void."

Father Joe, with a questioning look, gazed at Mr. Thorpe, then turned to Bob and asked, "What?"

"A tiny little detail, nothing much."

"Well, what is it?"

He did not answer, only smiled like a child with a secret.

Father Joe—head inclined, forehead creased—studied him, then turned to ask Mr. Thorpe, "May I see the Death Warrant, please?" Mr. Thorpe took it from his inner pocket and Father Joe, unfolding it, went back down the corridor to read it.

As Mr. Thorpe, Mr. Evans, and the two guards watched him read, Bob studied the brush marks in the fresh black paint on the door he was soon to enter. He told himself not to think about anything now, but rather practice the stilling of thoughts by mindless repetition: *Mary had a little lamb whose fleece was white as snow, and everywhere that Mary went the lamb was sure to go. Mary had a little lamb whose fleece...* There was movement among the others.

He looked to see Father Joe shrug and shake his head and hand the warrant back to Mr. Thorpe. Mr. Thorpe now took it and stepped aside to read it. As Father Joe and Mr. Evans watched him, the guards—one on Bob's right and one on his left, still holding the shanks that crisscrossed his arms in front of him—began talking quietly among themselves, past him.

"How's eleven o'clock tomorrow with you?" the bearded guard said.

"Can we make it ten? Johnny's got a Little League game at three."

"Okay," the bearded guard said. "I'll ask the Mrs. to

make her famous potato salad."

"Then we'll bring baked beans, hot dogs and buns. Can you bring the sodas?" the pockmarked guard asked.

A picnic! The guards are going on a picnic tomorrow. Bob closed his eyes, and fabricated the scene of their picnic at a lake. *While their children splashed in the water near the shore, the guards would swim, on a dare, all the way across the lake and back. Among trees and bushes their children would play hide-and-seek while their mothers—watching with loving but wary eyes—spread a blanket on the grass, heated beans and grilled hotdogs.*

Eyes still closed, he nodded to himself at the rightness of the scene.

Others would be at the lake as well. Sitting on the dock, a snaggle-toothed old woman in straw hat would slap herself on the thigh, rooting herself on, as she reeled in a strike. A single black mother, reclining on a patchwork quilt, would suckle her child in the scanty shade of longleaf pines.

Under an oak a son and his father would wax, together, his first car. The father would ask, 'Who's that on the radio?' and his son would answer the Bee-Gees. 'Not too bad!'

And away from the others, walking quietly among the oak and long-leaf pines, would be two young men. They would talk among themselves quietly, in voices not to be overheard. Now and then hand would brush hand as they walked together.

Father Joe spoke in a voice that quavered: "Is there anyone you would like me to contact for you?"

Bob looked into his eyes. There was the glisten of moisture just above the lower lid, a puddle. "Just Betty. Tell her goodbye for me."

"Who?" he asked.

"You know, Betty, from the prison store."

"I believe she's on maternity leave," Father Joe said.

"I know," he said and looked at the bearded guard. Half a dozen gray hairs grew among the black.

Again he closed his eyes. *Tomorrow,* he told himself, *though I will not be here, the guards will go on picnic. And they should go, for that is as it ought to be. And the lake will witness scenes similar to the ones I've imagined, for the world will go on, as it should.*

His mouth gaped open in astonishment. It opened further and further. *The world will go on! Imagine! It will go on. It must!*

With guards on either side—with arms still crossed across his chest by the handcuffs and shanks, and with eyes still closed—his shoulders began to jerk and his head to bow. *That's it! I've found it! The world will go on! There'll be continuance. Things will go on as they should! My death, or the death of any one person doesn't matter, for the world goes on. For ever and ever it goes on! Alleluia! World without end!*

With his head declined, he was laughing and crying with joy. He had found it, had found the answer, something to which he could cling, something that would help him over. He could go in peace now for he had found it. *An answer so simple and beautiful. My death doesn't matter! It goes on! Imagine!*

Father Joe put his hand again on his shoulder to help still his sobs. "Oh, my son, my son."

"Bob, if there's an error,"—the voice was Mr. Thorpe's—"this warrant is worthless!"

"What?" he said, composing himself. He wiped his nose on the shoulder of the suit the State had purchased for him.

"Is there an error in this?" Mr. Thorpe said, holding the document tightly in his hand and shaking it. He came to him and, feet from him, said, "Bob, listen to me now. Any error, no matter how small, makes this warrant an invalid instrument. Is there an error? Tell me."

And should he again endure—a month, maybe two away—again endure the horrible slow creep to the appointed time? He sniffled deeply. "Gentlemen," he said in words soft and non-incriminatory, "for over a month now, ever since the State put me on Death Watch, I have watched death. I have stared into the black hole and have seen my coffin gaping, waiting, and beckoning to me. I have seen fungus grow on my flesh. That's not a pretty sight, Gentlemen. And I have stared into that hole, feeling my stomach knot and a cold sweat chill me for as long as I am going to! So, Gentlemen! What thou doest, go thou, and do thou quickly!"

"Bob, is there a mistake?" Father Joe asked, a pleading in his voice.

Mr. Thorpe said, "You aren't trying to pull a ruse on us, now are you?"

He didn't answer.

Father Joe, standing close, asked in a loving voice, "Is there a mistake, Bob?"

"Yes, there is," he said.

His lips pursing, Mr. Thorpe looked at Mr. Evans, then at Father Joe, then at Bob. His gaze sunk deep into Bob. "Have the guards take the restraints off him, Mr. Evans," he said.

"Mr. Thorpe, I protest!" Mr. Evans said.

"That is your prerogative, Mr. Evans. You can protest all you want. You can put it in writing and in triplicate," he said, his voice rising. "You can send a copy to the governor if you want. You can have one filed in your personnel file, but that is an order, Mr. Evans! Take the damn restraints off him and do it NOW!"

Taken aback, Mr. Evans kept his eyes on Mr. Thorpe as he moved toward Bob. He reached into his side jacket pocket, took out a key and unlocked, one at a time, the handcuffs. The guards wound the chains around the wooden shanks while Bob rubbed his wrists.

Mr. Thorpe walked down the corridor to again read the document. He leaned against the wall, looked toward the others and called, "Mr. Evans, call the governor and inform him of the suspected error. Have him get legal going over the warrant. That's number one, Evans. Number two, announce in the chamber there's a delay. And three, have food service send up coffee. And do it now, Evans, all of it NOW!"

"Yes, sir," Mr. Evans said, and went through the black painted door into the death chamber, toward a telephone.

Mr. Thorpe began reading the document, flipping to the many attached pages.

Bob, looking left and right to the guards, said, "Does anybody have a cigarette?"

"Sure," the bearded guard said, gave him one and lit it for him with a disposable lighter.

"Thanks," he said, exhaling the first breathful.

"You amaze me, Bob," Father Joe said. "'What thou doest'? In all these years I've never heard you quote Scripture till now, the Scripture you read time after time in Negley's church."

"I know too much of it for a man to bear. But that doesn't mean anything, Joe. You know the Devil can quote it and twist it to lead you to perdition."

"Bob, you need not die. You have already what it takes. Just a tiny step further. Won't you take a tiny step further with me? That's all I'm asking."

"Joe, listen to me now....Won't you just listen?....You put it most elegantly a few minutes back when you said I'm scared shitless. I am scared because I don't know for sure what it is. But then everybody's got to say farewell sometime. My mother had to, my buddies in Nam had to. I just don't want to stutter when it comes time for me to say it. But I did stutter when the warden read those papers and I went off talking about Shakespeare and whatever other shit I was babbling about. Imagine, talking Shakespeare at a time like this! But getting back to dignity, Father! A man can die with dignity if he is in his own bed and has his family standing near. But I have to muster the dignity of being a man while strapped into a wooden chair with strangers gawking at me, waiting for it to happen. Maybe they're impatient for it to happen?

"Joe, help me die with a little dignity. It's difficult. Help me do it, my friend."

"You have no desire to live forever? It's possible," Father Joe said.

"Be honest. You've got a lot more education than I do, but couldn't that be just a vain imagining? Let the State do what it will, and I am no more. And tell me: Is there anything wrong with that either logically or aesthetically? And people have been dying since there have been people, and the world still goes on. Isn't that the important thing, that the world go on? That there be continuance? Think about it. Isn't that a mite more important than the death of a single man, that the world go on?"

"Scripture tells us…"

"Damn! Don't parrot that stuff, holy Fa-ther! I'm asking you! You, Joe!"

Mr. Thorpe walked toward them, the warrant folded and back in its sheath. "I don't see anything wrong with this," he said.

"Well, then, Gentlemen," Bob said, "shall we?"

"We may as well wait for the coffee," Mr. Thorpe said.

"Hey, both of you've been through this before. I haven't. And I want to get it over with. So, come on, guys, let's do it. I don't want to break down in there, not in front of all those witnesses, reporters. I don't want that in the newspapers. Let's give them the show they've come to watch!"

Father Joe put a hand on his shoulder. "Bob, it's never too late."

"Joe. Dear Joe," he said gently. "I'm not one of your dramatic death bed conversions, so get it out of your head. There'll be no orchestra with tympani pounding away and chorus of thousands." His voice was getting louder. "All creation shall not welcome me. My own Pa never did. And I just want to get it the fuck over with! Can't the two of you understand that?!" He broke into sobs. He fought them the best he could.

Mr. Evans opened the door to the death chamber and held it open as he spoke from it. "Mr. Thorpe, you'd better come talk with the governor—I'm getting nowhere. He keeps saying the warrant was reviewed and approved before he even signed it. And he says no way in hell is he going to wake anybody up at seven o'clock in the morning to go over it."

"He's worried about somebody's sleep while we're

talking about an execution! Tell him...Forget it, Evans! You just let me talk to that fat, slippery bald man," Mr. Thorpe said. The door, slung open with force, bounced with a thud against its stopper.

"One hell of a lot of protesters out there!" Mr. Evans said. "It's turning into a real show. Anita Bryant was even there with a bullhorn. She was railing about the deviants, but they've got her in a wagon now. Cameras, reporters. There must be four hundred Vietnam vets all in fatigues—lots with rifles—must be from all over the country. And just a little bit ago the Klan arrived in their robes, hating everybody and getting 'em all worked up. It's ugly and people are going to get hurt. The Highway Patrol's keeping the peace the best they can, and we've got guards staying over on overtime. No one's entering this place, no one's leaving. Let them try to storm it."

Can't we just get this over with! "Are we supposed to stay here?" Bob asked.

Father Joe shrugged.

"Well, uh, we may as well make it look like we're doing this right," Mr. Evans said. "Martin, Elliot, just hold him on the arms. Father, you go first. I'll follow." He stepped aside and pushed the door open.

So that's what it looks like! Bob thought.

CHAPTER 36

Over Father Joe's shoulder the chair was visible, a crude wooden thing, straight-backed and graceless. Above it hung a single fluorescent fixture. Three windows had been cut in the walls to reveal three separate chambers. In one, a dozen witnesses sat in folding chairs. In another reporters pressed to the plexiglass and shot glances between Bob and the pads on which they wrote. The third chamber, the administrative, was nearly empty—four men. In it Mr. Thorpe, holding a telephone, was moving his mouth rapidly and pounding the air with his free arm. Behind him, against the back wall stood two men—one, a redhead, in jeans with electrician tools hanging from his work-belt, and another, whose head was shrouded under a black hood, only the whites of his eyes visible. A paunchy man in white smock and with stethoscope around his neck sat on a bench apart from the others.

Lest he see those who had come to gawk, Bob closed his eyes and kept them closed as the guards escorted him to the chair, positioned him in front of it and with pressure on his shoulders had him move back and sit. His eyes were closed as the guards cinched a wide strap around his chest, bound his right leg to the chair, strapped his right arm to it, then the left. The tightness of the bindings pinched the skin and hurt.

There was the sound of a door opening and closing, the sound of tools jiggling. Then came the feel of something soft being placed on his head. Water, cold, was poured downward, streaming over his forehead, down the back of his neck and onto the jacket purchased for him. He caught a few drops on his tongue—salty. Something smelling of leather was pulled over his head. With a tugging it was adjusted so that his eyes, nose and mouth had a freedom from the snugness. A heavy cable was attached to the top of the black mask, its weight pulling downward.

He felt scissors cut off the lower portion of his right pant leg. He felt a cable being attached. There was the sound of people leaving the room.

Peeking, he saw Father Joe still standing on his right. *That's nice.* "Bye, Joe," he said.

Father Joe's face twisted. "Oh, my friend," he said, "let me just say a little prayer and assent yes after each sentence. That's all it would take, some tiny little acknowledgement. Acknowledge Him."

"Joe, please," he said, his voice soft and composed. "That's enough now. It's not going to happen. The State is going to hurl its thunderbolt at me. And Puff! Perception stops, I am no more. But if I'm wrong and there is a God, He'll know the intents of my heart. And He'll know the scars living inflicts and that I only tried to walk humbly."

"But if there is a God," Father Joe said, urgency in his voice, "you must acknowledge Him."

"But you know what?" Bob said, still calmly. "I can look back now and see something I couldn't see then. It should have been plain, but I didn't see it. I guess I was just stubborn and too proud to call it by its rightful name."

"Now is the acceptable time, Bob. Acknowledge His sovereignty and admit you've done wrong before Him."

"It didn't come in the package I thought it would come in…" Bob said.

Father Joe interrupted. "The time is slipping."

"Listen to me, Joe! Won't you fuckin' listen to me!"

"Okay, Bob, I'm sorry. Go ahead."

Bob glanced at the dozen or so assembled witnesses, then—through his black hood—back to Father Joe. He gazed at his friend's face, at the single tear running down his cheek. His words were gentle. "Joe, it wasn't packaged like I thought it would be. It wasn't all feminine and beautiful, but I did have love—love in its fullness."

Behind Father Joe he heard the door to the administrative chamber open. "Father?" It was Mr. Evans's voice. "It's time."

In a gesture of one moment, Father Joe raised a finger heavenward. His finger continued to point upward as he listened.

"He was homely, Joe. And I'm not queer, and yes he was. But we were lovers of a sort, I guess. And Joe?"

"Yes, my son?"

"Joe, I loved him and I miss him."

Father Joe lowered his finger. "But Bob you were never

meant to be the dispenser of life and death. Who appointed you to that exalted office?"

He was silent.

"Bob, it's not too late. You were baptized as a child. You know the Scriptures. The last shall be first."

He was silent.

Father Joe stood, waiting, expectant. He crossed himself. Bob closed his eyes. There was the sound of cassock swaying and the sound of a door closing.

He was alone now. His eyes were closed, but he knew dozens of eyes were watching him from the viewing chambers. *Don't look at them, don't think of them, don't think of anything now. Just get it over with. Relax now, no thoughts. Just a nursery rhyme. Say it over and over.* Yet even with his resolve he peeked and saw them. The reporters bunched up at the window. The witnesses in their folding chairs. One of them in the rear—a plain, cabbage-faced woman—moved a finger over the words of some book, the edges of the pages dyed red. Her lips moved as she read in her simple way. Perhaps he recognized her. *Don't try to remember. The world will go on,* he told himself. *Remember that. Not long now. Mary had a little lamb whose fleece...*

Unheard, Mr. Thorpe came from the administrative chamber to stand by the chair. He spoke into a microphone: "Robert Newell..."

That startled him and he jerked, his eyes shooting open.

"...would you like to make a final statement?" He held the microphone toward the slit in the leather mask.

Bob looked up at him, silent.

Mr. Thorpe lowered the microphone to the floor and

whispered, bending over, "What's the error, Bob? Announce what the error is. If there is one, we can't go through with this. And I don't *want* to go through with this!"

To endure again the slow creep of minutes? To watch the phosphorescence of fungus lighting the blackness inside my coffin?...No...Enough's enough. "May I just speak to the Father once more?" he whispered.

"But Bob, it would be murder."

"Mr. Thorpe," he said, his voice getting louder and louder as he spoke, "no way in hell am I going to do this again. I won't let you shave my head again. And you're not going to strap me into this chair again! And all those people aren't going to gawk at me AGAIN! So, what thou doest, SIR!"

"You leave me no choice."

"So what type of choice is it for me! And may I please just speak to the Father? Please, Mr. Thorpe?"

Mr. Thorpe sighed. "Of course," he said, and left.

As Bob fought back tears, he noticed the reporters in their chambers scribbled furiously on their pads.

Father Joe, draped in the purple stole of his office, came to him, making the sign of the cross as he came, a large, big sign of the cross. Standing next to the Chair, he said in a voice grand, sonorous and liturgical, "Yes, my son?" It was a voice of pomposity, such as would be used in a cathedral crammed with thousands.

Bob was taken aback. He sniffled. Then he spoke, slowly though, quietly. "No, uh...no, Joe...oh yeah, the cookies. If they're still there, will you take the cookies home to the girls like you said? To little Helen and Elaine? And...and my journal, you remember you said you'd take that, too, and put it somewhere safe and dry for me. But, uh, if Mr. Padgett asks for it, you can give it back to him. He tried hard, Joe, tried to save my life. And, uh…and continuance, Father. There will be continuance. The world will go on, you'll see, and fathers and sons will wax together his first car, and girls will practice with their pom-poms and their cheers. So this really doesn't matter. The world goes on, so it doesn't matter, now does it? Be honest."

"And have you nothing else to say to me, my son?"

Bob lowered his gaze.

Palm forward, making the sign of the cross, and with a grand and sonorous rising in his voice, "The Lord be with you…" he said. He waited for the response. Eyes met eyes. No response came.

He crossed himself and left.

Bob closed his eyes. There was the sound of a door opening. The sound of it closing.

"…And also with you," he whispered into the silence of the room. And those words from his lips had a timelessness and a rightness to them like the pealing of church bells. They reverberated in his soul, "…and also with you."

Just count the breaths now, don't think. One…Two…

And against the blackness of his lids there appeared to him the woman who comforted him in times of trouble. Dressed in simplest of house dresses, but starched and ironed, she came to him in a pale blue light. Swallows of blue and golden wing flitted and encircled her. Stretching forth her hand to him, "It is time," she said. "Take my hand, son."

He did. His head slumped downward and there were

visions.

~

In the chamber there was some hubbub, something maybe swooping downward, then back up. Persons looked up and around and then at one another with quizzical expressions. They queried one another. "Did you see something?"

~

"The Lord be with you," she said.

"...And also with you," he said.

And in a twinkling of an eye, the single swallow that had been circling above the prison — unnoticed by those who had gathered outside with their placards and their causes — was joined by a second swallow. They circled and flitted, ascended and swooped, joyously, the two of them, there in the morning breeze. Meanwhile, below, the fluorescent light over the chair flickered. Smoke or steam arose from the top of the black hood.

Gliding side by side, Bob said to her, "Then, does this mean God isn't mad at me for not acknowledging Him like Joe wanted?"

"Solemnly I tell you, my son, our Father is not less wise than the wisest of your psychiatrists. And He well knows how the pain and anger you felt at the death of your dog, kept you, for all your years, from calling on Him. He is loving, Bobby, and wise, and understands how the child becomes father of the man."

"Well, that's pretty nice of Him, now isn't it!" he said.

"That it is, my son. Is there anything you wish to see before we leave?" she asked.

"You mean I can?"

"Of course you can," she said, "but we mustn't tarry too long."

"The Lord be with you!" he shouted, such joy was in his voice.

"…and also with you," she said.

"Well, then!" he said, "Come on!"

And they were off. They swooped and circled over the heads of those gathered outside the walls of the prison with their causes. They darted over lakes and through meadows. In a town they circled a Texaco station where two farmers were filling a tractor with diesel fuel. And Bob shouted down to them, "And with you!"

In a twinkling they were circling the great spire of the Washington Monument. Then they swooped down, went past a wall of black granite with names inscribed. A woman was placing a bouquet of jonquils and irises on the ground before it. And Bob said reverently, "And also with you."

"Have you now seen enough, my son?"

"Oh no, not yet! There is still so much more to see!" he said.

"Very well," she said. And they skimmed the waves till they circled Big Ben, then onward again, to the Eiffel Tower, around it and through it, then onward, to something square and draped in black cloth, with thousands of men prostrating themselves to it. And Bobby said to them reverently, "And also with you." Then on to the Serengeti where he commented to the woman how cute the baby elephants were, staying close to their mothers. And to each of the places they visited Bobby gave his benediction to one and to all.

"We must go now, Bobby," the woman said.

"Oh no, not yet!"

"You may visit whenever you wish, but now we must go. Others are coming to greet you."

"Okay then," he said.

And they soared ever higher and higher, to the clouds and beyond. Before him, although there were stars, it was black. But behind him, receding, lay the world, blue and white against the black. In awe and longing he watched the swirl of clouds over seas, yet he heard a sound, faint. *Must be the music of the spheres I've heard about.* And as he listened, it began to sound just like the songs whales sing.

He pried his eyes from the receding world, and looked ahead. And it was whales, six of them, swimming through the stars toward him. And something was jumping, leaping toward him from whale-back to back. The something had ears, long, red and floppy. And he heard in his head a simple, child-like voice: *Infinite? I'm sorry, God, but dogs don't understand big words. But I sure hope you like being it, in-, infinite.*

"Rusty!" he shouted.

And tagging behind her, trying to keep up, came Quasi.

And last of all, gliding smoothly on the back of the last whale was Blaine, who raised his hand and called, "Hi, you big lug!"

"They are your points of reference, Bob. You are still you!" she explained.

While yet a ways off, the woman told him they would show him the way now, and would explain about working in the world.

"Work?!" he said. "Did you say work, Mom? You mean I don't have to sit around all day and just sing? Well that's good! Work always makes a man feel good about himself."

"Solemnly, I tell you, Bobby, it puzzles us how they ever thought they'd just idle their time away! How tedious! For verily I tell you, from this time until eternity, you will have your work to do. The work I've chosen for myself is to escort those who die alone."

"I wasn't alone. Joe was there."

"But you are my son, Bobby. You're special."

The whales and the others were almost upon them, and the woman said she would now entrust him to their guidance, for she had to return, for the lonely had great need of her. And yet a moment, and a shooting star blazed in the firmament, far, far, below him. And colors, the colors. The blues and whites set against the black.

"The Lord be with you, you big lug!" a voice he knew said.

And he leapt onto a whale's back, rushing to Blaine, throwing his arms around him, laughing and crying at the same time. "And also with you, buddy," he said.

As they embraced, Rusty and Quasi contained their joy under their best behavior, sitting side by side, their tongues drooping from their mouths, cocking their heads this way and that and watching them hug. Finally Blaine said, "Your mother is charming. And she's so very proud of you."

"Mom? Yeah, quite a woman, isn't she?" he said.

He nodded. "And you should have told me Mrs. Sloan has such a sense of humor. What a carp, Bob!"

"She's in heaven, too!"

Just then, Rusty and Quasi could wait no longer, but dashed toward him, jumping on him, and licking with their tongues. "Okay! Okay!" he said, kneeling down, as his dogs—like puppies—climbed on him, their tails frantic with joy.

The whale on whose back they were traveling, twisted her head around and looked up at them. And he heard words, although her mouth did not move. "Hey, what about us?" she said. And Bob, lying down prone on her, stretched his arms down as far as they would go. And she thanked him for everything he had tried to do for them.

"Well, I'm sorry I really couldn't do anything," he said.

She looked at him with a huge, loving and wise eye. "Of no creature, Bobby," she said, again without moving her lips, "does our Father expect perfect actions. He settles for good intent."

"That's pretty nice of Him, I'd say," he said, sniffling. He stood up, went back to Blaine and put his arm around the smaller man's shoulders.

Together they watched the blue and white orb recede. "Can I really visit there if I want?"

"From this point on, all the desires of your heart are perfected," Blaine said. "You are cleansed of the confusion of the world. Whatever you wish, shall be granted in your wishing it."

"What's this about working there?" he asked.

"If you wish," Blaine said. "Most of us choose to work there, not all. There are other worlds. I work with delinquent teens and scholars and writers."

"Could I help dogs having puppies and also have responsibility for whales?"

"You have only to ask and it is granted in the asking,"

Blaine said.

"Could I look out for orphans and the unloved, too?"

"Just ask."

"Well, that's pretty nice of Him, I'd say."

"That it is," Blaine said. "But I'd like you to consider working with writers, too. Whisper to them in their sleep. You have stories to tell, Bobby, important stories. The world needs to know the truth of things. They make themselves dizzy putting their spin on everything down there. They need a grounding in the fundamentals."

"I love you!" Bob said.

"You big lug! You know it's mutual!"

"Even here you're still encouraging me to go on!" Bob said.

"Yes. Love does that."

Below them, as they glided toward the stars on the back of the whale, a blue and white jewel glistened against the blackness. "Look at the colors, Blaine. The colors!" he said.

And, resplendent in light, with his arm around Blaine, and with Rusty and Quasi sitting at his feet, he raised his hand, and in benediction to the receding orb, said, "...and with you."

~

Robert "Bobby" Newell
Born 23 Sept 1950
Died 4 Apr 1986

EPILOGUE

Back at Florida State Prison, things continued on. The witnesses dispersed, the reporters went to their telephones, the guards went on coffee-break.

Mr. Thorpe went directly to his office in company with the doctor. Passing his secretary, he told her they were not to be disturbed. "Then you don't think he just fainted?"

"Only an autopsy will tell," the doctor said. "But I observed it and in my medical opinion, he was already dead by the time the switch was thrown. Even with a corpse you'd expect muscular contractions. There wasn't so much as a single twitch. But what was that commotion just as his head slunk down? Everybody saw it."

"But how? He was young, healthy," Mr. Thorpe said.

"Probably the strain of watching the clock tick off the seconds for the four weeks he was in Q-wing. Some might think that cruel. There is wisdom and mercy in having it come to us unexpectedly...I'd like permission to do an autopsy."

"No! God, no! We will not desecrate his body." Mr. Thorpe said, his hands going to his forehead. "Why then did I give the order to throw the switch?"

"You had your orders," the doctor said.

Mr. Thorpe shook his head. "Well, the State's will was done one way or another. And we can sleep safely now, all the good citizens of this great State."

"Was he that much of a threat?" the doctor asked.

"Yes, he was. He wanted a wife and family. You may go, Doctor."

Mr. Thorpe watched the door close behind him then moved to sit behind his desk. He paused. His hand found the button on the intercom to his secretary.

"Yes, Warden?"

"Alice, I'm going home. Inform Mr. Evans for me."

Meanwhile, Father Joe—slipping unawares into the Latin rite—administered Extreme Unction on Bob's frame as it lay on a stretcher in the hallway. Then he gathered, as promised, his journal and the cookies. Troubled ("It doesn't matter. The world will go on, so it doesn't matter.") he drove home.

Outside the gates he passed the Highway Patrol in riot gear and those who had gathered with their placards and their causes. He was troubled and needed Anna and his girls around him.

The next day, in the pauper's field outside the prison walls—a field no one had ever bothered to consecrate, though the oak and long leaf pine stand in silent guard around it—he conducted a funeral. His wife was there, his daughters and Mr. Thorpe. Joining them were Della, a cabbage-faced woman from Montana and her fine German Shepherd. "Bobby gave him to me, a present."

In the late afternoon—with guards on lookout observing—a tall man with a bit of gray parked a rented car on the approach to the prison. He got out and knelt at the fresh turned earth. Finally he stood to wander through the surrounding oak and long-leaf pine. He dug a wild violet, carried it and planted it on the grave.

Then he drove to the prison gate and asked a guard if he could speak to someone about his son's death.

Robert "Bobby" Newell
Born 23 Sept 1950
Died 4 Apr 1986

...and with you.

APPENDICES

~ A Personal Note from the Author ~

A shy person and something of a recluse, I avoid crowds and try to avoid any attention. I am not on Facebook or Twitter. What I have to say publicly, I say in my writings.

On occasion friends visit me and my dogs in our mountain home. Every two weeks I go to the market for dairy products, fruits, vegetables and Oreos. You'll recognize me in Walmart (Newport, TN) by the black armband I wear on the left. If you do, come up and say hello. I welcome people into my life. People are important.

Or if you're not in Newport and would like to send me an email, I will answer you. One-on-one works well for me, you see. It's the crowd or anonymous blather that gives me the heebie-jeebies, not one-on-one contact. And besides, email has proved to be a bridge to friendships.

Let me hear from you and you'll hear back. Promise.

Vann Turner
March 6, 2018
Cosby, Tennessee
vann@vannturner.com

~ Titles by Vann Turner ~
Available everywhere

Sometimes Lovin' is Hurtful

This title. Also available as Audiobook with Christopher Boucher as narrator.

To Forestall the Darkness: A Novel of Ancient Rome, AD 589

Sixth Century Italy was a desolate land. The Romans cowered under the brutality of their Lombard overlords until one of them, Titus, dares to rally them. After some success he rashly frees his 400 slaves. That act—**He's subverting the foundations of our State!**—compels him, bloodied, into a naked walk into banishment.

~

The setting is the twilight of Antiquity—the Sixth Century—when the traditions of Rome collided with the customs of the Germanic invaders. The Sixth Century was *the pivotal century.*

Even at this late date things could have gone either way. The Western world did not need to slip into an abnegation of everything human as it awaited the End of Days. There was still a chance that the accumulated culture of the Roman people—the skills, the technologies, the optimistic world-view—would continue. Titus Tribonius tries to make it so.

To Abandon Rome: AD 593

Banishment has stripped Titus of his wife. In his absence she is raped. In his heart a rage simmers. The Pope commands him to defeat the King besieging Rome. He agrees to defend the city but won't lead the people out to their slaughter. Pope: "Who are you to dare defy me?!"

~

Pitted against Titus's public life is his private life and his personal needs. He needs to avenge his wife's defilement and he needs—

somehow, someway—to survive the machinations that threaten to destroy him and to escape Rome with the other woman he loves.

Toward Northern Lights: AD 593-624

Part 3 of the Tribonian Trilogy, set on the coast of Scotland. Coming spring of 2019.

The Marine, the Lady & the Hag: An Adult Fable

A prequel to *Sometimes,* only 3000 words. eBook only. Available free at many retailers.

~ Acknowledgements ~

I CANNOT say Thank You to Lori Roberts.

To you, my friend, I must bow, my face almost to the floor. I had pulled from a drawer an old short story that I had written and I intended to re-read it to see if it had anything of worth. You, Lori, noticed it on the painted table and read it. "You have got to publish THIS!" you said.

I had written that short story in 1993 after I had gotten six rejection letters on *this* novel, the final rejection from an Editor-in-Chief—Yeah, it had gotten that far!—"While prodigiously inventive, it's just not my cup of tea." Those were his exact words. The character you met in that story, Lori, is the same Robert Newell as in this.

Months prior to your reading the story, on his deathbed my

husband had asked me to dust off this novel and publish it. I assured him I would, but first needed to finish my Tribonian Trilogy. Because of you, Lori, the third novel in that waits until next year. Thank you, Lori. And thanks to your hubby, too, Mike.

And Dan Jones. I'm indebted, guy, INDEBTED to you *and* Reta. Your editorial guidance, your sitting with me and talking over things, your research on certain facts…and your financial support. After's Bob's death never could I have purchased a block of 10 ISBNs without you. You've made it possible, Dan.

To Nancy Soesbee. I know, I was never supposed to tell, but thank you for proofreading FREE of charge. I know I told you I wouldn't but I have, and I guess our secret is now on bookshelves all over the world and even in the Library of Congress! Deal with it, girl! And thanks. (If any author seeks a quality proofreader, you may email me and I'll gladly forward your contact information on to Nancy.)

To my neighbors on our hill—Lenny & Susan Croote, Tony & Starla Myers—thanks for the friendship, the help, the visits, the dinners, the favors and the sharing of your dogs. Oh, and I can't forget to mention the brownies, cakes, pies and cookies. I'm blessed.

And lastly—But not really, because there are no hierarchies of things. That is a mental construct and a false one.—I thank the Pack. I thank our temporal pack, Zoe and Lexi. And I thank our angelic pack, Kelsie, Sophie, Gustin, Dale, Kylie,

Bonnie, Kismet and Blazer. In truth there is not a temporal pack and an angelic one. There is the Pack, simultaneously present, eternal points of reference.

Vann Turner
March 21, 2018
Cosby, Tennessee

CPSIA information can be obtained
at www.ICGtesting.com
Printed in the USA
LVOW13s0824080818

585929LV00005B/37/P